ABNEY KELLY AND THE YULETIDE SHENANIGANS

BOOK 1 OF THE ABNEY KELLY SERIES

SamiJo McQuiston

This book is dedicated to all the Fleetlings out there. You may not be Faeries, but you ARE pretty freaking phenomenal. Don't ever change… unless you want to.

ABNEY KELLY AND THE YULETIDE SHENANIGANS

BOOK 1 OF THE ABNEY KELLY SERIES

PROLOGUE

"I was getting bored waiting for you," a honeyed voice came from the bushes. "Though I always suspected you have a genuine fondness for the Fleetlings." A large cat-faced creature emerged, pale blue eyes glowing and lips turned up in a smirk. His curled horns brushed against one of the taller branches on the tree, and his clawed hands adjusted his dusty-cobwebbed vest as he moved from the shadows so that he could stand up straight. The stitches on his capris groaned as his red-orange tail coiled around his left foot.

"I told you, Io-" Algernon started, but the cat-creature covered his mouth quickly.

"And I told you! Never say my real name! It's Gumpbo Sherbert," he corrected him.

"I'm not using your stupid code names," Algernon replied matter-of-factly as his face rippled like disturbed water. Brown eyes melted away to reveal black shining orbs. The dark human-skin evaporated and was replaced by coarse black hair and flaring nostrils. His fanged teeth gnashed with impatience, and Gumpbo Sherbert shivered. Kelpies were ghastly-looking, even to other magical creatures.

"No code names!" Algernon hissed in his loudest whisper.

"I've been watching all the Fleetling movies; all the best and most successful missions have code names," the cat creature explained.

"We are *not* Fleetlings," Algernon reminded him.

"Where's the child?" Gumpbo Sherbert questioned, letting the code names go for the moment.

Algernon reached beneath his cloak and produced the bundle. The cat took the babe, un-wrapping the blanket and holding its sleeping form in front of him. "She looks so… unremarkable. Are you sure she's one of us?"

"I was there at her birth," Algernon spat, this time offended. "Stop acting like an imbecile."

"You were always too sensitive," the cat teased.

"Just get on with it," he said impatiently.

Gumpbo Sherbert held the child in front of him, sizing her up, and then closed his eyes to think before he spoke again:

"As above, so below, take this child and make her so.

Light brown hair, bright gray eyes, charming smile, features wise.

Do not stand out or cause a scene, ordinary now, you must seem.

Take my words and listen well, your true self hidden in this spell.

Short the time this form you'll take, upon my word this spell shall break.

Then truest form be found with friends, illusion shattered and ignorance end."

Algernon looked the child up and down, trying to seem unimpressed. To all who would gaze on her, even the Fae, she now looked as Fleetling-like and normal as any child of mortal birth. "It would've been better done in the old tongue," he lied.

"You're such a snob!" the cat retorted. "Words are powerful, no matter the language if spoken in the right way with the proper intent. Now it's your turn; finish the job. The parents will be home soon, and the sitter of babies will not sleep forever." Algernon gave the cat a quick glare and snatched up the still slumbering child, wrapping her back in the blanket and tucking her beneath his coat.

He walked toward the house, and even in the dark, he could see the vibrant pinks and purples adorning the exterior of the Victorian style abode. Wooden houses, gated yards—things had been much different when he dwelled Topside. Algernon remembered his time with Fleetlings. It was bittersweet. His Fae-self told him that he cared nothing for that time or any other, but his first twenty years lurked like a cavity, stinging whenever a piece of it lodged in his thoughts.

He walked up to the front door and silently turned the knob. Being Fae, silence came easily, and he was able to walk up the stairs unnoticed. He sniffed the air inquisitively as he reached the second floor. The wee Fleetling was down the left side of the hall behind the third door. Fleetlings had such a strong odor, due to the iron in their blood, that any Fae could smell one within a fifty-yard radius. Algernon held his breath as he glided down the hallway and crept into its room. The room was brimming with blue blankets, blue teddy bears; blue everything. Algernon felt fear creep up his spine. This child was a boy. He approached the crib and looked down at what was supposed to be a Fleetling girl child. "Dragon's Fire!" he swore in a whisper.

There was no time to get another family. The babe was already hours past the allowed youth limit; this would have to work. He took the Fleetling boy, placed him beneath his coat, and substituted him with the glamoured Fae. He had to admit the resemblance was seamless, besides the one apparent glitch…one was a boy and the other a girl. These kinds of shenanigans are what had tipped the Fleetlings off to what was occurring in the first place.

Algernon bent over the crib, placing his toothy lips on the child's cheek and spoke softly, "Have courage, small one. We will see each other again." With that, he dashed out of the house to find Gumpbo Sherbert, who was in the same place he had left him.

"You moron!" he accused him in a hushed tone. "How could you foul this up? You had a very simple job."

"What are you on about?" Gumpbo Sherbert replied.

"This Fleetling," Algernon said, pulling out the baby for dramatic effect, "is a boy!" The cat's sneer turned into a frown. "Fix it, you fool! I don't care how!" The creature did not wait for further insults or instruction. Without a word, he made a mad dash for the house.

Thirteen Years Later...

CHAPTER 1

JUST A DREAM

The morning sky had woken and stretched, leaving its pink and orange fingerprints on the sky. Abney sat exhausted on her window seat quietly studying the colors. The dream had woken her again. It was the same dream she'd been having for months. She would find herself at a masquerade in some old abandoned ruins overgrown with delicate orange-lace creepers, a myriad of flowers she'd never seen before, and trees with luminous silver leaves. The surrounding air would be lit by millions of glowing fireflies whirling gracefully between dancers who moved effortlessly in unison to music as old as time itself, their performance telling a story Abney wasn't able to grasp.

After a tap on her shoulder, she'd turn to face the unknown artfully with a slight bow of her head. The hand then reached for her, and she'd grasp it, following the stranger to the dance floor. Somehow, she always knew the steps, and her feet moved accordingly to the rhythm of the song. The dance was consuming. She could feel the music moving through her whole being, taking over as she moved from partner to partner, and the line between herself and the other dancers blurred. They became one.

One being careening into nothing until they disappeared entirely and became a mere extension of the song.

She felt everything at once. Love, malice, intrigue, boredom, lust, apathy, joy, and fear. It was overwhelming, yet she never wanted to feel differently ever again. Then, a golden cat mask would catch her eye, plucking her from the trance. It disappeared and reappeared as her eyes tried desperately to follow. Eventually, she would break away from her partner in search of the masked stranger. He eluded her. Every time she thought she was close, he appeared across the room from her, and she would fight her way through the whirlwind of bodies, determined to catch him. At some point in the chase, his back would appear tauntingly in front of her. She would reach out for his shoulder. Her heart would be beating so loud that it drowned out the music. Then as he began to turn, she would sit straight up in bed, breathing heavy and shallow at the same time.

It was always the same, every night. It never wavered or changed in even the smallest detail. Her memory of it was perfect and strangely exact. Who was behind the mask? Why, when she found him, did she wake up? Why did she feel like she hadn't slept a wink when she'd dreamed all night?

A loud thump shook the ceiling above her and startled her from her thoughts and onto her feet. Her hands were shaking, and her breath was unsteady, but she soon realized the source and resolved to settle her nerves. Abney pushed her mind to other things. It was the first weekend after Thanksgiving, and that meant it was time to put up their holiday decorations.

Her father was already dressed and buried in boxes when Abney descended the stairs wearing her housecoat and slippers. The back of his salt and pepper head was bobbing up and down as he fought to get their giant fake tree put together. It was like watching a cartoon, and she tried to stifle her laughter, but a chuckle escaped. He turned to face her and fell into one of the opened boxes. Abney's giggle grew to a full-blown laugh.

"Hey, kiddo!" He begged humorously, "Mind helping your ol' dad out here?" Abney grasped his hand and pulled him to his feet. "I'm so glad you're awake," he announced. "Now, I can put on the Christmas music. What should we start with?"

""The Carol of the Bells,'" Abney replied with enthusiasm. It was her favorite.

Her father pulled his phone out of his pocket. "I stayed up last night creating the perfect Christmas playlist on Musidora," he informed her while plugging the device into the speakers.

"I did the same thing." Abney showed him her phone.

"Great minds think alike," Dad said with a smile. "But I'm older, so mine first."

"But mine are always better," Abney protested.

"Exactly. We always save the best for last," her father insisted, not missing a beat. Abney rolled her eyes but let him win, this time.

"I'm going to make hot chocolate, any requests?" Abney enquired.

"Caramel and sea salt," he answered predictably.

Music erupted through the speakers, filling the house with the sound of bells. An immediate smile bursting onto her face, Abney put the milk on to boil and got the cocoa powder and sprinkles from the pantry.

This was her favorite day of the year. They would listen to holiday music, spend hours decorating the tree, drink hot chocolate, put up window clings, and lights would be strung on every available surface. At the end of the day, they would order a pineapple, jalapeno, and cream cheese pizza from Mr. Leung's #1 Pizza Buffet and make a final cup of hot chocolate to complete their sugar comas. Then, they would turn off all regular lights so just the holiday lights were glowing, and they would gaze at the tree for an hour or so before they grabbed blankets and ended the night watching *The Muppet Christmas Carol*.

"Good morning," a cheerful voice came from behind her. Abney turned and smiled at the wrinkled but sparkling-brown eyes that beamed at her. Her grandmother never left her room without dressing, and today was no exception. She wore long black slacks that accentuated her thin frame and a cream-colored turtleneck sweater. Her makeup was lightly and tastefully applied, the pearl earrings her long-deceased husband had given her for their fifteenth wedding anniversary adorned her ears, and a small silver ring with four petite diamonds encircled her left ring finger.

Reginald "Reggie" Kelly had been a soft and caring man. He'd built and repaired clocks for a living, which always provided nicely for his family. He'd dressed as Santa every year to deliver gifts to the homeless shelter, ran the cornbread stand at every county fair, knew everyone in town by name (it was a small town), and whenever someone mentioned him, there was always a kind word to be said. Granny missed him fiercely. He'd died eighteen years earlier of lung cancer. Abney never knew him, but Granny never took off her wedding ring.

"Good morning, Granny," Abney greeted her. "I'm making cocoa, would you like some?"

"No, thank you." she responded. "It cannot be healthy to start the day off with so much sugar. I'll make myself a cup of tea. You ought to consider a cup yourself. You look like you could use some caffeine."

"Suit yourself," Abney said with a mischievous smile and put her and her father's cups on a tray to take out to the living room.

Her father had just managed to get the white pre-lit tree up and was fanning out the branches. Abney set the tray down on the coffee table, grabbed her mug, and took a seat on an oversized crimson armchair. It was her chair. The place she felt the most comfortable.

Life was sometimes like a bad fairy tale. She was just a little too chubby for the regular clothes section. She was too short to reach anything on the top shelf. She was a bit too young to be taken seriously by most adults, and her hair was a little too short to be girly. She seemed always to be a little too much of this or not enough of that, but in her chair, she always felt just right.

"Looking good, Dad."

"Thanks, kid." He sipped his hot cocoa. Whipped cream clung to his handlebar mustache, and he wiped it away clumsily with his bare arm. Her father was unconsciously messy. Even with a belt, the back of his shirt always managed to come untucked. His hair escaped the gel at the front, leaving a perfect bobble of curls above his right eye, and his morning coffee stained his bowtie every day without fail. Abney found it charming, but Granny was always trying to get him to pay better attention to his appearance.

"Oh, for Pete's sake!" his mother exclaimed. "You would think I'd raised you in a barn! Use a napkin, not your arm!"

"Sorry, Mom," he replied automatically.

"The tree looks lovely," Granny said, joining her son on the couch. Abney looked at her family. It had been the three of them against the world for as long as she could remember. Her mother had never really been there for them, yet she hung over them like an ominous cloud. The little she had experienced of the woman didn't leave her eager for a repeat of the activity.

"It will look even better when it's decorated," Abney piped in.

"Well, we should get to it then," Granny replied.

The theme this year was under-the-sea. They had bought all sorts of different fish, octopi, seashells, whale, dolphin, and mermaid ornaments. Abney had made the tree topper herself by gluing a Santa Claus merman figurine to a large sea star and then gluing that to a paper cone she had made from construction paper. Granny had spent months sewing and hand beading the tree skirt. It was a lovely scene of a mermaid peeking from behind some seaweed. Dad was not crafty, so he merely paid for all the supplies the two ladies needed for their creations, which was much appreciated.

Abney went to the box labeled *ornaments* and unfolded the lid excitedly. She had been dying to do this for weeks. She looked lovingly at the collection of sea creatures. They were beautiful and sparkled almost magically. She picked up an orange and yellow octopus first, as it was her favorite, and she knew just where she wanted it. Then it was Granny's turn, then her father's, and then Abney's again. Between the three of them, the box emptied quickly, and the tree transformed into an ocean paradise. They frequently stopped to rearrange the ornaments, move the branches, and make sure that every creature was placed perfectly. They were nearing the bottom of the box when Abney noticed something that did not belong.

The cat masquerade mask looked up at her from the underneath the remaining ornaments. She reached in and pulled it out, questioning her family as she did, "Where did this come from?"

Granny and Dad looked at the mask, also perplexed. No one had seen it before. Abney's stomach turned, and she suddenly felt nauseous.

She couldn't explain it, but it felt like the mask was hunting her, and it had just found its prey. At that moment, the ceiling shook forebodingly, and all three looked up.

"I'll go," Granny stated with a worried look, and she disappeared up the stairs.

"I think it's time for a break," Dad announced nervously. "How about I make us some unicorn waffles, and you go take a shower?"

"Sure," Abney agreed, grabbing the mask as she headed up the stairs as well.

Once she was upstairs, she threw the mask onto her bed. How had it gotten in the box? Had it been there the whole time and that's how it got into her dream? She paced around it but didn't quite dare to touch it again.

"Abney, how many waffles do you want?" her father bellowed up at her.

Grateful for the distraction Abney replied loudly, "Just two, Dad!"

"You got it, kiddo," came the booming reply.

Forgetting the mask, Abney dove into her closet, and the first thing she saw was her school uniform. She frowned at the crest on the left blazer breast. It was a golden shield with a bouquet of white flowers in the middle. Ms. Ulyanna's Academy for Young Women, where any common weed would become a delicate flower. Abney unconsciously pinched her lips and gave a snort. "Delicate flower", that was her all right. She pushed it aside and grabbed her red Christmas sweater and a pair of comfortable black yoga pants.

✴

The steam swirled as she stepped from the shower and wiped down the fogged mirror. Green and blue hair hung limply around her chubby face, and her over-sized gray eyes looked dully back at her. She shook her head and was careful not to stare directly at the reflection. She hated looking in the mirror. It was always accompanied by a million voices telling her she was fat, ugly, and unwanted. It was too painful to face, so she avoided it as much as possible. Instead, she focused on styling her hair and applying a small amount of make-up, before fleeing the bathroom. A wave of relief hit her as she stepped back into her room and away from her condemning image.

Abney's room was more like a library than a bedroom. Where other girls her age had posters of Harry Styles and Arianna Grande, she had shelves and shelves of books. There was nothing she treasured more. Each book was a new adventure and a new life. She was only thirteen, but she felt like she'd already lived a thousand times over. She went over to her nightstand where her latest two books and audiobook sat. She was tempted for just a second to read a few pages.

"Breakfast, ladies!" Dad bellowed. Abney looked past her books, opened the drawer to retrieve her socks, and ran down the stairs.

✦

The day went exactly as planned. All the decorations were up, many cups of hot chocolate had been drunk, and the pizza consumed. Now, their house lights were dark, yet the inside glowed with thousands of multi-colored fairy lights. Abney was sure this was what it was like to live in a snow globe. It was a tiny isolated world of pure perfection that could only be made better by giving the ball a good turn and watching the snow churn around it. *If only I could tip our house upside down and produce snow.*

Abney, Granny, and Dad sat exhausted side by side on the couch, admiring all their hard work, as "The Nutcracker Suite" played in the background. Every year they were all confident that no tree could be more beautiful, and year after year, they seemed to outdo themselves. Abney felt pleased with herself. It had been her turn to pick the theme this year, and there had been grumbling from Dad's camp that ocean life would not make a very good Christmas tree, but here it was, and even he had to admit it was enchanting.

"Are we ready for the movie?" Granny questioned.

"I'll grab the blankets," Abney volunteered.

"And I'll make the cocoa," Dad said, standing to head into the kitchen.

Abney would watch *The Muppet Christmas Carol* at least ten more times before the season was through, but this time was always the best because she had been waiting for months to watch it again. Abney ran upstairs to collect blankets for everyone. Dad's was forest green, Granny's was baby pink, and Abney's was bright purple, but hers wasn't in the closet.

"Granny!" Abney hollered down the stairs. "Do you know where my blanket is?"

"If it's not in the closet, check your room," she replied. "And don't shout in the house."

"Okay!" Abney shouted down the stairs with an impish grin. She could hear her grandmother saying, "Well, she's definitely your child, Olly," as she walked past the stairs to her room. She opened the door and immediately recognized her blanket on the window seat. As she picked it up, the cat mask fell from beneath it.

"How did you get there?" she questioned and bent down to pick it up. It was beautiful. The mask was gold painted wood with black filigree markings. On the forehead, red gemstones were placed in a v and a few were spaced perfectly on the whiskers as well. A tremble ran through her body as she held it, and the air began to vibrate. Abney dropped the thing—half out of fear and half out of shock. Was it possible for a thing to feel powerful?

"Do we need to throw up a rope?" Dad jested.

"No, I'm coming," Abney assured them and moved away from the mask as quickly as she could. She then slid down the banister, balancing the blankets in her hands and landing solidly on her feet. Granny gave a disapproving look while Dad tried to hide his amusement.

"Young ladies do not slide down banisters," Granny chided half-heartedly.

"Good thing I'm not a lady," Abney replied in a good-humored tone.

"Oh Olly, do something with your daughter," she pleaded with a smile.

"Ummmm…don't sass your grandmother," he tried, but they both shook their heads at him. "Fine! Let's just get on with it then." He pretended at being wounded, but no one bought that either. Abney passed out the blankets, and they all settled in to watch her favorite movie for the millionth time.

CHAPTER 2

COW TIPPING

Abney's head was banging against the window of the bus on her way to the academy. It was a long way from Archer to Cheyenne every day, and the ride seemed endless. She was weary to the bone; it felt like she hadn't slept in months, and she did not have the energy to deal with school today. Her earbuds were tucked in snug, and the music up as loud as it would go. Whoever had thought all-girl schools were a good thing had clearly never spent any real time with teenage girls.

This was without a doubt the doing of the patriarchy and their juvenile fantasies, Abney thought irritably as yet another colorful marshmallow flew through the air and stuck in her hair.

She did not need the music down to know the comments they were making:

"Open up, fat girl. You look hungry!"

"Careful on the corners, Nick, the bus is a little heavy on one side. Wouldn't want to tip over."

"Hey, Abney! The circus called, they need their fat lady back."

"Just because one person made a song, doesn't mean you should try to bring all the booty back yourself!" The comments were all the same. After all, bullies only needed to be mean, not witty.

The school was coming into view, and Abney cringed outwardly. There was surely no worse place in the whole of the universe. The school had extensive grounds with several buildings, including its own gymnasium and greenhouse. A distinctive red brick made up the buildings that seemed to bleed into the winter scenery and reflect the doom Abney knew to be waiting for her.

The bus halted, and Abney's head smashed against the window harder than it had before. She massaged the bump with an annoyed sigh and stood up to wait her turn to exit the bus. As everyone filed out, she removed her earbuds. Ms. Ulyanna did not approve of distractions at school and had already appropriated two pairs of earbuds and a rather expensive set of headphones from Abney in the last three years. She learned to take them off before setting foot on school property.

"Earthquake!" someone shouted from behind as she exited the bus. Some of her classmates jumped and pretended their footing was unsteady. Abney gritted her teeth and marched through those ominous wooden doors. The school had the smell of old books with just a hint of disinfectant, which she liked. Her footsteps echoed on the pea-green tiles as she made her way through the maze of cold and lifeless halls. There were no billboards or pictures in their corridors. Ms. Ulyanna was rearing young women, not children.

Her locker was at the far end of the 7th grade corridor, and as with most days, Cotton Ludlow was waiting for her. She was a year under Abney, but she was terrifying, even to girls in more advanced years.

"Hey it's Fat-ney," she said, leaning against Abney's locker and twirling her finger through her blonde curls. Abney wanted to slap her buck teeth and chubby cheeks right off her face, but she didn't fancy fighting the pack of girls that would descend on her if she dared such a thing.

"Just move, Cotton," Abney ordered defeatedly.

"You know, I know a great tailor who could let your uniform out for you. That way you wouldn't look so much like a little pig in a blanket," Cotton offered, her eyes gleaming with evil.

"Cotton!" Abney exclaimed, losing her cool, but Angelique, Cotton's giant defender, had already stepped between them.

"What do you think…" Angelique started to threaten but was interrupted by Mr. Peterson, the arithmetic teacher.

"Don't you girls think you should be getting to class?" he suggested, looking over his circular spectacles at them.

"Yes, Mr. Peterson," the girls replied in unison. Cotton gave Abney a look that said this was far from over and moved on down the hall with her clique following close at her heels.

"Collect your things quickly, Ms. Kelly," the pudgy-balding-man instructed her. "If you're late, you'll be headed for the headmistress's office." He'd just saved her, and he knew it. Abney gave him a grateful nod and pushed her bag and coat into her locker, taking the necessary books and binder with her.

English Literature was her first class on A Days. She was relieved that it was absent of her tormentors and contained her one friend, Molly McGregor. Molly was average looking, nothing remarkable, brown eyes and brown hair. She was thinner than Abney, but not skinny. Her green rectangular glasses were continually sliding down her slender nose, and she had this remarkable ability to blend into the background. Everyone, except Abney, always forgot she was there. Molly was the only person at school that treated her anywhere close to human, so Abney felt particularly tuned in to her existence and more than a little jealous of her invisibility.

She slid into the seat next to her friend. "How was your weekend?" she queried.

"Oh my god, it was freaking phenomenal!" Molly said excitedly. "My mom got me the *Return to Labyrinth* mangas, and I haven't been able to put them down! They're everything I imagined a sequel to the movie would be."

"I loved the movie," Abney agreed wholeheartedly. "Maybe I'll have to check those out," she lied. Manga had never been her thing; for some reason she had never been able to get into the stories.

"I'll let you borrow them as soon as I finish," Molly offered, but

Abney knew, as long as she kept her mouth shut, Molly would forget her offer, and she would be free from the obligation of drudging through the things.

"Sure, that would be great," she agreed and dropped the subject permanently.

"Good morning, class," Mrs. De Silva said, calling them to attention. "Let's start where we left last week. What is the significance of Marmee pulling Amy from school? Why would her views have been considered radical for the time? Ms. Winkelmeir, you begin…"

❖

Abney felt like the living dead, moving from one class to the next in a drained daze. She desperately needed a nap. Luckily, her botany class was next, and as long as she got one of the desks at the back of the room, she would likely be able to doze unnoticed.

She and Molly left lunch early to make sure Abney got the seat she wanted. The room was blissfully empty, and they took stools in the back. Abney set up her books and binder in the most studious way that she could, while Molly put a notebook in front of her to help blend in, not that it was necessary. Molly had Drama this period, but she didn't want to go. Mr. Berlin always forgot her, so she never got any parts and always ended up on the stage crew. Plus, no one would miss her. She'd been over-looked so often, most of the teachers had begun marking her present every class to avoid embarrassment, and Ms. Thornberry, who never could keep the students straight, would never notice an extra person. Abney was grateful for the company. The girls pulled out their lunches and ate quickly. Abney, because she didn't want anyone else to see her eat, and Molly because she ate with Abney, and it seemed rude to eat slow.

❖

Cotton and her comrades sauntered into class last as they were always reluctant to leave the lunch hall. Luckily for Abney, this left them the desks at the front of the class. It was just bad luck that the one elective class Abney really wanted to take was also considered a bird course and attracted the lazier and unseemly sorts, like Cotton, just looking for an easy A. It was also the only reason she was in a class with both younger and older students. Electives were not year-specific. Abney felt she would be relatively safe until the bell rang, though the gang of girls was already eyeing her with malice.

Ms. Thornberry bumbled into the room in her usual disarray. She always seemed to be in a state of anxiety and distraction. One of the many forgotten pencils stuck in her black top bun fell to the floor, ending up under her foot, causing her to slip and slide into her desk while a cascade of papers buried the poor woman. Laughter erupted from the students as she tried to right herself. A few of the older students ran to her aid, picking up her papers and helping her to her feet. Abney considered going up to assist, but that would have put her within reach of Cotton, and that was not a pleasant prospect.

After the class had settled, Ms. Thornberry made an announcement. "I know it is cold out, and normally, we would just have a lecture today. However, our winter garden has started to bloom, and I thought it would be nice for us to venture out to the greenhouse."

Abney groaned. There would be no napping at her desk.

After collecting their jackets from their lockers, the class reconvened in the greenhouse. It was bright and warm in the glass room. The winter sun beat down, allowing the plants to drink it in, and creating an oasis in the frozen tundra. Vegetables were peeking up from the soil at the far side of the room, and flowers were in bloom all around. It was a welcome sight, though the heat was making it hard for Abney to stay awake.

"Doesn't this place just give you new life?" Ms. Thornberry remarked as another pencil fell from her hair onto the books in her arms. "Come on, girls, grab some gardening gloves; we have some new seeds to start over there. Ms. Ludlow, why don't you cut some fresh flowers for Ms. Ulyanna's office? Those tomatoes look ready for picking. Remember only the red ones, ladies."

Abney grabbed Molly and used the hubbub to steal over to the other end of the greenhouse and sit on the bench. She pulled out her book, and Molly pulled out her manga. They were introverts, united on the same bench, each in their own private world. She needed to close her eyes for just a moment...

Everything happened as it always happened. She found herself at the enchanted ruins, elegant dancing figures swirling around her, buffet tables full of irresistible splendor. She danced with the same partners, felt those same addictive feelings, and chased the ever-elusive cat mask. She hunted him single-mindedly and caught him as always. However, when she put her hand on his shoulder this time, he turned all the way around, and she did not wake up!

He was standing there in loose black slacks, glittering blue tailcoat, and his pale blue glowing eyes stared at her from behind the mask. At first, she froze in shock. She had never gotten this far before, but she regained her composure quickly and did the first thing she could think to do; she reached up for the mask. She had to know who he was. His furry hand was lightning-fast as he grabbed her wrist and shook his head.

"Not..." he started.

And Abney's eyes flew open as her face smashed into the cold soft ground.

"Now that's cow tipping," Cotton informed her posse. Abney tried to rub the dirt from her face and struggle to her feet as the laughter endeavored to tear her down.

The merriment roused Molly from her book coma, and she defended her friend. "Hey, what the hell, chipmunk cheeks?"

"Who are you?" Cotton asked, obviously confused about where the new girl had come from.

"You wouldn't remember even if I branded it on your dumb forehead," Molly accused and helped Abney up.

"Ms. Kelly!" Ms. Thornberry exclaimed from behind them. "What are you doing? That is Ms. Ulyanna's clover patch. She is going to be furious!"

"Ms. Thornberry, I didn't..." Abney tried to explain.

"No, no excuses," Ms. Thornberry interrupted, "You had better go see Mr. Burke and get yourself checked out. You seem to have some bruising on your face. You must be more careful! I will have to report this to Ms. Ulyanna. And you"—she turned on Molly—"do you belong in this class? Get to wherever you are supposed to be this minute."

Both girls looked stunned; someone *had* actually noticed Molly, but the look on Ms. Thornberry's face soon shook them out of it.

"Yes, Ms. Thornberry," the girls replied hopelessly. Abney headed toward the infirmary and Molly to her drama class.

"Moooo!" the voices of their classmates chased after her. Abney's ears radiated heat, and her stomach tied itself in knots. *Can't they just leave me alone?*

"Girls! Girls, that is quite enough!" Ms. Thornberry pleaded with the class.

"Moooo!" they continued, paying no mind to their teacher.

✳

Inspirational posters and superhero-themed workout regimens covered the walls of Mr. Burke's office. He was the sort of person who believed firmly in leading by example. How could he lecture students about the importance of healthy eating habits and exercise, if he was not the very embodiment of these things? His bookshelves contained all of the latest information on healthy diets, modern nursing practices, and holistic approaches for those who shied away from the wonders of modern medicine. He even kept a small set of weights in the room, to help keep himself from becoming complacent while he waited for injured or ill students to attend.

"25, 26, 27," he said aloud as he rotated his bicep curls.

"Uh…Mr. Burke," Abney interrupted him, "Ms. Thornberry asked me to report to you."

"28, 29, 30," he continued, "Always finish what you start," he said, then put the weights down and turned to face her. "Now, how can I help?" He studied her shrewdly at a distance before he came closer and asked, "May I examine you?"

Abney nodded her permission. He cupped her face gently and turned it from side to side looking baffled.

"Please remove your coat and roll up your sleeves," he requested.

Abney reached up to undo the buttons on her coat and noticed the ice-blue stains on her hands as well. Mr. Burke saw too. A thorough examination revealed the marks only affected her hands and face.

"What happened?" he enquired.

"I…fell into a patch of clover," Abney lied. Ratting on Cotton would only make things worse.

"Are you aware of any allergies you may have?"

"I get a rash sometimes from touching iron, but other than that, no."

"Are you feeling poorly or does it hurt?" he continued.

"I feel fine," she said in earnest. "It doesn't hurt at all."

"Have a seat while I look up a few things." He pulled several books down from the shelves and dove in enthusiastically. A series of head shakes and grunts followed. He flipped through page after page, apparently with no satisfaction to be had. He didn't look happy and was at a loss for what to do. "I suppose it's possible it's just some light bruising. Or a rash? You're feeling completely fine?"

"I feel normal."

"Well, I'm going to send you home for the rest of the day at any rate. If you start feeling strange or poorly, you should seek medical attention right away. Who is your emergency contact on file?"

"My grandmother," Abney replied.

"Go get your things from your locker and come straight back here. You'll wait for your grandmother in my office. I want to speak with her before you head home."

Abney went to collect her backpack with a small spring in her step. Granny would make her homemade chicken noodle soup, mint tea, and then she would finally get the uninterrupted nap she had been dying for all day.

✦

Abney woke later from a dreamless sleep feeling better than she had in ages. It was like waking from a fever. Suddenly, everything was clearer. She didn't feel nearly as tired or run-down. Her room was dark with the newly fallen dusk. She walked over to her window seat and sat to look at the faint but smiling Cheshire Cat moon.

She looked down at her spotted blue hands and felt her face. Still no pain. She didn't feel any different, and it didn't feel like a bruise. Maybe it was just a weird blue rash? She'd touched clover before though…at least, she thought she had. In any case, she had never heard of a blue rash. It was getting her out of school till it cleared up though.

The cat mask lay temptingly close to her feet. She picked it up. It wasn't such a scary thing. She felt nothing while holding it this time. Had she just been being silly before? Her imagination did tend to get away with her sometimes. She lifted it close to her face, but not touching, and looked through the eye holes, trying to prove to herself that being afraid of it was just nonsense.

Her room was shadowy, but she could see her unmade bed, the stack of books on her nightstand, her school uniform that had not entirely made it into the hamper, and something glittery in the corner of her room that she could not quite make out. She stood up and walked cautiously toward the sparkle. Suddenly, a pair of blazing blue eyes came into focus, and Abney dropped the mask and jumped back.

The eyes disappeared. Abney turned on her table lamp and walked over to the empty corner. Was she seeing things now? She picked the mask back up. It was stupid. Even childish, but maybe it would show her the eyes again? She pulled the mask close to her face and paused. She took in a deep breath. It was ridiculous to be afraid, so she closed her eyes and put on the mask. When she opened her eyes, the blue eyes were staring back at her. She ripped the mask off with a yelp, and the eyes disappeared again.

"Abney," Dad's voice betrayed his concern as he knocked lightly and let himself in. "Hey kiddo, are you okay?" he asked.

Abney looked at him pale and wide-eyed. She didn't know what to say. He would think she was crazy. She thought she was crazy!

"What's this?" Her father bent down and picked up the mask. He put it on and stuck his tongue out at her. He obviously didn't see what Abney had seen. She snatched the mask from him and looked through it again, but all she saw was her room.

Dad grabbed the mask back from her, "What's up?"

"Nothing." Abney shook off her visions convincingly. "Must have been a bad dream."

"I'm here," he reassured his daughter. "Nothing is going to get you." Abney smiled at him gratefully. "I think that rash is looking better already," he lied. "Why don't we go downstairs and see if we can't talk Granny into a game of Scrabble?"

"I like the way you think," Abney agreed. He always knew how to make her feel better.

CHAPTER 3

MADNESS

The peace Abney found the night before didn't last long. The blue rash didn't go away, so Granny called her out of school for a second day, just to be safe. That morning they watched a gooey Christmas movie and then went to the grocery store to get the ingredients for tortilla soup. By the time they got home, all hell had broken loose.

Her mother had escaped again. The police came, and Officer Frederick Frawley was still finishing up with Dad. All the cupboards were open, and their dishes and food had been thrown all around, bringing disarray to their usually well-ordered home. The Christmas tree lay in ruin, and several of the ocean occupants were in pieces around the living room. Dr. Armstrong was en route, and Granny was trying to put their lives back together. Abney was hoping it would all be over faster than it usually was.

"Thank you for bringing her back," Dad said apologetically.

"Of course, Oliver," the officer replied sympathetically. "There was no damage this time. Just a few people who got a good scare, but no one is pressing charges."

"Please let them know how grateful we are," Dad conveyed. "We're not sure how she's getting out, but rest assured we are doing our best to figure it out."

"Is the doc on her way?" Officer Frawley asked, concerned.

"She should be here any minute," Dad reassured him. The policeman patted him on the shoulder in a consoling manner.

"Don't worry," he said with more sympathy. "We all understand."

A maroon Saturn was pulling up outside. Abney watched from the living room window as a sensible black dress shoe appeared, followed almost instantly by its mate. Dr. Armstrong was wearing a black pencil skirt with a flattering navy blue blouse. She had her blonde hair pulled back tight in a French twist, and a smile played on her deep red lips as she approached the kitchen door.

Abney had always thought of her as a beautiful snake. She moved elegantly and precisely, always prepared to strike. She did not like the woman. Dr. Armstrong had always been polite to her, but the energy coming off her was venomous, and Abney avoided her to the best of her ability.

Dr. Armstrong knocked politely before letting herself in. "Oliver, Bonnie, Officer," she greeted the adults. "Where is my patient?"

"Upstairs," Granny replied worriedly. "I convinced her to take her medication, but she's been pacing around in a state. We're so glad you're here."

"Of course," Dr. Armstrong said without hesitation. "Let's head up, shall we?" Abney heard her grandmother and the doctor heading in her direction.

"I'll be up in a minute," Dad called from behind them. "I just need to finish up with Fred."

"Hello, Abney." Dr. Armstrong entered the room and acknowledged her, sending a chill up her back.

"Hello," Abney nodded in reply. The doctor paused, taking in the marks on Abney's face and then walked right up to her. Abney tried to back away, but Dr. Armstrong already had a tight hold on her chin. She turned her head from side to side curiously.

"What's this?" she asked.

"It's a rash," Abney explained. "I…I fell in a patch of clover."

"Interesting," the doctor stated with what Abney thought was a dangerous glint in her eye. "You should come with us today. I think it might be beneficial for your mother."

"I don't think it's…" Granny tried to intervene.

"On the contrary," Dr. Armstrong interrupted. "This may be the exact dose of reality she needs today."

"If you think it's wise," Granny relented but did not look convinced. "Come along, Abney. If you feel uncomfortable or scared at all, you just leave, okay? No explanations necessary."

Abney nodded. She would have defied Dr. Armstrong, and had on several occasions, but she did not have the heart to openly disobey her grandmother. She followed them up the stairs without a word.

The stairs to the attic were old, rickety, and groaned with the weight of the threesome. Dust and decay filled their noses, though it was not an altogether unpleasant smell. The door to Moira's room loomed in front of them. It was a well-made heavy wooden door adorned with exactly ten locks. Granny took the key ring from the nail next to the door and expertly unlocked the entrance.

Soft yellow padding adorned the walls behind the well-sealed door. It gave a false air of cheer, kept the occupant from hurting herself, and contained her many, many screams. Moira was sitting in a rocking chair, staring blankly into space. The chair rocked in a steady rhythm, back and forth, back and forth. Dr. Armstrong entered the room first, then Granny, with Abney bringing up the rear.

"Good afternoon, Moira. I heard you had quite the adventure today. Let's chat about it," the doctor coaxed in a calm but firm voice. "Where were you going?"

Moira's pale gray eyes looked up wildly as if her visitors had just appeared from thin air. She pulled lightly on her mousy-brown braid, trying to soothe herself, and caught her nail on one of her abundant rebellious curls that stuck out all over her head. Her cheeks turned a violent red with surprise, making her skin almost translucent in comparison.

She hadn't seemed to notice Abney yet, which was fortunate, as Abney did not bring out the best in her mother.

"Dr. Armstrong...I saw him today. I saw my Abner," her mother told them frantically. "He was just outside. I had to follow him. I have to find him. I have to rescue him. Don't you see? He needs my help."

"Moira, we've talked about this. You have a little girl, remember? She lives in this house with you," Dr. Armstrong reminded her.

"That's *not* my child!" Moira stood up and shrieked. "She's a monster! A fake, to make everyone think I'm crazy. But I. Am. Not. Crazy!"

It had been this way for as long as Abney could remember. Her father would not speak to her about it, but Granny told her that there were a few mistakes on the birth certificate they received in the mail. It listed her name as Abner Skylar Kelly instead of Abney Skylar Kelly, and the gender box was checked as male. Moira had been looking all over for her phone to call the hospital and have the corrections made when she took a nasty fall down the stairs and hit her head forcibly. She never recovered.

Moira latched onto the idea that she had a son and not a daughter. For the first few years, she thought the hospital had given her the wrong child and was trying to cover it up. She took care of Abney, hoping that someone would help her, and she would be able to switch the girl for the boy that truly belonged to her. However, when Abney was around two, the psychosis took a dangerous turn, and Dad caught her trying to drown their daughter in the bath. She had convinced herself Abney was responsible for the disappearance of her imaginary son.

She was institutionalized for a year while Dad re-built the attic to house her. As appalled as he was by what she'd tried to do, he knew she was sick and not in her right mind. He loved her. He couldn't leave her to rot in an asylum. So, he brought Granny to live with them. She provided care for Moira and helped him raise Abney. He also hired Dr. Armstrong to come bi-weekly to oversee the operation and apply her medical expertise to his demented wife.

"Moira," Dr. Armstrong was saying. "I've brought you a visitor." She beckoned Abney to come forward, and she shuffled reluctantly closer.

Moira's eyes softened for a moment, and she took a step toward her daughter. Granny stepped protectively to her granddaughter's side, but Dr. Armstrong grabbed her hand to let her know it was safe. Moira stroked Abney's hair softly and traced her finger down her face.

"I wish you kids would leave your hair alone," she said referring to Abney's vibrant locks.

Her gentleness iced over when her fingers reached that first pale-blue mark on her daughter's cheek, and she backed away.

"You've cut her hair to make her look like a boy…but this is *not* my son! *This isn't my Abner!* Her skin is blue, for god's sake. Blue!"

"This *is* your daughter," Dr. Armstrong insisted, unruffled by the shouting. "Her skin is *not* blue. She has a rash."

"And you all think I'm the lunatic," she said defensively. "Whoever heard of a blue rash?" Abney's stomach turned sour. She could feel her mother's mood turning dangerous. She backed up a few steps. "That monster is not mine!" Moira persisted.

Granny jumped in with her sternest, do-not-mess-with-me tone. "That's enough, Moira. Abney, go downstairs now, dear and shut the door behind you."

"Bonnie, I think—" Dr. Armstrong started, but Granny wasn't having it.

"I'm sorry, Dr. Armstrong; this has been quite enough for a thirteen-year-old, and my decision is final."

There was no need to tell Abney twice. She backed out of the room as quickly as she could with Moira's accusations ringing in her ears.

"Where's my son? What have you done with my little boy? You're a monster! A monster!" Abney slammed the door and didn't look back. She felt tears running down her face, and she wanted to get to her room as fast as possible.

Dad passed her on the way down the stairs and looked horrified to see her so close to the attic. "Abney, what are you doing up here? What's wrong?" he asked after her.

"Ask Dr. Armstrong!" Abney shouted at him and continued to her room without stopping.

Her run-ins with Moira had been few and far between. Granny and

Dad were very vigilant about keeping the two apart, but when it did happen, it always stung. Some part of her wanted her mother to recognize her, love her, be the mother she was always supposed to be. Unfortunately, Abney was always left with that heavy feeling of disappointment and anger whenever she crossed that woman's path. She knew her mother was crazy, it wasn't her fault, and there was nothing to be done about it, but that didn't make it any easier.

She slammed her bedroom door behind her. It was mildly satisfying, but she wanted to rip the shelves from her walls, destroy everything in sight, make everything as broken as she felt at that moment. It wasn't fair! None of it, none of it was fair! She threw herself down on her bed and cried until she knew there wasn't a drop of water left in her whole body.

Sometime later, Abney got up from her bed and found she was calmer but still angry. She needed to burn off some energy, get her mind on something else. She needed to take a walk. She put on her coat and headed out into the snow. Their yard was barren and lifeless with the exception of the white flakes falling softly to the ground. The pond and its fountains were frozen, and the weeping willow earned her melancholic name, as her limbs hung over in mourning for their lost foliage. The swing in her branches looked inviting though, so Abney dusted the snow from it and pushed herself back and forth. She climbed higher and higher. She wanted to fly, fly away from her mother, Dr. Armstrong, Cotton, Ms. Ulyanna's Academy, and the whole stinking town of Archer, Wyoming. If it weren't for her father and Granny, she imagined she would have left already.

She put her feet down, dragging them to bring the swing to a halt. She'd forgotten her gloves, and her hands were aching with the cold. She stuffed them in her pockets, stubbornly refusing to go inside. Once her fingers regained some feeling, she realized there was something in her right pocket, a twig or some other nonsense. She pulled her hand from its toasty hiding place to examine the object. The tips of her index finger and thumb were now completely blue, and a perfect four-leaf clover was perched between them.

Still feeling destructive, Abney rubbed the leaves all over her left hand until there was not a speck of pale pink skin left. It was strangely calming to watch the color of her skin change, almost as if by magic. Maybe she could rub it all over her whole body and never have to go to school again? She could join a freak show—if those even existed anymore.

"Abney," her grandmother's voice sang out. "Abney Skylar Kelly, you get in here this instant. It's too cold for you to be outside for so long."

Abney groaned but started to walk toward the door, and as she did, a terrifying realization hit her. Her whole left hand was blue. How would she explain that? How could she tell Granny she knew she had an allergy to the weed but had rubbed it all over her hand anyway? She shoved her left hand as deep into her pocket as the coat would allow and entered the kitchen.

Granny, Dad, and Dr. Armstrong were there to ambush her.

"Abney, Dr. Armstrong has something she would like to say to you," Granny said, giving Dr. Armstrong an unamused look.

"I did not mean to cause you any emotional distress," the doctor said with remorse. "I was simply seeking to help your mother understand things a little better. It had not crossed my mind how much it might affect you. I am sorry for the harm I have caused."

"It's fine," Abney replied, not fully processing the conversation. "All good, we're groovy, cool, or whatever." She just wanted to get herself and her blue hand upstairs so she could figure out what to do next.

"You seem agitated," Dr. Armstrong stated. "Is there anything I can do to help?"

"No!" Abney exploded. "Just leave me alone, all right?" She ran up the stairs with the adults calling after her, but she didn't stop until she had slammed the door purposely behind her and locked it. She knew she'd bought herself at least a half hour before anyone tried to come and console her. Her family believed in letting emotions cool before attempting conversation in the case of an argument.

Now she just had to figure out what to do. What could she do? How was she going to hide this, if indeed, that was even a good idea? Blue was not a normal color for skin, was it? Mr. Burke had looked pretty concerned when he saw it at school. Maybe she shouldn't be taking this so lightly? What if she needed serious medical attention? What if her hand's circulation was being cut off, and it was due to fall off at any moment? She had officially scared herself enough to reconsider showing it to Dr. Armstrong when a strange voice startled her from her thoughts.

"Just couldn't wait, could you? Had to get yourself thrown in a clover patch and spoil everything. You're two weeks early, you know? Agatha will not be pleased, no, not in the slightest," a giant-horned-cat-creature said in a deep yet musical tone. He was sitting at the foot of her bed and looking very annoyed. She backed into her door, ready to scream, but the cat shook his head and held his hand up. Abney found she had no voice; she opened her mouth, but nothing came out. *Run*, her brain screamed, *run*, but her body would not obey. She was trapped by an imperceptible weight and unable to move or speak. His blue eyes burned through her like they were on fire and stood out in stunning contrast to his brilliant red-orange fur.

"Let's not and say we did." the creature said, bored. "It should be obvious by now that if I wanted to hurt you, I could, and there would be nothing you could do. So, if I remove the spell can we agree you should be reasonable? Blink once for yes and twice for no." Abney quickly and carefully considered her options. There weren't many. Therefore, she reluctantly blinked once. The pressure disappeared immediately, but she didn't dare speak.

"Are you ready to listen?" it asked. Abney nodded. "Good." He continued, "You are a Faerie. And before you even start, yes, really, you are. If this is not sinking in, please direct your attention to your blue appendage. What kind, you may ask? I don't know and won't until I remove your glamour. When will I do this is probably the next question in your predictable little mind. The answer is: When I feel like it. With me so far?" Abney nodded even though she had no idea what he was talking about.

"Now, we have to contact your Doppelgänger and get to Tír na nÓg.

I could re-glamour you and make you do this properly, but there's no guarantee you won't go rolling around in clover patches or that you won't make a very foolish attempt to run away. Usually, I plan these things better. Nothing ever seems to go right with you though, so I really shouldn't be surprised. We're just going to have to fly by the seat of our pants. By the way, the name is, Snozbert."

She introduced herself shakily. "Abney Kelly." It seemed the right thing to do or at least the polite thing. She stuck out her hand robotically and regretted doing so almost immediately. Snozbert looked at her hand in a very dismissive manner.

"I named you, silly girl. Do you think I'd forget who you are?" he remarked as if he was speaking to the dimmest person imaginable.

"You named me?" she piped up.

"For the love of Pixies, can you focus?" he chastised her. "First things first, we need to call your Doppelgänger. He's probably in the middle of a game of Basnorts and not at all prepared for any of this. That's the way the ball bounces, I suppose."

"He?" Abney questioned. "My Doppelgänger is a boy?"

"I told you nothing has ever gone quite as planned with you," he snapped in her face. "Keep up! I'll be needing some of your hair, hold still." He snatched a hair from her head before she could object.

"Ouch!" she cried out, more in surprise than in pain.

"Oh, don't be so dramatic," he sneered and walked into her closet uninvited. "Where's a mirror?" He searched. "Ah! Here it is, hidden behind all these clothes. A mirror should be in plain sight to use it properly. Didn't you know?"

"I-I-I—" Abney stammered, but Snozbert cut her off.

"Fleetlings...not very intelligent. I knew I should have looked for better-educated parents for you."

"My parents are just fine," she said, referring more to her father and grandmother than her mother. "And you can't just go around talking about them like that."

"Don't get yourself in a state; you'll soon feel the same," he replied, paying no heed to the flash of temper. "Hold your hair, while I pull out your mirror, and do *not* lose it." He handed her the strand, and she backed up automatically to give him some space. Everything was happening so fast there was no time to process anything, so she went along with it because she had no idea what else to do. He placed the mirror upright against one of her bookshelves and looked at it from several angles. "This should be fine, I think. No time like the present to find out!"

"What exactly are we doing?" Abney asked, her curiosity winning out over fear.

"Calling for your Doppelgänger. Have I been unclear?" Snozbert retorted, irked by her ignorance.

"No, I…uh…I just never made a call with a mirror before," she managed to get out.

"I would think not," the cat affirmed. "Now, stand back and hand me the hair when I tell you to."

Abney took three giant steps backward.

"*Mirror, mirror on the wall: Do you know if I am short, fat, thin, or tall? Do you know the curve of my face? Do you know where every single freckle is placed? What color is my hair? What tint my eyes? When I look in your depths will I find disgust or surprise?*"

A booming voice erupted through the glass. "Io…"

The cat stopped him quickly. "Code names only," he insisted. The glass had turned to a swirly-jelly-like substance.

"Snozbert isn't your name?" Abney questioned. They pretended not to hear her.

"Very well, if we must," the voice played along. "What is your name this time?"

"Snozbert," the cat said matter-of-factly.

"Snozbert," the voice continued. "You do not have to make up a silly rhyme to summon me, and you know it. It sets a bad precedent with the students. I hate whimsy."

"I'll consider your request," Snozbert obviously lied, and Abney thought she heard the mirror groan. "I need Abney Kelly's Doppelgänger."

"He's not on the schedule for another two weeks," the mirror complained.

"Well, things have been moved up," the cat replied.

"What have you done this time?" the mirror said in an accusatory tone.

"I didn't do anything," Snozbert answered, slightly offended...but only slightly. "She got into a patch of clover. One of her hands is completely blue. She looks like a part albino Smurf."

Abney injected herself into the conversation. "Hey! I do not."

"Your input is not required," Snozbert said curtly.

"Quite right. You've caused enough trouble, young lady."

Abney did not appreciate being criticized by complete strangers.

"You two don't even know me," she defended herself, which only elicited hearty laughter from the ruffians.

"Do you have the hair?" the mirror asked Snozbert between cackles.

"Abney," the cat demanded, putting his hand in front of her face. Abney looked down to her hand; she had dropped it somewhere. She looked frantically at the ground and then to Snozbert, who pursed his lips in disapproval. He reached up quickly and plucked another hair from her head. Abney cried out again. "You have no one to blame but yourself," he informed her and then spoke to the mirror. "It's right here." Snozbert pushed the hair into the goo. A few moments later, the clone came flying through the glass at them. The cat caught it easily and steadied its balance.

"Are you going to be coming through?" the mirror asked.

"No. We'll take the river," Snozbert said.

"Very well," the mirror answered and solidified in front of them. Abney found it strange looking at herself but knowing it was not her. They were near identical down to the blue and green hair. There was one thing people were bound to notice though: she most certainly did not have an Adam's apple.

"No one is going to buy that this is me!" she lamented. "And why do we need a Doppelgänger anyway?"

"They won't notice a thing," Snozbert said. "You look rather like a boy already, and the only reason you noticed any difference is that you're Fae. Fleetlings will never be able to tell. And again, we need him so you can go to Tír na nÓg without being missed."

"I'm not leaving with you," she protested. "Not to mention, how will he know how to talk? What to say? He just met me. What can he even know about me? It will never work, and I'm not doing it."

"We have already established you *are* doing it…even if I have to drag you paralyzed and tongue-tied," Snozbert reminded her. "If you are worried about the Doppelgänger, he's been watching you your whole life. He will not give the slightest indication that he is not you. Also, it's only part-time for now."

"Really?" Abney said to her twin, trying desperately to get out of the situation, "Well then, what's my favorite book?"

"*Cart and Cwidder*, by Diana Wynne Jones. It's the first book of the Dalemark Quartet series," it replied without pause. Abney was taken aback; no one ever got that, not even Granny, and Abney had told her about the book more than once.

"Ummm…what about my favorite actor?" she continued, determined to prove he could not pass as her.

"Elijah Wood. You think he's odd, and you like that about him," he said very confidently.

"Favorite—" Abney tried to continue the quiz, but Snozbert's fuzzy hand was covering her mouth.

"We do not have time for this," he insisted. A knock came at the door.

"Abney? Hey kiddo, are you ready to talk?" Her father's voice came through the door. Abney wanted to call out, warn him, run to him, but Snozbert had her tightly by the arm, and they were rushing at her closed window. She put her free arm in front of her eyes and braced for impact.

CHAPTER 4

THE GIRL WHO *WAS* BLUE

Much to Abney's surprise, the glass didn't shatter, and there was no rush of wind as they plummeted from her second story window. In fact, they floated as slowly and gently downward as the snow surrounding them. Solid ground met her feet as they landed, and Abney found the courage to open her eyes. It was inky out. The only light was the gentle glow of the untouched snow. Her breath surrounded her like a heavy mist. She realized she was not wearing a coat, hat, or gloves, and it was freezing out. She began to shiver.

"Ah ha!" Snozbert exclaimed. "I knew you had a pond! Very convenient! Follow me." He pressed a button on his vest, and the wings on his back folded inward quickly and efficiently. Next, he strolled over to the ice. It was thick, dark, and foreboding, but the cat didn't seem the least bit concerned. Abney kept looking back at her house, hoping someone would notice them. She made exaggerated movements with her arms as soon as he turned his back, hoping to elicit a rescue. Even Dr. Armstrong would be a welcome sight at this point.

"They can't see you," Snozbert said over his shoulder, and Abney froze her motions. "Scream if you really must, but they won't hear you either. The Doppelgänger's protection spell keeps Fleetlings from seeing you both in the same space. While he's here, you're pretty much invisible." Abney nodded her understanding and swore under her breath. She would have to think of some other way to escape.

Snozbert walked around the pond, tapping on the frozen surface until he found a spot that produced a low sweet ringing sound. He then bent over and knocked smartly as if he expected someone to answer. To Abney's surprise, someone or something did. Three short knocks resounded from the frigid depths, and Snozbert replied with two short knocks followed by two unhurried knocks, then he took two quick steps backward. A large hole burned through the ice, leaving a perfectly circular window.

Snozbert pushed her forward. "Go take a look." Teeth chattering, Abney shook her head no. It was nearly arctic out, and she wasn't about to get near the open water, so that monster could push her in.

"I'm good," she told him. "I can see fine from here."

"I said, take a closer look," he persisted. Remembering that he could and would make her do it, Abney moved to the very edge of the pond and stared. "Closer," he hissed, losing his patience. "Get down on your knees and look closer!" This almost certainly ended with her going in head first, but what choice did she have?

She knelt down and peered timidly into the murk, but nothing happened. It was her turn to be peeved. "Yup," she spat. "Looks like our pond all right." She'd gotten down in the snow for nothing or so she thought. As she stood, she managed to spot the tip of one curly green tentacle, before another snaked around her waist and dragged her beneath the surface.

Pain stabbed her everywhere. The cold was utterly debilitating as she felt herself sink hastily through the icy abyss. She could feel things brushing against her, but the dark was too consuming to see anything. Her lungs were burning and begging for air. *I knew that beast was going to drown me*, she thought angrily.

That's when Abney's knees collided painfully with something solid, and she breathed involuntarily. Water did not rush in and overtake her though. Air—sweet, wonderful, dry air—filled her lungs. She coughed and water came up. She was alive, not dead, not drowned, and that was something.

She looked around. There was a strong salty smell on the eerie, glowing air. A drop of water plopped onto her forehead, and Abney looked up. There was water floating on the ceiling, an ocean above her head, held up by some invisible force. A loud thud shook the ground beneath her feet. She looked over her shoulder to see Snozbert standing there as if nothing had happened. Abney looked at him furiously, and he dared to look unfazed.

"Welcome aboard," a watery voice announced from in front of her. She followed the sound to a tall hooded creature dressed like a medieval monk. He was holding a long stick or some other object, and she could see long green tentacles protruding from beneath the hood. She had a flashback to just before she'd been jerked into the water. *What is he?* It didn't seem real. *Who's going to believe a beard accosted me?*

"It's rude to stare," he pointed out to her.

"Sorry," Abney replied, realizing she had been studying him for some time. "It's just I thought I was going to die...then I didn't. Now I'm..." She looked around, but she had no idea what to call this place.

"On a boat," the water-logged voice replied. "On the river Styx, if you want to be precise." Abney looked around again, noticing the wooden floor and siding around her. A boat at least made sense, however, the idea that there was water above and below her wasn't comforting. She felt slightly claustrophobic, and it only fed into the sense of panic that was starting to take her over.

"All right," she continued. "I'm on a boat with a talking cat and something with a tentacle beard. I'm cold. I'm wet..."

"You're not wet," Snozbert interjected.

"Yes, I am," Abney argued and seized her shirt for proof, but it was dry—not even a bit damp—and her skin felt warm to the touch.

"Thoughts are powerful, Abney Kelly," the cat told her. "You thought you should be cold and wet, and so you were. You should learn to discern what actually is before jumping to conclusions in the future." Abney looked at him, dumbfounded. How was it even possible? Snozbert, noticing her confusion, continued. "Close your mouth. Bewilderment isn't a good look for you."

"I just want to go home," Abney said, breaking into tears. She wanted her father, grandmother, and a cup of hot chocolate. "I don't want to be here with...with monsters!"

"I beg your pardon," the tentacle monk said, obviously offended.

"We're not monsters, any more than you are, girl with the blue hand," Snozbert said, unaffected by the outburst.

"For Pete's sake! I'm not blue! I have an allergy!" Abney snapped at him. Snozbert snorted and went to speak with the tentacled monk.

Abney walked sulkily over to the side of the boat and looked out over the water. It was the clearest blue she'd ever seen, and the fish and plants below glowed with neon colors that made them easily recognizable. It reminded her of being in a room with a black light. A cloud of pink caught her eye. It was moving up toward the surface, and Abney thought she could just make out a face at its center. A few seconds later, a long fish-like tail came into view. *It's a mermaid*, she thought and then doubted herself. *A mermaid? Why not? If I'm a Faerie, why can't there be mermaids too?* Abney waved at it, half believing it was real, halfway thinking she was as crazy as her mother. She saw a webbed purple hand reach up toward her in response.

The mermaid was completely identifiable now. She smiled and waved at Abney from beneath the surface. The mythical creature slithered gracefully back and forth in the water, doing tricks to amuse Abney. It was mesmerizing. Her webbed fingers beckoned for Abney to come in the water and join her. Abney felt tempted, but something in her stomach told her she'd better not. So, she pantomimed that she couldn't swim to the fish-woman, who made a pouty face and promptly disappeared.

Abney bent farther over the rail, trying to see where she had gone, but she was nowhere in sight. Suddenly, she felt a pair of hands yanking her backward from the railing as the mermaid exploded from the water with a horrifying shriek. Abney watched its pointed teeth snarl at her angrily as it fell back into the river.

"Not exactly like you see in the movies, are they?" Snozbert asked. "She is as likely to eat you as she is to drown you—just for fun. The River Styx is a dangerous place, best not to hang out too near the edge of the boat." Abney broke into sobs again. *What sort of hellish nightmare is this?*

Snozbert tried to quiet her. "Come on, blue girl, stop crying,"

"I'm not blue!" she shouted hysterically.

"Of course you are," he argued with a sigh and walked over to her. *"As above, so below, open her eyes, let her know. Faerie born, now Faerie be, I command you, Abney Kelly, to truly see."* Abney felt fresh, like she had just walked out of a hot shower. Snozbert turned to the tentacle monk and asked, "Do you have a mirror?"

"I might have, but I'm not giving it to you for that," he replied firmly.

"I'll owe you a favor," Snozbert offered, his voice heavy with meaning. The creature pretended to think about it, but even Abney could see he was eager to accept.

"It's a deal," he agreed greedily and handed Snozbert what looked like a small hand mirror, which Snozbert smashed on the ground immediately.

"Expandinium sproutoùx," he shouted with authority. Abney watched in amazement as the mirror shattered and rebuilt itself to ten times its original size in front of her. In its reflection, she saw a pale blue pudgy girl with short white hair, but not just white; greens and pinks danced through the strands like the northern lights. Her eyes were very large and silvery colored. Her nose tiny and nearly invisible to the naked eye. Abney would have missed it entirely if the surrounding oil slick-like freckles hadn't drawn her attention to the area. Her mouth was drawn down in concentration, but that only accentuated the perfect heart that her lips made.

"Who's that?" she asked.

"Do you often see people besides yourself in the mirror?" Snozbert remarked.

"That's me?" Abney questioned, unable to believe it. The reflection was wearing her clothes, but it couldn't be her. She checked the other side of the mirror to make sure it wasn't a trick. No one was there. She looked down at her hands and jumped when she noticed both of them were now completely blue. She pulled a strand of her hair out. It was white.

"Frost Fae by the look of it," Snozbert informed her. "It's a form of Pixie. I'm a Puca, and tentacle beard over there is a Cthulhui."

"Are you guys Pixies too?" Abney asked Snozbert, not sure of the different races or genomes.

"No," the Puca snorted. "We're Hobgoblins. Which are very different."

"I see," she said foolishly.

Snozbert outed her. "You don't. But you will. In two weeks, you'll start at either Mabon or Yule, I'm assuming. Those are two of the four schools in Tír na nÓg. They will teach you to interact correctly within Fae society. You will learn the names and how to identify the many different species of Fae. They will also teach you a trade, how to pay proper respect to the Elements, and of course, you'll learn magic."

Abney pumped him for more information. "Are those schools especially for Pixies? And what about the school I already go to? What about my family?"

"They're not your real family. Your Doppelgänger will handle your Fleetling school and life. I'm pretty sure we covered that already. As for the Fae schools, all Fae have talents that interact and correlate with certain Elements, and we school them accordingly. Mabon is located east of the city and houses those who are considered to have water-based talents. You will find Mermaids, Kelpies, Sirens, some forms of Nymphs, and Selkies, to name a few. North of the city, there is Yule, for the students born with air gifts. So you'll have your Thunder Birds, Fauns, Frost Fae, Banshees, Grim Reapers and that sort. To the west, Ostara, for those born with earthen gifts. It houses Flora-Fae, Centaurs, Leprechauns, Sylphs, Unicorns, and other life giving and healing Fae. Finally, to the south, Litha, for the fiery Fae. Such as Dragons, Demons, a few classes of Pixies, and the like," he informed her.

"What about Pucas and Cthulhuis?" Abney queried.

"Hobgoblins have a different school," Snozbert said in a tone that said the subject was now closed, but Abney pried anyway.

"What's the name of your school?" she asked.

"It's not important," he said, ending the discussion.

"Snozbert?" Abney said. "One more question." He raised his eyebrow at her in disbelief.

He nodded. "One more."

"If I'm a Pixie, shouldn't I have wings?"

"Not necessarily. Evolution isn't restricted to Fleetlings, you know. More and more Fae are being born without them as we use them less and less."

"Oh," Abney said glumly.

"Tír na nÓg, ahoy!" the Cthulhui sang out. Abney turned to view what, at first, looked like nothing but large stalagmites in a foggy cave, but as they entered the gloom, a grand underground city stretched out before them. The stone columns were like skyscrapers, full of windows and different colored lights. Mushrooms grew large here, like trees, and glowworms hung from the top of the cave, giving the city its unearthly glow. It was the most beautiful city she had ever seen. It was beyond words, a splendid trip into the unimaginable.

Her eyes darted here and there, trying to take everything in. Rainbows of crystals clung to the ground like underground bushes. Winged creatures were everywhere, zipping all around. She tried to get a good look, but they moved so fast it was practically impossible. She nearly fell overboard when the boat bumped into the dock, but Snozbert grabbed her shoulders and steadied her.

"This is unbelievable," Abney whispered in awe.

"This is Tír na nÓg," the Cthulhui said knowingly. She repeated the word and let it roll off her tongue. It all felt too fantastical. In her most vivid dreams, she could not have come up with this.

Snozbert got her attention. "Abney, this way."

He held onto her shoulders as he steered her through the docks and into a labyrinth of city streets. There were vendors everywhere, shops, and strange beings of every color, size, and shape imaginable and unimaginable. Some were single-colored and some multi-colored. Some had human-like mouths. Some had beaks and snouts. A few had wings, but most had none. There were ghost-like figures, willowy sirens, wart-faced trolls, Fae that were as tall as buildings, and Fae as small as ants. And color! There was so much color and in hues she could never have dreamed existed. Christmas trees covered in thousands of multi-colored lights were on every corner. Hypnum or sheet moss covered the streets. She wished she had her phone so that she could get some pictures for Ms. Thornberry. The thought of her botany teacher brought reality crashing into her heart, and her stomach cramped with a familiar fear. Would she ever see Ms. Thornberry or anyone from her home again?

Snozbert felt her tense. "You will get used to this life." He sounded almost comforting. "And you will see your Fleetling-family again, you have my word." Abney relaxed a little bit.

Looking to distract herself, she asked, "Snozbert, why do you call them Fleetlings?"

"Because their time is so fleeting. Barring accident or murder, we Fae live eternally. Their time is but a tiny blip, so they're called the Fleetlings," he explained. Abney nodded with understanding but felt sad at the thought that she would blink, and her father and Granny would be gone. It almost made her start crying again.

They stopped in front of a door with a carving of a tree whose leaves were drifting leisurely downward. It was a magical work of art, and it seemed almost insulting when Snozbert reached up and knocked on it lazily, but loudly, to get the inhabitants' attention. There was a ruckus from inside, and they heard something like shattering glass before the door swung open.

"Ah, it's you," a woman's raspy voice spoke. "Tell me, honey, what name are you going by now?"

He laughed. "Snozbert. Are you still going by the same dull name?"

The woman stepped from the shadows into view. "Yup, still Agatha." Agatha was very strange looking, like a creature that had once been human or at least humanesque. Her legs were large and stump-like beneath her skintight navy dress. Her hips were round and bumpy like cottage cheese, but her waist was quite long and slender. Her neck was drawn-out and boney, with a black hole in the center. Her skin was thin and wrinkled, and there were just a few wiry hairs sticking out on her well-rounded head.

"What kind of Fae are you?" Abney asked rudely. Agatha just laughed, a gravelly, phlegm-filled cackle.

"Agatha is a Fleetling…sort of," Snozbert told her. "Fleetlings who stay a long time in our lands experience…um…some strange effects."

"Oh honey, that was nearly a compliment," Agatha teased him.

"It was most certainly a compliment," he flirted with her. Agatha smiled, and Abney could see she still had all of her teeth, yellow and semi-rotted though they were.

Abney and Snozbert followed Agatha through the pitch-black entryway into a blue room. It was blue like the depths of the ocean and embellished with sage-green furnishings. Agatha motioned for them to take a seat on a couch that looked like a giant piece of padded coral. Abney noted that it was much more comfortable than it looked.

"Now, who is this?" Agatha's voice rattled at the Puca.

"Abney Kelly," he said, shaking his head in disapproval. "She took a roll in a clover patch, so here we are."

"How very inconvenient," Agatha commiserated with him. "I hope we can expect better behavior from you in future, honey," she directed at Abney, who felt rather put on the spot.

She challenged the accusation. "I did not roll around in clover. Cotton pushed me."

Agatha gave no quarter. "Then you must pay better attention to your surroundings. You can't be pushed over if you're not surprised."

"But I—" Abney started.

"Oh, never mind the excuses, sugar," Agatha told her. "Stand up, turn about. I need to get a good look at you."

Abney obeyed but managed to look hurt while twirling.

"A Snow Maiden," Agatha declared. "We haven't had one of those in a few years."

"Dragon's Fire," Snozbert swore. "I had her pegged for a Pixie or a Sprite."

"No, without a doubt, a Snow Maiden. It will be Yule for you, with special lessons at Litha in your free time," Agatha explained. "We have a few multi-elementals every year. Snozbert, if you wouldn't mind, she'll need some help until she can control it on her own."

"Control what?" Abney asked.

"Your emotions," Agatha remarked. "You, your skin, your hair, most of your organs are ice, but your heart..." The old woman shuffled over and touched her chest. "Your heart is fire. Too much emotion can melt you on the spot, and we don't want that, do we?"

"No," Abney agreed, picturing herself as an actual puddle on the floor. The Puca strode over to her and placed his hand over her heart. Abney tried to back up; she didn't like being touched by strangers, but Snozbert grabbed her shoulder and pulled her close. He placed his hand on her chest and whispered in a language she couldn't understand. A jolt shook through her. She struggled to catch her breath but managed to gulp out, "What did you do?"

"I've put a core of ice in your heart. It will help keep your temperature down," he stated. Abney's teeth chattered, and she felt herself shiver for a moment, but then the cold settled and felt quite pleasant.

"Feodora," Agatha called out, and a breathtakingly beautiful woman joined them. She had deep green moss like skin, which looked to have little bits of bark in it. Her hair flowed with vines and flowers, making it appear to have a life of its own. Her slender body and graceful movements gave the impression she was dancing into the room, yet she was only walking. "Feo, honey, take Abney upstairs. She will need a room in the Saxta Baba Wing. She will also need much cooler clothing. Send for the tailor," Agatha instructed.

"Yes, ma'am," the girl replied and pulled a tiny sleeping humanoid creature from her pocket and poked it lightly.

"Hey! What's the big idea?" it protested and stood up, shaking its wings loose from its back. It had butter-colored skin, wild blue hair, and no clothes.

"Go get DiGott," she ordered. "Tell him he's needed at Oberon House right away."

"After breakfast." The yellow head nodded at her hungrily. Feodora produced a tiny packet and tipped it upside down in her hand. The smallest worms Abney had ever seen fell out, and the little winged creature jumped on them like a wild dog, shoving them into its mouth as fast as it could.

"Now, be on your way," Feodora said. It flew up and pecked her on the cheek before dashing out an open window. "Follow me," Feodora bid Abney.

"Abney," Agatha called after them, and both girls turned to face her. "Welcome to Oberon House." Abney, unsure what to say, nodded her thanks and followed the green girl up the stairs.

CHAPTER 5

TÍR NA NÓG

The halls of Oberon House were vast and lengthy, each one a colorful, eclectic bohemian dream. Feodora moved quickly through the maze, never second-guessing a step. Abney tried to remember landmarks of sorts so that she would be able to leave if it became necessary. Turn left at the pig mask, right at the red hall with the elephant, right again at the Chinese vase, left at the wall of hats…or was it right? They had made so many turns that Abney couldn't keep up. They finally made it to a white hall with pale purple and orange snowflakes embellishing it. It was noticeably cooler, and Abney could feel her body relaxing into the chill. They stopped in front of a silver door.

"The Jack Frost Suite is open," Feodora said and opened the door. "We'll put you in here." Abney stepped into the ample space and spun around trying to take it all in. The walls were Prussian blue with silver, ice-like swirls painted flamboyantly over the top. A sparkling white canopy surrounded the round bed. She sat down on the edge and ran her hands over the soft silver comforter. The scent of cloves and cinnamon wafted up pleasantly.

"This is so cool!" Abney whispered excitedly, forgetting Feodora was there.

"It is charming," the green woman agreed. Abney hopped off the bed and continued to look around. There were many empty shelves, an armoire, a gorgeous Art Nouveau vanity, and what she supposed was a closet, but when she opened the door, she found that it had a thin, long bed and a small dresser. There was no color or cheerfulness to this room.

"Who sleeps here?" Abney questioned.

"Your Hobgoblin, of course," Feodora laughed. "He must remain with you until your twentieth year. You are not permitted to be unescorted in Tír na nÓg until then. The Queens would never allow it."

"I don't have a Hobgoblin," Abney told her earnestly.

"Io…or whatever his name is now"—the girl squirmed at almost giving the name away—"the Puca you arrived with. He is your Hobgoblin."

"Um…he's not mine," Abney replied, appalled. "We've just met. I don't own him."

"He is your assigned guardian." Feodora giggled, amused by Abney's bewilderment.

"And he's sleeping in here with me?" Abney gawked.

"No, he's sleeping in there." Feodora pointed to the closet. "He won't come out unbidden or spy on you, if that's what you're worried about." Abney stared at her. She wasn't comfortable with this situation at all, and she felt more than a little guilty that her room was so large, and his was hardly a cupboard.

A tiny yet deep voice erupted from the corner of the room. "Don't look so pathetic. It's just a Hobgoblin."

The girls turned and observed a newspaper floating in front of a large armchair. Ten small fingers grasped the sides, and two tiny feet stuck out from beneath it. The paper named itself, *The Korrigan Chronicler*, and the headline read:

Kringle Escapes! HAFWITS Suspected in Prison Break!

The paper folded itself, and the small man stood up on the chair to greet them. His pointed purple hat seemed a weak attempt to cover his equally pointed ears. Both Abney and Feodora watched as his delicate hands straightened the matching bowtie at his collar, drawing attention to his youthful face and blue eyes that sparkled mischievously. The yellow creature Abney had encountered earlier was sitting on his shoulder and flew back and landed on Feodora's outstretched hand. She petted it on the head with her finger and put it back in her pocket.

"DiGott," Feodora announced. "Good of you to join us."

He bowed sarcastically. "My pleasure as always. Doesn't look I have much to work with." The Elf looked Abney up and down in a way she did not appreciate. "Well, what is she so that I can get started?"

"A Snow Maiden," Feodora said with a knowing smirk.

The Elf's eyes lit up, and he nearly smiled genuinely but stopped. Abney got the impression he didn't want to give Feodora the satisfaction.

"You will need to be extra cold to help counterbalance your toasty innards." He clapped loudly, and a trunk with eight legs scuttered into her room. It seemed rather excitable.

"Lie down," DiGott commanded it. It whined, but the Elf was not having it. "I said, down!" The trunk's booted feet shot straight out, and the trunk landed with a thump. The Elf looked annoyed but opened the lid without chiding the chest further. "I'm thinking Ice-Spider Silk and Yeti Mucus," he chirped. Abney tried not to look disgusted.

"She'll need a Yule uniform and robes. Her sash should acknowledge Yule and Litha though, naturally," Feodora instructed him. "A few off-hour garments as well. As always, the school grants you one favor per four outfits with a max of three favors per student."

"Very well," the Elf grumbled, and the green girl left them to their measurements.

"Are favors valuable?" Abney asked curiously since this was the second time she had heard them exchanged.

"Usually," DiGott replied. "But favors from the school tend to cancel themselves out. By the time you graduate, you'll owe the school so many favors that you'll end up doing free stuff for them forever."

"Sounds like college back home," she admitted.

"Are women allowed in colleges now? My, my, how times have changed," the Elf said, intrigued.

"Yes." Abney replied, stunned. "Women can do anything a man can do."

"Is that so?" DiGott asked, amused. "Well, there's a few things I'd advise against, but I think I'll let you figure that out yourself."

She defended her gender. "Well, we've been going to college and working now, for-like-ever."

"Not for-like-ever," he mocked her. "You, young ones! You take so much for granted. When I was in school, women were barely let out of their houses, since they were little better than property. Be grateful that you were born into such a progressive time. It took years to break the girls in my class of their Fleetling stigmas."

"You must do this a lot." Abney pressed curiously, "How often do you get new students?"

"Oh, every year," the Elf told her.

"And no one told you women go to college or vote now?"

"Probably. I try not to remember too many of these conversations," he confided. "There's only so much you can say to a complete stranger, and I do this so often that it all sort of blends together. Who knows what I've said to whom? Certainly, not I."

Abney fell silent, why waste words on someone who was not paying attention?

A few hours later, Abney had school uniforms, regular clothing, and a few pairs of shoes. She was exhausted. There was no telling how long it had been since she last slept. Feodora came in, hung her clothing, brought her a nice cold glass of water, and saw DiGott out. Abney opened the doors and drawers of her armoire, searching for some pajamas but to no avail.

"Feodora," Abney said to get the girl's attention.

"Call me Feo. Feodora is such a mouthful."

"Feo," Abney obliged. "I need some pajamas so that I can go to bed."

Feo laughed. "Oh, dear. Fae don't wear pajamas. They're not good for sleep. It messes with your internal temperatures. Honestly, most don't even use the blankets; they just sleep on top of them."

"What do I wear then?" Abney said as the information flew right over her head.

"You sleep in the buff," Feo said more to the point. "You know, au natural."

"Ooooohhh," Abney said as the words sank in. "Wow."

✳

Abney woke the next morning believing the previous day had been a dream. She stumbled out of bed, searching for her slippers with her eyes half open. She couldn't think where they had gotten to. A draft of cool air blew against her backside, and she jumped up and patted herself down. She thought she'd felt a little extra liberated this morning.

Her eyes flew open fully. This was not her home or her room, and she wasn't wearing any clothes! A renewed sense of loss overwhelmed her. She wanted to burst into tears but kept it together until she pulled a thin icy shirt over her head, got herself into a pair of wide-leg matching pants and tied them at her waist.

She looked in the mirror accidently. Her initial reaction was to cringe, but having already caught a glimpse, she braved a full view. The white was rather pretty against her blue skin, and even though the reflection was strange, it wasn't as monstrous as she feared. That, however, did not help with the way she was feeling. It was a weird combination of calm and despair. There were no sobs or sniffling, but water gushed down her cheeks in wide unstoppable rivers.

A knock came from the Puca's door.

"May I come in?" he asked.

Abney wiped the tears away, very unsuccessfully, and replied, "Sure." The door opened, and Snozbert ducked through the archway into the larger room. He looked at her and shook his head.

"Abney Kelly, these," he said, catching a tear on his finger, "will do you no good. You must control your emotions. Your heart can still melt through the ice core if you get too worked up."

51

Abney understood and took a few deep breaths in and out. She pushed home and her family from her thoughts.

"Good," he said, acknowledging the effort. "Now, the showers are down the hall to your left. Get yourself ready. We have much to do today."

Abney was trying too hard to remain numb to argue; she walked out the door and headed for the bathroom.

✦

Sublime smells wafted from the bright white and yellow kitchen as Abney entered the room. It reminded her of what she had imagined whenever she had read about a quaint country cottage. There was even a vase filled with sunflowers and bluebells. It was like she had witnessed the scene in her mind a million times, never realizing it was a real place.

Sitting in the breakfast nook, she found Agatha, Snozbert, and four new faces as well. Two sets of what Abney assumed to be siblings, if not twins. They certainly looked near identical, aside from their genders. One set looked remarkably like Snozbert, except the coloring. The twin Pucas were milk white with strange eyes. Each had one blue and one green eye. The other set of twins had pale green skin, long aqua hair, and pointed ears. Both had an alien beauty and looked so much alike, that Abney almost missed that one was a girl; however, the one to the right was decidedly feminine looking, though she couldn't put her finger on precisely what gave that impression.

"Good morning, honey," Agatha greeted her. "Have a seat and grab some breakfast." There was a bowl of some pink paste on the table, near something that looked similar to pancakes. "These"—Agatha pointed to the blue-haired siblings—"are some fellow troublemakers." She pointed to the girl—"Zoey"—then pointed to the boy—"and Domino Doggett. They managed to get here on their own. Clever little buggers."

"Yes," the girl Puca agreed in a tone that was not complimentary.

"Cut our game of Basnorts right off," her twin complained.

"Yes, we're all so sorry for interrupting your game." Domino crossed his arms, and Zoey followed suit.

Agatha finished the introductions. "And this is Abney Kelly."

"And what are we? Chopped liver?" the girl Puca sniffed.

"No, need to get bent out of shape," Agatha smoothed it over. "Abney, this is Blythe and Wilbur. And before you start"—she looked at Snozbert—"Domino, Zoey, this is Snozbert...at least for the moment." The three young Fae nodded, and the Pucas seemed mildly pacified. Abney found herself thinking they were kind of touchy for creatures who seemed bored by everything.

✦

The sextet found themselves right in the middle of Tír na nÓg. The Pucas were looking about with their usual disinterest and Abney, Domino, and Zoey were running from one thing to the next, taking in the sights. There was a grow-your-own-furniture shop, where the chairs and sofas grew out of various pots and into some of the most ornate furniture Abney had ever seen. There were vendors of honeyed tree bark, steamed worms, fried blossoms, and oddly, there was a coffee and tea cart. Abney watched the vendor hand customers steaming cups. She could smell the rich bitterness from where she was standing, and coffee sounded so good. Then, she thought of her blue skin and comfortably frozen body. *Can I even drink hot drinks anymore? Surely, I've always been me on the inside? But then again, I had a lot of feelings back home, and I never melted. I think I'll put a pin in that for later.*

A movie palace caught her eye. This was another thing that reminded her of home until she saw the posters. *The Children*, starring Bluka Hornwrest, Jessa Aquiston, and Howard Mulgrave, looked like a scary movie. *Mushrooms Are NOT Food*, starring Stunondra Fickelfarret and Gustroferman Zablaster, looked like a comedy. She had never seen actors who looked like these did. They were not glamorous, nor did they have any particular beauty. Abney was very curious to see a Fae movie.

There were many more practical shops in view, selling herbs, groceries, clothing, and stationery; the biggest draw though, was the wing shop. An enormous window display showed a glowing pair of purple wings that flapped slowly and elegantly by themselves. Lovely gold runes decorated them and seemed to flicker in a specific sequence. Abney walked up and pressed her face to the window. She wanted wings.

Domino came up from behind her. "Wow!"

Zoey joined them, looking equally as transfixed. "Oh, we definitely need those."

"Not for a while yet," Blythe informed them.

"No, not for three more years," Wilbur agreed with his sister.

"They're very impractical," Snozbert said. "So outdated."

"They're beautiful," Abney replied, not giving a fig about what they had to say. "And you have some yourself," she said, remembering the jump and gentle glide down from her bedroom window. The other Pucas raised their eyebrows at him.

"Well, they can be useful, at times," he grumbled looking at the ground.

"You can apply for a learner's permit when you're sixteen," Blythe remarked. "Mind you, a set of wings will come with a heavy favor attached...and the schools don't pay for wings."

Abney had not been in Tír na nÓg long enough to realize how valuable favors were and why she should be wary of handing them out. At the moment, she didn't care what they would cost. She just knew that someday she was going to fly.

The first place they went after the Pucas pulled them away from the wing shop was the herbalist. Snozbert, Blythe, and Wilbur had come prepared with lists of supplies their young wards would need for school.

Yule: 1st Year Supply List

1 Stone Pestle and Mortar
25 Large Specimen Bottles
50 Small Specimen Bottles
Burdock Root
Ash Leaves
Poppy Seed

Vervain
Bishops Wart
Myrrh
Oak Moss
Cowrie Shells
Mandrake Root
Jojoba Oil
Book Carrier (Student's Choice)
Pack of Pencils
Pack of Pens (Any color, we really don't care)
6 Reams of Hemp Paper (Shame on you, if you get any other kind!)
Your Book (Don't try to take anyone else's. You will regret it!)

Unusual jars, weird concoctions, and unheard of spices populated the shelves. Dried herbs hung on every available surface, and there was a portly, short, storekeeper behind the counter. His beard was, in a word, magnificent. He had very cleverly sculpted it into a clock, with working hands and all. His handlebar mustache was much larger than her father's with three curls on each side. Abney felt instantly that she would like this fellow or at least like looking at him. The Pucas walked up to him with their lists, giving instructions to charge the purchases to the school, and he got off the step stool and started hunting for the supplies.

Abney and the twins looked around eagerly, picking up the oddities, putting them back, and having a guess at how to use them. Abney thought it was great fun. The twins seemed a little less awestruck, and Abney noticed Domino slipping things into his pockets, while his sister gave him very disapproving looks. Abney considered telling Snozbert but thought better of it. Being known as a fink wasn't a good way to start in a new place or a new school. The anxiety put a knot in her stomach though. She hated breaking rules or doing things even perceived as wrong. She had a guilty conscience, and even an accusation would cause a panic attack.

The Pucas signed a bill of sale on the school's behalf, and they headed out the door. The shame was weighing heavily on Abney's mind. She made it out the door without incident, and everything seemed to be okay until they heard Domino calling for them from the door of the shop. He seemed to be glued to the doorway.

Wilbur looked at him woefully. "You had better go on without us. It seems Domino has tried to make off with what wasn't his." Domino looked frightened as the gnome-like storekeeper confronted him. Zoey just looked annoyed. Abney felt relieved.

"He never learns," she told Abney.

Next, they visited Beatle Babich's Luggage, Etc. It was a clean and posh store, fancier than the Coach counter in Dillard's back home. Abney was sure someone was going to realize they didn't belong and kick them out at any second, but they didn't. The shop assistants were exceedingly friendly; in fact, they were the friendliest Fae they had encountered so far. Two winged Pixies dashed about, showing the girls different backpacks. There were bags with legs like frogs and would hop after you, colorful ones with parrot-like plumage that glided, ones with human legs, like the trunk DiGott had, and so much more. Zoey picked out a snake backpack, which slithered after her and seemed to be able to swallow almost anything she wanted it to hold. They discussed some larger items they planned to try to feed it later. The shop manager warned them that it was most particular about animals, though. It would not hold them and hid if it even thought it saw a mouse. Abney picked out a bag with bat-like wings. It was a bat-pack. Stupid jokes always made her laugh. Her father loved telling them, which was likely the reason she looked on them so fondly.

They made a few more stops to pick up pens, paper, and the like, but they were hungry after their busy morning, so they opted to stop at a nearby restaurant for lunch. Domino and Wilbur met them at The Left Side of the Mushroom, one of the more teen-friendly places to eat. Abney got the strange feeling that the Fae as a whole were not fond of younger Fae.

It was everything one would hope an *Alice in Wonderland* themed restaurant would be. Old chipped and stained teapots and teacups dangled from the ceiling, glowing with multicolored light bulbs. The round tables all looked like red mushroom caps and came equipped with matching fungus stools. The servers all wore an assortment of Mad Hatter-type hats, and there was a stick-insect looking Fae by the food counter wearing a Queen of Hearts crown; Abney assumed she must be the manager.

Much to her relief, she recognized almost everything on the menu. There was even a White Rabbit Hot Chocolate. She took the pin out of her previous thought. "Snozbert"—she looked at him with concern—"can I drink hot chocolate?"

"Unless you are aware of something I am not, I don't see a problem," he said quizzically.

"I'm mostly ice, I thought," Abney whispered, feeling rather idiotic.

Snozbert shook his head at her. "Your heart and your stomach are two different things. Don't confuse the one with the other," he informed her rudely.

Abney glared at him, but when it had no effect, she sighed and looked back at the menu. She decided on the Smiling Kimchee and White Rabbit Hot Chocolate. The Pucas all ordered The Caterpillar Bowl and water. Zoey had the Tweedle-Weed Salad, and Domino had the Bandersnatch Steak.

"What happened?" Zoey finally asked Domino after they had all ordered.

"I had to give it all back," Domino replied defensively.

"And…" Zoey pushed, knowing it wasn't everything.

"I have to work there one hour a day for the semester as penance," he admitted.

"Serves you right," she said unsympathetically. Domino stuck his tongue out indignantly in reply.

The rest of the meal passed in relative silence, the Pucas because they weren't feeling particularly talkative and the teenagers because it was awkward to talk with three guardians hovering over them.

Once everyone had finished eating, the stick insect looking woman strolled over to the table, "How was everything?" she asked.

"Wonderful! Thank you," Abney replied politely.

"Yes, wonderful," the others agreed.

"Glad to hear it," she said gratefully. "Now, what have you to trade?" Snozbert held out a handful of colorful pebbles, Wilbur produced a pocket mirror, like the Cthulhui had on the boat, and Blythe offered a bag of dried pink flowers. The woman nodded and gathered the items into a bag she kept at her waist. "What about you three?" She looked at the younger Fae, who, in turn, looked to their guardians. The Pucas were all smiling deviously.

"First lesson, little Changelings," Mugrott said. "Nothing is free."

"Changelings?" Domino questioned.

"That's what we call all newly awakened Fae," Wilbur explained.

"Oh...okay," Domino replied and rolled his eyes.

"You don't have anything to trade then?" the insect woman asked. The three teens shook their heads no in reply.

"Labor then." She smiled. Abney winced. She felt idiotic that she'd assumed Snozbert would cover her. A flush of heat came over her as she stood to follow the owner to the back. She had never been so embarrassed in her life.

Abney, Domino, and Zoey went to work. Abney was outside pulling weeds and gathering vegetables. Zoey was tasked with wiping down tables and mopping the floor, and Domino found himself in the front, following complicated directions for placing their live Christmas tree. They noticed several Fae around their age doing similar work. Abney was bringing in a basket full of lettuce when she heard Zoey asking another girl, "Did your Hobgoblin stick you with the bill too?"

The girl laughed in reply. "No," she said. "Most of the students like to eat here. The food is more familiar. We don't have much to trade though, so Pernella lets us work instead. As long as you put in ten hours a week, you can eat, drink, and hang out as much as you like. It's not a bad deal considering most restaurants charge in favors, and some of those can be pretty steep."

"This place is so weird. So, favors and trade are like the currency here?" Zoey asked.

"You get used to it," the girl said with confidence. "It's basically a barter system. Favors are the most valuable and can be redeemed for anything, so you have to be careful handing them out. Most Fae hold to a code that only allows them to ask for things within our laws, but not everyone follows the code. Trade is preferred. And you can trade almost anything. You never know what another Fae will find valuable. I'm Honali, by the way. I go to Litha."

"Zoey," she acknowledged. "My brother, Domino, and I will be at Mabon, I guess."

"What about you?" The girl turned to face Abney. Abney had only been able to see her vibrant orange and yellow hair from behind, but the full view was a little scary. Her skin was light blue and scaled, like a lizard. Her eyes glowed with red fire, and all of her many, many teeth were sharp and pointed. Abney tried not to look startled; Honali didn't seem to notice.

"Oh...uh...I'm...uh Abney, Abney Kelly. I'll be at Yule and Litha."

"Multi-elemental eh? What are you?" she asked. Abney didn't care much for being asked "what" she was, but assumed it was probably par for the course in Tìr na nÓg.

"A Snow Maiden."

"Sweet." Honali threw up the hang loose sign. "I'm a Dragon."

"Aren't you a little small?" Abney shot back without thinking.

"You were expecting something more like this?" Honali asked. Her body elongated. The pop of her bones as she grew was cringe-worthy, and her tail filled in like sausage into a casing. All her human attributes disappeared as her face became more angular and lizard-like. The food prep tables screeched as they were flung against the walls. Honali now occupied the majority of the room. Abney and Zoey were pressed back against the counters, trying to give her more space. Honali smiled wickedly and roared at them. No one dared to move. She shrank back down. "I'll admit that shape comes more naturally to me, but this one is more practical for school and pretty much everything, you know?" Abney and Zoey nodded in astonishment, but didn't say much else. Fear and shock had a hold on their tongues. Neither were sure how to react to what they had witnessed, so they both threw themselves into their chores and tried hard to pretend there wasn't an actual dragon in the room.

✦

It took them about an hour and a half to work off their lunch. Pernella was so impressed with their work that she offered them all jobs, which the Pucas declined on their wards' behalf. Being first year students was enough of a challenge. Pernella left the offer open to them anyway. Then, it was time for them to part ways for the afternoon. The twins had their meeting at Mabon while Abney and Snozbert headed to Yule.

Snozbert informed her that Yule was too far to walk; they would require transportation. He led her to a large hive shaped building that read RENT-A-BEE on the front. There was a cheerful Dwarf at the entrance that greeted them and haggled with Snozbert over the price. Abney was a little relieved that she would not be working this one off, as she heard the Puca include her in the bargain. It had been a long day already.

Snozbert paid the Dwarf with a handful of the colorful pebbles like she'd seen him give to Pernella and a cloth satchel whose contents remained a mystery. Then, they walked into the hive and found several large bees in stalls. Grooms were brushing, feeding, and checking over them diligently. They stopped at one of the stalls, and the groom led the bee out. It appeared to be very calm and friendly. Snozbert easily leapt onto the creature's back and reached down to pull Abney up. She hardly had time to process him telling her to hold on, before they were out the door and taking off.

The city was effervescent below them, glowing in the darkness. What a sight! Abney could see the largest Christmas tree she'd ever seen going up in a square below them. It towered above even some of the more massive stalagmites. She hoped she could talk Snozbert into taking her to see it later. The bee zoomed through the air quickly, and it was not long before they landed in front of a lavishly carved building. It was like someone had sculpted the Palace of Versailles out of rock and covered it with dozens of balconies, chiseled scenes that Abney had zero context for, and imported ornate stained glass for every window. It was intimidating.

"This is a school?" Abney asked.

"It's not as impressive as Mabon," Snozbert said. "But I suppose it passes as a school." Abney couldn't imagine a building more opulent than the one glaring down at her.

A luminous silver-haired Elf greeted them. He was so beautiful Abney could hardly look away from him. Snozbert helped her down and bowed to the Elf as he handed over the reins. The Elf smiled slyly at Abney. From the tips of her ears to the bottom of her toes a wave of warmth flushed through her, and she gave him an uneasy smile in return.

They walked through the enormous doors. This place was colorful, unlike Ms. Ulyanna's Academy. There were billboards with flyers whose words frolicked and pictures waved to get your attention. They advertised clubs, plays, concerts, sports, and an odd number of dance groups. In the center of the room was a 3D wall sculpture of what looked like Krampus. He was menacing with his crown of mistletoe and a whip cracking up around his head. *It's strange a school would have him as a mascot*, Abney thought. *He's the bad guy. He even eats children in some of the stories.*

She smiled though; anti-Claus myths had always fascinated her. Father Christmas rewarded good children, while Krampus punished the bad ones, leaving coal and switches in their stockings. They were good and evil, all wrapped up in a nice neat package. Abney found black and white stories very comforting. The real world was grayer, so full of uncertainty, and she liked to be sure of herself.

The first place they visited was the library, a circular room with books on every available surface. When you thought there was no more room for anything, all you had to do was look up, and bookcases floated, spiraling above your head like a knowledge vortex. There were more books than she had ever seen in her lifetime and more books than she could read in ten lifetimes. If there was a heaven, she had died and gone there. She wanted to stay in this room forever or at least as long as they would allow her. There was a great green worm reading behind a counter at the center of the room. It did not look up as they approached.

"Eh hmm," Snozbert coughed to get his attention. The worm looked up lazily.

"Can I help you?" he asked.

"We're here for Abney Kelly's book," Snozbert announced.

"The students do not arrive for two weeks." He dismissed them and went back to his book. "Come back then."

"Dean Freya instructed us to stop by today," Snozbert persisted. The worm put down his book, annoyed.

"Give me your hand," he instructed Abney. Abney felt hesitant but extended her hand to him anyway. She immediately wished she had made a better decision, as the worm's face dove at her hand and bit her index finger.

"Ow," she howled. "Why? Why would you do that?"

"Don't be such a Fleetling," he chided her. "Now squeeze your fingertip. We need a nice size blood drop."

"Why couldn't you have me prick my finger with a needle or something? Seriously? Was that necessary?" she spat at him.

"If we knew your true name, we could use that, but since you're only thirteen and haven't undergone your Binding yet, it's hardly a viable option. The only other way to locate your book is to mix your blood with my saliva since I am a Bookworm. The easiest way to do that is to bite you. Though, I suppose, we could have pricked your finger, and then I could've spit on you," he said arrogantly.

Abney squeezed her finger until a significant drop pooled. The worm whistled a low note. Several bookshelves leapt into the air to join the maelstrom above them, while seven shelves dropped down to take their place. The globule on her finger flew up on cue and zipped down an aisle. "Are you waiting for an invitation?" he grumbled. "Go after it! And touch only *your* book!"

Abney chased after the floating bead and caught up with it easily. The droplet was hovering as if it could read the titles on the books, though there were none. It must not have found what it was looking for, because it dashed down to the end of the aisle and made for the next. It did this three more times before it found its target. Once it found what it was looking for, it dove recklessly into the book, knocking it from the shelf. Abney jumped up to catch it. The book looked unremarkable, like a plain brown journal, albeit a rather large journal. All the pages were blank. It didn't seem unusual at all. She brought it back to the desk.

"I've got it," she said triumphantly.

"Bully for you," the Bookworm said without looking up from his book. "The Puca will show you how to use it. Now get out of here. I'm supposed to be teenager-free for another two weeks."

Abney looked at Snozbert, but he was walking away from her already. She jogged to catch up. The school was relatively easy to navigate due to the gaudy signs that hung clearly above every hall: Sciences, Reading Competency, Mathematics, Magic, Dance, Sports, Languages, Etiquette, and more.

They took the hall directly across from the library, labeled administration. This corridor was not as welcoming as the others seemed. It had a very solemn and serious feel to it. A small gurgle of foreboding rumbled in Abney's stomach. Snozbert stopped them in front of a tall gilded door and turned the knob confidently.

Abney paused to take in the intimidating Fae behind the enormous cherrywood desk. Dark gold eyes burned into them as they stepped into the office, and her black lips turned upward as she tossed her antlered head at them in greeting. She was breathtaking and frightening.

Abney leapt slightly when a dusky red hand with odd patches of feathers waved to get their attention from her seat at the side of the desk. Elongated-orange and yellow feathers cascaded from where hair would be on a person. When she put her arm back at her side, Abney noted her movements were graceful, regal even. It was difficult to tell with her beak, but she gave the impression she was smiling.

"Hello, Abney," the Fae behind the desk said. "I'm Freya Magnusson, Dean of Yule. And this"—she pointed to her feathered friend—"is Sadira

Chakroun, the Dean from Litha." Abney responded with a meek hello. "We wanted to save you a trip today. After all, it's just an informal meet and greet," she continued. "You will attend regular hours here, and twice a week, you'll go after school to Litha for Pyromancy lessons with Master Blewitt. He was supposed to be here today, but something...came up." She looked sideways at Dean Sadira.

"He'll be fine in a few days," Dean Sadira assured them.

"Oh, good," Abney said, unsure what the proper response was.

"We really just wanted to say hello and let you know that if you need anything, don't hesitate to come find us. It can be a bit of a rougher adjustment for our multi-elemental kids," Dean Freya said kindly. After a light knock on the door, a small blush-skinned humanoid came in. Her mint hair was in a loose bun, and she smiled pleasantly. It was hard not to like her almost immediately.

"Hi," she said shyly. "Hope I'm not too early."

"Right on time, Denisha," Dean Sadira acknowledged her.

"You must be Abney," she said with a big smile. "I'm Denisha, the guidance counselor, follow me please."

"It was nice to meet you, Abney," Dean Freya said in dismissal. "We will see you the day after the Yule celebration."

"Abney," Dean Sadira nodded in goodbye. "Your hobgoblin will be in to fetch you in an hour or so."

Abney followed Denisha to a smaller office where they picked three elective classes and one sport for her to take. She chose Introduction to Fae Literature, Glaciomancy, which was ice magic, and Elemental Sewing, which was like the Fae version of home economics. She didn't know about sports, human or Fae, so she picked Basnorts since she had heard it mentioned a few times. It didn't seem to matter much. She'd never been good at sports, and she didn't see that changing much, Fae or not.

CHAPTER 6

THE STORY OF NICHOLAS KRINGLE

A thick, stew-like fog encircled Oberon House. The Pucas were supposed to be taking them to see the enormous Christmas tree in the square, but there was no way to go out safely. If you stuck your hand into the mist, it disappeared before your eyes, and in general, had a strange-uneasy feel to it. Everyone was very content to stay in and help decorate the house Christmas tree in the Ocean Room.

The decorations were colorful and random; Agatha didn't do themes for her tree like Abney's family did, but it was still fun, and everyone chipped in. Blythe taught them to string popcorn, and Wilbur and Snozbert were taking colored glass beads and morphing them into different shapes and figures by request. It was like watching master glass blowers at work, but they never heated the marbles. They were able to manipulate them with their bare hands.

"I love Christmas trees," Abney said as she looked transfixed at the glowing masterpiece.

"It's a Yule tree," Feo said as she came in with a tray of sweet orange tea and began pouring cups.

"Is there a difference?" Abney asked curiously.

"Oh, most definitely. Christmas trees are a pagan tradition you know, taught to Fleetlings by the Fae," Feo said carefully. "Anyway, the most important difference is that a Yule tree is always a live tree. Fleetlings use fake trees and all sorts of nonsense these days. They've forgotten the traditions of old, but a Yule tree must be alive."

"I think it's time for a story," Agatha said from her armchair by the fire. She took a deep drag from her hookah pipe through the black hole in her neck. "Come closer, sugars, closer," she bid them, and they all sat on the floor near her feet. "You are all aware of the legend of The Santa Claus?"

"Everyone knows that one," Zoey replied.

"Ya, ya," Domino agreed. "The dude who knows if you're naughty or nice. We all know how it goes." Abney wasn't sure why but she suddenly felt edgy, and goosebumps rose on her arms.

"That's the one, honey," Agatha agreed. "I suppose you know him as a fat, jolly, man who passes out gifts?"

"Every December the 25th," Domino smiled.

"That's the version known to most Fleetlings," Agatha continued. "But I'm going to tell you the real story. Heed my words. They are much more paramount now than they have been in many years." The teenagers and Pucas moved closer to the fire, unconsciously wanting to chase away the dark and its accompanying shadows.

"This story starts out as all good tales do. Once upon a time, in a faraway land, there lived a lonely king. Not just any king though, The Winter King, Jack Frost, himself. Blythe, a little help please?" Agatha breathed out. Blythe whispered a few words and blew them into Agatha's smoke. A sad man appeared in the escaping vapor, and the story took to life as Agatha started to speak again, "He longed for a child to love and fill his days with joy, but no maid could carry the child of the frozen monarch. Frustrated and grief-stricken, he sought out the great witch, Baba Yaga.

"'Grandmother,' he begged. 'I am alone and childless. Is there anything you can do to help me? Is there a way for me to have a child?' Baba

Yaga thought for a moment, looked deep into his heart, and knew he was sincere. She decided to help The Winter King, but he must bring her three things: Snow, from the coldest peak, coal from the deepest mine, and a feather from the brightest Phoenix.

"So The Winter King scoured the Earth until he had everything the witch had asked for. First, Baba Yaga took the snow and patted it into the shape of a girl, then she picked up the coal and wrapped the phoenix feather around it, the coal ignited melting the feather into it. Finally, she forced the coal into the snow girl where her heart would have been. The winds picked up and whirled violently around them, but The Winter King and Baba Yaga stood fast, and when the snow settled again, a small pale girl stood before them. Her skin was blue, like a frozen glacier, and her hair white as snow, with a hint of the Northern Lights about it. The King loved her instantly, but as he reached for her, Baba Yaga stepped between them.

"'Nothing is free, Winter King,' she said. 'A time will come when I will ask you for a favor, and you must agree to do as I ask.' The King, being so close to his heart's desire could do nothing but agree. Baba Yaga released the girl to him with a warning.

"'She is snow and ice, but her heart is fire. She must never lose control of her emotions. You must teach her to remain calm in even the worst of storms. If she loses control, your daughter will melt and return to the water from whence she came.'

"This," Agatha said, looking at Abney, "was the very first Snow Maiden, and your distant ancestor. Her name was Orina. Orina grew kind and wise under the careful gaze of her father. She brought him contentment that he never thought was possible, and she, in turn, loved her father very much.

"When Orina was quite grown, she fell in love with a gentle auburn-haired man. His name was Cesare Kringle, but you will probably know him better as Father Time."

Agatha paused to let her words sink in. When wonder had registered on each of their faces, she began again. "The two fell madly in love, and it was not long before they were wed. The Winter King could not be angry with Cesare though, for Orina was happy, and that was all that mattered.

"They were all blessed again a few years later when Orina gave birth to a son, whom they called Nicholas. He was a rambunctious fair-haired child, the very soul of his parents, and the apple of his grandfather's eye. But no happiness lasts forever, and theirs was no exception.

"Nicholas was only seven years old when Baba Yaga came to collect on The Winter King's debt. When the witch arrived at the palace, she was granted admittance gladly. He would do whatever she wanted. She had given him so much happiness, and he wasn't sure he could ever repay her.

"'Winter King,' she said. 'Have you been happy these many years?'

"'Beyond measure,' he assured her.

"'And you, of course, wish to remain happy?' she asked.

"'Naturally,' he said, nervous for the first time.

"'Good.' The witch nodded. 'My price is your grandson. You have had a child to make you happy. Now I desire one of my own, to make me happy.'

"'No!' The Winter King exclaimed. "No! You must ask for something else. Anything else.'

"'My mind is made up. A bargain is a bargain. You promised to do whatever I asked, and this is what I want,' she insisted.

"'I cannot give you what is not mine to give,' he pleaded.

"'You will bring him to me, or Orina will return to snow,' Baba Yaga threatened.

"Faced with an impossible decision, The Winter King broke into Time's castle and led the boy away in secret. He took Nicholas to Baba Yaga's cottage and begged for forgiveness as the witch pulled his grandson from his arms. Then, they were gone, cottage and all.

"Orina and Cesare despaired at the loss of their son. They looked high and low, but no one could find him. Father Time grew forlorn. Still, Orina refused to feel anything but hope. She knew her son was out there somewhere, just waiting for her to find him. So, she left the lands of her husband and father and walked the world over, calling out her son's name, 'Nicholas! Niiichoolaaasss!' No one ever replied.

"The Winter King watched his daughter search in vain for three years before he could no longer bear her unhappy wandering. He took her to his castle and confessed all. He begged for her forgiveness and told her again and again how much he loved her, but she would not listen. Her heart grew inflamed with anger, sorrow, and betrayal. Nothing would soothe her, and the Winter King sobbed as his only delight, his only daughter, melted in his arms.

"After that, he shut the doors of his castle forever, and Jack Frost has not been seen since, contrary to what Fleetlings would have you believe," Agatha said in a low, sad voice. The group looked at her hopefully, knowing that it couldn't just end there, and they were right. She spoke after a moment. "That is far from the end though. Cesare was left empty and sullen by the loss of his family. He could not let things stand as they were; there was nothing he could do for Orina now, but he could go after Baba Yaga and Nicholas, and that is precisely what he did.

"He searched the realms of Fae and Fleetling for many years before he learned of a witch living deep in the Russian wilderness with a handsome young man who happened to have, startling white hair. This had to be his son. After so long, he was close, and he could almost hear Orina's voice urging him on. He combed the forests until he finally came across Baba Yaga's cottage. The cottage was notable due to the four large chicken legs that acted as stilts underneath it, to carry it away whenever the witch desired.

"He knew she would never just hand over the boy, so he came up with a cunning plan: He would trick the witch into returning his son. He transformed himself into an old man, with long gray hair, knobby knees, and a bad leg that required him to use a walking stick. He walked shakily up to the cottage and asked Baba Yaga if she could spare a glass of water. The witch looked him up and down and finally made a decision.

"'Come, sit here next to me,' she beckoned him to take a seat on the cottage steps, which he did rather nosily as his old limbs creaked and moaned with the effort of bending.

"'I have traveled far,' Father Time told her. 'And I am so weary.'

"'Nicky,' Baba Yaga called. 'Fetch a glass of water for our visitor.'

Cesare would have known his son anywhere, and there he was, a full-grown man now. He looked so much like him, except the snow-white hair and silver eyes that belonged to Orina. His old heart was weak, and he almost cried at the sight of his long-lost son, but he grabbed hold of himself.

"'What a strong young man,' he commented. 'I wish I had such a man to carry my pack and do my work for me in my old age. Things don't work as they used to, you know?'

"'I could get you a lad,' she offered the old man slyly. 'It would only cost you a favor.' Cesare had learned much from his father-in-law's dealing with Baba Yaga and declined.

"'I am too old to keep promises to anyone,' he complained. 'But I'll make you an offer. If you can guess my age, I will let you make me a boy, and I will owe you a favor. However, if you cannot guess, I will take your boy with me, and I will owe you nothing.' The witch studied him with clever eyes, lit her pipe, and did not look away from him as she smoked.

"'Very well,' she agreed finally. 'But you must grant me three questions before I guess.' Father Time nodded his agreement.

"'First, where were you born?' she asked.

"Time danced around the subject. 'The place I was born is a place no longer. It only lives on in an old man's memory.'

"'That is not much of an answer,' she said grumpily. 'I will turn you into a worm if you try to cheat me, old man.'

"'I would never cheat you,' he replied. 'That is simply the most honest answer there is about my birthplace.' The witch looked into his eyes and seemed to be satisfied with the truth of it.

"The witch continued with her questions. 'Tell me about your mother.'

"'I never knew her,' he answered. 'I was an orphan, doomed to walk alone throughout my life.' The witch's face lit up, and Father Time began to feel unsettled.

"'Now that is a lie,' the woman said. 'You had a lovely wintery bride and a son. You were not alone, Cesare.' Time stood up, taken aback. He needed a new plan and quickly. 'Did you think you could disguise yourself from me?' she asked. 'I am not nearly so old as you, but I know Time when I see him.'

"Cesare was panicking; he couldn't lose his son now, not when he was so close. Then something unexpected happened, the light went from Baba Yaga's eyes, and she gasped for air. He noticed a blade sticking out from the witch's heart, and his son, his Nicholas, stood behind her with a cruel and unforgiving look.

"'We must go, Papa,' Nicholas said urgently.

"'Cursed,' Baba Yaga rattled shakily. 'You're both cursed!'

"'Hurry, Papa,' the boy said, lifting Time over his shoulder and carrying him away from the witch's cottage as quickly as he could. Nicholas hauled his father many miles before he dared to stop.

"'Papa,' he said. 'Papa, you came for me. I never thought I would see you again.' Time touched his son's face lovingly. He could scarcely believe that, after so many years, he had him; he had his son.

"'Oh, if only your mother were here,' Time said with a tear in his eye. 'But now is not the time. We will talk when we are home safe and out of Baba Yaga's grasp.'

"'I killed her, Papa,' Nicholas said. 'We don't have to worry about her.'

"'You cannot kill Baba Yaga with a mere blade, my son,' Time informed him. 'You have maimed her surely, but she will be well soon and very angry. We must go and quickly.' Time then tried to remove his disguise; he needed to be himself because the old man had not moved fast enough, but he could not change back.

"He heard Baba Yaga's voice in his head. '*Cursed. You are both cursed!*'

"And from that time on," Agatha said knowingly, "Time was an old man. He ached; his joints creaked, and he had a new-found penchant for napping at odd hours of the day. He would never be a young man again. So Nicholas carried his poor old father to the nearest village where they purchased two horses and began their journey in earnest. They rode day and night, often stopping to swap their mounts for fresh ones.

"As they traveled, Nicholas began to change as well. His stomach became large and bulging, the youth drained from his face, and a long beard grew rapidly. By the time they reached their home, both were old men.

"For a while, they were content. Nicholas took to carving toys from the discarded branches in the forest to give to the Changelings that dwelled in the village of Swallow Song. It pleased him to make others happy and gave him a sense of purpose. Cesare found love again with the Faun Griselda, and it did not take long for them to gain a new member of the family. Peter Kringle was born only eighteen months after his father and brother arrived home from their ordeal with Baba Yaga. It really seemed their family was finally going to have their long deserved happy ending. That is, until the night Cesare finally told Nicholas what really happened to his mother…"

The clock above the mantle chimed, and a family of whales swam out from their hiding place in the clock face. They circled round and round until the number of chimes reached eleven. Agatha took another deep drag from her hookah and sighed.

"All right, sugars, it's getting late. We'll have to finish this story another time."

"But I thought this story was important," Domino argued.

"It'll keep." Agatha held her ground, and the Pucas ushered the teens up to their rooms. Abney ran the story through her mind as she ascended the stairs. There was more to that story, and Abney felt deep in her bones that knowing the rest was important, even if she didn't know why just yet.

"Are you having one of those absent seizures?" Snozbert asked her.

"No." Abney shook her head and realized she'd been paused on the stairs.

"Well, let's get moving then." He nudged her on. "Tomorrow is a big day."

CHAPTER 7

THE YULE MASQUERADE

Abney sat at her vanity getting ready. This was it. They were headed to the Yule Masquerade tonight, and tomorrow she would start her new school. Until this very moment, she felt that somehow, she was going to wake up. Then she would run down the stairs, ask Granny to make her a cup of cocoa, and she would tell her all about this extra bizarre dream. It was not a dream though; she was really in Tír na nÓg, and Granny was not waiting downstairs for her. Her heart felt heavy again, but there were no tears this time. Feodora knocked lightly on the door and let herself in.

"Would you like some help with your hair?" she offered. Abney nodded gratefully. Feo's delicate fingers worked deftly with Abney's short hair and managed two braids on each side of her head that met in the back. Then, she laced small blue flowers throughout. Abney admired the skill it took. She had never been able to do much with her hair, which is why she had cut it short in the first place.

A brush stroked her cheeks softly as Feo highlighted them with silver powder. Abney asked her makeup be left simple, she was going to be wearing a mask after all. So Feo stuck to applying some eyeliner and black lipstick and covering Abney's entire body in a fine white glitter.

DiGott had been working with her for three days on her costume. There had been arguments, yelling, and he had even thrown a bolt of spider's silk at her, but they had finally come to a compromise that pleased them both. Abney was going as a polar bear, and she would wear pants of a sort, and a skirt. Abney had wanted to have a pantsuit, as dresses made her feel awkward, but DiGott desired a full Cinderella-type ball gown. This way, they both won half of the argument.

The first part was a skin-tight white full body sock with hooks on the back where they attached a flowy white faux fur half-skirt, which didn't encumber her walking and gave the desired ball gown appearance. Then, she put a white bedazzled vest corset over the body sock. It smoothed out and accentuated Abney's curves in a very flattering manner. A pair of furry leg warmers then went over her calves and covered her legs up to her knees. Then the shoes! DiGott had made her a pair of flats that looked a lot like real bear paws but still managed to appear delicate and feminine. She pulled a pair of fingerless white lace gloves over her hands and finally reached for the mask. It was the most beautiful part of the whole ensemble. White and silver streaks gave the illusion of real fur, pale pink quartz settled in the corner of the eyes, and cream-colored pearls lined the cheeks up to the nose. Abney's mouth was the only visible part, aside from her eyes. She didn't just look pretty, she was beautiful, and for the first time in Abney's life, she knew it.

"You look just lovely," Feo said. "Now, I've got to go get myself ready. We're meeting in the entry hall in half an hour."

For the first time in years, Abney looked in the mirror without flinching. She found her image bewitching. *Why don't I look like this all the time*, she thought? The masquerade had been this big, daunting, horror-filled evening in her mind for over a week, but now she found she was looking forward to it.

✦

Just like the old fairy tales, a carriage picked them up for the ball; however, unlike any fairy tale Abney had ever read, a giant brown and gold chicken, which the driver referred to as Rooney, pulled them toward their destination. Abney wondered if the chicken was really so large or they were merely small? Faeries were sometimes very small in legends.

Those in the carriage were quiet with nerves and anticipation. The Pucas were meeting them there. Agatha would make an appearance later in some sort of official capacity but was not invited to the ball, because she was a Fleetling. So, it was just Feo, Zoey, Domino, and Abney.

Abney was reconsidering her odd burst of self-esteem. She looked beautiful for her, but she was nothing compared to the genetically blessed Sirens and Wood Nymph she was arriving with. Zoey wore a deer mask with a brass and cream-colored slip of a dress that complemented her light green skin and thin frame. Domino was costumed rather fittingly, like a raccoon. His gray and black suit fit him well and accentuated his gangly limbs and broad chest. Feodora outshined them all in her beautiful golden ball gown and sun mask. She was radiant and glowing. None of them could look away. Feo seemed to be used to this reaction and paid them no mind.

It was almost an hour later when they pulled up outside the ruins of an old castle. Abney saw familiar silver-leafed trees, orange lace flowers, and fireflies, hundreds of them. "I know this place," Abney said aloud.

"Us too," Zoey spoke for her brother.

Snozbert's voice came from behind her. "I should hope so. You've been here enough." Abney's eyes widened as recognition dawned on her. Snozbert was standing in front of her, wearing the cat mask, sparkling blue tailcoat, and black slacks.

"It was you?" she said, disappointed.

He mocked her. "You were expecting a prince or your one true love?"

Abney hated to admit it, but she had thought of her dream as highly romantic. Here was her dream, come to life, and her prince had turned out to be a sarcastic, bad-tempered, cat-faced, Goblin. How was that even fair? Domino and Zoey seemed to be having equally disappointing realizations.

"Had you waited to come here like good little Fae," Blythe said, "you would have put on your masks and been transported instantly to the masquerade tonight. It would have been way more epic. I suppose you're arriving in style this way at least. Most of the new Changelings will show up in their pajamas."

The teens, escorted by their guardians, entered the ruins, and everything was just as Abney remembered. The fountains of aqua drinks, tables of food and sweets, and the dancers moving in unison. It was like a musical where everyone knew all the moves, except for the new Fae, that is. Abney felt she could watch this scene for hours and never feel bored. Feo and Zoey were snatched up almost immediately by partners, and the Pucas went off in search of food, which left Domino and Abney standing awkwardly next to each other. Thankfully, out of the corner of her eye, Abney recognized Honali from the *Alice in Wonderland* restaurant, waving at her and smiling toothily. Even under her striking black and white owl mask, her sky-blue skin and yellow-orange hair were unmistakable. She walked over to them, squeezing easily through the crowd.

"Aloha. Abney, right?" she greeted her.

"Yes. And you're Honali?" Abney asked, even though she knew she was correct. Honali nodded.

"You look great!" the dragon-girl exclaimed.

"Thanks. I love your owl costume," Abney complimented her. She was never sure how to respond to praise; mostly, it made her feel uncomfortable.

"Ehhhhmmmm," Domino coughed.

"Oh," Abney said, embarrassed. She had completely forgotten about him. "Honali, this is Domino. You met his sister, Zoey, at the restaurant. Domino, this is Honali."

"Hi," Domino said, leering at Honali.

"Hey," Honali replied, oblivious to the look he was giving her. "Anyway," she said, turning back to Abney, "a bunch of us are meeting at The Left Side of the Mushroom tomorrow after school. It's a sort of school commencement bash. You guys should totally come."

"That sounds awesome," Domino answered for both of them. Abney felt resentful. She hated social gatherings. She always ended up sitting and nodding politely to some stranger who droned on and on while she wished she was at home with a book instead. It was better to get off on a good foot with her new peers though, so she nodded reluctantly.

"I'll be late," Abney warned Honali. "I have lessons at Litha after school."

"No worries, girl." Honali smiled. "Only squares show up on time." She laughed and made a box with her fingers. Then a red-haired girl in a snake costume came up and held her hand out to Honali to dance.

"Sümeyye." Honali grabbed the hand and pulled the girl into an enthusiastic embrace. "Abney, Domino, this is Sümeyye, my girlfriend. Sümeyye, these are my new friends."

She waved at them shyly. "Hello."

"We'll see you at the party." Honali grabbed Sümeyye's hand and winked at Abney before whisking the girl in the snake costume away. Abney and Domino stared after them. There were many same-sex couples on the floor; how had she not noticed before? This would have been a significant controversy among the Fleetlings, especially the ones in her hometown, but here it seemed the most natural thing in the world.

"Do you think she meant girlfriend girlfriend?" Domino asked Abney. "Or like a girl that's your friend?"

"I haven't a clue," she replied honestly.

"So, do you wanna dance?" Domino held out his hand to her. Abney immediately felt sick. She knew he was probably feeling sorry for her.

"You don't have to, really. I'm fine," Abney replied self-consciously.

"I wouldn't have asked if I didn't want to," he said charmingly. Abney was relieved and took his hand out to the floor. At first, they were both out of place, so they pulled out the goofy dance moves. Domino started with the shopping cart; Abney cleaned her ears. Then Domino waxed the car, and Abney tried to disco, but one of the other dancers knocked her into Domino's arms.

It was as if they'd fallen under a spell and found that they knew all the steps to the dance; it was in their blood, and they were powerless to stop their feet. Abney could hear a high sweet violin guiding her and directing the movements of everyone. Her heartbeat was rapid, and everything felt deliciously dangerous and dark. The music touched something deep inside, an infernal flame that burned with wickedness. Just when they were really getting into it, the melody stopped unexpectedly, and everyone batted their eyes like they'd just woken up. Silence dominated them, and then the crowds parted, revealing two women who were everything Abney had always thought Faeries should be.

They were arm in arm, strolling through the parted sea of Fae. The one on the right was tall with milk-white skin and vibrant red hair. Abney had never seen anyone with hair that color of red. She wore a black glittering ball gown with a matching *Phantom of the Opera*-style mask, and she had wings, real butterfly-like wings, which glowed mint green behind her. The one to the left had such dark brown skin that it was almost black. She wore a stunning white mermaid-style dress and a matching half mask like her counterpart. She also had wings that glowed red fiercely and fluttered delicately at her back. Everyone bowed in turn as they passed.

"The Faerie Queens," Snozbert whispered at her side. "The one in white is Titania, Queen of The Seelie or Summer Court. The One in Black is Mab, Queen of the Unseelie or Winter Court. They love and hate each other equally. They are both wonderful and terrifying. One day, you'll pick which lady to serve. Be aware: Both are beautiful and treacherous, and at the end of the day, they are much the same, though they'd kill you for saying so."

"They look surprisingly human, besides the wings," Abney murmured.

"They're Faeries, true Faeries. Their forms are very Fleetling-like, but don't let that fool you. They're as inhuman as they come, the last pureblooded specimens of their kind and the most powerful of our kind. Which is why we all bear their name," Snozbert replied.

"Why do they hate each other?" Abney asked as they drew nearer.

"Jealousy. They're lovers half the time and enemies the other half. Pray you never catch either of their eyes. It's a deadly place to be. If King

Oberon were still alive, I'm sure he would agree. Queen Titania married him after one of their bigger arguments. Mab, in her spite, refused to see Titania while he remained at her side. After one hundred and fifty years, Queen Titania lost interest in him and her fight with Queen Mab, so she killed him and took his head to her lover as an apology." His voice was barely discernable. Abney gulped in horror.

The Queens passed by, and Abney's knees almost buckled as she struggled to curtsey correctly. A trail of male and female Fae followed in their wake and sat dotingly at their feet when the Queens turned to face the court from their elevated platform. They looked sideways at each other with resigned contempt that put the whole atmosphere on edge. Then, without warning, they both smiled and looked toward the crowd. A barely audible sigh of relief swept through them all.

"Seelie Court," Titania addressed her people.

"Unseelie Court," Mab acknowledged in turn.

"Welcome to the Yule festivities," they said together. The crowd cheered, and Abney remained silent, trying to observe all that was going on around her.

"The Mother, after a long labor, bears The Sun God!" Mab declared.

"And so we pay homage to The Mother Goddess, who brings life to us once more," Titania said. "Salutations and welcome to the element Earth, warden and keeper in the west, mother and grounder to us all."

"Salutations and welcome the element Air, warden and keeper in the north, death bringer and change bearer," Mab opened up her arms.

"Salutations and welcome the element Water, warden and keeper in the east, purifier of us all," Titania invoked.

"Salutations and welcome the element Fire, warden and keeper in the south, father and seed bearer of all," Mab intoned.

"Our lady has made the journey from maiden to mother and now gives birth to the sun, making our lands fertile and giving to all the joy of new life," the two Queens said harmoniously. Two torchbearers appeared and bore a light to each lady. For the first time, Abney noticed a great log set a top of kindling. The two women smiled, and a shiver ran down her back as they lowered the torches, and the log blazed to life. Something powerful had just happened, but she wasn't sure exactly what it was. Cheers of joy erupted from the courts, and the dancing began again.

This time, Abney was swept away by a stranger in a frog mask. Her brain was screaming that she didn't know this person and to free herself from him, but something stronger kept her feet moving. The darkness was filling her again, and she was powerless to stop it. Something had woken up inside her, and she knew it would never go away. Fear shocked her awake, and she pulled away from the Fae in the frog mask, only to be caught by a pink-skinned female in a wolf mask, who twirled her under her arm, and then spun them farther into the swarm of Faeries.

When the music stopped again, Abney found herself disquieted, as if awakened from a trance, and it took her a minute to remember where she was. When she looked about, she saw Fleetlings, many Fleetlings, all around her age and most in their pajamas, looking frightened. Agatha and twelve other older and misshapen Fleetlings had appeared on the raised platform with the burning Yule Log and the Queens. Dozens of unmasked Pucas, Cthulhuis, Orcs, Cupids, and other Hobgoblins stood sullen and severe-looking, but separate from the rest of the court, even though they were scattered throughout.

"Now Seelie Court," Titania stood and addressed her people.

"Unseelie Court," Mab called to her people as well. "We welcome our newly born Fae. They hold no allegiances and to take advantage of or deal badly with them is to transgress against both courts. Consider yourselves warned."

"That is, until their twentieth year," Titania said cheerfully. "Then they become fair game." A low grumble of amused and approving laughter shook the court.

"Hobgoblins, escort your wards," Mab commanded. Snozbert appeared by Abney's side again, took her stiffly by the arm, and escorted her to the front of the platform with the rest of the Changelings.

"Deans, bring forth your banners," Titania directed. Abney saw Dean Freya bearing a white, blue, and silver banner with Krampus on the front. Dean Sadira bore an orange, red, and yellow flag with what looked like a flaming peacock on it. A short, stone-gray, and wart-covered woman, carried a brown, green, and white banner with a rearing Unicorn on it, and a shimmering-scaled man hoisted an aqua, sage, and gold banner with a Kraken on it.

"Present." Mab nodded. The Deans slammed the butt of the staff bearing their banners down at the same time and turned to face the crowd.

"I, Hansi König," the gray woman spoke gruffly, "stand as Dean of Ostara. The ground is mighty as it grumbles and shakes. We nurture all for the Mother's sake. If your thumb is green and soul full of mirth, then you belong with us in the element Earth."

"I, Freya Magnusson," the Faun announced, "stand as Dean of Yule. The wind can be gentle, or the wind may roar. Compassion and strength are at our core. If the balance of life and death is yours to bear, then you belong with us in the element Air."

"I, Thiago Gómez," the man's voice boomed, "stand as Dean of Mabon. Water washes away our dirt and sin. We are concerned most with what lies within. If you would see the best in every son and daughter, then you belong with us in the element Water."

"I, Sadira Chakroun," the Fire Bird sang out, "stand as Dean of Litha. Fire burns and consumes all in its path. Ours can be a way of love or wrath. If your soul is ablaze with passion and desire, you belong with us in the element Fire."

"You may belong to one, or you may belong to all," they spoke together. "Prepare yourself to find out. Hail and welcome to the Yule Ball." The Deans bowed to their audience and then to the Queens as they made their way to the back of the stage.

"First," said Titania, "we will introduce this year's troublemakers, the ones we should all keep an eye on. They arrived early and have no need of the Truth Seeing."

"There's always a few," Mab laughed.

"Abney Kelly," Titania instructed, "you will step forward." Snozbert pushed her up the steps of the platform and told her to kneel before the Queens. He did the same. "Abney is a Snow Maiden. She will attend Yule and Litha and lodge at Oberon House. Hail and welcome, Abney Kelly of the Fae."

The voices of the courts embraced her. "Hail and welcome." Titania lifted Abney's chin, brought her to her feet, and motioned for her to stand next to Agatha. Snozbert followed dutifully.

"Domino Doggett," Mab called, and he and Wilbur stepped forth. "Domino is a Siren and Gemini Twin. He will attend Mabon and lodge at Oberon House. Hail and welcome, Domino Doggett of the Fae."

"Hail and welcome," the court repeated, and Domino and Wilbur joined them by Agatha.

"Zoey Doggett," Titania beckoned, and Blythe pushed her forward. "Zoey is a Siren and Gemini Twin. She will attend Mabon and lodge at Oberon House. Hail and welcome, Zoey Doggett of the Fae."

"Hail and welcome," the crowd agreed.

"Now that our un-glamoured Changelings have been introduced, let us begin the Truth Seeing!" Mab announced. Looking from her place on the raised platform, Abney recognized the same fear she had felt the night Snozbert came for her. They were paralyzed and voiceless. The court was silent as Fae in lavender robes brushed through them carrying large wooden bowls that contained some sort of liquid, which sloshed noisily in the quiet. When they reached the front, they bowed to their Queens and handed the containers to the awaiting Hobgoblins.

"As it was, so it must be. We command you all to truly see!" Titania and Mab exclaimed together. The Hobgoblins dumped the liquid over the frightened teen's heads. Abney saw what looked like clovers in the opaque fluid. The glamour seemed to melt away like wax down their bodies until drenched Fae stood before them. She found herself remembering Blythe's words from earlier. This was a better show than Snozbert turning up in her room unannounced, but she was suddenly grateful Cotton had pushed her into the clover patch.

"Akira, Bashira, and Shion Matsumoto," Mab called out, "step forward." Three small, frightened Fleetling-looking girls stepped up. Abney noticed they were identical, with white sightless eyes and long black hair. She also noticed they seemed much younger than the other teens. She would have guessed them at only seven or eight.

"These three are special," Titania informed them all. "They cannot belong to any court, nor be schooled with the regular students. They are Fates, brought here before their thirteenth year to study with the Elder Fates." A gasp arose from the crowd as they all exchanged worried looks. Abney noted that they all seemed to be afraid of children.

"Do not fear," Mab interjected. "They will attend school on the Isle of Avalon. After tonight we will not see them in Tír na nÓg again, until they have reached their thirteenth year and are a proper age to be among us…supervised, of course." The atmosphere remained uneasy, but no one dared contradict the Queen. Mab continued, "We will welcome them now. Akira Matsumoto. Akira is the Future Fate and lodges on the Isle of Avalon to be reared by the Moirai. Hail and welcome, Akira Matsumoto of the Fae."

"Hail and welcome," the courts greeted. The other two sisters followed and were rushed out of the ruins before the rest of the Changelings were announced.

The ceremony went on for what felt like ages. Abney learned there were a total of thirteen houses like Agatha's in Tír na nÓg. There didn't seem to be any reason or rhyme to the placement of the young Fae; there were students from every school in every house. Snozbert explained this was to discourage rivalries and promote respect for each other, no matter what the individual Fae's talents or abilities were.

Seven new Fae were to join her and the twins in Oberon House: BlueMoon Jones, a Firebird who would be attending Litha; Shilo Finkelman, a Gnome who would be attending Ostara; Cozmo Hollingsworth, a Centaur who would also be attending Ostara; Devlin Sand, a Troll who would be attending Yule; Melinda Fairfax, a Gorgon who would be attending Litha; James Lockwood, a Banshee who would be attending Yule; And lastly, LaVern Dubois, a Merman, who would be attending Mabon.

"That concludes The Truth Seeing," Titania announced.

Mab released them. "Enjoy the rest of the ball. House Matrons, your earmuffs, please." The House Matrons all pulled the padding over their ears, and Mab nodded that the music could begin. Some went back to the dance; some went to look for food, and most of the school-age Fae gathered around their den mothers to meet their new housemates. Abney looked at Snozbert questioningly. He looked over to the Fleetlings and laughed.

"Ah, the music is too powerful for Fleetlings to hear. They would dance until they died. So, we provide them with special earmuffs."

"Oh," Abney said, a little shocked as Snozbert pushed her toward her new housemates. She received introductions to an additional fourteen returning students who would be living with her at Oberon House. There were so many names to learn, and Abney wasn't familiar with what kind of Fae half of them were. It was a bit overwhelming.

"All right!" Agatha shouted. "Oberon House residents, find your Hobgoblins and meet me outside! You all have a long day tomorrow! It's time we head home!"

Snozbert grabbed Abney before she could even process the thought to look for him. Several coaches waited outside to take the students home. Abney knew she should be exhausted and that her mind should be on sleep, but she felt energized and nervous. The rest of her night was spent tossing, turning, and worrying about what the following day would be like.

CHAPTER 8

MUST BE SANTA

"**Y**ou are all like trees, trees without roots. You have no idea about your origins, your culture, or your history. You know in your head that you are not Fleetlings, but you do not feel Fae at your core. You will though. You will! The first step is this course," Master Ibori said exuberantly and wrote *Fae History and Etiquette* on the board in wide swooping letters that his tummy partially wiped away. Half the class had to stand up to see what the Master was writing as he was only two and a half feet tall and the board was low to the ground.

This was Abney's third class of the day, and she was starting to feel the lack of sleep. She wondered whose idea it was to have a party the night before the first day of school anyway? Understanding Runes and her study period had gone well. Lunch had been short; her stomach was full, and all she wanted was a nap.

She fought the oncoming yawn and opened her book. The pages were blank and crisp, and Abney unconsciously breathed in, enjoying the smell of the slightly yellowing pages. She looked up at the board and copied *Fae: Origins* by Derya Gűngör onto the blank page. Abney watched, fascinated as words and letters populated the once blank book.

Master Hallewell had shown them how to use the books in first period. She had explained to the class that paper was precious because it came from living plants, and it was wasteful for them to print millions of copies of the same book, so these books were created to give them access to all books. All one had to do was close the book to clear the pages and then open it to the front page, write the title of the book and name of the author, and the text would appear on the pages.

Master Hallewell was very passionate about not wasting paper. She wouldn't even let them use their hemp paper to take notes. Abney admitted she'd never thought of books in that way, as words printed on the carcass of something real that had once enjoyed light, air, perhaps even had feelings. She felt a small pang of guilt as she thought of her room back home. She had hundreds of books.

Instead, Master Hallewell handed them each a miniature elephant called a Minelephant. They looked exactly like regular elephants except they were only about five inches high and spoke fluently in several languages. Abney's was called Audrey. The creatures listened to Master Hallewell's lectures with the students and could repeat anything they needed to hear again. They even answered questions if the questions pertained to the lecture.

"Let us first cover Changelings. As new Fae, a sense of identity will help you adjust. Now, who can venture a guess as to why Fae do not raise their own children?" Master Ibori asked the class. Not a single hand went up. The class, overcome with exhaustion, and having no actual idea why they had been dumped on their unsuspecting Fleetling families, remained silent. "No one?" he coaxed. "Very well, turn to page fifty-six in your books." Abney went to the page he indicated. The heading read, "The Almost Complete Destruction of a World," and a picture of an explosion with frightened dinosaurs running in front of it covered the page to the left.

"First, you must understand this. Fae *hate* children. They are small and always requiring help or needing things. They have poor hygiene habits, and quite frankly, they take up far too much time. This led to Fae children running wild with almost no supervision. Which in turn, led to the almost complete destruction of the world above as the chapter clearly states.

"That's when we were forced to take stock and evaluate ourselves. Having our children run amuck would simply not do, so we tried several foster situations. There is an entire generation here that was raised by otters, but ultimately, we needed a race a little more like ourselves. That's when we discovered the Fleetlings. They walked upright, had some minor language, but most importantly, they seemed to enjoy their young. Fawning over them and hardly ever taking their eyes off them.

"Early trials were not encouraging. They were most uninterested in adopting children. Their own children were the only ones that seemed to concern them, so we had to take further steps. At birth, Fae children were then smuggled in and charmed…"

"That's scandalous," James Lockwood spoke up. "I mean that makes us no better than those birds…ummm…"

"Cuckoos," another student offered helpfully.

"Yeah, Cuckoos," James said.

Master Ibori addressed him. "Mr. Lockwood, have you ever tried to raise a child?"

"Well, no. I'm only thirteen," James replied.

"Then, respectfully, you have no idea what you're talking about," Master Ibori spat. "Take your average Fleetling child, times their behavioral problems by ten, then add uncontrolled magical powers, and you'll come close to what Fae children are like."

"What happens to the Fleetling children?" a deep male voice asked from behind Abney.

"Tsk tsk, Mr. Carlson," Master Ibori scolded lightly. "That would be skipping ahead. Now, as I was saying, the newborn Fae are charmed to be exact replicas of the Fleetling children they take the place of. The charm makes you real Fleetlings for all intents and purposes. Thus, the Fae children get through their volatile years without destroying things or worlds and come to us better adjusted and ready to learn."

"If you can just suppress their powers by turning them into Fleetlings, why not do that and keep them here?" James asked critically.

"Because we do *not* like children," Master Ibori repeated. "Was that confusing for anyone else when I said it?" James gave up. The rest of the class shook their heads no.

"So, do we get to meet our real parents?" Abney recognized the voice of Devlin Sand.

"Maybe," Master Ibori said. "But not for many years yet. Some parents show up for graduation. Some don't. Fae don't usually feel familial ties like Fleetlings do."

"So how are we supposed to know our roots if we never know who our parents are?" a pink haired girl in the front row questioned.

"You don't need parents to have roots," Master Ibori informed them. "You are who you are. If you're an Ice Giant, your ancestors come from southernmost regions. From the lines of Lula StrongMountain and Combald Monstronomy. If you're a Banshee, your first ancestors were Darthula and Everhart of the Veil. And so on and so forth, et cetera, et cetera. Your final project this semester will be to research your progenitors. One will be easy because you couldn't be what you are without a parent being the same. A simple blood test will reveal the rest of your ancestry, and we'll go from there. Then you will write a twenty-page essay outlining your genome and what that means to you."

"Okay," the pink haired girl said with annoyance. "But if our parents don't come to graduation, is there a way for us to find out who they are? What if we want to find them?"

"Ms...?" Master Ibori enquired.

"Buckles, Margot Buckles."

"Ms. Buckles, if your parents don't want you, they don't want you, and there's nothing for it. If you find you have unresolved issues because of this, I suggest you seek therapy," Master Ibori replied. Abney couldn't see the girl's face, but she watched as her shoulders sank sadly.

"What about our names? Do we have different names than those given to us by our Fleetling families?" James spoke out again.

"Now that is a good question!" Master Ibori responded with a smile.

"Names are significant to the Fae, especially true names. If someone is in possession of your true name, they can make you do anything, so it is a heavily guarded secret."

"How do we figure out what our true names are?" Devlin asked.

"Another good question!" Master Ibori celebrated. "We are given them upon our Binding Day. Which is the day you choose whether to belong to the Seelie or Unseelie Court. On that day, your queen will whisper your name in your ear and upon doing so, bind you to her for all time. As I said, you do not hand this name out lightly, so most of us go by the names given to us by the Fleetlings. Keeps things simple. You may change it any time you wish though."

"When is Binding Day?" James enquired.

"Binding Day comes after your graduation," Master Ibori answered. "Please hold any further questions until the end of the lesson. Now, turn to page fifty-seven..."

Glaciomancy went by easy enough. The Master was a youthful and handsome Snow Man, which was the male version of Abney's species. The humor of his Fae-type was not lost on him, and he joked about it often. His name was Master Popov, but he asked that they call him Sasha or Frosty, if they preferred. The class liked his easygoing manner, but Abney was a little disappointed. In her limited experience, teachers who tried too hard to be friends with the students often did so at the expense of actually teaching.

A subdued horn sounded, and the students dispersed for the day. The majority headed back to their houses or to the party at The Left Side of the Mushroom. Not Abney though. She had one more class. Snozbert escorted her to the hive on school grounds, and she tripped over her robes while trying to mount the bee. She was still trying to get used to them. It was strange wearing the dark blue robe over her regular clothes, and the sash felt a little confining. It was white with the coat of arms for Yule and Litha at the top. Abney pulled at it, wishing it was looser.

The top portion of Litha was not as grand as Yule. It was a smaller stalagmite with a plain yellow wooden door out front and no other decoration. Once inside, there was a dark spiral grand staircase that went down for over a mile. The walls were covered with grim carvings, all vicious monsters and demons; it gave Abney the chills.

"Your mind is getting to you again." Snozbert observed the goosebumps on her arm. "You're practically a living ice cube. You shouldn't have goosebumps." Abney looked sideways at him and stuck her tongue out when she thought he couldn't see. The air grew warmer and warmer as they descended. Abney was sweating profusely by the time she reached the bottom, even with her robes, which were designed to keep her cooler.

Abney's mouth fell open. Where Yule had a large carving of Krampus, Litha had a waterfall of lava. It was terrifying and awe-inspiring. From the molten rock, a figure emerged and walked toward them. Snozbert looked particularly unimpressed, but he always was. Abney was delighted. The burnt creature approached them. Its skin was charred and cracked looking. It had no hair and no clothing. Its mouth turned up painfully in what Abney assumed to be a smile.

"Msss. Kelly?" it hissed.

"Yes, and this is…"

"Wortlister," the Puca interjected. Abney raised her eyebrows.

"His name is Snozbert," she corrected him.

"It is not," the Puca informed her. "It's whatever I want it to be, and now I want it to be Wortlister." Abney covered half of her face with her hand. She was mortified by the impression they were making on her new teacher.

"It'sss okay, Msss. Kelly," it said. "I'm well acquainted with Wortlisssster here. I know hisss love for code namesss. I am Massster Blewitt. If you'll follow me, we'll begin your lessson."

He took them to a classroom that was thankfully cooler than the rest of the school; it was still warm, but Abney at least felt like she could breathe. Unlike her other teachers, he did not write on the board or stand in front of her. Instead, he pulled two desks head to head, and they sat facing each other.

"Now, Msss. Kelly," Master Blewitt said. "Thisss isss not a traditional Pyromancy courssse, becaussse you cannot control fire in the usssual way. You ssshould not manipulate fire outssside of your body. It isss ill-advisssed for you to try to touch fire at all, becaussse your outer sss-hell, your ssskin, isss ice. Your insssides can handle the fire, but your sss-kin cannot. It can do you great harm outssside your body. Ssso inssstead, you mussst learn to control the fire inssside of you." Abney nodded that she understood.

"The first ssstep for you isssn't magic or reading, it'sss meditation. That'sss what our firsst lessssonsss will be on. You will learn meditation and ssself-control. Once you have massstered that, I will teach you how to manipulate and control that fire in your chessst. Today, you will sssit there and clossse your eyesss." Abney obeyed, shutting her eyes. "I want you to picture a ssscene in your mind that makesss you feel calm. Picture every detail to the tiniessst rock or piece of furniture."

Abney pictured herself in a giant library. Hundreds of thousands of books surrounding her. She could smell the dust and mold and feel her fingertips brushing against the spines of her beloved friends. Suddenly, she remembered what Master Hallewell had said about books. Shrieks filled the air, and books started diving off the shelves at her. She ran but could not escape their cries. Her eyes flung open, and she was breathing heavily.

Master Blewitt looked at her knowingly. "Sssometimes the place we asssume is the mossst relaxing is, in fact, not what we thought. Try again."

This time, Abney imagined the kitchen in her home. Granny's face covered with flour and strands of hair escaping from their usual order as she rolled cookie dough. Her father sat at the bar, sipping a cup of cocoa. His mustache held the evidence that there had once been whipped cream on top of his drink. Abney imagined herself laughing and talking with them. She felt the tension leaving her body. This was relaxing, familiar, and comfortable. She felt warm and safe.

Wham!

Abney, who had fallen asleep, startled and sat up, wide-eyed and heart racing. Master Blewitt jumped right out of his chair and was hiding behind the desk. The Puca was laughing. Abney realized he had slammed her book down on one of the desks. Master Blewitt stood up shakily and turned to face the prankster.

"Very amusssing. I…" Master Blewitt started.

"Wortlister," the Puca cut in quickly. "And your pupil was asleep." Abney looked at the floor sheepishly.

"Sorry."

"It'sss fine. Happensss all the time," he said. "Why don't we call it a day? I'll sssee you next Monday. Enjoy your holiday weekend." The Master still looked frightened, like he was reliving the shock again and again. Abney felt grateful to be going back to Oberon House until she realized she still had a party to go to.

✴

Abney went back to the house with the newly re-named Wortlister, to change her clothes, and then headed over to the Left Side of the Mushroom. Young Fae and their Hobgoblins crowded the restaurant. They were playing Fleetling holiday music loudly. She recognized "The Dance of the Sugar Plum Fairy" had been remixed with "The Arabian Dance" to sound trippy and hip. Red and green lights flashed all around, and the tree Domino had set up was fully decorated and shining. It was more like a Christmas party than a back to school party.

Teens were sipping some sort of green drink with purple whipped cream, eating cookies, cakes, and goodies of every kind. Giant Jenga had completely taken over one of the corners, along with other Fleetling board games and a few that weren't familiar to her. Couples kissed under the mistletoe and, oddly, none of the marvelously-hatted staff were in sight. Abney couldn't spot Pernella either.

"Abney!" Honali yelled in excitement and hugged her. Abney froze; she wasn't used to her peers touching her. "You don't mind if I steal her, do you?" she asked Wortlister.

"She's all yours," the Puca said and walked over to visit with some of the other Hobgoblins.

"Did you bring your boyfriend?" Honali asked. Abney blushed white.

"He's not my boyfriend," she replied quickly. "We're just housemates."

"Sure, whatevs, girl," Honali said unconvinced and dragged Abney by her hand to a table with a wide assortment of Fae. "Hey all, this is my new home girl, Abney. I've adopted her, so be nice."

"Lunetta," a very petite, yet chubby, Fleetling-looking girl said in introduction. "I'm a Hobbit."

"Abel," an overly buff youth with lavender skin and black hair stuck out his hand. Abney shook it cautiously. "I'm the most handsome guy here. Oh, and I'm a Djinn," he winked at her, making her feel uncomfortable.

"Gus." A skeletal arm reached for hers. Abney stared for a moment before she could force herself to touch the boney hand. It was hard, lacked any warmth, and when she tried to let go of it, the hand detached from its owner and clung to her. Abney shrieked and shook it off as the others laughed.

"For the love of Pete!" Abney exclaimed, not meaning to sound like her grandmother.

"Who's Pete?" Abel looked at her confused.

"He's…well…I don't know. He's just someone we do things in the name of in my family."

"Vive la Pete," one of the girls said with a slight French accent.

"Vive la Pete!" everyone shouted with smiles. Abney cringed and started looking around for an exit strategy.

Honali grinned. "She's never going to play with us again if you all scare her off the first day." She passed the hand back to Gus. He smirked, or Abney thought he did; it was tough to read emotions on someone who didn't have lips.

"I'm a Grim Reaper," Gus continued. "Nice to meet you." Abney nodded uneasily.

"Sabine," the beautiful girl with the French accent and glittering horn on top of her head announced. She didn't seem overly thrilled by the meeting. "In case you couldn't tell, I'm a Unicorn. You know, the rarest type of Fae there is?"

"And the snobbiest," Lunetta smirked. Sabine ignored the Hobbit and looked at her nails.

"I'm Sümeyye." A frizzy-red-haired Pixie stood up to grab Abney's hand. She was clearly embarrassed by her friends' bickering and rudeness. "We met at the ball. I'm an Autumn Pixie."

"I'm...I'm Abney," she stuttered, even though Honali had already introduced her. "I'm a Snow Maiden."

"What do you say, guys?" Honali asked them mischievously. They looked at each other, then stared at Abney with neutral faces for an uncomfortable amount of time.

"Goable gobble one of us, one of us! Goable gobble one of us, one of us," they chanted loudly all at once and banged their fists on the table! Abney stood absolutely still. Everyone was looking at her, and she wanted to crawl into a hole and disappear.

"What was that?" Abney looked at Honali wide-eyed.

"Haven't you ever seen *Freaks?*" Lunetta answered for her friend. Abney shook her head no.

"Well, it's something they do in the movie," Honali informed her. "We will have to discuss your movie education later."

"Sit down." Abel indicated she should sit next to Sümeyye.

"Now that you've been gooble gobbled, you'll never get rid of us," Honali teased and scooted into the booth next to her. The party had stopped staring at them and gone back to whatever they were doing.

"Right." Gus spoke up, "So, where were we?"

"We were waiting for Honali," Sabine said not looking up from filing her fingernails. "To do the toast."

"That's right!" Gus acknowledged. "We're short a glass now though."

"Hold up." Abel sprang to his feet. "I'll get it." He disappeared for a few seconds and came back with a glass of eggnog for Abney.

"All right everyone, glasses raised," Lunetta commanded, and everyone obliged. "Here's to a new year and new friends. To hard work and fun that never ends."

"To causing mischief and never getting caught," Gus cut in. "To new adventures and new battles to be fought."

Abel took a turn. "To new loves and to old. May our conquests be many and spirit bold!"

Sümeyye spoke up. "To fewer tears and more days of laughter. To getting through the year and it not being a disaster."

"To confidence in the face of stress," Sabine chimed in. "May we never forget that we know best."

"To friends that become family and always have your back." Honali smiled. "May our bonds be unbreakable and never shatter or crack." They all looked at Abney expectantly, and she rummaged through her brain in a panic.

"May...or...ummm...to...to always being able to find the right words and things to say." Abney tried to come up with a rhyme. "May your lips not sink ships and…. Keep trouble at bay?"

"Cheers," the group cried and clinked their glasses together. Abney took a swig of her eggnog and nearly choked; it was strong.

"What's in this?" Abney questioned them. They all shared a secret smile. Abel opened his jacket to reveal a flask.

"Homemade," he said proudly. "I have a talent for botany and distillation."

"That was pretty good, by the way." Gus applauded Abney. "I was working on what I was going to say almost all of break. I don't know that I could've come up with something on the fly."

"I was totally thinking the same thing," Lunetta agreed.

Domino greeted them as he approached the table with Zoey in tow. "Hey."

"You give new meaning to being fashionably late," Honali teased him.

"I know. I was working for Herr Koch, and he kept me late labeling different kinds of moss," he admitted.

"The herbalist?" Gus asked. "Wow, you work fast. Just got here and already have a job."

"It's more of a mandatory thing," Zoey smiled at her brother wryly.

"Shut up." He pushed her playfully. "So what did we miss?"

"Just the introductions," Honali said and introduced the group to the twins. "We were just about to start up Karaoke. Since you guys were last in, you can be first up." Her manner let them know, in no uncertain terms, that it wasn't up for discussion. Zoey seemed pleased, but her brother looked less keen on the idea.

Abel helped Sümeyye set up the machine and told the twins it was holiday songs only tonight. Zoey thumbed through the binder full of tracks until she found the number of one she wanted to do. Abney watched as Lunetta put a spotlight on her housemates, and the music started.

The twins were barely able to belt out the chorus before a bone-chilling scream brought the party to a standstill. The melody to "Must be Santa" was playing through the speakers, but not another sound could be heard until a second scream ripped through the air, and everyone dashed out to the street to see what was happening.

A Cherub was lying crumbled in a puddle of blood just outside. Wortlister pushed his way to the front. Abney watched his face turn from cynical to serious. "Hobgoblins, get your wards to their houses now!" he shouted with authority. Abney made her way to his side, and he held her shoulders protectively. "Wilbur," he called to his fellow Puca who had his hand tightly around Domino's wrist. They came forward. "Take Abney with you. I'm going to alert KRAMPUS Don't let them out of your sight and hurry."

Wilbur led them down the street hastily. Abney could hear voices behind them shouting in alarm:

"Has anyone seen the boy?"

"Where's Emmanuel?"

"It's Kringle! It's Kringle! Get the Changelings out of here now!"

Abney struggled to keep up with her fellow escapees. They were lean and athletic, and Abney was not. After a few blocks, she could hardly breathe, and Domino couldn't keep up either. So, the Puca stopped, picked them up, one under each arm, and fled. Abney felt fear infecting her, and she looked around wildly as Wilbur sprinted, holding them at his sides. Everything seemed darker than usual as a dense fog rolled in, dimming the normally glowing city.

CHAPTER 9

THE STORY OF NICHOLAS KRINGLE PART 2

They reached Oberon House safely only to find new chaos. Inside, everyone was running about, stoking fires and watering the Yule trees. Each Fae carried a switch in their hand and jumped at the slightest touch. Feo and some of the Hobgoblins brought blankets and pillows into the Ocean Room while everyone whispered fearfully.

"Hey," Agatha shouted and then whistled to get their attention. "Eyes on me. We will all stay in here for the night. They spotted Kringle outside The Left Side of the Mushroom. The Cherub Gilbert was found dead, and his ward, Emmanuel, is missing. These are not safe times, my little Changelings. Stay close to your Hobgoblins, travel in groups, stay as safe as possible. We will do everything in our power to protect you."

"Even then," Blythe commented darkly. "You may not make it out of this alive."

"That's enough of that, honey," Agatha said to Blythe. "Now, gather round everyone, gather round. It's time you all hear this." Abney listened contentedly as Agatha relayed the story of Nicholas Kringle again to the group, and her ears perked up when she finally reached the spot where they'd left off only a few nights before.

"And for a while, they were content. That is, until the night Cesare finally told Nicholas what really happened to his mother.

"One night, while they sat rocking by the fire, Cesare told his son the story of how The Winter King had made a bargain so that he might have a daughter and what Baba Yaga had asked for in return many years later. He told his son of how his mother had wandered, calling out his name and how she had died of a broken heart when she found out what had become of him. Nicholas had loved his mother fiercely, and the news of how she died enraged him. He was distraught, and he wanted his mother back.

"He began to brood and became isolated. He stopped playing with his brother and visiting the villagers. Despite his father's encouragement to go out and live a happy life, Nicholas continued his isolation. He stayed up late, reading old and dark books. Small animals started disappearing from Time's forest, and the trees were becoming angry. They murmured of Nicholas stalking through them and taking their creatures. Cesare was growing concerned but could not bear to confront the son he finally had back.

"Nicholas's heart filled with so much hate it started to turn black. Book after book turned up only one way to get his mother back, but he would need a very powerful witch, and he only knew of one with that kind of power. Baba Yaga. And so, like his father and grandfather before him, he set out to find the witch.

"He found her with surprising ease.

"'Come to get your youth back?' the witch laughed at him.

"'I do not mind being an old man,' he admitted, and this was true. He rather preferred it. It suited him better. 'I want you to bring my mother back.'

"'It is not possible,' she lied.

"'I've done the research.' He pressed her. 'I know you can, and I know the price.'

"Baba Yaga gave him a piteous look. 'Do not ask for this,' she said almost pleadingly. She had raised him from a young boy, and she was not heartless. 'She will only be a fragment of what you remember, and there will be no going back for you.'

"'There is nothing else I desire,' he said with finality.

"The old witch shook her head and grabbed his hand tenderly, but dropped it immediately as if it burned.

"'You've already begun the process.' she said sadly. 'You must have taken many innocent lives for your heart to be so black.'

"'I cannot turn back,' he said, a hint of woe in his eyes. 'I am ready, Grandmother. I know what my consequences will be. Now, name your price.'

"'There is nothing more precious I can ask for than what you are already sacrificing.' She frowned. 'I will take nothing from you in return, but I urge you to turn back now, for your own sake.' Nicholas shook his head defiantly. 'Very well,' the witch conceded. 'Give me your hands.'

"He held his shaking hands out to her, and she grasped them harshly and whispered a spell over them. Then, she dragged him over to one of her many shelves and pulled down a clear jar with an orange salve inside. She reached in, got a large handful of the slime and caked it on his hands.

"It took several minutes, but Nicholas's hands started to burn and tear as his fingers elongated, and his fingernails grew long and sharp."

"Sandy Claws," Domino joked and made crab-like pinchers with his hands. Agatha and the rest of the room stared at him like he had grown a third head. "Come on," he said. "Tim Burton, *Nightmare Before Christmas*…anybody?" Agatha was looking particularly put out, and no one dared answer him. "Sorry," he said. "Please continue."

"I don't know what a Tim Burton is, but you were sort of right," Agatha admitted. "It was originally Saxta Kogti or Santa Claws, so named because of the claws given to him by Baba Yaga, which brings us back to our story.

"After Nicholas's claws had grown in, he dropped to his knees and began to shiver as his heart turned to ice.

"'Claws,' Baba Yaga spoke eerily, 'to rip out the hearts of your victims and a cold heart so that you will not hesitate in your task. Be warned!

You will never be able to feel the summer again. Heat will melt your heart, and you will feel the pain of every life you have ever taken, which will likely kill you. You must travel in the cold. You will need a hundred hearts as pure as snow to bring your mother back. Come to me when you have them.'

"Nicholas nodded at the witch and set out to complete his dark quest.

"The world of Fleetling and Fae grew to fear the winter as Nicholas stalked their children to see which were bad and which were good enough to perhaps have that rare heart that is pure as snow."

"Well, a bunch of Christmas songs just got a whole lot creepier," BlueMoon spoke without thinking and apologized immediately.

"Why didn't they just set a team of Dragons on him?" Devlin asked. "If he can't handle heat, that seems like an obvious answer."

"Oh, brilliant one! Why weren't you born at the beginning of our troubles? We have feared this monster for many a year, but no one thought to bring in the Dragons." Wilbur shook his head. "Of course we tried that. Fae with fire talents can't see him. He has some sort of protection spell from Baba Yaga. We lost legions of good soldiers before we stopped deploying them. A few of the multi-elementals were able to see him, but their fire wasn't strong enough to do the necessary damage."

"That's convenient," Abney said. "The one type of Fae that can stop him, can't see him?" Agatha looked ready to explode. "Sorry." Abney looked at the floor, trying to avoid her glare.

"Anyone else?" Agatha asked crossly. "Or can we get on with this?" Everyone nodded for her to continue.

"Father Time watched in dismay as his son fell further and further into darkness. His grief riddled the lands, and they agonized with him. In vengeance for their woodland occupants and loyalty to Cesare, the trees called down another curse on Nicholas. From then on, even the smell of trees made him sick and touching them burned and left painful welts on his skin.

"It went on for years, many heroes fell before Santa Claws, and the numbers of lost children was sickening. Finally, at a loss, the two Faerie

Queens, Titania and Mab went to see Old Man Time to beg for his help. For you new Fae, this meant things were as bad as they could get. The Seelie and Unseelie Queens are not inclined to ask for help, ever. A Fleetling king also went. He, you will have heard of. His name was Arthur."

At this, Abney's face lost the haunted look of horror and exchanged it for a temporary one of delight. King Arthur, his knights of the round table, Merlin, they were real? She thought lovingly of her copy of *Le Morte d'Arthur* and made a mental note to reread it.

Agatha's voice faded back in, and Abney reinvested herself in the story.

"But Time refused to see them. He didn't want to acknowledge what Nicholas was doing. He wanted it to go away so he could remember his oldest son as he had been. Arthur was ready to give up and head back to do what little he could to protect his people when the Faerie Queens used their considerable power to wreak havoc in Time's Forest. The trees complained loudly, disturbing the old man's much-loved naps. Finally, he relented and agreed to meet with the threesome.

"They spoke to him of thousands of dead Fae and Fleetling children. Cesare looked weary to the bone. He loved Nicholas. He was the last part of his beloved Orina left in the world, but this could not be allowed to continue. He called his youngest son, Peter to him. Peter had grown into a tall, dark looking youth of fifteen, with long jet-black hair and cloven hooves.

"'Peter,' Time addressed his son, 'I worry I will lose you both, but my body is too old to go chasing after your brother. I need you to go and bring him back to me, alive. I will imprison him here. What has happened is not his fault.'

"'You have my word,' Peter vowed.

"Peter was young, but he was nobody's fool. He knew he would need more than just himself if he was going to bring his brother back alive. He asked King Arthur and The Fae Queens for soldiers to aid him in his task. The Faerie Queens sent a troop of Elves each. These Elves were not very fierce looking, but they were small, efficient, hard to catch, and expert at getting into places they weren't supposed to be. King Arthur sent his two best knights, Lancelot and Guinevere. And before a single one of you interrupt me," Agatha warned, "yes, Guinevere was a knight, not a queen, and a damn fine one at that. It's so sad how they rewrote her history. Instead of riding out of Camelot to battle with her comrade in arms, her name was drug through the mud, saying she ran away from her husband with another man. Complete nonsense!

"Anyway," she continued, "these mismatched allies formed the very first KRAMPUS squad."

"What?" Abney dared to cut in. "I thought Krampus was only one man, Fae, or whatever?"

"Ha," Blythe responded. "KRAMPUS stands for Kringle Retrieval and Mischief Patrol United Squadron. Nowadays, they are kind of like Fae police, but back in the day, they were real warriors."

"Well, in the Fleetling stories"—Abney found herself separating from humanity for the first time—"he's only a single person with many names, Black Peter, Belsnickel, Krampus, and so on."

Wilbur snorted. "Like one person could've brought down Nicholas Kringle."

"Well, how would I have known?" Abney replied defensively.

"Hey," Agatha said sharply. "I'm telling a story here!" Abney and Wilbur zipped their lips and looked at her attentively. She acknowledged their effort. "Good. Now, where was I? Oh, KRAMPUS had just formed, and the team was gathering its weapons. Peter, Lancelot, and Guinevere carried whips made specifically from the branches of the trees in Time's Forest. The Elves carried switches made from the same, and Cesare had one more gift for his son. A necklace with a tiny hourglass dangling from it.

"'Only at your darkest time, turn the hourglass,' he instructed Peter. 'It only works once, but it will summon help to you if you are ever in dire need.'

"KRAMPUS followed the trail of dead bodies around the globe and through the mists of the Fae, but Nicholas's dark magic seemed to always keep him just one step ahead of our heroes. A new strategy was needed. They would have to go on the offensive. So, they taught Fleetlings and Fae alike, to keep live trees in their homes. Firs were the hardiest, and everyone kept stockings by their fire, whether they needed to dry or not. If you found them weighed down with coal and switches when you woke, you knew that Nicholas was near, and to be on your guard."

"Wait, wait, wait," Domino interjected. "I thought switches and coal were for bad children."

"Fleetlings rarely get the stories straight," Agatha grumbled. "They are not for bad children. The Elves left them as gifts of protection. Haven't you been paying attention?" she admonished him. "A jolly-looking fat man sliding down your chimney is not a good thing. And without those gifts, many would not have survived!" Agatha announced. Domino looked a little scared but nodded that Agatha should go on.

"Anyway," she continued, "they finally cornered Nicholas in the small village of Kaplice, and a mighty battle raged where many Elves and Lancelot lost their lives. It came down to the two brothers. Just before Nicholas could land a killing blow, Peter turned the hourglass around his neck, and their father appeared between them. He grabbed Nicholas by his mighty talons and froze him in time. Nicholas was carried back to his father's lands and imprisoned in a wooden fortress.

"Time unfroze his son once he was secured, but never went to visit him again. The boy he knew was gone, only a black-hearted monster remained, and he could not bear the sight of him. Nicholas Kringle remained there, guarded by KRAMPUS until very recently when a group of pickle-headed nimrods set him free," Agatha concluded.

"HAFWITS," Abney remembered out loud. "I saw the headline on the newspaper DiGott was reading."

"Halfwits?" Zoey asked.

"Humans Aware of Faerie Waggishness, Indiscretions, Tomfoolery, and Shenanigans," Blythe enlightened them.

Shilo Finkelman laughed. "They couldn't have come up with something that didn't insinuate they were idiots?"

"They *are* idiots," Wilbur stated. "Which makes them the worst kind of dangerous. They thought we were keeping a sweet gift-giving old man captive to spite the Fleetlings. Now, they've released terror on us all."

"What about Orina?" Zoey ventured suddenly. "Nicholas killed thousands; didn't he get his mother back?"

"No," Agatha replied. "A heart as pure as snow is one in a million, to find a hundred? An impossible task. He could only have found half at best, by the time they imprisoned him."

Zoey pressed on. "Then why did he kill so many?"

"You only know the purity of heart when you taste it. A pure heart is said to taste like chicken noodle soup," Agatha replied with a raspy shudder.

"He was eating them?" Abney asked, disgusted.

"Enough for now," Agatha commanded. "Time for bed, sugars." She stood and the Hobgoblins handed out stockings with coal and switches inside to each of them. "Be vigilant," she warned and left the room.

Abney sat on a blanket near the twins. Everyone was whispering fearfully again. Abney turned her face to the fire. She somehow felt safer looking at it and at the same time she felt a terrible dread that it might go out. She'd never been scared of the dark, yet, now she was.

"Do you think he'll come here?" she heard Zoey ask.

"I don't know," Abney said and shrugged her shoulders.

"It's time to sleep!" Blythe commanded them. "If he comes, he comes, there will be nothing that can save you. So, sleep. Tired Changelings are slow, and your only chance will be to run."

CHAPTER 10

HAPPY HOLIDAYS

The headline from *The Korrigan Chronicler* read: **Cherub Found Dead Outside Local Hotspot! Changeling Still Missing!** No one had slept in their own rooms for several nights. They were allowed to, of course, but it felt safer in the packed Ocean Room. Agatha was sitting in her chair by the fire, smoking her hookah, and reading the article out loud. Nicholas Kringle was spotted the night of the back to school bash, but no new sightings or disappearances had been reported since. A picture of Peter Kringle looking very serious adorned the page, and his quote stated, "I will not rest until my brother is brought to justice and is no longer a threat to any realm." It was also mentioned that Cesare Kringle had declined to comment.

Christmas Eve loomed before them, bringing a mixture of relief and uncertainty. The first three days of school were officially over, and they were all headed back to their Fleetling families for a long weekend. Abney, on the one hand, felt joy. She wanted to see her father and grandmother, be near them and do all the usual Christmas things they always did. On the other hand, she was scared to death that they were going to notice that she didn't belong with them and that Moira had been right all along.

"You won't be able to tell them," Wortlister had warned her. "I wouldn't bother. Plus, what good would it do? It's Fleetling holiday time. Do you really want them to remember their Christmas as the day they found out they've been living a lie for thirteen years and had locked up a completely sane woman?" Abney meditated for an hour after that conversation. She had a lot of feelings about lying to the people who raised her.

Feo and a Cthulhui named Apollonia lugged a large mirror into the room. Of the types of Hobgoblins, Abney had found the Cthulhui the hardest to get used to. Their face tentacles moved independently, and they sometimes used them like extra hands. Their thick legs were elephant-like, and they had humanoid hands covered in different colors of frog-like skin. She caught herself staring at them too often and felt guilty that she had so much trouble looking away.

"All right, sugars!" Agatha stood to get their attention. "The Traveler is on his way. Line up with your Hobgoblins. Have a nice trip Topside. Remember to stay vigilant. Kringle could be anywhere. We don't want anyone else to go missing." The students lined up, carrying their backpacks and small gifts they had made for their Fleetling families. Abney stood behind the twins, who didn't seem especially excited to be going home.

"Do we have to go?" she heard Domino asking Wilbur.

"Doppelgängers aren't perfect. We have to send you back every so often to ensure the Fleetlings don't get suspicious," Wilbur said firmly, though he was obviously not pleased to be going Topside either.

"It'll be all right." Zoey grabbed her brother's hand. "You always have me, old bean," she said with a pretty decent British accent. Abney thought they both looked a little frightened, but she was too worried about her own problems to dig into it. Besides, it wasn't her business.

"Next," Agatha called out, and Domino and Wilbur stepped forward. Domino yanked a hair from his head, shoved it into the glass, and a tall messy-haired boy appeared in the mirror. He had a pirate earing in his right ear and tons of multi-colored bracelets around his wrists.

Agatha instructed him to reach for the boy's right hand in the mirror. The Fleetling reached for him as well, and he disappeared through the glass. His Doppelgänger came through to them, looking not like a Fleetling, but like Domino's Fae-self. Once Not-Domino gained his footing, he stepped to the side, to stand with the other replicas.

Wilbur stepped up and walked right through without hesitation. Zoey and Blythe followed, and then it was Abney's turn. Her masculine lookalike waved at her from the other side and reached out his hand. Abney reached hers out to his, and as they touched, she found herself back in her room—well, her closet. She turned and looked back into the mirror and found she was no longer ashamed of the person in there. Her hair was purple and pink now, but her gray eyes and curves were still the same. It was like seeing an old friend, and she cried.

She had no idea she would feel like this. Part of her had truly believed she would never see this place again, and here she was. A huge weight lifted off of her, yet she was trembling. It felt like she had been through so much in such a short amount of time, and it was just so wonderful to be home and feel safe.

Wortlister stumbled through after her and lifted up her chin. Abney looked down, wishing that she could just be alone for a few minutes. "Look at me," he commanded. "I said, look at me!" Abney looked up slowly. "Now, deep breath. One, two, three, exhale. Deep breath. One, two, three, exhale." She felt her tears dry up as she followed his instructions. "Good. Change your clothes and meet me in your room."

Abney emerged dressed in familiar yoga pants and a t-shirt that said, "Merry Christmas, You Filthy Muggle." It felt so normal, like she had woken up from a nightmare, but the large orange Puca in her bedroom reminded her that this place that was the dream for her not the other way around.

"Here," he said and handed her a blue Santa hat. "Go enjoy Christmas Eve with your family. I'll be up here if you need me. And remember, no confessions." Abney nodded and put the hat on. "Oh, and your family will smell bad to you at first. You'll get used to it."

"Why would they smell?" Abney asked.

"It's the iron in their blood. All Fae have a severe allergy to the deplorable metal. You'll smell it on them." he replied. Abney took a deep breath and prepared herself.

"Can I ask you something?" she stalled. Panic clawed its way up her spine, and she felt nervous about seeing her family again.

"Yes."

"Why didn't we just use the Traveler the first time to get to Tír na nÓg? I mean it seems like it would have been a lot less of a hassle," she said.

"I prefer the river," he replied. "And you needed some time to process things before I dropped you into the middle of that circus."

Abney nodded and tried to find the courage to make her feet carry her toward the stairs.

"Hey, kiddo," a familiar voice hollered up the stairs. "You ready?"

"Yes!" Abney shouted back, not sure exactly what she had just agreed to. She made herself walk out of her room and slid down the banister. The *Supernatural* Monopoly board was set up in the kitchen along with mugs of hot chocolate topped with mountains of whipped cream. Dad was holding the Impala, Granny had the hex bag, and Abney could see Bobby's flask laid out for her. "Patapan" was playing over the speakers, and the house smelled like Christmas tree scented candles. She stood in the doorway for a minute, drinking it all in, wishing it could always be this way. The new smell of her family was also becoming apparent. It was intense, metallic, and it turned her stomach. It was definitely worse than Wortlister described.

"Don't stand there looking all mopey," her father teased her. "You were gone for forever, and I'm dying to save the world from the apocalypse while beating the pants off you and Granny here."

"In your dreams, old timer," Abney said competitively and held her breath to take her place at the island.

"Oh really, you two." Granny shook her head with a laugh. "We all know I'm going to win." A pit grew in Abney's stomach. Even if she could tell them she was Fae, she wouldn't. She didn't want to lose this; she didn't want to lose them, and that knowledge didn't make her particularly proud of herself.

✦

Granny won Monopoly. Hot chocolate was drunk. Abney won Balderdash. Dad predictably lost all the other games (he wasn't very good at them), they watched *The Muppet Christmas Carol* again, and then they all went to bed. Well, Granny and her father went to bed. Abney snuck down the stairs after she was sure the others were sleeping. She snuggled up in her chair with her blanket and stared at their Christmas tree. Someone had repaired the ornaments Moira shattered, and the tree looked just as beautiful as it had before. There was something incredibly calming about gazing at the sparkling lights and glittering ocean dwellers. This was the safest and most content she had felt in the last two weeks.

Abney grabbed her phone, put "Little Soldier" on repeat, and stuffed her earbuds in her ears. She let everything go, deep breath in, deep breath out. It was going to be what it was going to be, no matter what. So, she dropped it all for the moment and admired their tree. It really was the most beautiful tree. Her eyes grew heavy, and finally, she slept.

✦

Christmas came and went with its usual pomp and circumstance. Gifts were given and received. They sang songs; games were played by some, and food was consumed in mass quantities by most everyone. Abney's family went to see the latest Hobbit movie, and Granny and Dad even spent a few hours in the attic with Moira. Abney opted out of the last activity, as recent events had opened her eyes. She now felt pity and an overwhelming sense of guilt when it came to her mother.

Wortlister stayed inside of her closet, reading and doing whatever it was Pucas did when they weren't hovering over their wards. Abney was grateful for the space. Having the alone time was nice. She could read in the living room, and it was utterly silent. Besides Granny running by her when there were thumps from the attic, no one bothered her at all. She could go to the bathroom, and there was no one in the stall next to her. In short, it was like heaven.

Once she decompressed, Abney spent some time baking with Granny, and she and her father started watching *Red Dwarf* from the beginning of the series again. She even ventured out of her comfort zone and called Molly to see how Christmas break was going. It didn't take long for her to realize that even though she was Fae, she still wasn't capable of a full-on phone conversation. Molly was also anti-social, so when Abney made an excuse to get off the phone, they were both immensely relieved.

Outdoors was becoming a new haven for her. Her Fleetling clothing was warmer than she liked, and being outside in the snow with her jacket off was as close as she could get to being comfortable. It gave her a chance to practice her Glaciomancy too. She enlarged the snowflakes as they fell in front of her. It wasn't easy—most of them disappeared completely—but she did manage a few hand-sized flakes.

"*Culivaře Flawix*," she whispered under her breath and concentrated on a single drop of white powder. She could feel the snow straining to hear her. Master Popov had only handled introductions last week, but the reading he assigned was very informative. According to *The Language of Winter* by Octavius Knotrump, the Elements had their own language, and while more experienced Fae did not need words, only intent, younger Fae were encouraged to learn the language and speak to the Elements often. They could be temperamental and stubborn if they felt the common courtesies had been ignored or one didn't talk to them enough.

Air wrapped around her like a hug, and an enlarged flake fell into her waiting hands. One thing about living on the desolate prairie was that neighbors were often well spaced, so she wasn't worried that anyone would notice what she was doing. She found it relaxing to be alone. She craved space, and that was hard to get in Tír na nÓg. Someone was always up in your face there.

When the light started to fade, Granny called her in, and they made bread while listening to radio shows on the oldies station. Abney was punching the dough down again when an emergency bulletin interrupted their program.

"*Amber Alert! Please be on the lookout for a nine-year-old girl, blonde hair, brown eyes, last seen wearing a purple snowsuit with a blue hat and gloves. Name: Shannon Nelson. She is reported to be in the company of an overweight man in his late sixties. White hair and white beard. Witnesses state the man was wearing a red tracksuit and matching hat. The suspect and Shannon were last spotted in Holiday Park near the train. This may be related to a string of missing children reported across the United States. Seventeen children have gone missing under similar circumstances with the same suspect described in the last three weeks. Please keep your eyes peeled and report any sightings to the Cheyenne Police Department immediately. Now back to our regular programming.*"

"Who could do such a thing?" Granny shook her head and frowned. Abney wanted to tell her the truth, but even as she thought about it, she knew how it would sound. Santa Claus kidnapping children? They would lock her in the attic with Moira. So, she said the only thing she could.

"A monster, Granny," she replied. "A monster."

✦

The rest of the weekend flew by fast, too fast. She was soon back at Oberon House with the other Changelings and their Hobgoblins. Everyone was tense, and the camp in the Ocean Room was alive and active. A second year Wood Nymph and her Hobgoblin had been found dead just the day before, and the boy from the party was still missing.

Abney was sitting in a circle with the twins and two of the new Changelings, Melinda and Cozmo. Everyone had their books out, studying different subjects. Abney was making a study guide and flashcards for her Herbology class. There were a ton of new plants she had to learn to identify and know their properties. Ms. Thornberry's class had not even begun to prepare her for the intensity of Fae herbology.

"I never thought I'd miss algebra," Cozmo said dramatically. "Have any of you read *Earth Tones*? I can't even pronounce half the words in here, and mispronunciations can be very offensive to the Elements. Look." He showed them a picture of Crater Lake in Oregon.

"Are we supposed to see something besides water?" Melinda asked, unsure of what they were supposed to be seeing.

"Looks pretty average to me," Domino said, unimpressed. Cozmo rolled his eyes and read the caption.

"The Pond of Tears, known to Fleetlings as Crater Lake, gets its name due to the tragedy that created it. A group of mermaids, known as The Land Fish…"

"Land Fish?" Zoey asked.

"Some mermaids choose to live on land. Much like you, Siren. When you get in water, you have a tail right?" Zoey nodded. "Mermaids are the same. They have a tail in the water and legs on land."

"Fair enough," Zoey said.

"Anyway," he continued, "the Land Fish decided that their power to use the Elements was really mastery of it. As they were 'masters', they stopped speaking with the Elements and paying the proper respects. The Elements took their revenge. Earth grew around their land legs, trapping them while water and lava combined beneath them to burn their feet with steam, and the wind blew bitterly against their backs. Over thousands of years of torture, their tears created the lake we see today. The Land Fish now live cloistered in the deepest part of the Atlantic Ocean. Like, what the deuce?"

"I feel like the moral to that story is: Don't get cocky," Abney cracked without thinking.

"Wow," Domino said. "You do have a sense of humor, after all." Abney blushed.

"I'm just saying that it seems like a pretty extreme punishment." Cozmo continued, "There should have been a warning or something. I mean, they just went straight for the thousands of years of torture. This place is so messed up."

"The description under the picture doesn't give every detail," Zoey observed. "Maybe they were warned?"

"Maybe," Cozmo conceded. "This place just gives the impression that it's much more dangerous than the Fleetling world."

"There's also more for you here," Abney said. "Here we can do magic, talk to the Elements, live forever. I would assume such great rewards would have to come with a heavier price than the Fleetling existence."

"A very wise statement…for once," Wortlister butted in. "Nothing is free, little Changelings. The greater the reward, the greater the price. You can live a boring life here too. Never taking risks or stepping outside your box. But how dull. You have a wonderful and terrible power. I think it's your responsibility to explore it to the fullest, come what may."

"Yeah, but what if we accidentally tick off the Elements and end up getting our feet burned off?" Cozmo argued. "Is it really worth it?"

"Definitely," Wortlister told him. "You take a risk getting out of bed every day. If you're going to live, you might as well do it loudly, or why bother? If you make the safe choice every time and live forever, what would you have to talk about? Take risks, be scared; hell, be terrified. You will be surprised what you can survive…"

"What risks have you taken?" Domino challenged.

"That is a story for another time," Wortlister said, suddenly looking far away. Abney didn't know why, but she felt sorry for him and put her hand on his. He looked at her sharply. "I am not to be pitied. I have lived. That is all." Abney removed her hand.

✦

New Year's Eve was upon them in no time, but there was no long weekend with their Fleetling families this time. The Fae don't measure time the way it's measured Topside. Not to mention, they deemed New Year a holiday where Fleetlings made the worst possible decisions, so having the Doppelgängers there wouldn't be especially notable. Instead, Abney found herself over at Niamh House where Gus and Honali lived. She and the twins had been permitted to stay the night. Lunetta, Abel, Sabine, and Sümeyye also had permission to stay.

Technically, it was a school night, but classes started later the next day because the elder Fae understood the students still liked to celebrate, even if it was just another day to the rest of them. They were all staying in Gus's room because it was in the basement and had stone walls. Therefore, they were not as likely to be in trouble for too much noise or unruly behavior.

They were each tasked with bringing something to share with everyone. Abel had made another diabolical concoction that Abney could hardly swallow. Lunetta made chips from thin sliced sweet potatoes, along with some sort of creamy dip. Sümeyye made a Turkish dish her Fleetling family enjoyed called Börek. Gus had managed to sneak Japanese sodas from Topside in his school bag. Abney and the twins brought a chocolate-cherry cheesecake that Feo helped them make. Sabine brought baguettes with Nutella, and Honali brought a hookah with choco-mint shisha.

This was all strange and alarming for Abney. Having sleepovers with boys and girls or having sleepovers at all, drinking alcohol, smoking? Granny most certainly would not approve. However, Granny also did not know Abney was Fae or how drastically life had changed for her in a little over a month. Tír na nÓg was not like home, so, maybe it was okay that she wasn't acting like she would have if she were back home?

She took a glass from Abel, sipped at it, and tried Honali's hookah. The drink was still disgusting, but the hookah wasn't so bad. She caught onto smoke tricks quickly and enjoyed making smoke rings. It was new and different. She was laughing and interacting with other beings, and it wasn't the worst thing ever. She was a little surprised by how easily she seemed to fit in and enjoy herself.

"Hey," Gus said to get everyone's attention. "I have an idea." He lit a bunch of candles, turned out the lights, and produced a glow in the dark Ouija Board. "Let's see what the spirits have to say about 2015. I'm a Grim Reaper, so we have nothing to fear, right? I can put them back in the Veil if the spirits get too rowdy."

"Cool," Abney said, going with the flow for once in her life.

"I don't know," Sümeyye objected. "Master Edwards says they're dangerous, even with a Reaper. You never know what you're letting in."

"Master Edwards is a wimp," Lunetta spoke up. "Come on, it'll be a blast."

"Oh, for Pete's sake," Abney said, feeling her buzz a little bit. "Let's just do it!"

"For Pete!" Abel agreed enthusiastically.

"Vive la Pete!" the others yelled with wide grins.

"Okay, but if this goes sideways, I want it known I said it was a bad idea," Sümeyye pouted.

"Pete will remember when everything is just fine too." Abel pinched her cheek and laughed.

"Me first." Honali volunteered and put her finger on the planchette. The others followed suit. "Do we have to say some magic words or something?" she asked.

"Nah, that's just a gimmick they use in the movies," Gus said. "I just need to make the Veil a little thinner here." He got up, looking very serious and tapped his scythe three times. "Now we can ask questions," he announced.

"Is someone there?" Honali asked. The planchette was still for a few moments and then jerked their arms to the side of the board that indicated **YES**.

"How many girlfriends will I have this year?" Abel jumped in.

"Hey!" Honali looked at him sternly.

"What?" he said. "You got your question. Not my fault you wasted it on something stupid." The triangle leapt to the number **8**, and Abel looked especially pleased with himself.

"Will Abel get anywhere with any of them?" Lunetta asked. The planchette dived for **NO**. Everyone but Abel laughed.

"You guys," Gus said seriously, "don't be rude to the dead. Welcome spirit. I'm Gus, and these heathens are my friends." The group went around introducing themselves, feeling bad about the breach in etiquette. "Who are we speaking with?" Gus asked, keeping up the decorum. The planchette remained on **NO**.

"Now, who's being rude?" Abel said under his breath, and Honali slapped him upside the head.

"Respect the dead!" she told him. "She…he…it…whatever did not have to come through the Veil to answer our questions."

"Maybe it doesn't have a name?" Lunetta guessed, "Do you have a name?" Their hands were pulled slowly over to **YES**.

"Well, can you tell it to us?" Gus asked politely. The triangle jolted over to **NO**. "I suppose we should just get on with our questions then?" Gus shrugged his shoulders.

"Will Herr Koch let me out of my indentured servitude early?" Domino asked. The planchette didn't move. **NO**.

Honali took the next question. "Will my real parents come to my graduation?" The triangle didn't move. It remained on **NO**.

"Harsh," Lunetta patted Honali's back, though the dragon girl looked more annoyed than hurt.

"Will I be Queen of Dreams at next year's carnival?" Sabine asked like she already knew the answer. The spirit did not disappoint, and the Planchette jumped over to **YES**. Sabine glowed triumphantly.

"Does Moira know what I am?" Abney spoke up suddenly. This time it went for the letters. **S H E S U S P E C T S**, the board answered, making Abney feel a little queasy.

"Does the Fae I like, like me back?" Zoey blushed. The triangle moved to **YES**.

"Ooooo!" the group teased her together, but Zoey didn't seem to mind.

"Will I pass my sacred geometry class?" Sümeyye finally joined in. The board was quiet for a moment and then slid down to **NO**.

"Uh oh," Gus teased. "Sümeyye failing her first class…hell might actually freeze over."

"Why will I fail?" she asked, panicked. It went for the letters and spelled out. **N O T F A I L**. Everyone looked confused now.

"Well, why would I not pass then?" she interrogated it. Staying in the letters, it jerked their fingers around more violently than it had before. **D E A D**, it said and spelled it again for them. **D E A D**.

"What do you mean dead?" Abney blurted out. She wasn't sure why she'd shouted. It was just too much, too morbid. Couldn't they have fun without it taking a dark turn? The room was silent, and it felt like all the air had been sucked out. After what seemed like hours, the planchette moved again. **K R I N G L E**, it spelled out to them. They all removed their fingers in fear. Gus stood up and banged his scythe again, closing the Veil. Sümeyye had lost all of her color, and Honali grabbed her hand.

Lunetta tried to soothe everyone. "It's just a game." Poppers and screams went off around them, causing the teens to hit the floor as they waited for a monster to come bursting in. Abney stood up first.

"It's midnight," she said, recognizing shouts of celebration and not fear. "Just midnight."

CHAPTER 11

PLANS

The purr of sewing machines polluted the air. The noise was over-whelming, and Abney kept losing her concentration. She was struggling to make a pair of elephant bell pants from Mermaid Scales and Yeti Mucus. The mucus is what the Fae used instead of thread, and it was very temperamental. Abney's kept getting too warm, melting, and ruining her stitch work.

"Keep your mucus cold, Ms. Kelly." Master Sjögren's voices vibrated in her cranium, and one of the Rat Queen's heads looked over her shoulder. "Also, add more starch. You want it much thicker if you want it to set right." The Elemental Sewing Master was brilliant, tolerant, but mostly creepy.

Rat Queens or Kings were one of the only types of Fae that were not born Fae. When seven or more rats' tails become irreversibly knotted, their souls also become intertwined, causing the rats to gain a sort of hive mind and heightened awareness. A Rat King/Queen was then born from that consciousness. Master Sjögren was, in fact, eleven separate rats, all about five feet tall, and each dressed in different colored robes that fitted over their heads. They moved circularly, seeing all things at once, and did not use their mouths to speak. They were telepathic, which one would think would limit them to a singular voice, but no, each of their distinctive voices could be heard melting together as they whispered in one's head.

Abney wiped out her stitching and began again. This was the first time in her life she had struggled with any class besides physical education, and it wasn't just Elemental Sewing. Glaciomancy and Understanding Runes were kicking her butt too. The only course she felt good about was Pyromancy, and that was because all she had to do so far was meditate.

It didn't help that she was distracted. The Ouija Board's prediction had them all spooked. They had already taken steps to try and secure Sümeyye's safety. One of them walked with her and her Hobgoblin, Hatsuko, at all times. She was sharing a room with one of her housemates and avoided being out in the open whenever possible. They hadn't told any of the Hobgoblins or their house matrons what the Ouija Board said, because they weren't supposed to have the thing in the first place. A meeting had been set for later that night at The Left Side of the Mushroom so that they could make a decisive plan. If Kringle was coming for Sümeyye, they most certainly were not going to sit by and let him take her.

Abney had mixed feelings about being involved with all of this. Sometimes, she wanted more than anything to go back to hanging out with her books; friends seemed to be trouble. Then again, Sümeyye was a lovely girl, and Abney would never be able to live with herself if she walked away, and Sümeyye died. Also, she had had fun with them, even if it always ended badly. So, she would meet with them and at least see what they could come up with.

Master Sjögren interrupted her thoughts. "Ms. Kelly…Ms. Kelly, your stitches are melting. Wipe them out and start again. Remember, more starch!" Abney groaned loudly, which earned her stern looks from three of the Master's heads. How was she supposed to do any of this with a psychotic mythological being walking around, killing people, and eating their hearts? Luckily, class was almost over. She still had Herbology left, but then she could head out to meet her cohorts.

✦

The Left Side of the Mushroom was sparsely populated. Most everyone was going straight from school back to their houses these days. Pernella said they could have whatever they wanted, provided they cleaned up after themselves and brought in some fresh vegetables from the garden. Zoey tagged along with Abney to get out of the house, and Domino was to meet up with them after his shift at the herbalist.

"I don't think the newbies should be in on this," Sabine said in a low voice. Their Hobgoblins were only three tables away, and they didn't want them to know what they were up to.

"They were there when this happened too." Honali went on to defend her assertion. "We're going to need all the help we can get."

"They're not really one of us," Sabine argued. "We don't know them well enough. They might not be trustworthy. We just met them."

"All right, Captain Wonderful," Honali conceded. "How do you propose we protect Sümeyye from Kringle without extra help? Have you gained some ninja-like powers I'm unaware of?"

Sabine glared. "Whatever. They're here anyway."

"Since that's settled," Honali said to Sümeyye, "what are we going to do? We're already guarding you to the best of our ability, but what good is that going to do in the long run?"

Abney spoke up. "In the story, Agatha told us KRAMPUS had to hunt him down to stop him. Maybe that's what we should do? Go after him, before he comes for Sümeyye."

"What would we do if we actually caught him?" Lunetta questioned. "If Lancelot, Guinevere, Black Peter, and two troops of elves couldn't defeat him…how will we?"

"I'm totally going to die." Sümeyye hid her head in her hands.

"No, you're not," Honali said emphatically. "We're going to figure something out. Nobody is going to take you." She removed Sümeyye's hands from her face and laced their fingers. "I won't let anything happen to you."

"Maybe we could find Baba Yaga," Zoey ventured. "She created this mess. Maybe she can fix it?"

"Nobody has seen hide nor hair of her for hundreds of years," Sümeyye said.

"Couldn't hurt to look," Zoey continued.

"Well, right now all we have is hearsay. Verbal stories repeated to us. Why don't we all do some research? There might be some detail or information that may help us that isn't in the versions we've heard. If nothing else, we may get a lead on where to start," Abney offered.

"Man, I hate homework!" Abel complained and instantly backpedaled, after looking at Sümeyye's face. "But...anything to save a friend."

"What'd I miss?" Domino joined them.

"Assignments," Gus informed him. "We're all on the Santa Claus research team now."

"Fun," Domino replied, taking a seat conspicuously next to Honali. "Hey," he said, looking her up and down.

"Hey," Honali responded with a skeptical sideways glance and then looked him square in the face. "You know I'm into girls, right? And this"— she held up Sümeyye's hand with their fingers still intertwined—"is my girlfriend."

"Oh, yeah. I wasn't..." he lied.

"I think you were," she persisted.

"I think you'll find you're into Fae in general," Wortlister interrupted them. "It's rather limiting only to be interested in one sex. You'll find that truer as you get older and the centuries roll on."

"I think I know what I'm into." Honali whipped her hair around to look at him.

He shrugged. "Suit yourself. Now, what are you all up to over here?"

"The same thing we do every night." Honali laughed. "We're gonna take over the world." Wortlister looked at her hard, but he couldn't tell if she was kidding or not.

"Uh huh," he said, not quite believing her, but he went back to his table. The Hobgoblin table was full and just as colorful as the Changeling's. Naturally, Blythe and Wilbur were there along with Chasha, a blue and violet Cthulhui who was Lunetta's guardian. Luke, a wild looking Brownie who was somewhat reminiscent of Pig Pen, was Abel's Hobgoblin. Mary-Lou, a golden drooling Orc, cared for Gus. Beau, a petite, curly-headed Cupid, was Sabine's Hobgoblin. Arjun, a Cthulhui with turquoise eyes, was Honali's Hobgoblin, and Hatsuko, a deadly, dripping wet Rusalka, was the guardian of Sümeyye.

Zoey summed up the situation. "So we'll research Kringle, keep our ears to the ground for information about Baba Yaga, and we'll all continue taking turns staying close to Sümeyye."

"For Pete's sake." Abel put his hand in the middle of the table. Abney shook her head; she knew he was making fun of her.

"For Pete's sake," she said, rising to the occasion and putting her hand in. The others followed suit.

"Vive la Pete!" they yelled.

There had been no waiters since the incident at the back to school party, so Pernella brought them out a plate of heavily peppered cheese fries and a round of Mulled Slithy Tove Brews, a green, hot, creamy, apple flavored drink. Purple whipped cream mountains covered the tops, while caramel and orange sprinkles drizzled all the way down the sides of the glasses. They were so pretty you almost didn't want to drink them, but they were also too delicious to let get cold. The young Fae grabbed them greedily and dug into the fries.

Emmanuel Medina Found Dead! The Hunt for Kringle Continues! *The Korrigan Chronicler*'s headline announced. The students were feeling the strain, fear, and grief associated with the loss of their classmate. He had been missing for a while. They all knew it was coming, but that didn't make it any easier. Abney had never even met him, but the sadness was catching, and she couldn't help feeling devastated for him. He must have been so scared and alone before he died.

KRAMPUS guards were everywhere now. The students were no longer allowed to take the bees and walked in large secured groups or took the bubble busses, which were very popular with the students. The vehicles were quirky looking and pushed out bubbles all around them as they rode to their destinations. It was clean energy transportation, run on the current created by a combination of glow energy and friction from the bubbles as they endeavored to escape the bus.

Master Blewitt now met with Abney at Yule after regular school hours, so that she didn't make herself a target by traveling in too small of a group. The lessons with him were going pretty well. She was getting better at keeping her cool, even when the Demon did things to purposefully scare her or make her angry or sad.

Wortlister and all the other Hobgoblins followed their wards closer than ever, making it harder to explain all their research and seemingly unusual attachment to Sümeyye. "Are you in love?" Wortlister had asked her. "You seem to be very interested in your friend."

"No," Abney responded, annoyed. Love? He thought she was in love at a time like this? Not to mention she was Honali's girlfriend. How could he be so thick?

She didn't feel comfortable asking Agatha more about Kringle, but she was finding Balthazar, the Bookworm in the library, very helpful. He gave her a list of titles that he thought would be helpful: *Fleetlings ARE Stupid: The Real Story of Santa Claus* by Alyssa Golightly, *Frozen Kingdom: The Unofficial Biography of His Royal Highness, Jack Frost* by Lura Sweetwater, *Of Coal and Switches, a KRAMPUS Story* by Ted Vasser, and *The Gray Witch* by Holland Hill, a biography about Baba Yaga.

She was also discovering how cool her book was. She could write notes in the margins, highlight sections, place bookmarks where she needed them, and even after she had cleared her book, she could write the title in again, and everything would be there. At times, she wished she could have all the books in front of her for comparison, but she took notes on her hemp paper and, to retain extra information, bribed her Minelephant with lemon/lime Snack Packs that she had smuggled back from her house during Christmas. The Minelephant was technically only supposed to remember stuff from Master Hallewell's class, but she was willing to trade the extra work for extra food. After all, an elephant never forgets.

Sümeyye was also very studious and made arrangements to study with Abney at The Left Side of the Mushroom, or LSOM, as she had begun to call it. Abney showed up with her list and book. Sümeyye had shown up with several books, her own book, and a list.

"Where did you get books?" Abney asked with amazement.

"The librarian at Ostara," she said. "I smuggle books to her from Topside, and she lets me check out real books, instead of handing me a list; it works. I hate not being able to reference other books when I need them. With our books, you have to wipe out what you're reading, write in the new title, make notes, wipe that out, and go back to your original book. I'd much rather have it all available in front of me." Abney was understandably jealous.

"Unbelievable," Abney shook her head.

"If you give me a list, I can get you whatever you want," Sümeyye offered. "Just get them back to me in a reasonable amount of time. Fernanda gets all anxious if I have them out too long."

"That would be amazing!" Abney said. "I'll make you a list after we finish here."

So far, they'd found out a lot of interesting facts: Like Black Peter's mother had refused to marry Father Time because she didn't trust Nicholas. Guinevere chose not to go back to Camelot after the battle of Kaplice. Instead, she moved to Tír na nÓg, married an elf, and lived to the ripe old age of three hundred and seventy-five. Baba Yaga hates summer and moves her cottage around accordingly to keep cool. Nicholas Kringle was said to have fathered over one hundred children, and Jack Frost had a harem of over one thousand Fae during his heyday. But nothing super helpful, except the fact that they would likely find Baba Yaga in a colder climate. Discouraged, Abney handed Sümeyye a list, picked up her book, and deposited it into her fluttering bat-pack. They were going to have to dig deeper and get much longer lists.

CHAPTER 12

THE BOAT TO AVALON

The students were all in their rooms, packing to go Topside for the weekend. Abney was relieved to be going home. She was looking forward to visiting with her dad and grandmother, reading in her chair, and relaxing in general. The research was going nowhere. They had no better answers than they began with, and school was increasingly challenging. It was time for a breather and where better to get one?

She'd brought some of her Fleetling clothing back with her last time so that she could change before they left. She was sporting stretchy black corduroys and a blue and white plaid long-sleeved shirt. The clothes looked strange on her Fae body, but she knew it would be more normal looking once she was home and "human" again.

Someone was knocking on the door that led into the hallway. "Come in."

"You're going to want to change," Wortlister told her as he entered the room.

"Why?" she asked, confused.

His expression was dark, and Abney could see the worry on his wrinkled forehead. "Home visits have been canceled for the foreseeable future. You'll need to pack your regular clothing and anything you need for school. We're all leaving."

"What? Why? Where?" Abney listed off her questions.

"Three more students and their Hobgoblins have been found dead. We couldn't protect you here or Topside. By royal decree from both Queens, we are moving out of the city. They haven't disclosed the location to us yet, but you need to get packed. They're sending a bubble bus for us in one hour."

"Who was found dead?" Abney asked sharply with sudden panic. "Who was it?"

"They haven't released the names yet. Get packed. Knowing the victims' names won't make them any less dead," he told her emotionlessly. Abney wanted to stomp on his foot with all her might, but she kept her cool.

"Don't look so glum," Wortlister said over his shoulder. "You're finally going to get some pajamas since you'll be sharing rooms. You love pajamas."

Abney shook her head and focused on packing. The sooner it was done, the sooner she could find her friends.

✳

There was no way for her to check on the others. Feo wouldn't let her borrow her little messenger Pixie, and even if they had been allowed cell phones in Tír na nÓg, they'd never work this far underground. Zoey and Domino sat next to her on the bus. They had identical looks of concern on their faces. Abney hoped they would be able to catch up with the others wherever they were going. The bus dashed down one street and then turned right onto another. There was something familiar about this route, but she couldn't quite put her finger on it.

"It wasn't Sümeyye," Zoey chanted like a prayer. "It wasn't her." They were all feeling guilty. They hadn't looked hard enough, put in enough effort, and now their friend might be dead. There couldn't be a worse way to let someone down.

"It's going to be fine." Domino stroked his sister's hair. "We're going to get to wherever we're going, and she'll be there, you'll see." Abney noticed he was not particularly convinced. She pulled out her book and started reading through yet another account of Nicholas Kringle's life. She couldn't let worry engulf her. Sümeyye was out there somewhere, she hoped, and she was going to need to double her efforts if they were going to save her in time.

The bus turned left and then right again. Abney gazed down from her window through the bubbles to the mossy street below. She remembered now. This was the way Wortlister had taken her to Oberon House that first day she had learned that she was Fae. She stood up slightly, and the harbor came into view.

The docks were chaotic with students running here and there. Abney, Domino, and Zoey held hands so they didn't lose each other as they looked for their other friends. They found Gus first, then Lunetta, but no one else before they were forced to board one of the ships. Gus and Lunetta had not seen Sümeyye, but they thought she was with Sabine. They all crossed their fingers.

"Listen up!" a lofty-orangish Mermaid shouted and lifted her hand to her large pouty lips for an ear-piercing whistle. Abney admired the way her scales glistened under the glow from the worms above. "My name is Captain Eliza. This is my ship. While you are aboard, you will listen carefully and obey orders. The river is dangerous, stay away from the railings. If you are told to do something, do it without delay. This may save your life. If you are caught disobeying orders or endangering others, there will be severe consequences. There are hammocks and a galley down below. It's best you stay in that area. If you must be on deck, again, stay away from the railing! Any questions?"

"Yeah," Gus shouted. "Where are we going?"

"We'll tell you if we get there," she replied morbidly.

"Did she say *if*?" Lunetta asked them wide-eyed. "Like, seriously, if?" The others only nodded and headed into the bowels of the ship to claim a hammock.

Below deck was pretty sparse. The hammocks were stacked three high. There was a toilet with a shower curtain in front of it and a small galley where a yellow man with octopus tentacles was stirring a pot and had a cigarette hanging from his lips.

"These are some sweet digs," Domino snarked.

"Not really," Abney countered, missing the scorn in his voice.

"I was being sarcastic." Abney looked at him and shrugged an apology.

"There are eight other boats. The others have to be on them," Zoey said and looked worriedly out one of the portholes. "They're okay. They have to be okay."

"There's no use worrying ourselves sick," Lunetta observed. "They're probably just fine. We'll look for them when we get where we're going. If we can't find them, then we'll worry."

Zoey moped. "What else are we going to do?"

"Well, we're stuck here together; we might as well use this time to compare notes," Gus suggested and looked around. The Hobgoblins were all on deck, standing guard or helping with the ship, and the other students were all huddled in their own little groups, discussing their own fears. There was no danger of anyone discovering their plans.

"The only thing I've found so far," Lunetta confided, "is that Kringle is more susceptible to damage from weapons made from the trees and bushes in Time's Forest. Wood from other places will still harm him, but it's more like a rash or a sting. Apparently, Time's Forrest was particularly spiteful toward Old Saint Nick. That large tree in the square was brought in from there as a deterrent. Can't say how much good it did."

"I didn't come up with squat," Gus admitted. "Nothing that we didn't already know." Zoey and Domino faired similarly. Abney told them about Baba Yaga likely being in a cold place, but there were a lot of cold places in the realms, so again, not super helpful.

"Well, that was next to useless," Domino concluded. "What do we do now?"

"More research," Abney proposed. "Balthazar gave me another list of books to look into. There's like twenty on here. We can cross off any that we've already read and divide the rest."

Domino groaned. "I guess."

"Let's have a look," Zoey said with more enthusiasm than her brother. They crossed off three books immediately and split the rest up. Who knew how long they were going to be on this boat? At least it was something to do.

＊

They'd been on the river for three days. Abney, Zoey, and Lunetta had developed horrible seasickness from the choppy water. Gus and Domino brought them buckets and fresh water, but nothing seemed to make it more bearable. Even the crisp air on deck didn't help because of the all-consuming fog that kept their minds from making sense of the sway of their feet. Abney had motion sickness as a child, even riding in the car made her ill, but they'd been able to combat it by letting her have a front seat. The more she could see, the less sick she was, and she could see nothing in this.

"Did no one bring ginger or peppermint?" Wortlister complained. He pretended to be caring for the children, but Abney suspected him of having a hint of motion sickness himself. In either case, the herbs would have been a boon.

"I'm so sick of being sick," Zoey sobbed dramatically.

"Yeah, and I'm sick of you—period," Domino replied.

Zoey threw her pillow at him. "You're sick of me? That's rich, considering the last thirteen years..."

"Oh, stuff it!" Gus snapped at them. "Your bickering only makes it worse!" The twins stuck their tongues out at him at the same time.

"When will we get where we're going?" Abney moaned at Wortlister.

"Not sure. It's not a place you get to by going a certain distance or direction. It's in a place between realms, and it moves around quite a bit. You sort of search for it, and it eventually finds you."

"What?" Abney questioned. "Why is it always something stupid here? Why is nothing ever easy?"

"Whining won't get us there any—" Wortlister started.

"Hey!" Lunetta shouted to get their attention. "Do you feel that?"

"I don't feel anything," Domino remarked.

They stood still and listened. There was no lapping of water against the sides of the ship or jostle from the waves. There was nothing.

"Exactly," Wortlister said, now intense and alert.

Abney's stomach felt a small amount of relief, but she also knew the boat should not be this still. Something was wrong. A thunderous roar erupted around them, and there were screams from the deck. Wortlister ran for the stairs, taking them three at a time. Abney, fighting her own illness, followed behind him. She wasn't sure why. It seemed like a bad idea, but her feet were moving, and she soon found herself on deck. Domino and Gus bumped into her on their way up.

The mist obscured everything. They could hardly make each other out even though they were mere steps apart. Another bellow crashed around them, and then the boat became wobbly again but in a frightening, weightless way. Everyone stood fixed to their spots, barely breathing and looking around carefully. Abney wished she had stayed in her hammock. A shiver ran up her spine. She could smell dirt, salt, and something else. Ash?

"Abney," Wortlister said in a hushed voice, "take your friends and go below deck, now."

A large stone head barreled into view, and Abney's body would not move. "I think it's too late," she hissed through her teeth. Everyone ducked like it would hide them, but it didn't. The colossus glared at them with furious glowing green eyes and began to spin with the boat still in hand. It felt like the swings at amusement parks, the ones that turned you so fast you ended up sideways. Those who were farther out on deck were thrown against the rails as the centrifuge picked up speed. Abney could hear the screams of her classmates and watched helplessly as Domino and Gus were flung backward down the stairs to the lower deck.

Captain Eliza had used her belt to secure herself to the helm while she shouted in vain at the creature, "Goromiser! Goromiser The Terrible! Hear me! We mean you no harm!" When that had no effect, she tried other languages but was getting nowhere. Abney wasn't sure it could hear her.

Meanwhile, Wortlister, Wilbur, and Blythe kept their balance better than most. They collected the remaining students and Hobgoblins and tossed them gruffly below deck. The ship changed direction again. The momentum threw Abney to the opposite side of the boat. She tried to catch the rail, but her hands slipped, and she fell head first into the gloom. *I should scream; if ever there was a time, this is it,* but she found she was too scared to open her mouth. *I'm going to die! I'm going to die! I'M GOING TO DIE!* Her mind raced.

"Gotcha," Wortlister's voice came from above her. She was no longer falling. His hand was grasping her leg tightly. Relief flooded through her, and then she did what she had not been able to earlier, she screamed. "Shut up and stop squirming," he growled, trying to lift her up.

"I'm not squirming!" she shrieked at him. "Pull me up!" The ship changed directions again, and Abney could make out an enormous stone hand clutching the bottom of their boat. It shook them violently; Wortlister lost his hold on the rail, and they were both plummeting. He hissed angrily as their fall halted abruptly.

"I thought I was very clear about everyone staying away from the railing," a robust feminine voice stated. Captain Eliza had hold of Wortlister's tail, and Wortlister still had Abney by the foot. Abney tried to breathe. She could hear the captain calling for assistance because she didn't know how much longer she could hold onto them. The boat jolted violently, and they were falling anew. Abney found another scream. There was no telling how far they were falling or how fast, but certainly they would never survive. She closed her eyes.

Then she hit something hard, but softer than she thought it would be, Wortlister landed behind her with a death grip on her leg. She didn't dare open her eyes yet. She heard Honali's familiar voice. "You guys okay?" Abney's eyes snapped open. She recognized the dragon girl's vibrant blue scales.

"Oh my god, I'm so happy to see you!" Abney said and hugged her friend's elongated neck.

"Just fine back here...in case you were wondering," Wortlister said sharply.

"I got you guys!" Honali turned and gave them a toothy grin. "This is one of the few times that this form is practical!" She looked like she was having a great time.

"Why didn't you use your wings?" Abney accused Wortlister. "You used them when we jumped out of my window; why not now?"

"I'm not wearing them." He looked down. "Not really supposed to have them." A howl zoomed past them.

"Hold on!" Honali instructed, and they dived.

Abney closed her eyes again, and she could feel Wortlister's hands grasping her around the waist. Her chest was on fire or warmer than usual. She'd thought she was going to die there for a moment. She worked on her breathing, remembering that it was not good for her to be over emotional about anything. Baking with Granny, she thought, I'm baking with Granny, and Dad is making hot chocolate. They stopped and were hovering again. Honali stretched her long neck back, placing Captain Eliza behind them on her back. The captain was wide-eyed and trembling.

"This is exactly why wings are not outdated," Captain Eliza rattled. "Everyone is, like, noooo, they cost too much. We don't need them anymore. My scaled patootie! I'm getting a pair as soon as this ridiculous journey is over."

Honali was circling upward again.

"How did you find us?" Abney asked her, "This fog is insane."

"I have exceptional hearing," Honali said. "You guys were so loud, I could've found you with my eyes closed."

A bird-like screech pierced their ears, and light blasted around them. "Look," Honali urged them. "It's Dean Sadira." They watched as a flaming bird approached the giant's face and shrieked again, stopping the attacker in its tracks.

"Goromiser, Moirai, Priestesses of Avalon!" the bird thundered. "Hear me! I have brought the children of the Fae to lodge here for safety. We mean no harm. Please allow us safe passage."

The giant studied her, apparently searching for any hint of dishonesty. When he was satisfied, he placed the boats in his hands back down gently and sank into the river. The mist cleared, and a blindingly bright day greeted them. *There's sun in the place in between worlds,* Abney thought gratefully. Tír na nÓg had a dark beauty, but she missed this. There was just something about sunshine on your face.

The rocky head half-submerged itself in the water, leaving only a small normal looking island visible. You would never know that a monster lurked only a few feet below the surface. They were able to clearly identify trees, buildings, and what looked like vast gardens. Honali glided downward to the shore where Dean Sadira was awaiting them and the ships.

The Dean greeted them after they landed. "I'm glad to see you are safe. It took us a while to figure out what was happening. We could hear screams, but we didn't know where they were coming from. Thank goodness Ms. Kekoa here has more courage than sense or we might have lost you." She acknowledged Honali for her bravery. Back to her more humanoid form, Honali nodded her head modestly.

"Yes, I believe a few favors are owed." Captain Eliza inclined her head. "Honali Kekoa, you may collect your favor anytime and ask for anything."

"I am similarly indebted," Wortlister said begrudgingly.

"Me too," Abney agreed, hoping it was the correct thing to say.

"I just love flying." she blushed. "Really, I don't expect…"

"To refuse a favor is bad form," Dean Sadira corrected her. "It is our way. You will take what is owed."

"Well…thank you…I think." Honali looked uncomfortable.

"Look, they come," Captain Eliza pointed out.

A line of horse-drawn carts led by three women on horses was coming down the side of the mountain toward the shore. The women were completely bald and white, like someone had doused them in baby powder. As they drew closer, Abney could see their eyes were cloudy, sightless, and their horses were blindfolded.

"The Moirai," Dean Sadira said ominously as the horses pulled up in front of them. "Clotho, spinner of the thread. Lachesis, dispenser of the thread. And Atropos, she who cuts the thread." Dean Sadira bowed, and Wortlister pulled Abney and Honali to their knees with him.

The women spoke as one. "Rise Sadira Chakroun, Phoenix and Dean to Litha." Dean Sadira stood. Honali went to stand as well, but Wortlister pulled her back down.

"We have come seeking shelter for the Changelings," Dean Sadira stated, not looking up from the ground. "Nicholas Kringle hunts again, and we cannot protect them in Tír na nÓg. Please allow them sanctuary."

"You bring danger here," they said. "He will hunt his prey to the ends of the worlds. Avalon may not be immune."

Dean Sadira spoke respectfully. "The Faerie Queens would not ask if we had not considered all other options. You have The Mists of The Goddess and Goromiser the Terrible as protection. They are safer here than anywhere else."

"You ask a lot and put the young Fates at risk. Avalon is not an asylum. You should seek safety elsewhere," they replied.

"We need all of our strength to hunt Kringle," Dean Sadira pleaded. "We are exposed if half of us must protect the young. We will leave sufficient Masters to continue their lessons, and their individual Hobgoblins will remain as extra protection. Please, Great Moirai, you are their best chance."

"No," they said with finality. "We cannot take such risks. Not with the responsibility of young Fates. You must go elsewhere."

Dean Sadira looked very uncomfortable. "Queen Titania thought you might feel this way," she said in a shaking voice. "She reminds you of the debt owed to her by each of you. She will forgive all three obligations for this one favor. She reminds you this is also a kindness because, technically, she only needs to forgive one." The women hissed angrily and looked at the shrinking Dean with burning indignation that made their eyes glow red.

"Anchor your boats and bring the Changelings ashore." They scowled. "You will have sanctuary, and you will tell Queen Titania we will not forget a favor this badly inflicted." Dean Sadira nodded. "Abney Kelly, Honali Kekoa, and…"

"Wortlister," the Puca stood up, blocking his real name again. The Moirai smiled.

"Wortlister," they acknowledged. "Rise and ride with us. The others will join you shortly." For feeble looking women, they pulled their guests strongly up onto their mounts and rode expertly.

"You have questions for me, Abney Kelly," Atropos said as they followed the trail up the mountain.

"If you didn't intend to let us stay," Abney ventured, "why did you bring all the carts with you?"

"We knew the Queen would call in her favor and that we would have to grant it to her. For that is our way. We would also be remiss in our duties as guardians if we did not protest your presence. New Fates have been born into the world, and our time draws to a close. If anything happens to the young Fates, more will not be born for thousands of years. If one is gone, the others are blind. There must always be three Fates for all to have the sight," Atropos replied.

"Oh," Abney said.

"You have another question," the Fate stated.

"Do you know my future?" Abney couldn't help herself. How many times did you get to meet Fate?

"I know of several of them," the old woman noted. "The future is not set in stone; there are many paths to take."

"What will I be like, you know, when I'm older?" Abney questioned. She hoped she might be beautiful, accomplished, important, or at least one of those things.

"You will be yourself but older," Atropos declared. Abney felt frustrated. That wasn't an answer. "The future is a delicate thing. It is not wise to go about speaking of things that may or may not be. What will be, will be. You would do better to face things as they come rather than try to divine every outcome. A little mystery keeps life interesting." Abney nodded, though she still wasn't pleased.

✳

The home of the Moirai consisted of several shallow outer buildings carved into the side of the mountain. Once inside, secret passages opened up and led deep into the ground. The passages were bright, as if bathed in sunlight, but Abney could not find the source. They followed the Fates to a long dining hall. Broth and crackers had been set out, along with a bitter smelling tea. Abney's stomach grumbled; she hadn't been able to keep anything down in days, and her belly was crying out in hunger.

"Sit, eat," Lachesis encouraged them. She did not need to tell Abney twice. She leapt over to the table, sat down, crushed crackers in her hand, and dumped them into the broth. Honali and Wortlister watched her with amusement.

"What?" she said through a mouthful. "I'm hungry."

"Obviously," Wortlister snorted.

Honali smirked. "Don't listen to him. You do you." She broke her own crackers into the broth and slurped lazily.

"We must go greet the others," The Moirai announced. "Help yourselves in our absence."

"Wait!" Abney shouted louder than she meant to. The women turned around. "Is Sümeyye okay?" How had she not thought to ask that before?

"No more questions, Abney Kelly. You will find out soon enough," they said and left. Abney felt so stupid. How could she have forgotten about Sümeyye? Why had she wasted her time on questions that didn't even receive proper answers?

She remembered she hadn't interrogated her friend. "Honali, did you see Sümeyye before we left?"

"No. The only one of us I could find was Sabine. We were on the same ship," she said.

Abney spoke with concern. "I thought Sabine was supposed to be with her?"

"No, I'm sure she's with Lunetta," Honali replied.

"Lunetta was with me. So were Zoey, Domino, and Gus," Abney told her. Both girls pushed their food away, looking sick. Where was Sümeyye?

CHAPTER 13

THE LIVES OF TREES

Between her Fleetling life and Fae life, the holidays were getting a little ridiculous. They had barely gotten through Yule, Christmas, and New Year's, and now it was Imbolc. Abney planned to boycott Valentine's Day. There were just too many holidays, and she never had a valentine anyway.

The Changelings found themselves busier than ever. Classes were large now as students from every school were all together. Each Master taught multiple classes, which were all overly full, so it was necessary to pay very close attention because there wasn't much time for one on one training. Abney and her friends found themselves more occupied than most with their extracurricular activities eating up the majority of their time.

Sümeyye turned up safe, much to everyone's relief. She'd been with Abel on one of the other ships and hadn't been in danger. The whole group had forgotten it was his turn to be with her. They decided to keep a written schedule on who had Sümeyye and when after that so that they didn't panic unnecessarily again. Also, Honali convinced Arjun, her hob-goblin, to teach them how to use insects to send messages.

Insect language was basically tapping rhythmically near the bug's feet so that they could feel the vibrations. The bug would then crawl onto your hand and tap out the response similarly. They all needed to have paper and pen nearby to figure out how many taps and the correct rhythm for their messages. It wasn't as fast or as convenient as a text message, but it was a way to keep in communication when they needed to.

Imbolc was a very sacred holiday to the Fae. It marked the beginning of spring, and every awakened Fae cleansed themselves in order to commune with the Earth Mother. It was a day to solidify their connection to nature and reflect on the spiritual side of their existence. Abney and the newer Changelings were naturally nervous, but the elder Fae were there to guide them through.

"Has everyone got their groups of four?" Master Keo, the Fae History and Etiquette teacher from Mabon, asked them. Abney was holding hands with Honali, Lunetta, and Zoey. The ritual called for a person gifted in each element to be in the circle. Each student wore off-white robes with sashes of black, white, blue, and red. "Good." She nodded at the teenagers. "You may begin."

Lunetta went first. "Hail and welcome, Element Earth. Bury us beneath you so that we may grow anew in your womb and emerge full of the strength and wisdom to be better versions of ourselves." The smell of fresh dirt filled their noses, and a warm pulse beat through their hands.

"Hail and welcome, Element Air," Abney spoke shakily. She was nervous that she would not be able to open the Element to the others, but she continued. "Blow over us and through us. Open our hearts with your mighty roar. Teach us to embrace change as nothing can remain the same forever." Abney concentrated and opened herself to share the energies inside her. The others shivered as the cold wind blew through them.

"Hail and welcome, Element Water," Zoey said in turn. "Wash over us and leave us clean. Immerse us in your purity and leave us ready to receive the love of the Goddess and The Horned One." It was like being thrown into a pool, but they were all dry.

"Hail and Welcome, Element Fire," Honali finished. "Engulf us in your flames, burn away all that is undesirable and leave us ready for the

Mother to birth us again. Teach us to burn bright and defiant against the darkness." This was the hard part. They had been warned not to let go of each other's hands or break the circle. Honali opened up and fire burned through them. Abney bore it better than her companions because of her own Fire gift. Lunetta and Zoey struggled against the others and managed to hold on just long enough for it to do its work.

"We are cleansed by the Elements Earth, Air, Water, and Fire," they said together, "and open to their lessons." They broke their circle and walked to the table next to them. Each girl lit four candles that sat nestled in fir wreaths. A black one for Earth, a white one for Air, a blue one for Water, and a red one for Fire. Once they lit the candles, they placed the wreaths on their heads and lined up to go through an ominous wooden door, one at a time.

"Don't be afraid," Honali reassured them. "It's just a walk through the woods. You reflect on the cleansing you've just received and your spiritual goals. It's not as scary as it seems." Lunetta nodded. She and the dragon-girl were a year ahead of them and had undergone the ceremony before. Abney still felt nervous.

She stumbled over her robes as they moved forward. Thankfully, Zoey caught her from behind and righted her. "Thanks," Abney said, grateful for not landing on her face. Her hands flew up to her crown of candles to straighten it. The last thing she needed was wax falling in her eyes. Lunetta disappeared through the door. Abney's heart rate accelerated, and she worked on her meditation exercises to control it. It was her turn next.

The door opened, and Abney made her feet carry her through. It was black as they shut the door behind her. Even with the light from her candles, she couldn't see a thing. She was frightened, but she pushed herself to take one step and then another. Something began to crunch beneath her feet, and she looked down to see snow. When she looked up again, she was in a forest, the trees were naked and the light was gray, but she could see.

The forest was vast, intimidating, and her sudden clarity of vision didn't make her feel any better. As far as she could see in every direction, there were just trees, nothing but barren trees. *Which way do I even go,* she thought? The air carried a soft feminine voice on a gentle breeze. She closed her eyes to listen. At first, it sounded like gibberish, the language was foreign to her, but slowly the words changed, and she was able to understand what was she was hearing.

"Welcome, child of nature. Daughter of the chosen people. Walk with us. Walk with us and among us. Do not be troubled. You are safe here. Walk with us." Abney felt all of her inhibitions melt away.

Her spirit felt lighter, joyous. She wanted to run, jump, and dance. It was like being at the Yule Ball, where her feet moved of their own accord, but that had been dark magic. This was light magic. Orbs of softly glowing lights surrounded her, and she spun with her arms wide open. She flitted from tree to tree, touching the bark and feeling the spirits within. It was like listening to a thousand stories at once and still hearing each one distinctly.

They told her of countless seasons, of the children who had played beneath them, of the lovers who had carved their initials in them, of the old people who walked by them day after day murmuring their stories where they thought no one would hear, but someone had. It was millions of lives lived, millions of lives watched in silence. It was the best and worst of the world at her fingertips as the trees whispered their secrets.

She wasn't sure how long she'd been wandering, but it didn't seem to matter. Even naked, the forest was beautiful. There were streams, birds, squirrels, and other small animals. There was so much life here, despite the cold. Then, she saw it. Blooming beautiful pink and green through the snow. She recognized it from her studies at Ms. Ulyanna's Academy. It was an *Anacamptis Pyramidalis,* commonly known as a Pyramidal Orchid. She reached down to touch its soft leaves. The first bloom of spring. She wasn't sure how she knew that it was, but her whole being told her it was true. It spoke to her of death and rebirth, of joy and sorrow. It was the story of life itself, and she wanted to cry and laugh all at once.

"You made it!" Lunetta appeared with Sümeyye at her side. They both gave her unnatural crooked smiles. Abney waved at them, and a snowball clocked the side of her face. She turned to face her assailant. It was Honali, and she was laughing so hard she almost fell over. Abney rolled her own snowball.

"*Culivaŕe Flawix,*" she spoke and listened for the Element's reply. Her snowball grew three times its original size, and she tossed it at Honali, who found herself buried in snow as the snowball grew again right before it hit her.

"That's cheating," she complained with a laugh, and the snowball fight began in earnest. Everyone joined in the game. Students were running, using magic, and throwing snow. For the first time in a long time, they were free, wild, without a sense of terror or hesitation. The multicolored circles floated gently between them, lighting the woods and making it seem like an enchanted forest from a fairy tale.

They were at it for hours. They made snow forts, engaged in a snow war, ran wild through woods just because they could, and danced in firelight when the will-o'-the-wisps beat their drums and played their flutes.

If being Fae was like this all the time, Abney thought, I don't think I'd ever wish to be human again.

✶

The next day, everyone was more at ease and spent the day relaxing, reading, or spending time with their friends. The light was dim in the cell Abney shared with Zoey, Domino, and Dermott MacDonald, who lived with them at Oberon House. The Hobgoblins had done their best to keep students who already lived together in the same cells. It kept the disruption of the move to a minimum or at least that was the thought behind it.

The large number of students overwhelmed Avalon. There hadn't been enough rooms for everyone, so a good portion of them were sharing cells in the dungeons. There were three stone walls per cell, four cots, and a door of flowery wooden bars. There was pretty much no privacy. Bathrooms were sparse, and shower tents had been erected outside to clear up some of the lines.

They were also living freely with Fleetlings. All of the priestesses of Avalon were humans who possessed innate magic of their own. It wasn't like Faerie magic; it was more like productive wishing. They were able to channel their energies to influence things around them. Abney found them very interesting and highly informed about the worlds of Fae and Fleetling.

Domino sat down in front of her cot. "Mind if I cop a squat?" he asked.

"By all means," Abney said and went back to reading.

"Do you think we're going to be able to stop Kringle, I mean, really?" he asked. Abney thought about it for a minute, closed her book, and rolled on her side to look at him.

"I don't know," she admitted. "The reality looks pretty bleak, but we have to try. I don't know about you, but I could never face myself again if something happened to Sümeyye and I didn't do everything I could to prevent it."

"Yeah, I guess," he said lazily. "It just feels impossible. It's too hard. We're just kids."

"I would say we're more like teens than kids, but kids or teens or whatever, lots of young people accomplish some pretty amazing things. We won't do anything if we start out already defeated," Abney lectured.

"Did anyone ever tell you you're weirdly positive?" he complained with a smile.

"Not really," she admitted. "But I guess I never talked much to anyone before I came here."

"Why not?" He tilted his head with interest.

"I was the fat girl. No one cared much about what I said. They just needed someone to make themselves feel better. I did talk to this girl, Molly, but never outside of school," she told him. "We were on opposite sides of the same coin. She was too invisible, and Cotton Ludlow would say it's impossible to miss me. We didn't have anyone else, so we had each other."

"People are kind of crappy everywhere, aren't they?" he said, frowning.

"The kids at school were mean to you?" She looked at him with raised eyebrows.

"Not the kids at school. They were all right. My dad's pretty awful though, and Mom's always strung out on something or other. Doesn't make you want to go home much," he confided without looking at her. Abney reached out to touch his shoulder. She wasn't sure it was the correct thing to do. She'd never had to comfort someone outside her family. He looked up at her with sad eyes. Abney noticed his face was getting closer to hers. She flushed and sat up quickly. Fortunately, Zoey walked in, so they did not have to discuss what he was about to do. Domino scooted rapidly backward when he noticed his sister.

"What are you guys up to?" she accused them with a frown.

"Nothing," Abney said abruptly and picked her book up again.

"Nothing now." He threw the accusation back at his sister. Abney held her book closer to her face to hide her blush.

"I can leave," she offered.

"No!" Abney shouted and grabbed her hand. "Stay. Nothing is happening." She wasn't sure why she was so freaked out, but she worried Domino would try it again, and she wasn't sure she wanted that. She wasn't sure she didn't want it either. It was confusing.

"I guess you can stay." He gave Abney a wicked grin, and she buried her face back in her book. Zoey and Domino took up their usual bickering as they read through some scrolls the priestesses had provided regarding Baba Yaga. Dermott came in a short while later, quoting a poem by Pan.

"'For a weak and foolish wanderer, am I; my sights set only on the sky. My feet are nimble but sightless be; they lead me wrongly out to sea.'" he recited lyrically.

"Oh, not another poem," Domino complained.

"Shhhh, you uncultured swine," he replied in good humor.

Abney cracked a smile.

"'At sea, I am soaked and cannot get dry; yet still I stare upon the sky.'"

Domino hit him squarely in the face with a pillow, and Dermott tackled him. Both boys ended up rolling around on the ground laughing.

"Come on, Abney." Zoey reached for her friend's hand and grabbed her jacket. "We'd better let the boys play."

Abney nodded her agreement, hopped over them, and out of the cell. She hadn't needed a coat since they had removed her glamour. The girls followed the winding path up to the gardens. They had more freedom here, which Abney liked. Wortlister didn't haunt her steps. The Hobgoblins were set to guard duties and other tasks, leaving them only enough time to check in on their wards a few times a day.

"You should be careful," Zoey said to her once they were outside.

"Of what?" Abney asked, concerned.

"My brother," she answered seriously. "I love him, but he's a clown. He'll only play with you like a cat does a mouse." She stopped them, putting her hands on Abney's shoulders. "You're a nice girl, Abney, and my friend. Don't trust him in that way. You'll only get hurt." Abney blushed, and she felt ashamed. She was the fat girl; of course he was playing with her. She felt sick that she'd considered it for a second.

"No, I uhhhhh…" she stuttered. "I would never…"

Zoey grabbed her face. "No, you misunderstand," she said. "He's not too good for you. You're too good for him. He does this to all girls, Abney. I just don't want you to be one of them. I don't want to lose a friend."

Abney was shocked and didn't know what to say. No one but her grandmother and father had ever tried to protect her, and that's what Zoey was doing.

"Don't worry," Abney consoled her. "You won't lose me. I'm smarter than that…I think." The truth was Abney didn't know if she was that smart. She wanted to be, but her feelings were all mixed up at the moment.

Zoey smiled at her. "You are." She put her arm through Abney's to continue the walk. "You just need to remember that you're better than that."

They made a right at a sizeable barren bush and collided with a shorter old man.

"Oh my gosh," Abney bent over to give him a hand up. "I'm so sorry!" Zoey offered him her hand too, and the girls pulled him up together.

"No harm done," he said with good humor.

"I feel awful," Abney apologized.

"Gardeners belong in the dirt." He laughed. "Ain't nowhere I ain't been before."

The girls apologized again. The gardener assured them he was fine and went back to trimming the dead branches. Abney and Zoey continued on their walk.

The class crammed into the dining hall. A few of the students were lucky enough to have snagged chairs; Abney had not been so fortunate and sat on the ground among other students of her year. Introduction to Fae Literature was her favorite class. They studied books she'd never heard of, and she was thrilled with the new variety she now had at her fingertips.

Due to recent happenings, they had brought forward a book over a thousand years old entitled *Silent Bells are Ringing*. It followed a young Sprite named Isodanelli, who lived in the forest village of Swallow Song. Nicholas Kringle terrorized her village and the surrounding area. It was a dark tale as the girl was captured and forced to watch as her friend's heart was ripped out of his chest, and she eventually became a victim herself.

Master Sjögren's voices melted into their heads. "A sinister story for somber times." She was teaching four classes now, Elemental Sewing, Intro to Fae Literature, Contemporary Fae Literature, and The Complete History of Trolls. The chosen Masters had arrived two days after the students and were teaching multiple classes as the majority of the faculty had stayed behind to aid KRAMPUS in the hunt for Kringle. "Let's start off with questions," she announced.

Abney's hand shot up in the air before she realized what she was doing, and the Rat Queen nodded that she should speak. "Why does Kringle only go after children?" This was the first time she had asked a question in front of her new classmates. She swallowed hard and waited for them to ridicule her, but her question was met with only interested silence as they waited for the Master to answer.

"That's not strictly a book related question," the voices said sternly. "But we will answer anyway. Only children hold the potential for a pure heart. Adults have experienced too much to be unspoiled, and as you've heard, even most children have already seen too much to possess the required innocence. He attacks children because they offer the only chance at a heart as pure as snow." You could have heard a pin drop in the hall. Everyone looked at Master Sjögren with the appropriate amount of fear.

"Oh," was the only response Abney could think to give.

"Miss Kelly, since you seem to have had the only question, please begin reading aloud from page seventy-three, second paragraph," Master Sjögren instructed.

"*The village elders are setting up trees in each of our dwellings after speaking with a pair of Fleetlings, who came to us with an Elven escort. It is a strange thing to do. I think a tree will look out of place, but Zora says we'll find a way to make it more suitable,*" Abney read from her book.

They read a few pages together and then gathered into groups to discuss what they had learned. Abney felt strangely attached to the girl in the story and was not looking forward to her inevitable death. It was causing her anxiety about Sümeyye to boil over. They still didn't have any idea of how to save her, and Abney was growing more attached to her new friends every day. She no longer thought about whether having friends was worth it; now, she just worried about how to keep the one in danger alive.

"Ehh…hmm…" The Harpy-girl next to her coughed and slid a note under Abney's palm. Abney looked at her and thought she saw her flicker, like a hologram. The girl continued to stare at her book as if nothing had happened. Curious, Abney went to read the note, but the girl's hand covered hers again. The hand was definitely solid. This time, when Abney looked at her, she met her cool blue eyes and the girl shook her head. "Not here," she whispered. Abney pressed the note into her palm and put it into her pocket for later.

✦

After class, Abney went down to her cell, which was thankfully empty. She pulled the note from her pocket and read:

Midnight, by the statue of Morgan le Fay, in the garden. Come alone.

CHAPTER 14

THE MIDNIGHT GARDENER

"I don't think you should go," Audrey, her Minelephant, warned her. "You don't even know this Harpy. Why would she slip you a note suddenly? Something's fishy. Just throw the note away."

"I'm not giving you extra food to tell me my business," Abney grumped back at her. "I need your help to find a way to stop Kringle from taking Sümeyye."

"And how did you find out she was in danger?" the Minelephant asked. "Hmm? Messing with a Ouija Board. Stupid! Stupid! Stupid!"

"Audrey, help me study or be quiet." She tossed a piece of lavender crumb cake at her.

"What is this?" She frowned. "What happened to the lime Snack Packs?"

"I told you." Abney raised her eyebrows in annoyance. "There are no home visits right now, and you went through all I had pretty quickly. So, suck it up, or we'll go back to your original feeding arrangement with no extras." Audrey glared at her but ate the lavender crumb cake anyway.

"Can you at least bring something savory next time? I'm tired of sweets," Audrey pleaded.

"Sure, I'll bring you something tomorrow," Abney agreed.

"I don't think you should go either," Zoey offered.

Domino jumped in. "Why not?"

"Because the Minelephant is right. We don't know that girl and something could be up." Zoey slapped her brother on the back of the head.

"We're pretty safe here. I think she should go," Domino persisted. "What's the worst that could happen?"

"The note is really from Nicholas Kringle. Abney goes up to meet him. Sümeyye tries to stop her from being kidnapped and becomes Kringle's next victim." Zoey looked down at Domino from her top bunk.

"You're such a Debbie Downer." He stuck out his tongue at her.

"I'm going," Abney said decisively. "What if she can help us? Plus, Domino is right. This place is pretty safe."

"How do you know she wants to help us?" Zoey asked. "She can't know about Sümeyye. It's not like it's common knowledge. So, what can she want? I just have a bad feeling."

"I don't know," Abney admitted, "but I have to find out."

"At least take someone with you," Zoey pleaded. "Going alone is a bad idea."

"I'll agree with that," Domino conceded. "Take someone with you. I'll go."

"The note says to come alone. What if she backs out when she sees two of us?" Abney pointed out.

"Take the Minelephant," Zoey suggested. "She's small; you can put her in your pocket, and she can make quite a racket if something goes wrong."

"No way! I'm a Brainiac, not a risk taker. You need a whole library memorized? I'm your Minelephant, but I don't do potentially dangerous secret spy missions," Audrey stated.

"We'll all sneak you extra food for a week," Zoey offered.

"Two." Domino upped his sister's offer. Audrey's ears perked up. That was a lot of extra food, and there wasn't a Minelephant alive who would turn their trunk up at an offer like that.

"Fine, scraps from all of us for one month." Abney looked sideways at the greedy Minelephant. "And that's the final offer." Audrey walked back and forth and furrowed her brow like she was thinking about it hard. She didn't want to do anything out of her comfort zone, but that was a lot of food to walk away from.

"Fine!" she shouted angrily at them. "But if something goes wrong, I'm going right to Wortlister!" They all nodded their agreement and went back to their research. The twins thought they had found a way to summon Baba Yaga in the scrolls, but they were still working on the translation with Master Hallewell, who assumed they were just very ambitious students.

✦

Dim torches lined the corridor as Abney crept along silently, not wanting to alert anyone that she was out of bed at such a late hour. Sweat darkened her armpits. The sweater was killing her, but she had needed something with a pocket large enough to carry the Minelephant, and a cardigan was the only thing she could find. Audrey felt awkward and bulky in her inside pocket. She had to hold the sweater on the opposite side so that it didn't end up noticeably lopsided. Voices ahead of her forced her into a dark closet filled with brooms, mops, and buckets. She held her breath as they passed. It sounded like a pair of Hobgoblins.

"What are you doing? Why is it so dark?" Audrey whispered loudly. Abney reached in her pocket and covered her mouth. The voices were getting louder.

"I miss the days when we just had to follow the little riffraff around. I've been scouring pots and cleaning all day. Our punishment was to become the guardians of the young Fae, not to be servants," a rich smoky feminine voice complained.

"I prefer scrubbing to guarding," a lighter male voice said. "I hate my ward. Stinky, entitled little wretch. I wouldn't mind if Kringle got him as long as he left me alone."

"If only, my friend," the other voice laughed. Abney was appalled.

Does Wortlister feel that way about me? And what did she mean by their guardianship being a punishment? Abney waited for the Hobgoblin's voices to fade farther down the hall before she dared to set out again.

She made it out to the garden near the statue. No one was there yet. The figure of Morgan le Fay loomed over her. She had been the most powerful priestess Avalon had ever seen. She was fierce looking with her mostly bald head and single braid wrapping around her shoulder like a rope. Morgan's brows were drawn down in determination. Abney thought she must have really been something. At a time when society treated women as little better than cattle, she had stood toe to toe with kings, advising them, and inflicting her wrath when she deemed it necessary. Abney admired her. She wished she could be that strong and determined. The statue version of the lady looked like she had never second-guessed a step in her life.

"Terrifying, isn't she," a merry voice spoke behind her. Abney jumped, and Audrey sounded off. She was loud for such a small creature. Abney desperately tried to cover the Minelephant's trunk, but Audrey bit her and yelled as loud as she could. "Help! Heeeelp! He's going to kill us! We're going to die! help!"

"Audrey..." Abney tried to get a word in. "It's just the gardener. Calm down."

"I'm too smart to die like this!" Audrey wailed. "I should never have listened to you, even for a month's worth of scraps!" Avoiding her mouth, Abney lifted the Minelephant out of her pocket and showed her the gardener. The sweet looking old man stood beside her. Thick wiry muttonchops covered his face, and a wooden pipe stuck out from his turned-up lips. "My, you have a set of pipes on you." He laughed. Audrey was silent, looking from Abney back to the gardener.

"It's just the gardener," Abney explained. "But thanks to you, I'm sure the whole island is awake, you chicken."

"I've known some brave chickens," the gardener observed.

Abney glowered. "Fine, then. She's a coward."

"I'm a scholar! Not some action hero," Audrey said, still shaky. "I'm never doing anything like this again."

"Fine with me," Abney replied, annoyed, and shoved Audrey back in her pocket.

"I suppose I should ask what a student is doing out of bed at this hour."

Abney looked around. The Harpy girl had probably heard the racket and run off.

"I…I couldn't sleep," Abney lied. "I thought I'd go for a walk."

"She's a liar!" Audrey shouted up at them. "She was out here to meet some strange girl and got me all tangled up in this nonsense. I'm not going down with the ship!"

"You rotten fink!" Abney cursed. The gardener only laughed.

"You ladies have nothing to fear from me," he said. "Your secret is safe." Abney breathed a little lighter.

"Thanks," she said to the gardener and lowered her eyes to glare at the Minelephant.

"Why don't you have a seat with me? Does an old man good to have some company every now and again." He sat down on a nearby bench and patted the space next to him. Abney sighed inwardly. She hated speaking to strangers but obliged him since she wasn't doing anything else at the moment, and if the old man felt so inclined, he could march her straight to Dean Sadira.

She did have to at least let Zoey know she was safe. She slyly scooped out the moth she had in her other pocket and placed it on the bench next to her. She tapped the bench impatiently so that it looked like she was just nervous.

"Tell me, how's school going? I rarely get to have a conversation with anyone. It would be nice to hear about someone else's day." The old man smiled.

"Well, I guess it's okay," Abney said. "Right now, we're reading this book about a girl who was murdered by Kringle. It's pretty depressing." She kept eye contact with him so that he didn't notice her tapping. There really wasn't a reason to keep it from him, but she felt she should anyway. The moth took off from the bench, and Abney could see it heading toward the dungeons from the corner of her eye.

"Ah, *Silent Bells are Ringing*? I know it well," he said. "A fascinating perspective on that situation." The smoke from his pipe circled his head like a halo.

"A dark perspective for sure," Abney agreed.

"Such a sweet girl and such a terrible fate…" he remarked.

"There you are!" Wortlister fumed and emerged from the dark. "I've been looking for you everywhere! Why aren't you in bed?"

"I couldn't sleep," Abney said, glaring down at Audrey, daring her to say something.

He turned on the old man. "Who are you?"

"Why, I'm just Ol' Chris, the gardener," the old man replied in a syrupy voice.

"I've never seen you before," Wortlister stated suspiciously.

"I've seen him more than a few times," Abney stuck up for him.

"You be quiet," he said and grabbed Abney by the ear to drag her back to the dungeons.

"Wait," Ol' Chris called after them. "I have something for the girl." Wortlister paused, but Abney could see he was a volcano just waiting to blow. The old man jogged up to them, stuck out his gloved hand, and pushed a worn green leather book at her. "You may find this an interesting companion to the book you're reading." He winked slyly and walked away from them. Abney put the book in her pocket and followed Wortlister inside.

"Don't you ever do something this reckless ever again," he lectured her. "Have you somehow missed everything that has been going on around you?"

"I brought the Minelephant with me," Abney said, holding Audrey up to show him. "Plus, I thought this place was pretty much Kringle-proof."

Audrey sucked up to Wortlister. "I was against this from the start."

"Oh, be quiet," Abney snarled and shoved the protesting Minelephant back in her pocket.

"And what did you think a five-inch-high Minelephant was going to do to help you? This place is safer, yes, but impenetrable? No! This was an incredibly stupid and naïve move. I'll just have to keep a closer eye on you from now on," Wortlister said crossly as they marched downward.

✦

Abney was feeling sick as Wortlister helped her attach her riding helmet. She was about to participate in her first Fae sport, Basnorts. She'd tried everything imaginable to get out of it, but it was mandatory because morale was low, and the Masters thought it was just the way to raise everyone's spirits.

There were three types of mounts, and she chose to ride a chicken as they seemed the least terrifying. The grasshopper's large alien eyes felt cold. Also, they spit, and she wasn't up for a jumping-spitting ride. The salamanders weren't bad, but Basnorts was played with croquet mallets, and they seemed too low to the ground to make hitting the ball easy.

Wortlister lifted Abney easily onto the chicken's back and instructed her to take the reins. The chicken turned to look at her. One golden eye curiously studied her and then disappeared as the head faced forward again. "This is Juliet. I think she likes you." Wortlister smiled, but it wasn't comforting. He then handed her a blueish-purple mallet and a large ball. "Remember, drop your ball when you hear the whistle blow. The wickets have clear numbering at the top. Just make your way from one to the next, and try to stay on your mount."

"Do I have to do this?" Abney asked helplessly. "I hate sports."

"Yes," Wortlister said and gave the chicken a gentle pat on the behind to get it moving. Abney jostled about in her seat, trying to hang on for dear life.

The course had been set up on one of the large lawns in the gardens. The wickets were huge, large enough for three or four mounted players to fit through at a time. The other first years collected near the wicket labeled #1. Abney did her best to steer Juliet, but it seemed more likely that the chicken knew where to go.

Zoey and Domino pulled up next to her, Zoey on a chicken and Domino on a salamander. Abney didn't notice the cold, but she assumed it was chilly based on the clouds of condensation escaping the other students' mouths. Everyone looked nervous. They were about to be set free on each other, and no one was quite sure what was going to happen or how to handle the situation. They looked around at their classmates. It looked like they had everyone, so what now?

Wilbur stepped onto the field with an unnatural glow of happiness. Abney shook her head. This was not going to be good. He put a silver whistle in his mouth and blew. It was hardly necessary as all of the first-year students were already staring at him silently in fear. "Listen up!" he commanded them. "I'm looking forward to a good dirty fight, but there are a few rules. If you touch another player's ball, you're out! If you touch any ball with your hands, you are out! If you fall off your mount, you are out! If you leave the field of play, you are out! Magic is permitted! The first one to get their ball successfully through every wicket or the last player still on their mount wins. Blythe, turn the wickets on," he called out to his sister. She turned a stone rod in the ground, and the wickets took to life.

Abney and the others watched transfixed as the wickets morphed. A huge crack appeared in the ground under the first archway, and the earth visibly shook. The second wicket had become a solid wall of water, and Abney could see large shadows swimming around in it. The third had a cartoon-style tornado moving quickly back and forth from end to end. The fourth blocked out the last four as it roared with fire.

No, freaking, way, Abney thought. *I'm not doing this. They can't make me.*

Wilbur blew his whistle again. "Let the game begin!" The field was entirely still. No one moved a muscle. The Puca rolled his eyes dramatically and swirled his arms in large circular motions. A spray of small pebbles pelted them, and their mounts scattered and reared. The melee had begun.

Abney dropped her ball and attempted to whack it with her mallet, but missed again and again. She just wanted off the field, but she couldn't get Juliet to move. She kicked the chicken with her heels and yelled, "Giddy up!" Juliet turned to give her a cross look. "Sorry," Abney mouthed. A stream of water shot at her head. Abney ducked in time but dropped her mallet. Then something hot slammed into her leg, and the chicken took off. Abney threw her arms around Juliet's neck and hung on for dear life.

"Oh my god, oh my god, ohmygod!" Cozmo went zooming past her. Zoey was still seated. It looked like she'd made through the first wicket and was headed for the second. Domino's lizard was taking him in circles, and Melinda Fairfax had somehow already urged her mount outside of the field of play, Abney noticed jealously.

Her classmates were falling to the ground all around her, and a few of the more coordinated ones were trying to get their balls through the second wicket. Abney's eyes widened with panic as she watched what looked like a Mosasaurus eat one of her classmate's balls. *Nope, nope, nope*, Abney shook her head unconsciously. She started looking for a way to get off the field. It was a circus of injured bodies and still-mounted riders.

A ball of water came hurtling from Domino right at her head. It struck but did not knock her off. Abney took sharp breaths in as the sudden wetness shocked her body. An emotion that rarely ruled Abney took over: Anger. "*Zephyrus phearrow!*" she shouted. A bolt of wind laced with fire darted at Domino, completely throwing him from his mount. Fear and rage took over completely. She couldn't focus, and her temperature rose quickly. The last thing she remembered was wiping sweat from her brow, and then it all went black.

✦

When she came around, she found herself crammed in her cell with the whole rest of the group. Honali was stroking her hair. The twins stood behind her, looking concerned, and Abel, Sümeyye, Sabine, Lunetta, and Gus stood behind them. "She's awake!" Honali announced. A wave a relief swept through the room.

"Don't you ever scare us like that again." Zoey pushed Honali aside and hugged her.

"Move it!" Wortlister shouted at the group, and they parted to let him through. "I should never have let you play," he said. "It's just a game. I never thought it would affect you this way."

"Really? You had no idea a real-life *World of Warcraft* battle scene would freak me out?" The anger returned to Abney's heart.

Wortlister tried to soothe her. "It's only a game. Deep breath in, deep breath out. You melted through your ice core. It would damage your heart for me to put another in. You will have to be extra conscious of your emotions now."

Abney closed her eyes and breathed in and out, slowly mastering her anger. "Why did it melt during the game and not when we fell off the ship?" Abney asked, perplexed.

"I'm sure the ship incident melted it at least part way. What did you in was that fire trick you added to the wind you threw at Domino. I'm pretty sure Master Blewitt has told you more than once it was ill-advised to try to control fire that doesn't come from inside you. You're lucky you didn't kill yourself. You got emotional and messed up, kid," he said.

"I was scared! Of course, I got emotional. I was angry. And don't call me kid!" she blew at him. "Only my dad calls me that!"

"Uh, huh," Wortlister said, as if that explained it all. "Anger is a force of nature. You were like a volcano that was ready to blow. It was probably building up for a while. We'll have to work on your anger issues."

"I don't have anger issues!" Abney shouted, contradicting herself. The room grew uncomfortably quiet.

"Sure you don't," Sabine snarked. Honali covered her friend's mouth and smiled at Abney. Abney glared at them but let it go.

"On the plus side," Domino said excitedly, "you won! You were the last Fae still mounted, even though you were passed out." Abney had never won any sport in her life. She tried to smile, but it came across as more of a grimace. She never wanted to play Basnorts again.

✦

Abney found herself confined to her cell for a week. Master Blewitt wanted her emotions under control before she would be allowed back out in the general population. Their lessons now lasted four hours a day for the foreseeable future. She was permitted visitors. Many students stopped by to congratulate her on the win, but she didn't feel like a sports hero. It was pure dumb luck that she stayed on her mount after passing out. It didn't require any talent. Her friends dropped by often to bring her homework from her other classes and entertain her while Wortlister fussed over her like a mother hen.

"Be careful," she told him. "Someone might think you actually like me." He only snorted and walked away, but Abney knew the truth. He liked her.

All of her friends were scouring the place for the Harpy-girl from her literature class so that they could explain what had happened and see what the girl had wanted to meet Abney about, but no one seemed to know who they were talking about. No one remembered a Harpy having Intro to Fae Lit during that hour. It was all very strange and mysterious. As soon as Abney was better, she planned on doing some investigating of her own.

With her enquiry into the Harpy being put off, she spent her spare time reading the book the gardener had given her. It didn't have a title, was handwritten, and it seemed to be the journal of Isodanelli herself. Abney wondered where the old man found it. It was much more detailed than the book her class was reading.

According to the diary, the relationship between Changelings and the elder Fae at that time was tense, to say the least. There were no home visits for the young Fae back then. They ripped the children from their Fleetling families, never to see them again. Abney felt sadness at that. Isodanelli loved her Fleetling family as much as Abney loved her own human family and struggled to adapt to her new Fae life.

Most interesting though, according to the journal, the book got it wrong. Kringle did not kidnap Isodanelli with her friend Casper. She was not taken at all. When her friend went missing, she decided to try to save him and did everything in her power to get him back. She found a way to contact Baba Yaga, and the witch led her to Casper and ultimately her own death. The best part was she had left step-by-step instructions on how to contact the infamous witch.

They would need a new moon, a silver chalice, a drop of blood from each traveler, ceremonial wine, Zoey to translate a few runes, and a large mirror. Only three of them would be able to go, and considering the danger, Abney immediately ruled Sümeyye out. She and two other lucky volunteers would have to go…but who would willingly face this with her?

CHAPTER 15

THE WITCH'S COTTAGE

It was a beautiful day to be outside in the gardens. The air was crisp with just the slightest hint of a breeze. Abney, Zoey, and Domino were on their hands and knees harvesting Vervain. When they left Tír na nÓg most of their school supplies had been left behind. Luckily, the gardens of Avalon were extensive, and almost any herb one could possibly need grew there.

None of the Fae Masters who came to teach the students had a vast background in herbology, so one of the priestesses had volunteered to educate them. Priestess Hillevi was blonde, large chested, and good-humored. She seemed to enjoy teaching and had a very hands-on approach to their lessons.

"Who can tell me one of the many uses for Vervain?" she asked the class as they gathered their herbs. Zoey's hand shot up.

"Zoey." Priestess Hillevi nodded for her answer.

"Arthritis," Zoey said proudly.

"Very good. Do you know you know why it's helpful?"

"It's an anti-inflammatory," Zoey answered.

"Well done!" The priestess applauded her. "How about you, Domino? Do you know any of the uses for Vervain?"

"Cure for headaches?" he guessed.

"No, try again," she urged him.

"I don't know," he admitted. "I didn't read the chapter."

"Then we will have a special study session after class." She smiled at him. Domino groaned. "How about you, Abney? Do you know any of the uses for Vervain?"

"It helps with coughs and asthma, also because it's an anti-inflammatory," Abney said.

The priestess smiled. "Very good."

"Showoff," Domino murmured.

"What was that, Domino?" Priestess Hillevi asked.

He tried to cover. "I said hats off to Abney because she obviously studied." Priestess Hillevi didn't look like she believed him for a minute.

"Smooth," Zoey laughed at him.

✳

After that morning's classes, they gathered in Honali's cell. Her roommates were all out, enjoying what they were allowed to of the Ostara festivities. Wortlister explained that the majority of this holiday's activities were for Fae who had undergone the Binding and were not appropriate for the Changelings. Abney wasn't an idiot. She knew that Ostara was the basis for Fleetling Easter. She also knew what the bunnies and eggs represented, but she didn't want to embarrass herself or Wortlister, so she kept her mouth shut.

Sabine commanded her attention. "Abney! Focus! We don't have a lot of time to prepare before the others come back."

"Sorry," Abney said absentmindedly and turned her attention back to her friends. If this worked, Abney would be going to visit the infamous Baba Yaga tonight, along with Abel and Honali. Abel had the most magical abilities. Honali could transform in an instant and cook any threat to a crisp, and Abney was just a brave volunteer.

"Domino," Honali asked, "did you get the silver chalice from the temple?"

"Is a frog's butt watertight?" he quipped smugly.

"I've never really given that any thought," Abel said, consumed by the idea. "It's going to drive me crazy. I can't stop thinking about it now. Is a frog's butt watertight?"

"Amphibian skin is absorbent, not waterproof," Lunetta informed him. "Satisfied?"

"No," Abel admitted. "I'm going to google it next time we're Topside."

"Whatever," Honali shrugged her shoulders. "Sabine, did you get the mirror?"

"Naturally," she replied, not looking up as she applied metallic blue polish to her nails. Abney didn't think she had ever seen anyone obsess over their fingernails the way Sabine did.

"Abel, the ceremonial wine?" Honali questioned.

"They didn't have any in the cellars that met the requirements. So I brewed us a special bottle. I had to speed up the fermentation process with magic, so I hope it's all right." The others cringed. Abel's drinks never tasted great, and boy did they pack a punch.

"Zoey, you were able to work out the translation with Master Hallewell?" Honali moved on to her next friend.

"Yes," she said. "I was worried we wouldn't get it done, but I think it's right."

"Think?" Lunetta asked.

"We couldn't find exact matches for a few of the runes, so we filled it in with what seemed like the most logical translation. If the incantation is real, it will work," Zoey replied confidently.

"Well, that's reassuring," Gus said sarcastically. It was getting easier to read his skeletal facial expressions, though it still involved a lot of guesswork. He seemed to only have two modes, humor and sarcasm, so that helped.

"I have faith in you, sis." Domino slapped Zoey's back.

"Gee, thanks!" She smiled at him and crossed her eyes.

"What am I supposed to do?" Sümeyye asked.

Sabine had an odd nice moment. "Staying out of the clutches of Kringle until we can figure out how to save you seems like plenty."

"I feel completely useless," Sümeyye continued. "I need to do something."

"You are helping," Lunetta responded. "It's going to take all of us to keep the portal open long enough for Abney, Honali, and Abel to cross over, have a chat with Baba Yaga, and get back."

"I should be going," Sümeyye argued. "It's not fair for you guys to be in danger like this."

"Nonsense, we're your friends." Sabine looked up from her nails. "We wouldn't be very good friends if we didn't have your back."

"I guess," she relented, but Abney could see the guilt on her face.

"Hey"—Honali grabbed her hand—"no one is making us do any of this. Every Fae who's here is here because they want to be. We take our own risks, and we're all aware of what that means."

"And if you're not comfortable with us doing it for your sake"—Lunetta smiled—"then we'll do it for Pete's sake."

Abney laughed. "You guys have to let that go."

"Never!" Abel cheered. "Vive la Pete!"

"Vive la Pete!" everyone yelled and put their hands in. Sümeyye seemed to feel a little better after that.

"Hey, what's going on?" Honali's roommate, Cherry, burst in.

"Nothing, just hanging out," Honali lied easily.

"Well, Ostara has officially become an adults-only activity, so can you all find somewhere else to hang? I need a nap," she said rudely. Honali made a crude gesture as soon as Cherry's back was turned, and the gang dispersed to finish their preparations. It was going to be a long night.

✦

The darkness of their cells was always the same, whether it was high noon or midnight. Domino had taken Dermott to one of the other cells for a boys' night that he would sneak away from at the earliest possible moment as it would take all of them to hold the portal. They had all crowded into Abney and the twin's cell and appeared to be studying when the Hobgoblins checked on them twice already.

It was ten minutes to midnight when they laid out their tools to prepare; no Hobgoblins would be roaming now. The moon was high in the sky, and the official Ostara ritual was set to begin right at the stroke of twelve. Sabine propped the mirror up against the dresser, and Zoey was running through the words for the incantation with everyone while Sümeyye stared anxiously at the cup.

"Are we ready?" Honali asked.

"What about Domino?" Gus asked. "I thought we needed him."

"We do," Zoey said, "but not right away. It's probably good he'll be late. A fresh chanter can only strengthen us."

"Let's do this then," Sabine said, not looking at her nails for once.

"First," Sümeyye said, "a drop of blood from each passenger into the chalice." Abney, Abel, and Honali stuck their hands out, and Lunetta pricked their fingers quickly and efficiently to cause the least amount of pain. Abel scrunched up his face and sucked air through his teeth, but the girls remained impassive and quiet. They squeezed a drop of blood each into the cup. Abel then opened his bottle, swirled it around like people did in the movies and poured the "ceremonial" wine in. Sümeyye gently moved the cup in a circular fashion to mix the fluids.

Mirror, Mirror, Traveler, we call on you, Sabine said and waited for a reply.

A familiar liquid voice filled the cell. "This had better be good. I was just with the most delightful Sylph. It's Ostara, you know."

Dèsolè, Sabine said, shoving the chalice into the gooey reflection before the Traveler could reply. Then, she turned it upside down and forced the mirror to drink.

"You don't want—" the Traveler tried to say, but they were already chanting.

"Baba Yaga, Baba Yaga, Baba Yaga!"

The mirror flashed to an image of a cottage held up on four large chicken legs. It was daytime there. It looked peaceful, quiet, not scary at all. Then the witch opened the door and came out. Her hair was long and silver, her eyes small and beady, and her nose stuck out a good way from her face.

"Who dares disturb me?" she looked directly at them. A chill ran through them all. Even Abney had goosebumps. *You are scared and think you should have goosebumps, so you do,* Wortlister's voice nagged in her head. *Thoughts are powerful, Abney Kelly.* She shook off the offending bumps with determination. The last thing she needed right now was that Puca in her head.

"I, Honali Kekoa, seek you." Honali stepped forward.

"I, Abel Poitier, seek you." Abel stood beside his friend.

"I, Abney Kelly, seek you." Abney took her place next to them. Her knees were knocking, but she held her ground. She was in it now, so best to go with the flow.

"You are children; go away," she snapped and turned to go back into her house.

"We have called on you with our blood. You must grant us an audience," Abney demanded, sounding much braver than she felt.

Baba Yaga turned, looking annoyed. "What makes you think a child like you can make me honor anything? If you were within arm's reach, I'd cut you up and make stew from your eyeballs," Baba Yaga growled. Abney lost her voice. She was officially frightened.

"Is the Great Baba Yaga too afraid to honor the call?" Honali challenged her. The witch looked at them curiously now. She squinted her eyes and made up her mind.

"Come then! My Bright Dawn, My Red Sun, and My Dark Midnight retrieve our guests." Three horsemen appeared, one white, one red, and one black. They were still for only a moment and then galloped full bore at the mirror.

"Now!" Zoey yelled. And the others began the chant.

"The road is open, the road is wide, so it shall remain, with us as your guide. Complete your task and do not roam, listen for our voices, and you will find your home. Pure is the heart. Pure is the host. The witch may not harm you as long as we do not abandon our post." They said this over and over rhythmically.

The white horseman's arm reached through the mirror and grabbed Honali, the red reached for Abel, and the black snagged Abney. Charges in hand, the riders placed the young Fae at their rears and galloped back to the cottage. Abney clung to the rider's back. She was so petrified she dared not look up. Instead, paralyzed, she stared at the ground, watching the horse's hooves trample mud and snow beneath them.

The journey was short, and the riders deposited them before the cottage and rode out of sight again. Abney, Abel, and Honali stood frozen and gazed at the daunting stairs. They had read and re-read so many versions of the tale of Nicholas Kringle with the many different variations of Baba Yaga and her cottage, but none of the accounts had managed to do the real thing any justice.

The chicken legs were large with white and gray feathers, and the toes twitched and scratched with impatience. Steps floated just above the ground and led up to the small wooden house. They could smell oranges, vanilla, and peppermint escaping from the doorway, and strange wind chimes clanged disturbingly in the breeze.

The witch called out to them. "Don't stand there like a Gorgon looked at you wrong. Come in. I haven't got all day." Honali took the first step; Abney and Abel followed. The inside of the cottage was just as strange. Dead birds hung by their feet from the ceiling along with flowers, herbs, and one rabbit. A fire roared at the back of the house with a covered pot hanging from a spit. A small bed was to the left of the fireplace, but most of the room was taken up by a large table covered in books, parchment, and a wide assortment of jars. Baba Yaga sat on a wooden stool and shoveled a spoonful porridge into her mouth.

"You've interrupted my breakfast," she charged them.

"Sorry," Abney and Abel murmured.

Honali was more direct. "We need your help," she stated.

"I suspected as much. No one ever stops by to see how I am," she grouched.

"Uuuhh, how you doin'?" Abel ventured. His voice went up half an octave on the last word. The witch gave him a look that made him take a step back.

"Kringle is going to come for one of our friends. We need to know how to stop him," Abney blurted.

"He's out?" Baba Yaga asked, looking sad for a moment. "For how long?"

"Since before Yule," Abney answered.

"This is unfortunate but not my problem. Go away."

"How is this not your problem?" Honali asked. "As far as I can tell from the legends, this is all your fault. The blood of thousands of children is on your hands."

"My, my, aren't you a brave *devushka*." Baba Yaga stood up, looking terrifying, but Honali didn't shrink away. The witch laughed. "Of course, you're a Dragon. Dragons know no fear, even when it would serve them better. What else do we have here? A Djinn? Yes, I think so. And you..." The witch's voice trailed off as she looked at Abney. Abney tried not to tremble as the witch stared her down. "A Snow Maiden. Maybe you are not as hopeless as I thought. I think I will help you." Abney felt uneasy; why had Baba Yaga changed her mind after looking at her? "Tell me how you know your friend is in trouble?"

"Well, we used a Ouija Board," Abel admitted.

"Messing with things you don't understand." Baba Yaga shook her head. "Did no one tell you those boards are dangerous? Also, spirits do not always tell the truth. What would you have done if the spirit refused to leave? How do you know it went back to the Veil?"

Honali defended them. "We had a Grim Reaper with us. He made sure that the spirit went back."

"A teenage Grim Reaper who does not even know his true name yet? Better to have him than not, but still not very smart," the witch chided them. "No use in crying over spilt milk though. We will proceed, assuming the spirit is not a liar. Stopping Nicholas is no easy task. He is old and powerful. It will take sacrifice."

"We're willing to do whatever we have to," Honali assured her.

"You will give anything?" the witch asked.

"Anything," Honali agreed.

"It's a bargain! Come, sit," she instructed them. She shuffled a deck of large cards expertly between her hands. "Now, each of you pick a card and lay it face down on the table in front of me." She spread the cards out like a fan in front of them. They each grabbed a card from a different place in the deck and set it in front of her. She flipped them over one at a time. "The Devil, The Three of Swords, and The Hanged Man. Two major arcana. This is largely in the hands of fate. You may only be able to do what you were born to." She closed her eyes, and when she opened them again, only the whites were visible. Her voice changed, it became high and child-like.

"*Nine warriors, two grieving men, one mother, one daughter, the broken girl, the ice dragon, and the forest,*" She spoke. "*These will be the players of our tragedy. You must trap the grieving men with the forest, weaken them with cold fire, and sacrifice the daughter. Should you fail, the worlds of Fae and Man will know a new age of darkness. The dead shall rise, and all will bow before the Wraith Queen.*" The witch's head slammed suddenly against the table. Abney, Abel, and Honali looked at each other wide-eyed.

"What do we do?" Abney asked her friends.

"Uhhh…Baba Yaga?" Abel reached for the old women slowly. "Ma'am, are you okay?"

She snatched his hand out of the air without lifting her head. "Do not touch me, *negodyay*." Her words came muffled from the table. She raised her head upright again. "Have you understood?" She looked at them quizzically.

"There are nine of us in our group of friends," Abney replied. She'd started analyzing the prophecy right away. She always fancied being a modern-day Sherlock Holmes. "I think we're the warriors."

"Very good. What else?" Baba Yaga asked.

"I'm not certain about the rest. I'll need more time."

"No time." The witch shook her head. "I will interpret for you. First, I must know, Abney Kelly, how far are you willing to go to help a friend? There will be much danger, but you are the one who may lose her life."

"I don't understand," Abney told her. "Kringle is coming for Sümeyye, not me."

"You are the daughter, or more likely, the many-times-removed great-granddaughter of Nicholas Kringle," she informed them.

"How would you know that?" Abney questioned her.

"Aren't they teaching genealogy in those schools anymore? You're a Snow Maiden. I made the very first of your kind from snow, coal, and a Phoenix feather. Her name was Orina. You can only be what you are through her. She had but one son. You, my dear are of the Kringle bloodline and a critical part of this quest. Again, how far are you willing to go?" the witch asked.

"...and sacrifice the daughter." Abney heard the child's voice in her head again. *Sacrifice? As in die?* She had been willing to stand shoulder to shoulder with her friends, but this was starting to sound more like a solo mission. *Do people actually volunteer to die?* In books and the movies, ya, heroes never seemed to fear for their own safety. In fact, she was sure most heroes had a weird death wish. She decided she needed more information.

"What will I have to do?" she asked Baba Yaga.

"Smart girl," the witch said, "unlike your friend. It is better to know what you're agreeing to before you jump in. You will require four items. Out of the four, there are three your friends may help with. First, you will need to go to Time's forest and forge a rope from the bark of the trees and dogbane that grow there. Second, you will need to procure The Torch of The Wyvern Dragon. Third, you must convince She of the Glass Heart to willingly give you a piece of that heart. And lastly, you will need a sacrifice of love.

"You will lure Nicholas to a location that you have prepared by binding all of the windows and doors with the rope you have made. This will make escape difficult for all of you, but it is your best chance to keep him trapped. This place must have a fireplace. You will light the hearth with the Torch of the Wyvern Dragon. It's a cold heat, but heat nonetheless. It looks like ice fire. He will not suspect it is weakening him. This is where you come in, Abney. You must find a way to get as close to him as possible without injury. Then, you must overwhelm your emotions with love. This is very important! If you do it with fear or anger, you will fail.

Just before your heart destroys you and Nicholas together, one of your friends will have to stab a piece of the glass heart through your back and into your heart. It must be done at this precise time for the glass to combine with your heart properly to save you. Even with it, you may die in the attempt. Is this understood?"

Breathe…one, two, three… I'm not the hero type. Then again, I wasn't the friend type a few months ago. Maybe I can do this? But what if I die? I'm not ready to die. What if Nicholas survives and kills them all? "I understand," Abney said, though she wished she had said, "Nope, I'm out."

Baba Yaga looked at her with a half-smile. "Very well." She nodded. "You will take this." She handed them a golden tree pendant on a string. "Wear the pendant around your neck. When you are ready, make sure everyone holds hands, run your finger counter clockwise around the perimeter three times, and it will take you to Time's forest and back, once and once only. The rest you will have to figure out yourselves."

"What sort of payment do we owe?" Abney asked. By now she knew nothing Fae-related came without a price.

"A bargain was struck. In exchange for my information, your friend offered me anything. I intend to collect that from her later." Baba Yaga smiled toothlessly. Honali shrunk a little for the first time since they had arrived. A favor owed to Baba Yaga was no small thing. "Now be gone with you. I don't have all day to play with children." She whistled, and the horsemen appeared again. "Take them back," she commanded.

Abney accepted a hand up from the black rider. Whispers echoed around them. They could hear their friends leading the riders back to Avalon. *"The road is open, the road is wide, so it shall remain, with us as your guide. Complete your task and do not roam, listen for our voices and you will find your home…"*

*

The horseman tossed them roughly back into the cell. Their friends looked at them, stunned. How long had it been? The way they looked, it must have been a while. The chanting stopped, the witch's cottage disappeared, and Sabine dumped the rest of Abel's homemade brew into the gooey mirror before it solidified. They were hoping the Traveler would be too drunk to remember exactly what happened and therefore could not rat them out to the Hobgoblins or Dean Sadira. Domino was noticeably still missing.

"How long were we gone?" Abney asked.

"A second, if that," Sabine informed her. "What happened? Did they decide just to throw you back?"

"We must have been gone at least an hour," Abel said confused.

"No," Lunetta said. "You went through the mirror, and it spat you right back out."

"We went to the cottage. Baba Yaga told us what we have to do and what it would cost," Honali said, looking a little weary. Abney was confident that she had not meant to end up owing Baba Yaga a favor. She was just so brave. She always leapt before she looked.

"Tell us what happened," Lunetta demanded. Bells started ringing all over Avalon. The explanation would have to wait. The group stood up and looked outside the cell to see what all the commotion was about. Domino jogged into the room.

"Is this a normal Ostara thing, or did you guys get caught?" Domino's gills flared breathlessly. He'd obviously run quite a distance.

"Neither, I think," Gus said.

Wortlister was running down the hall, looking a bit disheveled and pulling his vest on. "Come on, you idiots," he said, grasping the cell bars to catch his breath. "Akira, the new Future Fate has had her first revelation. Everyone is meeting in the temple to hear it."

"What did she predict?" Abel asked.

"Something about nine warriors in water or nine warriors and a daughter, not really sure. They're reading the whole thing in a few minutes; come on," Wortlister said and ran ahead of them. Abney, Abel, and Honali looked at each other and ran after the Puca.

Master Fù, the Fae History and Etiquette teacher from Mabon, was one of the most grotesque Fae Abney had come across so far. He told them his kind were called The Nasnas, a subcategory of Grim Reapers. He had half of a body, one leg, one arm, one eye that was pitch black, half a mouth with jagged, chipped teeth, all covered in a sagging gray deathlike skin. His other half was missing completely so all of his organs were visible when he turned to the side. Also, his touch was extremely deadly, so he wore a pink elbow-length rubber glove at all times and made sure everyone gave him ample room to move about.

"Can anybody tell me the one situation where you would not bow to the Queens?" he asked the class. They looked around at each other.

"I thought you always had to bow to the Queens?" Zoey whispered in Abney's ear.

"Speak up, Ms. Doggett!" Master Fù encouraged her. "The rest of the class can't hear you!"

"I said…" Zoey cleared her throat. "I said that I thought that there were no instances where you would not bow to the Queens."

"Correct! It was a trick question! Clever of you to spot it. You will always bow, even if you're a one-legged hop-along like me." The Master tapped his leg. Abney shook her head. He was feigning frailty when he moved faster than most four-legged Fae on a good day. Half a body hadn't slowed him down in the slightest.

"Now, who knows when it's appropriate to seek an audience with the Queens?" the quiz continued. Melinda Fairfax raised her hand. "Yes, Ms. Fairfax?"

"Only if you become aware of an immediate threat to the Fae; otherwise, the Queens will seek you out when they desire to speak with you. You never speak unless they address you first," she said

He congratulated them and continued with the lesson. "Very good. I am pleased you all seem to be paying attention." Abney had never been so grateful to be in class doing something semi-normal in her whole life. School, she was good at school. Study, learn, take tests, make flash cards, write essays, all of this she was more than capable of. Adventures, facing bad guys, visiting witches? That was all way out of her skill set. She almost had an anxiety attack thinking about it.

"Hey, are you all right?" Zoey whispered to her. "You've gone completely white." Abney did feel a little flushed.

"I'm fine," she fibbed. "Just tired today."

"Okay," Zoey relented but looked suspicious.

How could she tell any of them how scared she was? She felt like the world's biggest coward. Everyone else was so ready to jump in, so prepared to risk everything, and here she was, wondering if she could go back home? Back to her Fleetling family and leave all of this behind. Some of it had been fun and exciting, but mostly she was terrified. Abney just wanted to feel normal again.

CHAPTER 16

INTO THE WOODS

The class was nervous. Whispers polluted the air, and there was a general feeling of unease. Master Sjögren was nowhere in sight, and they were never late. It was very out of character for the brainy Masters who never forgot anything. "Where do you think they are?" Esha whispered to Abney. Esha was a nosey Bookworm. Well, she was more like a Book-grub at this point, but she was always up on the latest gossip and goings-on. Frankly, Abney was grateful to have flown under her radar for so long.

"I don't know," Abney replied. She was only half listening, half looking for the Harpy-girl who had passed her the note. She had not seen her since that class, and come to think of it, she didn't remember seeing her before that class either. Esha would know though. She knew everyone. "Hey, what happened to that Harpy-girl who used to be in this class?"

"Ummm…there was never a Harpy in this class." She looked at Abney over her glasses.

"Are you sure?" Abney asked.

"Most definitely," she replied. "My memory is eidetic. Bookworm, remember?" Esha moved her tail in circles while pointing it at her face. What the heck? Abney thought. Am I losing it? After everything that had happened and was happening, she wouldn't be surprised.

"This class will come to order," a deep voice commanded from behind them. Everyone turned to see who was giving commands. A tall stringy Fae with an elongated horse face stormed into the room. He seemed to be in a foul mood. His fang-like teeth ground together noisily, and his black eyes were dull with melancholy.

"Master Sjögren is indisposed. My name is Algernon Schimmelpfennig. No, you do not have to call me Master Schimmelpfennig as it's rather a mouthful. I'm not fond of the Master part either. You will address me as Algernon. I will be teaching this class until further notice. Any questions?" The class stared at him in stunned silence. "No? Good! Where have we left off? You"—he pointed at a shrinking Pixie—"with the unreasonably long nose, answer."

"We're on chapter eleven of *Silent Bells are Ringing*," she stammered while trying to cover her nose. A couple of boys were snickering at the back.

"What are you genetic rejects laughing at?" Algernon turned on them. "You think you're superior to Ms.—" He looked at the Pixie again.

"Amari," she replied meekly.

"Thank you." He nodded at her and looked back at the boys. "Gentlemen, you are so okay with the way that you look that you dare laugh at this unfortunate looking girl? Well, let's all have a good look at you then. Stand up! State your names."

A reddish-brown Troll stood up, looking ashamed. "Alex Tinker."

"Angus Scott." A purple and aqua scaled boy stood.

"Stefano Esposito." The last boy stood without an ounce of shame. His blue and yellow Phoenix feathers ruffled proudly.

"Right! Up to the front and bring your books. Come on now!" he demanded. "The class doesn't have all day." The boys shuffled to the front of the class. "Wonderful! You will stand here for the rest of the class so that we may observe what stupidity and narcissism look like. Now, everyone read chapter eleven silently. Your voices are already making my soul numb."

The class stared for a moment in astonishment and then began to read. Abney got the feeling teaching wasn't this guy's ideal job. She was happy to be reading alone though. She hated reading in groups. Reading out loud took too long, and it eliminated some of the magic when she had to share a story with anyone.

"Psst…" Esha tapped Abney's shoulder, trying to get her attention. She tried to ignore her since Algernon had made it very clear he wanted silence. "Psst…" she persisted.

"What?" Abney whispered, without looking back.

Esha spoke quietly. "My pen is out of ink. Can I borrow one?" Abney nodded and reached up to pull the bat-pack down.

"Excuse me." Algernon stood up. "Chubby blue girl, what are you doing?"

"I-I-I was just getting a pen," she stuttered. It felt like the walls were collapsing in to crush her. She had the undivided attention of the class, which was the last thing she wanted, ever.

"Algernon,"—Esha snaked her way out of her seat—"sir, the fault is mine. I asked her to get me a pen."

"How noble of you," he snapped. "You can join these three clowns as they stand and read silently. And you…" he paused waiting for Abney to fill in her name.

"Abney Kelly," she said in the loudest voice she could muster, which was barely louder than a mutter. *Breathe…one, two, three… There's no ice core; you can't be this upset. Breathe…one, two, three… I'm at home with Granny. I can smell cinnamon rolls and chili. Dad is bumbling about, looking for his glasses that he forgot were on top of his head.* She had to rein herself in and quickly. She was starting to sweat.

"Ms. Kelly," he said a little quieter. He seemed almost pacified as he looked at her, but regained his fire in an instant. "Learn to follow directions and tell your classmates no, or you will spend our next class front and center, reading chapter twelve aloud."

"Yes, sir," Abney replied, her voice calmer than she felt.

"Very, well," he nodded and went back to the desk, picked up the newspaper, kicked his feet up, and shook the newspaper out in front of him. "Read silently. Not a peep or rustle until I excuse you." The class remained absolutely quiet for the duration.

✦

After class, Abney walked briskly out to the gardens. She needed air, space, no people, and to scream, anything to let out the tension that was overwhelming her. The brisk walk turned into a run, and she burst into the garden full-bore, screaming aloud. She was angry, angry at herself for getting attached to people, angry she couldn't have her old life back, angry she might not have a life at all here shortly, and angry that she felt so helpless to do anything about any of it.

"Whoa there," Ol' Chris greeted her. "You all right?" Surprisingly, Abney did feel a lot better.

"I think I'll be all right," she replied. The statement wasn't completely dishonest.

"I thought that Minelephant of yours was pretty boisterous, but I think you might give her a run for her money." The old man laughed. Abney frowned. *Does he really have to compare me to Audrey?*

"Sorry." She tried to sound apologetic, but it came out with just a hint of annoyance. The gardener noticed.

"You are feisty today. Why don't you come with me?" He smiled. "Let's see if we can't get this day turned around for you." Abney followed him. She was supposed to be meeting Zoey and Sabine, but she didn't feel like it at the moment. She would apologize later.

The air was crisp, but there were no puffs of steam coming from Abney or the gardener. She wondered what type of Fae he was, evidently something of a wintery persuasion, but what? They walked through the mostly naked garden. A few buds were braving the spring cold, but most of the plants were still hibernating, waiting for warmer spring weather. Ol' Chris led her into a greenhouse. There were seeds, pots, and dirt everywhere. It was very disorganized. Abney was not fond of disorganization. It made her mind feel messy. It was also warmer than she would have liked.

"Here ya go." He handed her bulbs in a paper packet. "See that empty tray right there? Good. Fill all the slots to the top with dirt, then dig your thumb in to make a large hole in each, put one bulb in each hole, cover it up, and then we'll give them a little water."

"What are we planting?" Abney asked while using a small shovel to pour dirt into her tray. She was happy for the distraction. Gardening was so relaxing, effortless. She barely had to think about what she was doing.

"Galanthus, more commonly known as Snowdrops. My mother loved Snowdrops. She used to gather them from the fields near our home. We always had vases filled with them," he told her, smiling gently at the memory.

"My grandmother likes bleeding hearts," she confided. "We have a lot of them around our house during the summer."

"Ah, a wonderful flower indeed. We plant a few of them here as well." He nodded while dropping seeds into his own tray. "So, what seems to be the trouble, young lady? You can tell me. Nobody talks to or listens to old gardeners, you know."

"It's just a lot," Abney stated. "This time last year I was human. I had a family I loved; school was not exactly pleasant, but it was manageable. Now I'm lost. Everything is strange; nothing is comfortable, and I feel like I'm in over my head." She tried to keep the explanation as simple as possible.

"Ah, yes. I can't imagine what that must be like. I'm very, very old. We still lived with our parents when I was a boy and knew all about the Fae from the very beginning. To be dropped into this at your age? Nasty shock, I would think. The majority of Fae aren't what you would call great parents. They're too self-absorbed. My parents were wonderful though. My father could be cruel at times, but mostly, he was kind, and he loved my mother more than anything in the world. I miss them all the time," Ol' Chris said. Abney listened contentedly. It was nice to hear someone else talk. "Have you had a chance to read the book I gave you?"

Abney looked at him gratefully. "Oh, my gosh, I almost forgot! Yes, I read it! Where did you find it? Is it the actual journal of Isodanelli?"

"Many old things have made their way to Avalon over the years. It may or may not be her actual journal. Who can say? I would assume it is, at the very least, the inspiration for the book. Again an educated guess at best." He shrugged his shoulders.

"Abney Kelly!" a shrill voice shouted behind her. Abney and Ol' Chris turned to see Zoey with Sabine following behind. "We were worried sick!"

"She was worried," Sabine corrected Zoey. "I haven't decided if you're worthy of worry yet."

"Thanks," Abney stuck her tongue out at the Unicorn. "Sorry, I just…"

Ol' Chris stepped in. "It's my fault, ladies. Not as spritely as I used to be. Ms. Kelly here was on her way to meet up with you when I asked her for assistance. Thank you very much for your help." He winked at her. Abney nodded her thanks.

"It's no problem."

"Let's go then." Sabine shivered. "It's cold out here."

✳

It worked. Not exactly like they expected—in fact, not at all like they expected—but it worked. Snow and evergreens were everywhere as far as Abney could see, but not a single one of her friends was in sight. They'd held hands tightly, while Abney traced the outside of the medallion, and the spinning started slowly but picked up speed quickly. It was like being in the eye of a tornado. Their legs lifted off the floor and were pulled backward until they were looking straight down at the floor, holding onto each other's hands for dear life. Abney held onto Domino and Lunetta for as long as she could, but the force eventually pulled them apart and spun them in different directions.

"Maarrcooo!" someone shouted. Abney thought it sounded like Zoey. It was coming somewhere from her left. Abney turned and started walking toward the voice.

"Polo!" Abney answered. She heard at least two more Polos that had mingled with hers.

180

"Maarrcooo!" the call sounded again. This time more Polos answered. They were getting closer too. Abney started running. She could see movement just ahead of her. She picked up speed.

"Maarrcooo!" Zoey yelled with her hands cupped over her mouth. Abney burst through the bushes and ran into her friend's arms. The girls hugged gleefully. "Oh my god! I was so worried when I didn't see any of you."

"Me too," Abney agreed, still hugging Zoey. Another body crashed into them. Gus's bony arms reached around them. After that, they were attacked on all sides until nearly everyone had joined them.

"We freaking made it!" Abel roared. "Hoo-yah!"

"Is everyone here and accounted for?" Zoey pushed everyone apart to do a head count. "We're missing someone." The group looked around.

"It's Sabine," Sümeyye announced, looking worried.

"Sabine!" Abel's deep voice rang out.

"*Quoi*," she snarled from behind them. She was pulling leaves from her normally perfect cotton candy hair. "Ugggg! I broke my freaking nail!"

"Maybe we should have left the princess back in Avalon." Lunetta smirked at the unhappy Unicorn.

Sabine glared at her. "Oh shut up."

"Guys, kill each other later." Honali pushed between them. "We have a mission remember?"

The girls stood down but traded angry glances. They needed to find bark and dogbane. Everyone had their own large satchel so that they could get as much material as possible back to Avalon with them.

"Let's split up. Does everyone have their partner?" Honali asked. Abney paired off with Sabine, Lunetta with Gus, Honali with Sümeyye, and Zoey with Domino and Abel. "Good, let's get to it. We'll meet back here in two hours. Remember to tie a ribbon every twenty feet or so. That way we can get back to each other."

"Hands in everyone," Zoey commanded, and the group followed orders.

"Vive la Pete," she said.

"Vive la Pete," they said together and broke apart.

The group split up, with each team taking a different direction. Abney and Sabine were on bark duty. They were to keep an eye out for any dogsbane as well, but their main focus was to strip bark. They started right where they were, looking for branches and dead trees as that was the best place to find plant fiber.

Sabine was surprisingly adept at stripping bark. Abney had thought she would be more of a hindrance than a help, but she was working through branches faster than Abney. They worked an area and then moved on, tying a yellow ribbon to mark their path. The girls barely spoke. Abney hoped it was just because they were working so hard, but she had a feeling it was more because Sabine didn't want to talk to her. It was hard to tell with her though. Every time Abney thought she was nothing but a shallow, self-absorbed mean-girl, Sabine would do something entirely out of character that made her think she wasn't so bad.

They walked around fifty feet from their last gathering point and started again. They tied one of their ribbons around a nearby tree and began to work. The wood in this area seemed to be all really old or dead, which made the girls' job easier. Abney's hands started to ache as she gathered. *That's weird; it's not like I'm doing anything hard.* She put the sticks down, shook out her hands, looked down to stretch them, and screamed. Her hands were wrinkled and spotted with age. She reached up to grab her face and discovered she had jowls.

Sabine was ambling over to her. Abney noticed she was annoyingly still perfect, with only a few crows' feet around her eyes that even suggested she had aged at all. "Come on, we're in an aging pocket; we need to move on quickly before we are too decrepit to escape." Sabine grabbed Abney's hand.

"I'm not going anywhere." Abney snatched her hand back. "Who are you? Why are you grabbing me?" Abney was genuinely confused. She didn't recognize the woman in front of her. She didn't recognize this place. Something was wrong. She knew that she knew what it was, but she couldn't remember.

"Don't be stupid." Sabine grabbed her hand again. "We have to leave this area now or die."

"Do I know you?" Abney asked her hopefully. Sabine pulled at her hand again, but Abney still would not budge.

"Abney, we have to go," the Unicorn said with a grimace, and then everything went dark.

Abney awoke a short while later with Sabine lying next to her, still unconscious. A black-haired Faun was standing over them and poking Abney with a stick. "What happened?" Abney asked groggily.

"I had to knock you out to drag you and your friend out of the aging pocket. You're a very uncooperative and heavy old lady," she said.

"What's an aging pocket?" Abney questioned.

"A few tales suggested there might be weird pockets of time where you might age rapidly or grow young, but most of the information said nothing about it at all. I didn't think it would be relevant," Sabine said, sitting up and cradling her head.

"They're real," the Faun confirmed.

"Why the hell didn't we cover them before we came here?" Abney said, now slightly upset.

"Well, I wasn't sure it was actually a thing. There isn't a lot written about this forest." Sabine shrugged. "I don't like to speak on matters I'm unsure about."

"Well, since we're Fae trying to kill Santa Claus, I would think that any mythology would be relevant and helpful," Abney snapped.

"Point taken." Sabine raised her eyebrows.

"What are you girls doing in this forest?" the Faun asked when she was finally able to get a word in.

"Admiring it," Sabine said curtly. "We fancied a walk."

"It's too dangerous here," the Faun said. "You should not be here. Children are not safe here."

"We're not children," Sabine retorted.

"Are you less than one hundred and fifty years old?" she asked them. Both girls nodded yes. "Then you are children. Get out of here while you can."

"We have to finish our walk first," Sabine insisted.

"I see." The Faun shook her head. "Your lives are your own to waste. You have been warned."

"We really won't be here long," Abney stated, hoping to pacify the stranger. A startled look crossed the Faun's face, and she took off into the brush.

"Well, that was a close call," Sabine said and got to her feet. Then she headed over to a tree that looked dead and dug her knife in to start stripping it. Abney, still annoyed and a little achy, knelt to gather larger tree limbs to do the same when the birds all screamed and flew out of the branches above. Both girls froze. Abney looked over at Sabine and held a finger up to her lips. There was a soft crunch of snow beneath feet. Crunch, squish, crunch, the steps came closer and closer. Sabine managed to roll herself under a log, and Abney pressed her back into one of the trees, trying to stay out of sight.

"Come out. I know you're there," an older male voice commanded, but neither girl moved. "Abney Kelly and Sabine Comtois, I do not enjoy hide and seek. Come out now." The voice knew them. There seemed to be no reason to pretend they weren't there, so Abney stepped out from her hiding spot. Sabine followed her lead grudgingly. A figure in a blue hood stood before them. His long beard, which hung down to his knees, was all that was visible of his face. In his right hand, he held an elegantly carved wooden walking stick. Abney got the impression that he couldn't manage without it. "Much better. Tell me, what are you doing in my forest?"

His forest? That means he's…

"You're Father Time?" Sabine looked at him suspiciously.

"Cesare, please." He gave them a slight bow of his head. "I already know your names. Now, tell me why you're here and how you got here?" Abney and Sabine exchanged worried looks. What should they tell him? The truth might not be the best idea, but he already knew who they were, so lying to him might be ill-advised as well.

"Man, I already told you why we're here," Abel stepped out from behind the old man, followed by Zoey and Domino. Sabine pinched her lips in contempt. The jig was definitely up.

"I know what you told me," the old man said patiently. "I want to hear what your friends have to say." Abel gave her a pleading look, and Abney knew they had lied through their teeth. There was no way to know what they had said, so she did the only thing she could: She told the truth. The old man listened without interrupting, and when she finished, he remained silent for a while, apparently considering their plight. He removed his hood to look at them. The hood hid many things, including soft green eyes and many, many wrinkles. None of them had ever seen anyone who looked that old. His eyes stopped on Abney.

"Orina," he whispered, and his eyes clouded over with grief for an instant, but he shook himself, and the moment was gone. "All Snow Maidens remind me of my late wife," he said offhandedly and smiled at them. They all nodded; it made sense. In the legends, Cesare loved Orina very much. Even after all this time, it was hard for him. "I think you all better come with me."

They followed Time through the forest to his castle. On their way, they found Sümeyye, Honali, Lunetta, and Gus, all crawling around the forest floor as much younger versions of themselves. They carried their friends until they were out of the youth pocket and grew large enough to walk on their own. There was a lot of confusion, bumbling, and unanswered questions as they followed the ancient man. No one dared complain though.

Time's castle was not what Abney had expected. In her mind, there were tall white towers capped in blue and balconies with red draping flags, but that was not what stood before them. Instead, it reminded her of St. Basil's Cathedral with its colorful ice cream towers and gingerbread looking walls. She was ravenous just looking at it.

"Is anyone else hungry?" Abel said out loud. The others smirked and raised their hands but did not speak. Abel had a gift for saying what everyone else was thinking. Time didn't seem to notice the comment. He simply held up his hands, the gates flung open, and he motioned for them to follow. As they traipsed through colorful green, orange, and yellow gates, the aromas of apple pie and fresh bread wrapped around them like a warm hug.

"I feel like Hansel and Gretel," Sabine whispered in her ear. "And not like in a *I just found a candy house* way. More like *we're going to be fattened up and pushed in an oven* kind of way." Abney nodded. There was something not quite right about this place.

Inside, the rooms were warm, inviting, and cozy. She had expected it
to feel more like a museum. Cesare led them into a large study with comfy
couches and a roaring fire. He pulled a long cord next to the fireplace and
sat in the nearest armchair. A big hairy monster came in and grunted to
announce his arrival.

"Ah, Hugo," Time greeted him. "Bring us some tea and warm cookies,
will you? Oh, and some of those chocolaty marshmallow things."

"Mmmmm." Hugo bowed and exited the room.

"Now, tell me again, about your meeting with the witch and how you
came to be in my forest?" he commanded. This time, Honali obliged him.

"You're lucky she didn't boil your bones. She eats children, you know.
And I cannot say I am pleased that anyone is out to kill my son." Time
frowned at them. "But I cannot say I blame anyone for trying to preserve
their own life either. It is quite the conundrum. It's not easy, you know.
He's my flesh and blood, but I know as well as anyone what he's done. It's
not his fault though. It was that witch. Poor boy just wants his mother
back.

"My sweet Orina. She was so beautiful, much like you." He looked
at Abney. "I suppose there would be some family resemblance, you being a great-great-great-great-great-granddaughter or something to that
effect. I've seen them from afar but never actually met any of Nicholas's
progeny before. It's just too painful. In my mind, Orina is one of a kind,
truly unique yet here you sit, looking at me with her face and her eyes. It
breaks my heart. If only you had her voice, her thoughts, her effortless
way of laughing and telling me that I was too serious for my own good."
He looked distant and happy for the moment. "She was always right, you
know."

Abney looked at him with confused emotions. She hadn't thought
about that aspect before. This was the only actual family she'd ever met,
though he was undoubtedly many, many generations removed. She had a
family. A real family and not a stolen one, though she didn't see this turning into Sunday brunch or anything. She might want to get to know this
man; then again, it felt disloyal to her Fleetling family. They had raised
her, and he was a complete stranger.

"Man, I gotta ask," Abel said. "Why didn't you go back in time to save your old lady? I mean, you *are* Father Time. It seems like an easy fix."

"Time travel is not that simple," he said. "You can't zip through it willy-nilly. It's very complicated. Let's say I went back to before Baba Yaga created Orina and a snowflake falls in my hand that was meant to fall into the hand of a small village girl, whose hand gets cold as a result, and she runs home to warm her hands. On her way there, Jack Frost catches sight of her. Seeing the little girl running ignites his longing for a child of his own and that prompts him to seek out Baba Yaga. If I am there to catch the snow, that girl's hands might not get cold as fast, and she might never cross the Winter King's path, and Orina might never exist, or it might take place much further in the future, and she turns out completely different. If she no longer exists, my memory of her disappears as well, and she's lost to me forever."

"Whoa!" Able responded. "That's crazy-complicated."

"Everything must happen exactly as it did for her to exist. A memory of her is better than to have never known her at all. Nothing is worth the risk of that." The old man shook his head. Even the idea of her never coming into being was painful to him. "Not to mention my role is not that of a time traveler. I'm more of an archivist. I keep the memories and stories of the world. I was never meant to change things, only observe them."

"Well, this has been lovely," Sabine announced as she stood up. "But we really must be getting back to Avalon before someone notices we're missing." Abney noticed she was trying too hard to seem pleasant. Something was off. Sabine wasn't the type to suddenly be polite for no reason. She snapped out of her fantasies about family and paid attention. Something was wrong here, but what? Cesare seemed like a nice old man. Everything was warm and inviting, not scary, but something in her stomach was still shouting *danger*.

"Ah yes, of course." The old man stood and walked over to pull the bell to summon his servant. He appeared quickly. "Hugo, order the forest to bring several bags of bark and dogbane, make sure it's suitable for making rope."

"You're going to help us?" Honali asked with surprise.

"This is not helping," he said. "If I had not interfered, you would have gathered as much on your own. I am simply not hindering you. I will do nothing to help my son. Nor will I lift a finger to bring him down." He walked them through the castle and back to the courtyard, where they found their satchels overflowing with the supplies they needed to make the rope. The others went to grab their bags, but Cesare grabbed Abney's shoulder and held her back.

"You do look so like her," he said, looking at her. "I will tell you one more thing, granddaughter. She of the Glass Heart is hidden by the Faerie Queens. Be careful. It would be unfortunate if they were to find out you were after their treasure."

"Thank you," Abney replied, trying to pull away from him.

"Don't come back here," he growled in a whisper and pushed her toward her friends. Abney was happy to be leaving. She picked up her bag, slung it over her shoulders, and squeezed between Zoey and Lunetta. Abney's finger circled the amulet again, and they held on to each other for as long as possible, which was not long at all.

CHAPTER 17

THE BAD WEEK

Morale was getting low in Avalon. The rooms were overcrowded. Classes were overcrowded. You had to wait in line for over an hour to get a shower. Tempers, in general, were terrible. Not even a game of Basnorts could cheer them up. Everyone's schoolwork was suffering, and the Masters were becoming increasingly testy themselves. As a result, Dean Sadira announced that there was going to be a three-day weekend. Since Kringle's activities had ceased for the time being, the Changelings were going Topside to visit their Fleetling families, and the adults were being shipped back to Tír na nÓg for some R n' R.

Abney watched in amusement as Wortlister packed his bag. He seemed flat-out gleeful, which wasn't even remotely normal for him. "I'll be in your closet, of course, if you need me, but I know you'll understand when I say I would prefer if you'd get lost. For three days at least. There will be silence and no one to fight over bathrooms with! I can't wait! Are you packed yet?"

"Already done, Mr. Sunshine," Abney goaded him. She couldn't help it. He glared at her over the new moss-stitched vest she'd made for him and stuffed it in his bag.

"Teach me to be in a good mood around you," he grumbled and turned his back to her. Abney could tell he was smiling. She was secretly pleased he packed his vest. He had seemed less than enthused when she gave it to him. Now, she knew he liked it. "Well let's blow this popsicle stand!" Wortlister announced and headed for the door. Abney could swear she saw him skip.

✦

Home. There was nothing quite like it. They arrived just before dawn. Abney changed into some comfortable yoga pants and an overly large long-sleeved shirt. She ran her hands over her books, rolled across her bed, picked up her blanket, and went to sit in her window seat to watch the sun come up. Deep purple crept up like a flower sticking its head up from the soil and then bloomed brilliant orange and red as the sun emerged.

Wortlister had hastily tossed her out of her closet as soon as they came through the mirror and shoved pajamas under the door when she reminded him she still needed Fleetling clothing. She was happy to have the alone time too, so she didn't blame him. She was on the third book of Artemis Fowl, and that was her only plan for the whole day. That and hot chocolate, so many cups of hot chocolate, and maybe sushi if she could talk her dad into it. To say the food in Avalon was bland would have been putting it mildly. She was looking forward to some spicier cuisine.

"Hey, kiddo," followed a knock on her door. Abney jumped up, flung the door open, and wrapped her arms around her father. His smell was repulsive, but it felt so good to see him, she didn't care at all. "Are you okay?" he asked while hugging his daughter back.

"I missed you," she said almost tearfully.

He laughed. "Not that I'm not thrilled, but we did see each other last night."

"It seems like longer," she said, not letting go.

"Is this about your therapy appointment today? I love you, kid, but you're still going. Ten thousand hugs couldn't change my mind."

"Therapy?" Abney pushed back from him, looking baffled.

"Don't look so innocent." He shook his finger at her. "You know full well you've been out of sorts and moody for the last few months. Dr. Armstrong thinks you could benefit from talking to a therapist. Get dressed. We're outta here in an hour and a half." He patted her head and strolled down the stairs. Abney stared after him in utter disbelief. *Therapy? I'm going to therapy? I'm going to kill that Doppelgänger*, she fumed.

"Did you hear what my Doppelgänger has done?" Abney flung the closet door open angrily.

"No." Wortlister didn't look up from his book.

"He landed me in therapy! *Therapy*! What did he do?" Abney complained.

"No clue," he replied. "But it sounds like a personal problem."

"Personal problem?" She stuck out her hip and braced it with her right hand. "You said he'd been watching me my whole life. That he would act just like me."

"Well, it's not a perfect system; they're not meant to be Topside for so long. Let's be fair though. You could use a little anger management." He grabbed her some jeans, a Princess Bride t-shirt and pushed her out of the closet again. Abney punched the door behind him and spent the next five minutes shaking out her hand; the door was much harder than she had anticipated.

"Dr. Appleblossom said that you refused to speak with him the entire session," Granny scolded her while looking back from the front seat. "Therapy can't help if you don't use it properly."

"She's right, kiddo," her father said without taking his eyes from the road. "You're going twice a week until something improves. Might as well use the time wisely."

"I don't know him." Abney crossed her arms and glared at them. What she wanted to say was that she had started to say a million things, but stopped herself. Almost everything she had to say was completely unbelievable, sounded absolutely insane, and would most definitely land her in the attic with Moira.

"You can't get to know him if you don't speak with him," Granny said.

"It feels a little creepy confiding in an old man," Abney asserted. This was her safe place, her place to relax, and now it was all messed up.

"He's not old; he's in his early forties," Granny corrected her.

"Are you setting me up on a date or with a therapist?" Abney snapped.

"Abney Skylar Kelly," Dad growled, "you apologize to your grandmother right now." Abney paused, she had hardly ever heard her father raise his voice, and hearing it now only made her angrier.

"No. You apologize for taking me to see a therapist. I'm not Mom! And I won't let you keep me prisoner in the attic!" She knew that statement wasn't fair, but she didn't care. Her father pulled the car over and turned to look at his daughter. He was furious.

"When we get home, you go straight to your room. I will decide what your punishment will be later. Until then, I suggest you remain silent," he said through gritted teeth. Abney glowered back at him but did not speak. She couldn't remember the last time he'd looked like that. The rest of the car ride was quiet on all fronts.

✦

Abney tried all day to read her book, but she would turn several pages and realize she hadn't read a single word. Her mind was racing. She felt helpless and angry. Nothing was going right. Nothing was easy. Why couldn't just this one thing go according to plan? Her father came up to let her know she was grounded for the next two weeks. Granny had not said a word to her since the incident in the car. All in all, everything was a mess.

Her phone chirped, and Abney almost fell off her bed. No one ever texted her, so her phone was still in her possession, even though she was grounded. Who even had her number?

"What r u doing?"

Abney looked at the number—it wasn't a Wyoming number. Where was the 970 area code? She texted back.

"Who is this?"

"Zoey, duh."

Abney could see her friend smiling in her mind. She forgot she'd given them her number.

"Forgot I gave you my number. I'm grounded. How's it there?"

It turned out Zoey and Domino didn't live that far from her. They were in Fort Collins, Colorado. It was still an hour drive, but it was closer than most places.

"Want us 2 liber8 u?" Zoey replied.

Abney was considering the offer when she heard familiar sirens pull up outside their house.

"TTYL. Mom drama."

Abney sighed and opened her door to listen. Officer Frawley's familiar voice carried up the stairs.

"This is the third time this week." he notified them. "Oliver, you have to do something. She's breaking into people's homes. I know you're doing your best, but this can't continue."

"I'm not crazy," Moira stated. "I need my freedom, so I can prove it. I have a son, Fred, a boy. He needs me." Guilt swelled up in Abney like never before. Moira wasn't crazy, not really. She did have a son, and she had never given up on him. She found herself thinking of her Fleetling mother in a whole new light. Abney couldn't imagine what she'd gone through and being locked up in the attic for all that time. Tears threatened to flood her eyes, but she held them back with a now well-practiced coolness. *What am I doing to this family?* She moved into the hallway so she could see down the stairs.

Dad tried to pacify the officer. "Dr. Armstrong is on her way. She will be taking her to a more secure facility tonight." Abney had never seen her father look so defeated. She felt even worse for fighting with him now. Granny was leading Moira up the stairs. She looked Abney right in the eyes.

"Someday, everyone will know what you are," she hissed at Abney. "This isn't forever. I'm going to get my son back. You'll see!" For once, Abney didn't look at her with hate or anger, just pity and guilt. Moira noticed the change. "Wait," she jerked her arm away from Granny and walked up to Abney before the older woman could stop her. "You're different. You look different." She sniffed Abney's hair. "You smell different. What's changed?" Abney backed up, trying to get away from her.

Granny reached them and pulled Moira firmly back toward the attic. "Moira, she's getting older is all. She's still the same Abney we've always had. Come on now. Let's get upstairs. Dr. Armstrong will be here soon. Abney, I think it's best if you go back to your room." Granny looked at her sternly, and Abney knew she still wasn't forgiven for her earlier outburst. She went back into her room and shut her door. She spent the rest of her weekend locked away in what remained of her safe space. She wanted to make up with her father and grandmother, but didn't know how. She was angry, scared, and she couldn't really explain it to them, so why bother?

✦

Back in Avalon things weren't going awesome either. Master Blewitt was struggling to help Abney control her inner fire. Without the ice core, this was difficult at best and, at worst, very dangerous. So far, she had petrified herself by cooling her fire down too much and melted the fingertips off her left hand when she had given it too much of a bang. Luckily, Fae healed quickly, and her hand was only in bandages for a few hours.

"Focusss," he commanded her. "You mussst know yoursssself. Feel your heat, feel your cold, they mussst remain ssseperate and yet work together. Let the flamesss of your heart lick at the ice of your ssskin, but not melt through it. You mussst be in control of yoursssself at all timesss. Try again." He held his hand over his head, likely expecting further failures.

Abney did not disappoint. She was meant to guide her inner fire up and out of her mouth like a dragon without melting into a puddle. She managed not to melt, but the fire never seemed to make it out of her throat. The best she managed was large clouds of hot steam, which helped vent off her emotions, but also left her voiceless. Her throat ached, and she was almost certain her vocal cords had melted completely. She waved at Master Blewitt to get his attention and then pointed to her throat.

"Yesss, yesss, you'll be fine in a few hoursss." He crossed his arms scornfully and nodded. "Again. Thisss time really focusss on ssseperating the heat and the cold."

Abney breathed in deeply. Her throat was burning. She concentrated. She could feel the coolness of her skin, the iciness of her touch. She furrowed her brow and searched for the heat in her heart. She could feel the flames flickering inside her chest. She willed the fire to climb upward without touching the rest of her. Feeling confident, she opened her mouth wide, and steam flooded the room.

"Not quite." Master Blewitt shook his head. "You did ssseem more confident thisss time. All right, let'sss try it again!" Abney groaned inwardly since she could not make any sounds at present.

"Come on, you can do better than that," Wortlister provoked her. Abney gave him a challenging look. He petted her head with a wicked smile, and she swatted him away.

Abney closed her eyes and blocked them out. She tried thinking of home, but she found that too stressful at the moment. *Where is relaxing? Where are there no worries, no stress?* She found herself thinking of the old gardener in the greenhouse and imagined she was filling a tray with dirt. She picked up a handful and let the cool potting soil fall between her fingers. She could smell the faint scent of wood chips mixed in. Her heart rate was nice and slow. She saw her fire in her mind's eye and pushed it upward, being mindful that it did not touch any of her other parts. She opened her mouth and pushed it out. There was still a good deal of steam, but a small spurt of actual fire came out this time and singed Wortlister's eyelashes.

"What the..." Wortlister jumped back too late. Abney chuckled soundlessly, and Master Blewitt was positively sizzling with laughter. "It's not funny." He frowned. "Do I have any eyelashes left?" Master Blewitt looked for him. They were all gone.

"You ssshouldn't be trying to get a facial while a ssstudent is learning." Master Blewitt snickered. "And Abney! Wonderful! You did it! It'sss a little sssspark, but next time will be easssier. We'll call it a day. Sssee you Wednesssday!"

Abney pulled her bat-pack down from where it was floating and hugged it against her chest. She was headed to see Sümeyye. They were going to do some research on where the Torch of the Wyvern Dragon might be. Abel and Gus were working on how they were going to get out of Avalon without using the Traveler. Boozing him up on a holiday was one thing, but going for round two was foolish. One should never court fate if it could be avoided.

"Dongle Muffin!" Wortlister exclaimed, bringing Abney out of her own thoughts. To her horror, she realized he was addressing Algernon.

"I told you to never call me that." The long horse face clouded with anger.

"You were never any fun," Wortlister stated.

"Io—" Algernon started, but the Puca grabbed his mouth.

"And I told you, it's Wortlister, Algernon," he smiled at the Kelpie. Abney shook her head.

"Well, I'm refusing to speak to you, no matter what you call yourself." Algernon stormed away.

Abney looked at him angrily. Algernon was teaching Intro to Fae Lit now, and Wortlister had undoubtedly just made her a target of the unruly Master. He looked at her and understood what she was thinking.

"He'd be unpleasant no matter what," he told Abney. "His mood's been sour for four hundred years."

Great, Abney thought and went to meet Sümeyye.

✦

The twins and Dermott had fifth-hour classes on Mondays, so Sümeyye and Abney were able to study in relative quiet for once. They had been combing through scrolls and book lists. The librarian in Avalon was more willing to loan out books and manuscripts, but she was also less helpful. Whenever they asked her things, she would shrug her shoulders, point at the card catalogs, and ask if their legs had been painted on or if they had suddenly gone blind.

"I see lots of references to the Wyvern Dragon, but absolutely nothing about a torch," Sümeyye announced in frustration. "Do you think it's maybe *a* torch lit by the Wyvern Dragon and not *the* torch?"

"I don't know," Abney croaked. "Have we had any luck in locating him?"

"You guys are looking for the Wyvern Dragon?" Hatsuko, Sümeyye's Hobgoblin, looked up from *The Korrigan Chronicler*. "Why?"

"Honali thinks they may be related somewhere down the line. She thought her fire felt cooler than normal during her last Pyromancy class."

"That's ridiculous," Hatsuko said. "An Ice Dragon is almost as rare as a Unicorn. She would've been identified as such already if she possessed any Air talents. But if you must keep yourselves busy with silly fantasies, I suppose I could indulge you." She stood and walked over to them, dripping water everywhere as she did. Hatsuko was a Rusalka. Rusalkas were a deadly water Hobgoblin that found joy in drowning whatever wandered too near the water's edge. She moved with a dangerous grace, like a cat stalking a mouse.

"I happen to be an old friend of the Wyvern Dragon. He prefers to be called Vern." She sat down on the cot with the girls. "He was living in the Arctic last time I heard from him. That would be the place to start."

"Any idea how we can get out to find him?" Abney asked sweetly.

"You know very well Changelings are not allowed out of Avalon." She smiled. "But I am getting bored. I suppose I might be able to help you. None of the other Hobgoblins can find out of course." Abney and Sümeyye nodded conspiratorially. "All right, give me a few days to work something out. I'll let Sümeyye know when we can go. The rest of you had better find a way to slip your Hobgoblins for a few hours."

Their plans were progressing as they sat braiding their plant fiber into rope. However, their confidence was also starting to falter. Some part of it had seemed like a game up until this point, a grand adventure, but it wasn't looking as fun at the moment. They were braiding rope to trap a murderer and that had a sobering effect on all of them.

"This is all getting out of hand," Sabine said. "I think we should tell someone what's really going on."

"If we tell someone," Honali replied, "they probably won't let us finish getting everything we need. Baba Yaga gave us an exact list. I'm not willing to gamble Sümeyye's life on that."

"I kind of feel like *not* telling the adults is gambling with her life," Sabine said seriously. "We're in way over our heads. Look at this!" She held up the rope she was braiding. "We're trying to braid rope from instructions Gus found on Google. And if the Google instructions don't have us braiding this stuff correctly and it breaks or doesn't work, then what? We need help!"

"I normally disagree with Sabine, well, because she's Sabine. But I think she may have a point on this one," Lunetta said. Everyone stopped braiding and looked at her.

"I think hell just froze over," Gus said, leaving his mouth open for dramatic emphasis.

"Shut up!" Lunetta chucked a pillow at his head. Abney stayed quiet, but she was inclined to agree with Sabine as well.

"Let's just get through this next part," Sümeyye said. "We have help from an adult. Hatsuko will be with us the whole way. Once we have the torch, we can re-evaluate. Maybe she'll be willing to help us with the rest? We should wait to see how this goes first though."

"All right," Sabine conceded. "But once we have the torch, I want everyone to consider telling one of the other adults. This isn't fun and games. Sümeyye could actually end up dead."

"Agreed," Honali relented. Everyone else nodded and got back to work. They had a lot of rope to braid, and it wasn't as easy as the instructions made it look.

CHAPTER 18

THE DEVIL

Besides the night of the prophecy, no one had seen the younger or elder Fates at all. It was like they had disappeared when the rest of the Changelings arrived. The elder Fates had been very vocal about their disapproval of the arrangement, but they'd honored their debt to Queen Titania. Abney looked for the Elder Fates, hoping to pester them with more questions, another reason they were probably hiding. With powers like theirs, who wouldn't have questions? If they were out in the open, students and masters alike would bombard them with enquiries.

That's why Abney was surprised to find Akira wandering alone in the gardens. She'd been looking for Ol' Chris, but he was nowhere in sight. It bothered Abney that she didn't see him right away. He'd always been around before.

The small girl greeted her. "Abney Kelly." Abney recognized her voice as the voice of Baba Yaga the night they'd gone to the witch's cottage.

"Akira." Abney acknowledged that she knew who the girl was. Her sightless eyes were unsettling. There was just something about when little kids looked creepy that made it worse.

"Abney, I have to speak with you," she said and grabbed her hand. Abney looked around as if there might be someone else with her name hanging around. When she realized how stupid that was, she moved closer to the young Fate.

"Okay," Abney agreed reluctantly.

"Your father has been watching you. He knows who you are, but you do not know him. He means you harm," she whispered urgently. "Beware the male who came into your life recently."

"Who is he?" Abney asked intrigued and scared all at once.

"Akira Matsumoto," her sister Shion said disapprovingly, "you should not be here."

"You know what I saw," Akira accused her. "How could I say nothing? How can you say nothing?"

"It is not our job to interfere. What will be, will be. We cannot prevent or encourage events. The elders will be furious," she lectured.

"They won't know anything if you don't squeal," Akira suggested.

"Please tell me who he is," Abney pleaded, but Shion grabbed her sister's hand and dragged her away.

"Look for a male who recently made an appearance." Akira turned back to warn her again and then shoved her sister. "You 'fess up too." Shion gave her sister an angry look.

"Fine!" she yelled. "The Wraith will point you in the right direction. That's all I'm saying."

"Where do I find this Wraith?" Abney asked. She knew she was pushing her luck.

"The same place you found her before," Shion replied, and the young Fates turned to leave.

"Wait," Abney said, accepting she would get no further information. The girls stopped for a moment. "Have you seen the gardener?"

"Gloriana is over in the roses." Shion nodded down the path.

"No, I was looking for Ol' Chris," Abney said. The girls gave Abney a puzzled look.

"Gloriana is the only gardener in Avalon," Akira stated.

"Who's the old guy wandering around here all the time then?" Abney asked them. The girls shrugged together.

"Males are not typically allowed here," Shion said. "He had to have come here with all of you. We have to go now. We're not supposed to be out with the other students."

Abney watched them leave in baffled silence. Who the hell had she been talking to all this time? If he wasn't the gardener, who was he? She decided she would ask the others. Someone had to know who he was and where he had gone.

✦

"I knew there was something wrong with that old man," Wortlister chided her. "He certainly didn't come with us."

"How was I supposed to know?" Abney countered. "You met him. Why didn't you?"

"How was I supposed to focus on him with you sneaking out like a bloody idiot?" Wortlister shouted. He'd gained a slight accent that Abney had never noticed before.

"Oh what, you're British when you're angry?" Abney laughed. The situation was so tense she wasn't sure what caused the breakdown, but she was laughing so hard she was crying.

"Not, British," Wortlister sniffed. "Irish. Americans think every UK accent is British." Abney's laughter didn't stop, and it was infectious. Wortlister was sitting on the floor, laughing with her in no time. It was a few minutes before either of them could gain any composure.

"I'm sorry," she croaked, still chuckling. "I didn't know you grew up in Europe."

"Hundreds of years tends to morph accents, and anger tends to bring our basest selves to the front, along with old habits." He smiled at her.

"So, do you think in a few hundred years Fae won't be able to tell where I was born?"

"Maybe." He settled into his native cadence a little more.

"Fair enough," she said, shaking off the last of her giggles.

"Seriously, Abney"—Wortlister grabbed her chin and turned it toward him—"no running around alone. The Minelephant does not count as not alone. Try to stay out of trouble. It's more dangerous than usual out there right now." Abney could see he was concerned and not just superficially.

"You do like me," she squealed in her girliest voice, because she knew it would annoy him and hugged the big cat. He scrunched his nose and looked down at her.

"Don't go getting a big head." He pushed her away comically. "I'd sell you to Kringle in a heartbeat if I thought he'd take a black hearted creature like you."

Abney gave him a big grin. They both knew he was lying.

Later that day, after classes, Wortlister escorted Abney to Lunetta's cell and went to take his turn in the kitchen. Lunetta shared a cell with Sabine, Sümeyye, and one of Abney's old housemates, Zander Ambrosia. He was thankfully elsewhere, and the girls were alone. The others were supposed to be joining them anytime now but hadn't shown up yet.

"Who do you think your father is?" Lunetta asked. "And who could be the Wraith?"

"I don't know. Someone who's shown up recently, but the only new Fae I can think of is Algernon, and it can't be him. I hope it's not him. I do have an idea about the Wraith though. I thought it might be the spirit from the Ouija Board. That's the only thing that makes sense, right?"

"Spirits and Wraiths are kind of similar, I guess. It does seem to make the most sense. But why can't Algernon be your père?" Sabine asked. "Just because you happen to take after the parent that was a Snow Maiden or a Snowman, doesn't mean you're not half Kelpie. I'm half Menehune. Haven't you done your genealogy test yet?"

"They took our blood samples back to Tír na nÓg two weeks ago, but the results haven't come back yet. Master Fù extended the final deadline again because we can't finish our projects without them. I hope he's not my father. He's awful," Abney replied.

"Why did he take over all the Literature classes anyway?" Lunetta jumped in.

"He told us Master Sjögren was indisposed, but they were at all their other classes that day," Abney said. "Maybe they had them teaching too many classes?"

"Maybe," Sümeyye agreed. "It's pretty weird though. I think we should find out more about him, just to be safe. There's that new art teacher that showed up around the same time too. What's his name? Master…Master… Master Ricci. I feel like he was brought in to boost morale though. Have you seen him?"

"No, but I thought you liked girls?" Abney cocked her head to the side.

"I find both males and females attractive," Sümeyye said matter-of-factly. "And he's gorgeous. He's one of those taller Woodland Elves with blueish-silver hair, brilliant lime green eyes, and that Italian accent. It gives me chills." The Pixie smiled devilishly. "I hope he's not your dad. Otherwise, this conversation could be weird later."

"Is she talking about the new art Master again?" Honali laughed as she walked in.

"It doesn't bother you?" Sabine verbally poked at Honali.

"Nah, I know who she loves," she said and kissed Sümeyye's hand. The Pixie blushed.

"Knock it off," Gus yelled from behind Honali. "Love is gross. You guys probably have cooties."

"Only boys have cooties." Sabine stuck her tongue out at the Grim Reaper. Abel, Zoey, and Domino arrived right behind Gus.

"So, what's the plan?" Abel jumped on one of the cots and sat cross-legged.

"Right now, we're waiting on Hatsuko," Sümeyye said. "She said she found a way to get us into the Arctic and back this evening. While we're waiting, I've been doing some research about Tarot cards since you guys met with Baba Yaga, and I think you may find it interesting." The others nodded she should continue. "I think the Wyvern Dragon is The Devil, not literally of course, but in Tarot, he represents greed. Dragons are known to hoard treasure. The Hanged Man must be Abney, as he represents sacrifice. And the Three of Swords must be She of the Glass Heart, though I can't tell you why. There's, like, no information on her at all."

"Well, thanks for the Tarot lecture, but how does this information help us?" Sabine questioned.

"It doesn't really. I just thought it was interesting," Sümeyye replied. Sabine groaned and shook her head.

"Does everyone have their winter gear, besides Abney and Gus, of course?" Zoey asked. "We should probably get ready. Hatsuko should be here any minute."

The teens pulled on snow pants, heavy boots, and coats that Hatsuko found in one of the storage closets. Abney and Gus wore just their regular clothes with snow boots. Gus was technically dead, and Abney was ice, so they wouldn't be affected like the others.

"Are you all ready?" Hatsuko's rich smoky voice snuck through the bars.

The teens jumped up. Time was of the essence, and they needed to hurry.

"Something feels off," Sabine whispered in Abney's ear as they followed the Rusalka out of the cell and out into the hall. "I think we should tell Beau or Wortlister."

"We promised to see this through, but as soon as we get back, I'm with you. We need to tell them," Abney whispered. She was feeling anxious about this adventure as well, but what choice did they have?

✦

They reconvened in the temple where a nervous looking priestess was waiting for them. Her hair was a curly mop of red, and her eyes blazed an unearthly blue. She kept looking around and jumping at every sound. "What took you so long?" she whispered loudly to Hatsuko.

"Calm down, Keeva. It takes a while to get this many Fae in here unnoticed," she replied. "Are you ready?"

"As I'm ever going to be," Keeva nodded reluctantly. "You'd all better stand back. Once the portal is open, you go through one at a time. I'll open it back up in two hours. Don't be late, or you won't be getting back." Keeva made a series of complicated hand gestures and spoke in a very harsh language; Abney thought it might have been German, but the accent wasn't quite right. Bright pink and purple lights circled out from her hands, leaving a giant black hole pulsing before them.

"One at a time," Keeva reminded them.

204

"Vive la Pete!" Honali shouted and jumped through first.

"Vive la Pete!" the others called after her. Abel ran up to go next.

"How is she doing this?" Abney asked Hatsuko. "I thought Fleetlings couldn't do real magic."

"Keeva is a Wizard, so she's only half Fleetling; she's also half Fae. Their powers are not as elementally-driven as a full-blooded Fae. There's a bit of chaos to them, and they aren't bound to the same rules we are. Therefore, things like portals and transport come a lot easier for them. She was quite the find." Hatsuko smiled.

Sümeyye stepped up and leapt through the portal.

"She doesn't seem thrilled to be helping us," Abney observed.

"Blackmail victims are usually not happy, last time I checked." Hatsuko shrugged.

"Blackmail?" Abney raised an eyebrow.

"Later, Miss Nosey. It's your turn to go through." Hatsuko gave Abney a push. "Let's not wear out our Wizard."

Abney was even less thrilled about this now, but she wasn't going to leave all her friends on the other side, so she walked up and stepped through. It was like stepping into Jell-O. She fought her way forward, toward the glaringly bright light. When she reached the other side, it was so white her eyes ached. Her friends were waiting with their arms wrapped around themselves as a defense from the cold and the wind. Hatsuko popped out behind Abney, and the portal closed with a loud pop.

Abel shouted to be heard above the wind and pointed to a large black spot in their alabaster surroundings. "There's a cave about one hundred feet that way. He's got to be in there!" The others only nodded. The wind was so strong it was stealing their breath as they marched toward the black hole.

Inside the cave, most of the teens and Hatsuko did their best to shake off the cold and catch their breath. Abney had to catch her breath from the wind, but she wasn't cold. Gus was completely fine and had no complaints.

"**Who goes there?**" a great shaky voice boomed.

"It's only me, Vern," Hatsuko's voice sang out. "I've brought you some visitors."

"Hatsuko?" he questioned and moved out where they could see him. Where Honali was more like a vibrant version of a Medieval Dragon, Vern was long and snake-like, more like a Chinese Dragon. His scales were pure white and shimmered like mother of pearl. He had ten legs on each side and moved in an s-shape. It gave Abney the chills. She hated things with too many legs. The max amount of legs in her mind was eight. Octopi, spiders were all okay, any more than eight legs—a big nope.

"It is you! What has it been? Three hundred years or so?"

"About that," the Rusalka agreed, "you always pick the most unpleasant places to stay. Makes visiting hard."

"I see you have brought me a good deal of company," he roared.

"Vern, you're scaring the kids." She laughed, looking at the wide-eyed Changelings. "Maybe a less intimidating form is in order?"

He laughed loudly and disappeared in a swirl of snowflakes. When he appeared again, he had the look of youth in his scaled skin, and his long white hair hung down past his waist like a cape. His irises were such a pale blue that they were almost invisible. He was breathtaking.

"Is this better?" He smiled at them with guile. Everyone swooned slightly except Hatsuko, who shook her head with amusement.

"In a fashion, I suppose it is," she said. "Though I think they'll be just as intimidated by your beauty."

"Well, I can only be one or the other." He shrugged.

"Don't you have something you want to ask him?" Hatsuko prompted.

"Oh, right." Honali shook herself. "We are looking for The Torch of the Wyvern Dragon, or I guess...your torch?"

Hatsuko looked at Abney and Sümeyye accusingly. "I thought you said this was about genealogy?"

"Errrr," Abney murmured. "Well—"

"We lied," Sümeyye jumped in. There was no real reason to hold the truth back at this point.

"Obviously." Hatsuko shook her head. "What do you want with blue fire?"

Honali inserted herself into the conversation. "We can't tell you... yet." Some information had to be given out at this point, but it wouldn't do to give the whole game away. The Rusalka looked at them suspiciously but relented. There wasn't anything she could do to make them tell her, and if she went to Dean Sadira, they'd bust her for taking them out of Avalon.

"You must tell me," Vern demanded. "Otherwise, why would I hand over something so valuable?"

The teens huddled up. If they told him, he might turn around and tell Hatsuko, and they weren't sure it was a good idea to tell her yet. On the other hand, they needed that torch.

Honali spoke for them. "We can't tell you, but if you help us, we are willing to offer you favors from each of us."

He considered this for a moment. "I live in a cave in the Arctic. What need have I for favors?" he asked them. No one had a good answer. "What I have need of is company. I'll tell you what; I will take a single favor from the Snow Maiden in exchange. Once you have completed school and undergone your Binding, you will come here to live as a companion for no less than one hundred years. It is lonely here, and you are the only one besides the Reaper who would do well in the cold. If you will do this, I will give you what you ask."

Everyone looked at Abney, expecting her to turn him down because they would have, but Honali stepped up before anyone could say anything.

"No." she declared. "One hundred years is a big payment for one torch. That's not a fair deal."

"The torch will burn forever, so I would say it's worth more than one hundred years," Vern asserted. "And one hundred years for a Fae is not that long."

"I'll do it!" Abney shouted as much to her surprise as to everyone else's. Honali grabbed her arm and pulled her aside.

"What are you doing?" she hissed through her teeth.

"We need that torch, right?" Abney asked in her normal voice.

"Of course we do, but not at that price," Honali said, still whispering.

"We have to be getting back. If we're going to make the portal, we don't have all day to negotiate," she replied. Then, in a lower voice, she said, "Not to mention we have seven and a half years to figure out how to get me out of it." Honali didn't look happy, but she nodded.

"I'll do it," Abney said loudly again.

"It's a bargain." Vern smiled viciously. "I'll be right back." He turned around and disappeared into the caves.

"I hope you know what you're doing." Hatsuko shook her head at them.

Abney sighed. "I hope so too."

It didn't take long for Vern to return with a torch that burned with a blue flame.

"I have to ask," Sümeyye said. "Is this *the* torch or just *a* torch?"

"It's just a torch." He smiled. "I can breathe fire whenever I want, so there can most definitely be more than one."

"I knew it." Sümeyye beamed.

"Now, Snow Maiden—" Vern started.

"My name is Abney. If I'm going to be here for one hundred years, you should at least know my name."

"Abney," he corrected himself. "I will expect you in eight years, right after your Binding Day. Remember: A Fae's word is their bond. You will have no choice but to honor our agreement."

Abney nodded glumly. She wasn't sure she'd live long enough to deliver on her end of the bargain, but he didn't need to know that.

"All right, my little Changelings," Hatsuko said, "time to go or we'll miss our portal. Vern, it's always a pleasure."

"Come back when you can stay longer," he encouraged his friend.

"Absolutely." She smiled, and they headed out of the cave into the blizzard. It was worse than before outside. The wind was so strong it was hard to keep themselves upright, and most of them struggled with the sub-zero temperature.

"Where's the portal?" Gus shouted.

"I can't see anything out here!" Honali shouted back.

Suddenly, a bright circle of green and yellow appeared before them. They assumed it was their portal home until they heard yelling on the other side and twenty warmly bundled humanoid figures burst through. There was shouting, and Abney and her friends found themselves surrounded. Abney and Gus thought they could smell humans, but the other's noses were so frozen they couldn't smell anything. Hatsuko stepped out in front of them protectively.

"Hatsuko, do you have the girl?" one of the figures asked.

"I do. Has Kringle accepted my deal?" she asked. The Changelings all looked at her stunned. She had betrayed them.

"He has," the figure spoke again. The voice was female, and it sounded familiar to Abney, but she couldn't place it.

"Then they're all yours." Hatsuko stepped aside and let the figures come at them. Honali transformed immediately and sent a warning shot of fire at the intruders.

"I wouldn't," Honali growled at them. A rope with two balls flew up and wrapped around Honali's mouth, slamming it shut. Then the onslaught began.

They tried to run, but it was too windy, and visibility was low. They were surrounded. Abel opened his arms to call on the Elements but ended up with a pair of iron shackles on his wrists. Abney could see smoke rising from his skin where the metal was touching him, and he was screaming. She tried to call on Air to increase the winds and provide them with more cover, but she was too frightened and couldn't concentrate. Iron shackles clamped over her wrists, and an involuntary scream ripped from her mouth. She had never felt such agony in her life. It didn't take long for them all to be captured, except for Gus, who had dropped his black robe and was hiding. His bones were indistinguishable from the snow.

Brilliant pink and purple lights broke through right next to the yellow and green, and Dean Sadira burst through with Wortlister and the other Hobgoblins close behind. Their captors seemed genuinely surprised. Wortlister was at a dead run for Abney. He jumped and landed a hard kick into the chest of the figure holding her, freeing Abney and sending her jailer flying backward.

"Run for the portal now!" he growled at her and dashed after another one of the marshmallow-like beings. Abney didn't hesitate. She ran for the colorful circle her rescuers had come through as fast as her legs would carry her in the snow. The handcuffs were weighing her down, and a bolt of electricity shot through her each time they slapped against her skin, but she pushed forward. She reached the portal, but before she could jump through, a body crashed into her, knocking her to the ground.

"Got you!" announced a muffled voice from the snowsuit. Abney gulped, trying to catch her breath.

"No, I have you!" Vern thundered onto the scene and swallowed her would-be kidnapper in one gulp. "Yuck, Fleetling!" he burped.

"They are human!" Abney exclaimed.

"There's no time for this!" Vern picked her up in one of his enormous hands and tossed her through the portal. Keeva was on the other side with sweat trickling down her face. Abney could see she was trying desperately to keep the gateway open.

"What the hell is going on over there?" she demanded. Abney threw her arms in the air and shook her head no. It was a mess, the whole thing was a horrible mess, she couldn't even compute the words to reply to Keeva. She was in shock. How had it all gone so horribly wrong?

✦

It took a while for Abney's friends and what was left of the rescue party to come back through. It took even longer for the elder Fae to get the offending restraints off the Changelings. Abney and her friends all had welts going up and down their arms, and the skin at their wrists looked melted. There were a great many injuries, but they captured Hatsuko, and the majority had made it back through to Avalon. Zoey and Sümeyye were not among those to return. Gus thought he'd seen them dragged through the other portal, but no one knew for certain what happened to them.

"What were you doing out of Avalon?" Dean Sadira screeched. They were in deep now and lying flat out or by omission wasn't an option anymore. So they sat down and relayed most of the story to Dean Sadira and their Hobgoblins.

"You should have told someone the minute you got a warning from a spirit," the Dean scolded them. "That was HAFWITS out there, and they are clearly still working with Kringle. To what end? Who knows? But this is very dangerous. Do you realize that your friends are likely already dead?" Abney hung her head. She was so worried about Sümeyye and Zoey that she was downright nauseous. The others looked equally as guilty.

"Luckily, they didn't get who they were after," Wortlister interjected and looked coldly at Abney. "Before we executed the Fleetlings who didn't make it through the portal, they admitted that they had been looking for one Fae in particular…a Snow Maiden."

Abney's mouth dropped open. "What do they want with me? The spirit never said anything about me." Abney vomited, and steam filled the room. She couldn't hold it in anymore; her friends were probably dead, and it was her fault. They'd been after her. The Hobgoblins looked annoyed, but Wortlister went to get a mop to clean up the mess. They had to deal with the smell until he got back.

"We don't know what they wanted, but you will most definitely not be finding out any time soon," Dean Sadira said. "From this point on, the lot of you will be segregated from the rest of the student population for *their* safety. I sent for a ship already, and Agatha of Oberon House has agreed to keep you all as safe as is possible at this point. Master Schimmelpfennig will accompany you and attend to your lessons."

"Can't we use the Traveler to get back?" Lunetta interrupted her, remembering the boat ride there being particularly unpleasant.

"No. Using the Traveler opens Avalon up to dangers from others who may try to enter while you leave. Which is why we didn't come here that way in the first place. You're lucky the Fates are only banning you until Kringle is found and not permanently. I highly recommend that you all stay out of trouble from here on out. The next step will be expulsion. That may seem pretty light sentence in your limited Fleetling experiences, but for Fae, it means death. If you cannot learn to control your magic, you are too dangerous to keep around and will face public execution."

All of the Changelings looked at their feet except Abel; he looked up and raised his hand. The Hobgoblins looked at him with disapproval, and Dean Sadira tried to ignore him, but he seemed oblivious and only waved his arm more urgently. Dean Sadira put her hand on the side of her face, shook her head, and relented. "Yes, Abel?"

"Ma'am, I just want to know how you found us? Not that I'm not totally grateful for the rescue, but how did you know to come for us?"

"When Keeva couldn't re-open the portal to let you all back through, she became worried and came to warn me. At great expense to herself, I might add. Wizards are not welcome among the priestesses of Avalon. She lost her position to save you." The Dean glared at him. "I then summoned your Hobgoblins, and we followed her to the temple. It took us a few minutes to figure out how Hatsuko was blocking her, but once we removed the wall, she opened the portal, and we were able to get through."

"Oh…" He shook his head.

Abney looked up in recognition. That's what Hatsuko had been blackmailing her with, and she had lost her place among the priestesses anyway to save them. If it was possible, Abney felt worse than she had before.

Honali's hand shot up. The Dean nodded for her to go ahead.

"What will happen to Hatsuko?" Honali asked.

"You will find out tomorrow before you leave," the Dean said. "Now, back to your cells. I don't want to hear the tiniest peep that makes me acknowledge your existence until you leave tomorrow. Am I clear?"

"Yes ma'am," they all agreed and hurried to comply.

CHAPTER 19

REBELS WITH A CAUSE

The whole of Avalon woke to the clang of bells, loud and relentless. Abney hadn't slept at all. She'd cried until she was sick and cried some more. Everything had gone wrong, and everything they were trying to prevent, was brought about by those same actions. She felt helpless and frustrated. How were they going to save Zoey and Sümeyye now?

"Get up," Wortlister commanded her, but Abney turned her back to him, determined to stay where she was so that she could continue wallowing. Wortlister was in a foul mood and not prone to putting up with attitudes on a good day. He jerked her up by her arm. "You will get up, Abney Kelly, to see this. You and your friends seem to think all of this is a game. It's time you had a reality check."

"You think I think this is a game?" she sobbed while holding her heart at bay. It had become increasingly easier to control her fire, even when she was distraught. It was as simple as compartmentalizing, and she did it almost as easily as breathing now. When her heart felt like it was going to explode, she would vent some of the fire off, which made steam pour from her nose, ears, mouth, and nether regions. At the moment, her cell looked like a Turkish bath. "Sümeyye and Zoey are probably gone forever, and it's my fault! I do not find this amusing or think it's a game."

Wortlister softened his look a little. "I'm sorry for your friends. It's a high price to pay, but you don't have a choice. You have to get up. This is mandatory for everyone." Abney nodded and asked him to leave so she could get dressed. Typically, she would have done this in the bathroom or one of the dressing tents outside, but since Domino and Dermott slept elsewhere last night due to all the steam, she was actually free to dress in the cell, after she tied a blanket to the bars for privacy of course.

The gardens were full of students, Hobgoblins, Masters, priestesses, even the Fates, both young and old, were there. A raised gazebo had been erected and was viewable from every angle in the garden. Abney wondered if they were to be shamed in front of all their peers before the daunting trip back to Tír na nÓg. She tensed a little at the thought.

A resounding gasp came from the other side of the garden, Abney and those near her all stood on tiptoe trying to see. Then the Faerie Queens came into view—Titania in a stunning strapless green summer dress and Mab in a pastel-blue romper. Neither woman looked happy to be there; in fact, Abney could feel their cold fury from twenty yards away. Not a single soul dared to speak.

Titania commanded their attention. "Fae and citizens of Avalon, yesterday our community fell prey to a terrorist who traded two of our Changelings, your classmates, wards, and friends to the known murderer, Nicholas Kringle, in order to undermine the authority of our rule. The War of the Realms was over three hundred and fifty years ago, yet some insist on carrying on as if there are still battles to be fought. Bring the prisoner forward."

Two guards in heavy armor escorted the frightened yet defiant looking Hatsuko to stand before the Faerie monarchs. Her legs were trembling visibly, but her gaze was angry and hateful. The guards forced her to her knees and pushed her head down. The Queens glared at her, Titania in distaste and Mab in amusement.

"Tell me, Hatsuko"—Mab lifted her chin—"what have you to say for yourself?"

"I have nothing to say to you," Hatsuko hissed venomously. "Rebels!" she shouted to the crowd. "Goblins! Never give up, never surrender. We are not slaves or servants! We are goblins! Not hobbled goblins! Not Hobgoblins!" Her voice started to give out. "We belong to no one but ourselves! We have no Queens!" At that last statement, Titania brought up her hand, and Hatsuko's voice disappeared.

"Bring forward the coffin and the Evermore," Mab commanded. Muffled cries of shock shook through the horrified audience.

"Wortlister," Abney whispered, "what's an Evermore?"

"It is fruit from The Tree of Life," he whispered. "It is often used to allow Fleetling's to live here when one catches the eye of the Queens. It takes away all need to eat, drink, sleep, use the restroom, and effectively stops them from aging, as long as they eat it every seven days."

"Why would they give her the Evermore? She'll already live forever on her own," Abney asked.

"It doesn't affect magical beings the same way. When Hatsuko eats the fruit, it will pull her into fevered nightmares. All of her magic will drain from her over the next seven days. When she wakes, she will be trapped, powerless, but still immortal. She will slowly sink into madness as time marches endlessly on," he told her. "It's a fate worse than death."

Abney watched with new terror, now that she understood what was going on. The coffin was laid down at the feet of the Queens. Hatsuko's fear was more apparent now than it had been. There was no more anger, only dread. Mab leaned forward and whispered in the Rusalka's ear, and all of her emotion melted away. She moved like a puppet on a string, walking to kneel before the red-headed queen who was holding a purple and silver heart-shaped fruit. Queen Mab held it out to her, and Hatsuko ate it from her hands, pink juices dripping down her face. She looked like a repentant sinner receiving communion. Abney's stomach turned.

"What did Queen Mab say to make her like that?" Abney whispered to the Puca.

"She invoked her true name," he said. "And now you know what it means to be a subject of the Faerie Queens. Whichever court you choose, whichever lady you follow, they will have your name. You are powerless when commanded with it, which is why you will never give it out, ever, to anyone besides the lady who gave it to you. You can follow orders happily, or they will make you. This Faerie life offers a lot, but there is a price. There is always a price."

Hatsuko stood, her face still wet and dribbling leftover juice, and then lay down in the coffin. Titania closed the lid, looking pleased with what they had done. Everyone remained silent, afraid to move or draw attention to themselves. Abney scarcely dared to breathe.

"Take this as a warning." Titania's face darkened again as she looked over her subjects.

"We will not tolerate rebellion. Aiding Kringle in any way will land you with the same fate as the Hobgoblin in this coffin," Mab announced. "Now, back to your classes or whatever else you're supposed to be doing."

Abney and Wortlister turned solemnly to go back down to her cell. "Where are they taking the coffin?" she asked.

"Into the Veil, to the Graveyard of the Undying," he said hoarsely. "Believe me when I say that is all you ever want to know about it."

The ship was quiet. Abney and her friends had belowdecks all to themselves, but Captain Eliza forbade them from going up on deck until they reached Tír na nÓg. There was not much said between them as the journey progressed. At least this time, they had brought plenty of mint leaves, which were very effective against the motion sickness. To pass the time, they had taken down the hammocks and used the pillows to make a fortress that was surprisingly very comfortable.

Honali was understandably devastated; Kringle had her girlfriend, but Domino was inconsolable. He told them it was like half his soul was missing. He didn't seem to know how to function without his sister. The others were also realizing how much they had come to rely on both of the girls. Zoey was like the mother of their little group. She comforted them when they were sad, gave good advice whether or not they needed it, and always made sure they remembered what they were supposed to. Sümeyye was a bit of a know-it-all, but in a very humble way, and she was unfailingly kind. She always made sure their plans were as sound as possible and that there were no holes in the data. No one could have predicted that Hatsuko would turn on her though.

"I've never heard of The War of the Realms," Gus said, looking at his friends who were all lying lazily in a circle.

"Me either," Lunetta said. "I tried writing it in my book, but nothing came up."

Arjun, Honali's Hobgoblin, ducked into their fort. "It won't be in any surviving book."

Blythe followed him in. "I don't think now is the time."

"Why not?" Wortlister challenged from behind Abney. He had hardly left her side since the Arctic Incident. "After what they just saw, they're bound to have questions."

Beau, Sabine's Hobgoblin, joined in. "I agree with Io...Wortlister." Soon, all of the Hobgoblins were crammed into the fort with their wards.

"Where's Algernon?" Mary-Lou, Gus's Hobgoblin, asked. "He won't approve of this conversation."

"He's lecturing Captain Eliza on the finer points of sailing," Arjun said. "They'll be bickering for hours."

Blythe finally nodded in agreement. "Let Wilbur tell it then. He's the storyteller."

"I'm not up to it," Wilbur objected.

"I'll tell it," Wortlister said. "Unless someone else wants to?" No one else volunteered.

"It wasn't so very long ago," he began, "goblins were free. We were not under the rule of the Faerie Queens. We had our own realm, called Ra Sor Gadradon, our own laws, and system of governance. We had no true names and, therefore, could not be controlled. Despite this, the realms of Faerie and Goblin existed side by side with little or no conflict. That is, until the day Queen Titania's son, Prince Sabra, fell in love with Regina Zarita, wife of Reignor Jasper. A Reignor is like the Goblin version of a president.

"Needless to say, a good deal of drama ensued. Regina Zarita left her husband for the prince, but the Queens would only let her stay in Tír na nÓg if she agreed to be named. To be with her love, she relented and was the first Goblin to receive a true name. Being named is against the very nature of a Goblin, and the whole of Ra Sor Gadradon was enraged.

"Goblins and Faeries hurled insults at each other, skirmishes began, and soon a full-blown war followed. It lasted for twenty-five years. The Fae won. The Faerie Queens destroyed our cities, monuments, and literature. We were enslaved, given names, and given the jobs the Fae did not care for, which included captaining the ferries between realms and, of course, guarding their young. They also stripped us of the title of Goblin. They re-named us Hobgoblins so that we would always remember they hobbled us, and we no longer belonged to that once proud race of Goblin. We are but a sad remnant, shadows of something they erased."

"Well that explains a lot," Abel said. Everyone sat quietly. Abney had known taking care of the Changelings was a much-resented task, but she had never thought that Wortlister was a slave. Abel was right. It did explain a lot. It explained why Wortlister slept in a closet, why Hobgoblins had such prickly personalities, why they did not attend schools in Tír na nÓg, and made sense of the conversation she had overheard while hiding in the hallway closet in Avalon.

"Why isn't it in our books?" Abney asked.

"The Queens don't like the way it reads. No matter how you put it, enslaving an entire race and destroying their home sounds bad. They just pretend it has always been this way, and no one likes to disagree with them—for obvious reasons," Wilbur replied.

No one spoke; what could they say? Sorry our people destroyed and enslaved your people, and now you have to take care of us whether you like it or not? How do you apologize for something you didn't do, but feel somehow responsible for?

"It's not any of your faults." Blythe read their faces. "It is what it is. There is nothing that can be said."

"Hatsuko seemed to blame us," Honali said.

"She didn't. She just valued her freedom more," Arjun replied. "There isn't much most of us wouldn't give for our freedom, but I can confidently say, most of us draw the line at exchanging children for it."

"Yes, she is the exception," Blythe agreed, "not the rule."

The next two days went by at a snail's pace. Everyone was quiet, withdrawn, and lost in their own thoughts. So much had happened, and Tír na nÓg wasn't the safest place to be, but their own actions had gotten them booted from Avalon. No one was thrilled about it, but they understood why they were considered a danger to the other students.

Agatha was waiting for them with a bubble bus when they docked. She didn't look impressed.

CHAPTER 20

HOME AGAIN, HOME AGAIN

"**W**ell, aren't you a sorry bunch of screw-ups?" Agatha's phlegmy voice lectured them on the way back to the house. "One safe haven in all the realms and you managed to get yourselves thrown out. Not the brightest bulbs in the box, are you?"

"Man, we already know we screwed up, lady," Abel complained. Everyone else hung their heads.

"And Gods willing, you'll hear it from every shmuck from here to Timbuktu. That way the information may eventually force itself into your thick skulls." Agatha shook her whiskered chin at them in disapproval.

Abel continued the argument, not realizing it was futile. "I'm telling you, man, we get it."

"Shut up!" Lunetta slapped the back of Abel's head. "You're making it worse."

"Ow, I'm just trying to defend myself, a'ight? Jeeze." He rubbed the back of his head like it hurt.

Agatha zinged him again. "Why don't you try to defend yourself from your own stupidity? Then we'll be getting somewhere."

"Ouch!" Gus laughed.

Algernon put his foot down. "That's enough. None of this is amusing. And I doubt any of you will be laughing when Kringle comes for you."

No one laughed or made a peep after that. What could they say? They'd readily signed their own death warrants and put everyone who was on the bus with them in danger. It wasn't a pleasant thought.

When they reached Oberon House, Feo was waiting for them at the door. She looked more concerned than anything and was the first and only being to offer them any sympathy in the whole situation.

"Oh, you poor dears!" she exclaimed and hugged each of them as they walked through the door. "I've made some hot lavender tea. It's waiting for you in The Ocean Room. Abney and Domino will show you where that is. Hobgoblins and Algernon, why don't you follow me, and I'll get everyone all settled in."

Abney nodded and took the lead. The tree they'd decorated was still up, an inferno was churning in the fireplace, and she could see a steaming kettle surrounded by cups waiting for them. Abney picked up the pot and poured the tea, handing the cups out to her friends before she sat and took one for herself. Grief was working its way through them. Shock and denial flooded over them like a raging storm, followed by anger, so much anger that it was pouring from them into every nook and cranny in the room. Not even Feo's tea could calm the tension.

"We should be doing something!" Domino slammed his cup down and spilled his tea.

"What? What are we supposed to do?" Honali exploded back. "Don't you think I'd be out there to get Sümeyye if I even knew where to begin to look?"

"So what?" Domino argued. "Do we let them die and sit here like stool pigeons waiting for Kringle to pick us off?"

Sabine put her two cents in. "We wouldn't even be in this predicament if anyone had listened to me."

"Just what everyone needs right now, another I-told-you-so from princess perfect," Lunetta replied crossly.

"Everyone just needs to cool it." Abel put himself between them.

The bickering parties turned on him. "Shut up!" Abel sat down.

This time, Lunetta interjected. She'd calmed down enough to be semi-reasonable. "Come on, you guys. Fighting with each other won't bring them back."

"At least it makes me feel like I'm fighting something," Domino huffed and stormed out of the room. Gus stood to go after him, but Sabine grabbed his hand and shook her head.

"Let him go," she counseled. "He needs some time alone."

"He's right. We should be doing something," Abney said with steam rolling out of her.

"What can we do though?" Honali almost sobbed. "We don't even have the torch anymore."

"That's not entirely true," Gus offered, pulling an unlit torch from his sleeve. "I snagged it from Dean Sadira's office as we were being escorted out."

Sabine pointed out the obvious. "It's not lit though."

"He said it would burn forever," Gus said. "So, there must be a way to re-light it."

"How though?" Sabine pushed.

"I don't know!" Gus shrugged with annoyance.

"Well, that's super helpful," Sabine snapped.

Feo came in just in time to save them from a serious row. "I think it's time for everyone to have a rest. Abney, why don't you head up to your room, take Mr. Gus with you. He can stay in Namid's room for now. The rest of you follow me."

✦

Abney woke in her room. It was pitch black. She ran her hands over the soft velvety texture of her blanket that she hadn't realized she'd missed. The familiar smell of cinnamon and cloves caught her attention, and she smiled. It was so lovely to have her own room again. Then she remembered Zoey and Sümeyye. Steam gushed out of her suddenly, and she got up to get dressed.

She pulled on some comfy wide leg pants and a baggy shirt to head downstairs. The rest of the house seemed to be asleep. Abney walked into the kitchen and put the kettle on to brew some of Feo's special sleepy-time tea. She needed to sleep more, she knew she did, but her mind was racing a million miles an hour.

"Hello, Ms. Kelly," Algernon said as he entered the kitchen. Abney startled and almost dropped the full kettle but caught her balance in time.

"Errr…hello…sir," Abney greeted him.

"Algernon, if you please. Master and sir don't sit well with me," he said almost like it was a recording. Abney realized he must make the request a lot.

She gave him a half-smile, put the kettle on the burner, and started looking for the tea.

"Algernon, would you like a cup? Feodora has a killer sleepy time tea here somewhere."

"Sure, why not?" The hint of agitation that always seemed to linger in his voice was gone. Abney had to climb on the counter to find the tea she was looking for but eventually found it and made a cup for herself and one for the Kelpie.

"Have a seat," he instructed her. "The night is sometimes too long, isn't it? There's too much to think about." Abney nodded and sat at the table. She wasn't exactly comfortable with it, but she didn't think she had the option to refuse.

"Why did you think you and your friends could take on Kringle alone?"

"It wasn't about taking him on alone. It was about saving our friend. We found out she was in danger from the Ouija Board, which we weren't supposed to have, so we tried to fix it ourselves."

"You know, the amount of trouble you would have been in for the Ouija Board would have been considerably less than the trouble you're in now," he said. "And with the help of the elder Fae, your friends might still be with us."

Abney became defensive. "Well, we didn't, and they're not."

"I'm not getting on your case, so please, calm down. Mistakes are how we learn. You learned a tough lesson. Don't waste it or begrudge yourself the knowledge gained."

"Whatever." Abney sighed and took another drink of her tea. He smiled despite her attitude. Kelpie smiles were unsightly at best, and Abney shivered a little at the grin.

"You remind me so much of your mother," he said dreamily. That got her attention.

"Who are—" Abney started.

"*And when they've caressed me, as oft times before, I will never play the wild rover no more, and it's no, nay, never, no, nay, never, no more!*" A slurring Irish accent sang out loudly.

Wortlister burst into the room. "Abney! Dongle Muffin! I was worried when you weren't in bed young lady. You wee devil, you. *No, nay, never, no mooore. Will I play the wild rover, no never, no more.*"

"Are you drunk?" Abney asked.

Wortlister denied his condition. "No. No, I'm just grand. Thanks for asking." He made pistol fingers at her and winked.

"You're plowed," Abney asserted.

"Am not." He hiccupped.

"You couldn't walk a straight line if I drew it for you," Abney bantered, enjoying herself just a little.

"Shhhh," Wortlister said. "Your lips are blinking at me."

"Bedtime, Ms. Kelly." Algernon practically pushed her out of the kitchen. "I will take care of this."

"But, my mother..." she protested.

"Later," Algernon said finally. "Now, go."

Abney couldn't wait for the next morning. She ran to the Arthurian Wing and threw open Honali's door. Honali sat bolt upright, smoke pouring from her nostrils. Abney had startled her.

Abney ran in without apologizing. "He said he knew my mother. He said he knew my mother. It has to be him. He has to be my father, and we're all in danger."

"Whoa, whoa, calm down." Honali held her hands up. "What happened?"

"I was making tea, and Algernon came into the kitchen, so I made him a cup too." Abney was speaking at a million miles an hour. "Then he was all valuable lessons, blah, blah, blah. P.S. you remind me of your mother!"

"Did you ask what he meant?" Honali asked. "What else did he say?"

"Nothing. Wortlister stumbled in drunk as a skunk, and our conversation ended. Algernon scooted me out of the kitchen so he could deal with it."

Honali gawked. "Wortlister was drunk?"

"I was shocked. I just never pictured him doing anything fun." Abney smiled a little, thinking of it. "And he was singing."

"I wish I would have been awake to see that," Honali replied enviously. "What are we going to do about Algernon though? After what the Future Fate said, we can't take this lightly. He knows you, but you didn't know who he was. It has to be him."

"I don't know, but we're not safe," Abney said.

Honali made a plan. "You go grab Gus and Lunetta. I'll go get Domino, Sabine, and Abel. We'll meet in your room. Domino knows how to get there right? This house is a freaking maze." Abney nodded that he did, and they parted ways.

It took around a half hour for everyone to find their way to Abney's room. They looked tired and like they'd much rather be sleeping, but they sat patiently and listened as Abney relayed what had just happened in the kitchen and then reminded them of her conversation with Akira. Algernon had to be her father; they weren't safe with him around and needed to do something.

"This is wonderfully discouraging and all, but what are we supposed to do now?" Sabine asked. "Do we run? I don't think the Hobgoblins or your House Matron are going to listen to us after all the *manigances* we've gotten up to. And we'd run the risk of them letting him know that we know, which seems to be the only card in our deck right now." The group considered that for a moment.

"We're going to finish what we started," Abney said with sudden clarity. "It's the only thing we can do, the only thing that may get us out of this mess."

"How are we going to do that?" Abel asked. "We're still missing the piece of that broken girl's heart, and the torch has gone out. I'm not going back to the Arctic. The only thing we do have is the rope from Time's forest, oh and you, Abney, as long as we're willing to sacrifice you. I don't know about y'all, but I've lost enough friends this year."

"If we do nothing, we'll probably all die anyway," Lunetta said. "I'm for doing something, anything, just so we're not sitting here waiting."

"Let's take a vote," Honali suggested. "All for continuing our quest, say aye."

"Aye," Abney spoke up. Lunetta, Gus, Honali, and Domino agreed.

"Nays?" Honali asked as a matter of order.

"Nay," Sabine and Abel said glumly.

"The ayes have it. Motion to continue quest carries. Now we need a plan," Honali continued, in keeping with the rules of order.

"Gus, do you still have that Ouija Board?" Sabine asked, resigned.

Gus nodded. "Yeah, it's in my bag."

"Go get it," Sabine commanded. "We can't be in any more trouble than we're already in. That spirit started this. You're going to drag it back here. We have some questions that need to be answered, and this time we're not settling for anything but direct answers. You're going to trap it here until we get everything we need."

"It doesn't work—" Gus protested.

"I don't care; you'll figure it out." Sabine gave him a cold stare. "Go get it!" Sabine was intimidating when she was cross, and no one contradicted her or spoke until Gus came back with the board.

Gus got the board ready and banged his scythe three times loudly. He looked worriedly at things the rest of them couldn't see. "The spirit we want hasn't come through. Give me a minute," he said and disappeared into thin air. They all starred after him. He'd been gone a few minutes when they began to worry.

"Do you think he meant to disappear like that?" Abel asked.

"God, if we lose someone else right now, they're definitely going to lock us in coffins with Hatsuko," Lunetta said.

"What if we can't trust this spirit?" Abel asked. "It might be lying."

"I don't think so," Honali said. "Remember Shion said the Wraith would point us in the right direction."

"What if it's not this spirit? And aren't Wraiths and spirits different? We could be talking to the wrong ghost all together." he persisted.

"It's a chance we're going to have to take. Plus, we haven't been talking to any other spirits, have we? It's the most logical conclusion," Sabine cut in.

Gus reappeared just as suddenly as he left.

"I've got her," he said. "We've met before, so, we can dispense with the pleasantries. Dragging a spirit through is different than them coming through of their own accord. We won't have much time before one of the underworld guardians comes looking. Be quick. Ask your questions. She isn't happy about being here, but I won't let her go."

"First, you're going to tell us exactly who you are," Sabine demanded. The planchette was still for a few moments, and then it began to spell.

ISODANELLI

"Like, the Isodanelli from *Silent Bells are Ringing?*" Lunetta jumped in. The planchette jerked their arms over to **YES**. Everyone paused for a moment. That's why she'd come through in the first place; she was still trying to stop Kringle, even after her death.

"Are Sümeyye and Zoey still alive?" Honali asked. Everyone's hearts were in their throats, Abney noticed they were all holding their breath. The planchette remained on **YES**. Tears of relief streamed down Honali's face, and Abney felt a weight lift from her chest. There was still time.

"Well, you sent us down this path," Sabine accused the spirit. "Tell us where we can find She of the Glass Heart."

MISTMARROWCASTLE

"Crap," Gus said. "That's here in Tír na nÓg, right on the border between the Seelie and Unseelie Courts. There will be guards from both sides. All treasures that belong to the Fae as a whole are kept there so that no one faction has control of them. It's pretty much the Fae Fort Knox."

"One problem at a time," Sabine said, taking in the information. "How do we re-light the torch from the Wyvern dragon?"

HANDITTOTHESNOWMAIDEN

"Really?" Gus asked. "That's it?"

The planchette dove down to **YES**.

"Where's the torch?" Lunetta asked Gus.

"In my room," he replied. "But I have to stay here, or she'll bolt."

"I'll go get it," Lunetta volunteered. "Where in your room?"

"On the vanity," he said, and Lunetta ran out to grab it.

"Are you the Wraith?" Abney asked, "The one Shion told me about?" The planchette stayed at **YES**. Abney realized that the spirit could easily be lying, but she felt better anyway, and the others seemed to be breathing their own sighs of relief.

"Lastly," Sabine said, "where can we find Kringle?"

HEWILLFINDYOU

"So, he'll bring the fight to us then," Abney said. "At least that's one thing we don't have to hunt down. We're going to have to go straight up *Home Alone* on Oberon House though. I can't imagine Agatha will be happy."

"I got it." Lunetta rushed back into the room, torch in hand. She handed it to Abney, but nothing happened. Abney looked at it for a second. She was of ice and fire, just like Vern. There had to be a way for her to make it work.

"*Flawix.*" Abney invoked the name of snow and concentrated on moving the fire from her heart up her throat and out of her mouth. The fire came out blue, just like Vern's. Abney was proud of herself. She re-lit the torch, and she hadn't burned her throat or anyone else. It was a triumph! She needed that at the moment.

Sabine nodded in approval. "There's one thing taken care of."

Abney walked over to her fireplace and placed the torch in the grate. It should be safe there, for now.

"Are we done with Isodanelli?" Gus asked. "I'd rather get her back before something unpleasant comes to fetch her."

"Thank you for helping us," Honali said before Gus let her go. The lights flickered, and for a moment they could all see the ghost of a girl with a hole in her chest. She nodded at them briefly and then disappeared. Gus closed the Veil, and the group stared after her for a few minutes before anyone moved or spoke.

"We're going to need help," Abney said. "As soon as Wortlister sobers up, I'll talk to him. If we can convince him, he'll convince the others. We just have to make sure Algernon doesn't find out. If we're right about him, he means me harm, which can't be good for the rest of you either."

"If he won't agree," Honali said, "remind him he owes me a favor, then tell him I'm calling it in." They all nodded. Algernon was right about one thing. They needed to learn from their mistakes. They wouldn't bumble into this alone. This time, they would have help.

"Vive la Pete," Sabine said seriously.

"Vive la Pete," they all agreed somberly.

CHAPTER 21

THE NYXMADRA

"**W**hy is it that just when I think you can't do anything stupider, you seem to up the ante?" Wortlister moaned into his coffee.

Abney pleaded her case. "Do you really want to sit here and wait for Kringle to find us? We have to do something,"

"Did you completely block out the part where Dean Sadira threatened you with expulsion, which will lead directly to public execution?" He covered his head with his hands.

"Sitting here and doing nothing is a death sentence too," she argued. Wortlister sighed and gulped down the remainder of his coffee.

"I'm dying. I can't talk to you about this right now." Wortlister had still not recovered from his performance the night before.

"Wortlister, I need you to put your big boy pants on and listen to me. We know Kringle sent HAFWITS after me in the Arctic. We know he'll come again. I don't want to sit here and wait to die. Let's go down swinging." She looked at him thoughtfully.

"You're just a kid. You don't understand what it is to go down swinging," he said miserably. "You think you're invincible, but you're not, and this is incredibly dangerous. You're risking the lives of everyone who lives here, not just your own. Can you live with yourself if you get everyone killed?"

Abney thought about it for a minute and then looked him square in the eyes. "I can live with it if it means we fought. What I couldn't live with is if he shows up here and kills everyone and we didn't fight or try to save ourselves. I don't want to be a sitting duck."

"No," he said. "Now that's the end of it."

"I'm sorry you feel that way," Abney said as she prepared to pull out the big guns. "I wanted to do this the nice way, but you left me no choice." Wortlister scoffed. "Honali said to remind you that you owe her a favor. She's calling it in."

He glared at her with his mouth open. "This is a suicide mission!" he complained. "I will talk to the others, but I can't guarantee everyone's going to be willing to help or that they won't sell you up the river once they hear what you're planning."

"Not Algernon," Abney sad quickly. "You can't tell him anything. Everyone else is fine."

"I wasn't planning on including old sourpuss, but out of curiosity, why not?"

"I ran into Akira, the young Future Fate, in the gardens in Avalon. She told me to be wary of a male that recently came into my life. She said that he was my father, and he meant me harm. Algernon and that art teacher were the only ones who were male and new around that point in time. And then, last night, before your lovely serenade, he told me he knew my mother. It has to be him."

"Recent is a broad term, especially in Faespeak. Is that the exact terminology she used?"

"Yes, that's exactly what she said," Abney replied. "But who else would it be? He said he knew my mother."

"Well, I'm sure your mother knew more than one Fae, but I see your point. We'll leave him out for now," Wortlister agreed reluctantly. "Feo is bringing me a tonic for my headache. As soon as it kicks in, I'll go speak to the others. Do *not* do anything until then. Do you understand?" Abney nodded.

"No, I need you to say you understand," he demanded. "That way, if you go gallivanting off without me, I won't feel bad when you end up dead, either because Kringle got you or because I strangled you myself."

"Yes, I understand," she said loudly and with great exaggeration.

A few hours later, the Hobgoblins and Changelings gathered in Abney's room. It seemed everyone was agreeable to do something, though they hadn't quite figured out what that something would be. The teens told the Hobgoblins almost everything they knew and what still needed to happen. They decided to leave out the part about Abney possibly dying when she blew herself up to kill Kringle and the part where she had agreed to move to the Arctic for one hundred years after she finished with school. They would cross that bridge when they got there.

"Mist Marrow Castle is impossible to get into," Wilbur said, shaking his head. "Both Unseelie and Seelie guard it. It has shields preventing us from just flying in. Walking in would require badges and security clearance, and we don't have that kind of time. Moreover, I don't even know where they would keep a prisoner in there. I thought it was for magical artifacts only? I think it's a bad idea to blindly trust this spirit, especially when it's sending us all into certain death."

"Shion said it would point us in the right direction, and you already said you were in. Stop complaining. What we need is a plan," Abney said, taking charge. There was no room for doubters at the moment.

"I might have an idea," Wortlister volunteered with a grimace, "but it's going to cost." Someone knocked on the door. The whole room went silent with anticipation.

"Who is it?" Abney called out.

"Algernon."

"Coming," Abney ran to the door and composed herself before she opened it just a crack so that the others remained hidden.

"I thought we might continue our discussion," he told her.

"I'm sorry," she said, feigning illness. "I'm not feeling very well. Can we do it later?" Algernon squinted. Abney could tell he didn't believe her.

"All right, later then," he said and turned to leave.

"Sounds good," Abney agreed.

"Give the gang my regards," he said over his shoulder.

Abney flinched and watched him walk away in uncomfortable silence. "He knows something is up." Abney shut the door and returned to her spot on her bed.

"But he doesn't know what it is yet," Honali said hopefully. "We'll need to be more careful."

"Well, what's this plan of yours?" Blythe asked Wortlister.

"We could call Penelope," he said weakly. A chorus of nos and negative sentiments followed from the Hobgoblins. Wortlister covered his eyes and waited for them to quiet down. "Who has a better idea then?" There was complete silence. Abel raised his hand. "Yes?" Wortlister glared at him.

"Who's Penelope?" Abel asked.

"Trouble," his Hobgoblin, Luke, answered.

"Are there any better ideas?" Wortlister asked again. Everyone shook their heads. "I didn't think so. Wilbur, are you still in contact with Bash?" Wilbur nodded uncomfortably. "Get a hold of him and tell him we need to speak with Penelope."

✳

Before she even entered the room, everyone could smell her. Her odor was like earth and wind, danger and adventure. They could have heard a pin drop in the Ocean Room as the group waited for her to join them. The first thing the group saw was a patchwork newsboy cap as she rounded the corner. Then her head turned up to reveal jade colored fur, a shrewd ferret-like face, and a snout like a pig. Her eyes were bright and golden like sunlight. She snaked into the den fluidly and with great alertness. She stopped in front of Wortlister and wrapped her tail around her legs in a very cat-like fashion.

"Penelope." Wortlister tried to smile, but it looked painful.

"It's been too long," she said. "What name are you going by these days?"

"Taticus." He changed his name again. Abney sighed—she wished he'd pick a name and settle on it.

"I—" Blythe cut in, looking annoyed.

"Taticus," he corrected her before she could give him away.

"Now is not the time for your silly code names," Blythe glared.

"You're starting to sound like Algernon. We should all probably have code names since we're going on a mission," Taticus replied. Abney could see he was very excited by the idea of code names for everyone.

"If you don't mind"—Penelope slithered in between the two Pucas—"can you tell me what the mission is before I commit to a *nom de plume?*"

"Fair enough," Taticus agreed. "But if you join us, I'm going to call you Snoozle."

"Well, now that I know what I'm getting into"—she batted her eyelashes at him—"tell me the rest."

Taticus invited their guest to sit and explained only the part about needing to break out a friend who had, through no fault of her own, ended up imprisoned at Mist Marrow. He also suggested that while they were freeing their friend, Penelope and her crew might be able to liberate a few Fae treasures as their payment. Abney now realized how steep the price was and that, if caught, they were, without a doubt, going to end up entombed next to Hatsuko.

"This is a dangerous business." Penelope smiled, clearly thrilled by the prospect. "I will review it with the rest of the family. Expect my answer in the morning." She tipped her hat to them and made her exit. The Hobgoblins all looked wary, but the Changelings were feeling invigorated. Things were in motion. Their plans were coming to fruition, and that was both exhilarating and terrifying.

"What kind of Fae is she?" Honali asked after Penelope had exited.

"She is not Fae," Arjun replied. "She is Ramidreju."

"What's that?" Abel asked.

"They're mountain-dwelling creatures with a society of their own. They do not have true names and have no allegiance to anyone but themselves. They like shiny things, treasure, anything that has great value," Taticus informed them. "They run in families, kind of like the Fleetling mobs. Penelope's family is called Nyxmadra. They are the greatest thieves in all of the realms, which is why we need them."

"I've read something about them," Lunetta said. "Aren't their pelts considered some sort of magical cure-all?"

"In Fleetling mythology, yes," Chasha, Lunetta's Hobgoblin, replied. "And the Fleetlings nearly hunted them to extinction around seven hundred years ago. Unfortunately, their pelts have no magical properties. So, the sick Fleetlings remained ill, and all of those Ramidreju lives were lost for no reason at all."

Lunetta shook her head. "You all have no grasp on this happily-ever-after stuff, do you?"

"Until Disney came along, there were no happy fairy tales," Taticus told them. "Read the real *Grimms' Fairy Tales*; they're gruesome, just like real life. There's no such thing as happily ever after. It's more like, holy crap, somehow I survived."

"My, you're cynical today," Abney said with a sly grin.

"Give it a few hundred years, and you will be too," he said knowingly.

✦

The reply came early the next morning attached to something that strongly resembled a bottle rocket that exploded in the entryway into a purple and fiery

YES!

It held shape for almost five minutes before fizzling out and turning to ashes by the door. Algernon had been incensed and demanded to know what was going on. Agatha claimed it was the darn Pixies two stalagmites over, which seemed to satisfy the Kelpie, but then she winked at Abney. It hadn't occurred to her that Taticus would have told Agatha, but it made sense. She had sent Algernon on an errand just before Penelope arrived, and they would need her help if they were going to have a showdown with Kringle in her house.

Algernon sat the Changelings down for lessons later that morning, which lasted for several hours. It mostly consisted of him delegating reading assignments and telling them to be quiet. They could hardly sit still or concentrate, so Algernon let them go, after telling them they were the laziest doomed students he had ever encountered.

Taticus and the other Hobgoblins were waiting to take them to LSOM, where they would be meeting the Nyxmadra Family. The air was the usual amount of muggy and cool at the same time, and they could smell the fried blossoms from the vendor two streets over. Walking outside was nice. They were supposed to be under house arrest, but Agatha argued it was good for their mental well-being, and they would be going out in a large group, so where was the harm?

Pernella bowled over one of her waitresses to get to them. "You're alive!" she shouted and hugged each and every one of them, Hobgoblins included. "I never thought any Fae would say this, but I missed you kids."

"Puh." Honali smiled. "You missed the cheap labor."

Pernella gave her a light tap on her face. "The cheek on you," she laughed. "Go have a seat, the Nyxmadra have prepaid, so order whatever you want."

"A round of Mulled Slithy Tove Brews then, my good lady." Gus bowed theatrically and brushed his teeth against her hand. It was as close to a kiss as he could get.

"Oh, get on with you. I'll bring you my new special with the brews. I think you'll get a kick out of it." She herded them to a private room just off the kitchen. It had a large round table with plenty of chairs. The Nyxmadra family and a badly scarred Dwarf were waiting for them.

Penelope stood to greet them. "Welcome friends. I'd like to introduce my sister, Lavinia, brothers, Silvanus and Bash, my cousin Boris, and my parents, Rosella and Manfri. The Dwarf is a close associate by the name of Keme. You'll have to forgive his silence. You see, he had his voice box removed as part of a ritual to sever him from his true name. He is probably the only free Fae alive today. Have a seat." They all stared at him, impressed. He simply nodded and glared back. "Family and Keme, this is the group I was telling you about, the ones who are going to help us become the most famous thieves of all time."

The meeting began. Bash brought a set of old blueprints from when they'd first erected the castle. There had been many additions and subtractions over the years, and they were going to need a better idea of what it looked like now. Fortunately, the Hobgoblins already had a plan for getting the inside scoop. There was an Unseelie guard who was very smitten with Blythe. She'd been deflecting his advances up until now, but she was suddenly going to find him irresistible. He was very proud of his job at Mist Marrow, and Blythe didn't think it would take much to get him to give her a tour, after which they would be able to update the blueprints.

Pernella interrupted their meeting at this point to bring in the Mulled Slithy Tove Brews, and her brand new Eat Me special. She had created tiny cakes with little arms and legs that leapt into your mouth of their own accord. Watching them walk around was entertaining. However, it was a bit disturbing when they jumped up into your mouth so you'd eat them. Once everybody had marveled at Pernella's creations and sipped their drinks, it was back to business.

Penelope had an idea about how they were going to get in. They would need to tunnel in from over a mile away. Ramidrejus were famous for their digging abilities, and Keme was a sort of explosives expert. She said she believed they would be able to tunnel right in easy enough. It was what happened when they got inside that would be tricky. They would dress as guards, use prosthetics to disguise their faces and split up. Taticus and his group would go after their friend, and the Nyxmadra would go after treasure of their own. They would have a very short window of time to get in and get out. Going unnoticed was impossible, but with any luck, they would be halfway back through the tunnel before someone caught on. Then Keme would blast the tunnel behind them to smithereens, and they would run to meet Honali, who would fly them all to safety.

This was not the best plan Abney had ever heard. Their chances of getting caught were roughly seventy percent, even if they executed it perfectly. It relied heavily on everyone being able to find what they were looking for quickly. At the moment, they had no idea where She of the Glass Heart was, and the Nyxmadra had no idea which piece of treasure they were going to go after. Then, they had to get back to the tunnel and at least halfway through it, before Keme blew it sky high. Abney was not athletic, and running with an explosion behind her was not an exciting prospect. It seemed to be the only plan with any hope of success though, so they were all in, for better or worse.

The plan solidified and agreed upon, the Hobgoblins and their wards walked back to Oberon House. Wilbur kept a close eye, and as soon as they were out of earshot of the Nyxmadra, the rest of the Hobgoblins started to voice their concerns again. Apparently, no one trusted them in the slightest. Abney was baffled, she had found them very charming for the most part. Keme was intimidating, but other than that, they had been jovial and polite. She liked them.

"They're bad news," Beau warned. "We shouldn't be trusting them."

"They're going to use us as a diversion, get what they want, and leave us to pay the price," Arjun agreed.

"I'm counting on it." Taticus smiled. "We're going to be one step ahead."

"How do you plan to do that?" Wilbur asked. "Ramidreju are renowned for their cleverness and conniving. How do you plan to stop them from getting one over on us?"

"Trust me." Taticus nodded. "I've got this all in hand."

CHAPTER 22

THE THREE OF SWORDS

The tunnel was much smaller than Abney imagined. She, Gus, and Luke were able to stand up hunched over, but Abel, Mary-Lou, Blythe, and Taticus had to crawl. They were all growing increasingly worried about this tunnel as an escape route. The way it was built, only the Ramidreju could move easily and quickly through it. Taticus mumbled something about it being all a part of Penelope's plan to escape quickly while leaving them holding the smoking gun.

Taticus's plan was simple. They arranged for Wilbur, Domino, Lunetta, Chasha, Sabine, Honali, Arjun, and Beau to meet the Nyxmadra at eleven that night, while Taticus and his team would arrive exactly one hour earlier. They would grab a piece of glass heart, meet Wilbur's team in storage room 237 and get back in time for them to beat the Ramidreju out of the tunnel, thus, securing their own escape and leaving the Nyxmadra to fend for themselves. The Hobgoblins all insisted the double cross was necessary as Penelope would most certainly find a way to get her people out while trapping them to take the blame. After walking through the tunnel, Abney was inclined to trust their judgment.

The tunnel stopped abruptly. They looked up. The hole above led into a storage room. According to Blythe's intel, She of the Glass Heart was at the southernmost point of the basement. It was a bit of a jaunt from their current location, but they were confident they'd be able to collect their treasure and make it back to meet Wilbur in one hour.

Taticus lifted Abney onto his shoulders. "Boonspit, you're heavier than you look," he groaned.

"Get bent," Abney wiggled a bit to annoy him. She slid the piece of cardboard out of the way easily. Taticus lifted her up with some dramatic groans, and Abney scurried up to the floor. It was pitch black. She had to turn her headlamp on. The room was full of crates, boxes, and old paintings, but no guards. "We're good to go." She stuck her head down and waited for Mary-Lou so that she could give her a hand up. One by one, they climbed up through the tunnel.

"So far so good," Blythe mentioned nervously. Paranoia had its hooks in them. Trouble seemed to be lurking around every corner, whether it was or not. They dressed in the aqua and gold striped uniforms of the Mist Marrow Sentinels, and Feo had disguised their faces expertly with prosthetics. Abney gained a hook nose, a half-moon scar just below her left eye, and black hair. Taticus pinned his ears back, tucked his tail artfully out of sight, and dyed his fur blue. He was the most unrecognizable of the lot.

"This way." Taticus took the lead. He opened the door slowly and peeked his head out. "All clear." They took the hallway to the left, which was at least well lit, so they all turned off their headlamps and hid them out of sight behind one of the crates. The halls were almost as confusing as the ones in Oberon House, but Taticus guided them through expertly. He and Blythe had gone over her observations and the old blueprints over and over again until they both knew the way through the storage rooms like the back of their hands.

They reached the entrance to the cell with little difficulty and no guard sightings. A light shone through a barred half-moon window, and they could hear something pacing around on the other side of the door. An eerie soprano voice began to sing.

"*The maid of Albion has a heart full of woe.*
Love has betrayed her and laid her so low.

Her heart of crystal is broken on the floor,
On her knees she tries to repair her core.

Yet as she gathers another suitor does pass,
But he does not slow and leaves with a foot full of glass.

Pieces and pieces from her they have stole.
Will they ever give them back so that she can be whole…"

"Hello?" Abney said softly.

"I'm not hungry. Weren't you just here? Leave me to my work. How am I to get out of here if you won't leave me be?" the sweet high voice scolded them.

"I'm not a guard," Abney said. There was a shuffle of feet, and a lovely but messy brunette with violet eyes approached the window.

"Not my usual guard, for sure, but I recognize the uniform. What do you want?" she said crossly.

"It's a disguise," Abney said and wiggled her fake nose about to show it was false. "We need your help."

"Ha! And how am I to help you from here? Hmmm? If anyone needs help, it's me! Away with you!" she argued and walked away from the window.

"Please, our friends are in danger. Nicholas Kringle has them. We need a piece of your glass heart to stop him," Abney begged.

"That's all anyone ever wants: a piece of me," she lamented. "What about me? Don't I deserve to be a complete person? All anyone ever does is take, take, take! I'm sick of it. I don't even know you, and you have the nerve to ask me to give up my only chance to be whole again."

"What do you mean your only chance to be whole again?" Abney asked.

"I made a deal. Don't you know? I suppose you don't. No one knows

I'm here. Poor Maurelle! Poor lonely, forgotten girl. Gave her heart away till there was nothing left, then made a deal with a Faerie Queen to get it back. I was mortal, frail; she promised I would never be any of those things, ever again. She ripped my heart from my chest and burned it until it was glass, which she shattered into a thousand pieces. If I can put it back together, my heart will never break again. I will be free of sadness, don't you see? I've been rebuilding for so long that I can't just give it away, or what would I have been here for all this time?" She paced back and forth fervently as she spoke. Abney noted she was mostly talking to herself.

"Lady, how long you been in there?" Abel asked. He was frightened that their mission's success hung on the cooperation of a clearly unstable woman.

"I'm not certain. There's no night or day down here. Just lamp light and shadows, shadows and lamp light," she replied. "Last time I saw the sun, it was November, in the year of our Lord 1231."

"I know who she is," Taticus announced suddenly. "She's the Lady of Loch Rannoch."

Blythe stared at him. "You're joking."

"Who's the Lady of Loch Rannoch?" Abney asked them.

"She is," Taticus said to spite her.

"You know what I meant." She arched her eyebrow at him.

"In the legend, Mab didn't turn her heart to glass, but she did shatter it in a thousand pieces and lock her away. She promised the mortal if she could repair the broken heart she would never be hurt again. Unbeknownst to the lady, Mab took a piece with her so that she could never repair it and would never be able to leave. Tears of unrequited love are a potent ingredient, and the Lady of Loch Rannoch was well known for the string of lovers who always ultimately left her for other women," Taticus informed them.

"She lied to me?" the lady questioned.

"Obviously," Blythe replied. The lady broke down in a series of piercing shrieks. The group glared at Blythe. "What?" she asked. "It's true."

"She's going to bring a whole battalion down here with that wailing," Mary-Lou complained.

"Shhhhh!" Abel tried to console the weeping woman. "Lady, you gotta be quiet, okay? You're going to get us all caught."

"I care not!" she shouted back at him.

"Come on, please don't cry," Abel said with all the charm he possessed. "A beautiful woman like you should never cry." It didn't work.

"Stop crying this instant, or I will make you," Taticus threatened. Abney was wondering why he hadn't silenced her already. Then again, she was quite pitiful. It seemed too cruel to do that to her as well.

"I am the most pathetic creature ever to live," Maurelle sobbed. They noticed her hands grasping the bars of the window desperately as she cried. "I was never going to be able to repair it. I'm naught but an idiotic saddle-goose. That deceiver!"

"We have to take her with us," Abney said.

"That's not part of the plan," Mary-Lou reminded them. "Queen Mab won't think kindly of us taking her toy."

"Oh please," Maurelle begged. "I beseech you. Do not leave me here. I will give a piece of my heart gladly if you will but take me with you."

"Baba Yaga did say she had to give it to us willingly," Gus said.

"Dragon's fire!" Taticus swore. "Lady, can't we do anything else for you? Anything at all? I swear we will do it. Breaking you out of Mist Marrow is just not in the plan. We're all going to end up in here or worse if we try to take you."

"Do you not see? There is naught else I could want," she said, tears falling beautifully down her cheeks. "It is all I want, and I will not give you a piece of my heart if you do not take me with you." Taticus covered his eyes with his hand. Abney swore she could hear him saying, "Breathe…one, two, three…" under his breath.

"All right then! I hope you're all comfortable with being entombed for eternity while slipping into madness. I guess I am," he blurted, uncovering his face, and pulling a set of lock picking tools from the pocket of his guard uniform.

"Oh, bless you!" Maurelle cried. "Bless you all!" They could hear glass clinking as the lady gathered her heart to take with her. Taticus continued to swear under his breath. Abney's heart was racing a million miles an hour, and she was venting a considerable amount of steam. She could see Hatsuko's face with juice dripping down it and the marionette-like movements she made as she put herself in the coffin. She shuddered, but what else could they do? They couldn't leave Maurelle here. The lock clicked open.

Lady of Loch Rannoch was waiting with a wide-eyed overeager look. The dress she wore had once been dark red, but it was faded and in tatters. Her long brown hair was wild, and she smelled like she hadn't bathed in a couple of hundred years at least.

"Oh, thank you!" she exclaimed and ran to hug Abney. Abney noticed that Maurelle was not warm like other Fleetlings, which gave her an idea about what might be done with the lady after they had what they needed from her. She patted Maurelle's back awkwardly.

"It's all good, but we've got to get going," Abney said, backing out of the embrace. She tried desperately not to breathe in.

"Come on," Blythe said, pulling the lady off Abney. "My brother will be waiting." They snaked through the halls in silence and did not encounter a single guard. Nor they did they see another living being as they made their way to the storage room 237. It was all starting to feel terribly wrong. They entered the storage room where Wilbur was waiting.

"Blythe, we were just starting to worry," Wilbur announced as they all filed into the room. "Who is that?"

"She of the Glass Heart, but you will know her as the Lady of Loch Rannoch," Taticus said to the group. "And for today, your sister's name is Fen Foofer; we discussed this."

"No one agreed to your stupid code names," Blythe shook her head.

"Put her back. Put her back now!" Wilbur demanded.

"We can't. Baba Yaga said that she had to give the piece of her heart willingly. The only way she's willing to do that is if we get her out of here," Taticus replied.

"We're all going to end up in the Graveyard of the Undying," Beau said.

"Have you guys run into any trouble?" Chasha asked. "Besides the obvious?"

ABNEY KELLY AND THE YULETIDE SHENANIGANS

"No." Blythe replied. "And it's starting to make me nervous. How about you?"

"Penelope, Lavinia, and their cousin Boris—" Sabine started.

"You mean Snoozle, Butwhack, and Greenweave," Taticus tried to correct her.

"Whatever." Sabine rolled her eyes. "Anyway, they were missing from the party that came through with us, but other than that, we haven't had any trouble at all."

"That's not a good sign," Taticus said worriedly. "Snoozle isn't one to leave all the fun to her brothers."

"Well, let's get out of here then," Wilbur said. "We don't want the Nyxmadra to beat us to the tunnel."

Everyone nodded and headed out two by two at three-minute intervals so that they wouldn't be such a conspicuously large group. Blythe took Maurelle, and Abney and Taticus were last out. Abney traipsed back and forth as Taticus timed their departure to the second.

"Ready, Boonspit?" he asked her. She groaned and shook her head. He wasn't going to let it go. So she ignored him, and they walked out the door. The halls were still empty. They both sucked in a deep breath. Nothing to worry about yet. They zigged and zagged through the vacant corridors. As they made the last turn and entered the room with the tunnel, they found an entourage awaiting them. One Abney recognized from *The Korrigan Chronicler*. It was Peter Kringle.

"Hello," he said. "You must be Abney Kelly." Abney nodded affirmatively, trying not to fill the room with steam. All of her friends, including Honali and Arjun, were gagged and bound at the guards' feet.

"My father gave me an idea of what was going on. I suspected you'd end up here eventually," he said in a gruff voice. "Don't worry. There will be no punishment, for now. The Queens have given me leave to use any means necessary to get rid of Nicholas. Though I do have to say that it was a bold move to sneak into Mist Marrow and take the Lady of Loch Rannoch."

"She has to give us a piece of her heart willingly, this was her price," Taticus said.

"Silence, Hobgoblin!" Peter said harshly. "This is a conversation between my niece and myself." Taticus looked annoyed but remained quiet.

"That was her price," Abney agreed, steam billowing around her. She wasn't sure how she felt about the niece comment. She thought she should feel something, but she was too caught up in her current circumstance to really process the idea.

"You're a brave girl," he said. "I was waiting to see if you were going to fight despite warnings that you should not. I am proud of you. However, taking on Nicholas with a group of Hobgoblins and your young friends is not the wisest decision. You will need help, and we're here to assist."

"Then can you ungag and untie them?" Abney asked looking at her friends' helpless faces.

"Oh, well, yes. All but the gang of Ramidrejus," he said, looking at Penelope. "They showed up an hour before your group and tried to make off with the Seven League Boots and the Twenty-Year Earmuffs." He motioned for the guards to release Abney's friends.

"Twenty-Year Earmuffs?" Abney said, looking skeptical.

"Earmuffs made from the beard of Rip Van Winkle. They allow the wearer to sleep for twenty years at a time, uninterrupted," Taticus explained.

"Why would anyone want to do that?" Abney asked.

"When you live forever, sometimes a twenty-year break is nice," Peter explained. "In any case, they're not citizens of the Fae, so they won't end up in the Graveyard of the Undying, but there will punishment of some sort. You're lucky we were waiting for you, or they would have gotten away with the treasure and left you all to take the blame."

"I knew it!" Taticus exclaimed. "Dragon's fire, Snoozle! Do you always have to play dirty?" The Ramidreju shrugged playfully even though she was bound tight.

"And you," Peter said, taking back control of the conversation and looking at Abney, "can take a piece of the Lady of Loch Rannoch's heart, but she must stay."

"She can't," Abney said. "We already told you. Baba Yaga said she must give us the piece of her heart willingly. Her price is her freedom. If you put her back, it won't work properly." Peter considered what Abney had said for a moment then spoke to Lady Maurelle.

"What will you do with your freedom?" he asked. "You've been here for over seven hundred and fifty years. The world has changed a lot. Also, you are no longer human. Well, no longer mortal. I can't recommend going Topside. They'll probably lock you away in an asylum, and as soon as they realize you don't age, they'll slice you up for experiments. You'll have to stay within the magical realms. Avalon may be an option."

"I would prefer to be as far away from the Fae as possible," Maurelle said.

"I have an idea about that," Abney said. They all looked at her with interest. "The Wyvern Dragon is in the Arctic, and he's lonely. She wouldn't be with Fleetlings, and she'd be pretty far away from most Fae."

"And it might get you out of that deal we had to make," Sabine mentioned offhandedly.

"What deal?" Taticus looked at Abney.

Abney winced. "Well…I may have had to agree to spend one hundred years with him as soon as I get out of school in exchange for the torch." Taticus looked ready to explode. "But we have a nice solution here, don't you think?"

"We will take Lady Maurelle with us for now," Peter said. "I will agree to nothing regarding her until I've had a chance to speak with The Queens." Everyone nodded. That was the best they could hope for. "Now, we will reconvene at Oberon House. Plans need to be made, and I want the full story; nothing is to be left out." The Changelings gave each other sideways glances but nodded their agreement. "Good. Shall we?"

CHAPTER 23

THE GLASS DAGGER

Back at Oberon House things were tense. Tough decisions had been made, and a heavy commotion was brewing over the latest of those choices. Abney hid, listening with uncertainty as her accusations jailed her potential enemy.

"Where are you taking me?" Algernon challenged. "I demand to know what is going on this instant!"

Abney could hear the shouts from their schoolmaster as the KRAMPUS guards dragged him from his room to be jailed elsewhere. Abney felt immense guilt. They were not one hundred percent certain that he was her father, but it was agreed that it was too risky to have him around for the time being.

"Taticus!" Algernon bellowed. "Where are you, you damned fool of a Puca? If this is one of your jokes so help me...Io..." The sound of his voice was suddenly muted. Abney imagined the Hobgoblin's hand covering Algernon's mouth. Taticus had an uncanny ability to intervene right before someone gave away his real name. Abney could hear the Puca's voice, but she couldn't make out what he was saying. Algernon's voice, in contrast, was very clear.

"Of course, I'm not!" he said indignantly. Abney crept closer to eavesdrop better.

"You were the one who brought her to me to glamour," Taticus said.

"You know very well that doesn't make me the father," Algernon fumed. "It means I was convenient. I am here to protect her, and you know it. Now, let me go this instant!"

"Sorry," Taticus said with an actual note of regret. "This is too important to justify the risk. There will be a blood test. You'll be released as soon as we have the results."

"Of all the stupid—" Algernon started, but then his voice was muffled. *They've gagged him*, Abney thought. There would be no further information she could gather here. She was rather hoping Algernon would admit to being her father, just so that she could be certain at least one danger was out of the way. She sighed and tiptoed quietly back to her room.

Abney, Domino, and Honali were going to be allowed to stay at Oberon House for the showdown, but the rest were moving to Puck House. Mame, the house matron for that residence, was the only one who could be convinced to take in the troublemakers along with their guardians and Feo. Abney and Honali were helping Lunetta and Sabine pack.

"I don't like leaving you guys here." Lunetta shook her head, fighting back the tears. "It feels like we're never going to see each other again."

"Of course, we're going to see you again." Honali hugged her. "Girl, Abney and I are tough as nails. It's the boys you gotta worry about. They act all macho, but they're a bunch of sissies. That's why we're sending Gus and Abel with you." Abney patted Lunetta's back awkwardly. She wanted to be a comforting, but just trying made her personally very uncomfortable. She always ended up having the opposite effect.

"Don't mess this up," Sabine said coldly and then surprised everyone by hugging Abney. "Be careful."

The girls headed downstairs. Abel and Gus were waiting, suitcases in hand.

"Girls always take forever," Abel complained. "We been waitin' here for, like, twenty minutes while y'all been packing your dainties and whatnot."

"Shut up." Lunetta punched his arm playfully.

"Try to stay out of trouble. You know, basically, do what I wouldn't do," Gus said.

"Vive la Pete," Abney said, putting her hand out.

"Vive la Pete." They all put their hands in sadly.

Gus and Abel walked out first. The girls had another group hug before they departed with their Hobgoblins and Feo. Abney, Domino, and Honali watched them go from the window of the Ocean Room. Steam clouded around them as Abney tried not to cry. She wondered if she would ever see any of them again.

It was really happening. There was going to be a fight, and she didn't feel prepared for any of it.

The next thing they had to figure out was the piece of Lady Maurelle's heart. It was in a thousand tiny pieces, none of which were long enough to stab through Abney's back and reach her heart. Both Wilbur and Taticus were talented glass melders, but neither of them felt comfortable trying to make the pieces into a weapon. It was a one-shot deal, so Peter offered to take them to see a Dwarf he knew that worked at Hephaestus's Weapons and More.

Maurelle found the city shocking after being locked up for so long. She wasn't used to the number of beings or loud noises. She stayed very close to Peter, clutching the handkerchief with the pieces of her heart in it to her chest. The rest of the group walked at ease, enjoying being out of the house.

When they reached Hephaestus's, the place was buzzing. The sign in the window read: *Excalibur Replicas Coming Soon! Pre-Order Yours Today!* There were maces, wands, swords, staffs, all infused with magical properties and labeled with outlandish claims. The Lance of Tears makes an opponent sob uncontrollably so that you never have to actually fight.

The Bracelet of Laka: Win every dance-off without even trying. Pie's poisoned darts: Your enemies can't find you if they're drowning. Abney wasn't sure if she was impressed or appalled. Maybe a little bit of both.

"Gunther! Good to see you!" Peter proclaimed and shook the hand of the blue-gray Rock Troll standing behind the cash register.

"Pete, my man." Gunther came around the counter and pulled him in for a back slap. "What are you in for today? I can get you one of those Excalibur replicas on the house if you're interested."

"I might be," Peter said, momentarily distracted. "That's not why I'm here though. I need to see Nigel."

Gunther nodded. "Needing something custom then. He's in the back. You know the way."

Peter nodded and led the group down a short hall and under a large rubber flap that acted as a door. Behind the rubber door was a stout, muscular dwarf. He had snow-white skin, matching hair, and even his eyes lacked the slightest pigmentation.

"Nigel!" Peter yelled with the same amount of enthusiasm he'd shown Gunther.

"Pete!" Nigel greeted him with a toothy smile. "What can I do ya for?"

"I need a dagger made of very special glass. I was hoping you might be able to help me?" Peter asked.

"Anything for you! What kind of glass are we talking about?" Nigel beamed at the prospect of a challenge. Peter motioned Maurelle forward. She shuffled toward him, still wary of strangers and undid her bundle. "That's not very much to work with. Are we melding it with something else?"

"The blade can only be made from this glass, nothing else," Peter replied.

"You may not have it all either," Maurelle said protectively. "I'll allow you to have one-fourth of what is there, no more."

"And you are?" Nigel asked eyeing the Lady. She did clean up well.

"I am the Lady Maurelle." She curtsied very formally.

"And I am very pleased to meet you," Nigel said and kissed her hand.

"Nigel," Peter said to get his friend's attention. "I need you to focus. Time is of the essence here."

Nigel looked back at his friend obligingly. "It will be a challenge," Nigel said and stroked his braided beard. "We'll have to go with something closer to a rapier, obviously much shorter though."

"It needs to be long enough to pierce a heart from the back," Peter explained.

"I don't hold with stabbing through the back; it's cowardly," Nigel said, obviously reconsidering the help he had offered.

"The person who's back it's going through is well aware of what is happening," Peter said. "Isn't that right, Abney?"

"It is." Abney stepped forward. "It will be going through my back." The thought made her a little queasy. She sat down to avoiding vomiting again.

"In that case," he said, "have a seat. It'll take me about an hour." Maurelle handed over the part of her heart she was willing to relinquish, and they all took a seat to wait while Nigel got crafty.

One hour later to the second, Nigel presented them with a small but lethal weapon. The glass blade was needle-thin but visibly sharp. "I made the hilt from some colored glass I had lying about, but the blade is one hundred percent the material you supplied me with." The hilt was lovely, with greens and purples swirling around and a red heart visible just at the top. "I call her Le Coeur de Maurelle." He bowed to the Lady of Loch Rannoch. She blushed and hid behind Peter.

"It's precisely what we needed. Thank you, my friend." Peter shook his hand again. Nigel put the delicate dagger in a wooden box and handed it to him. "I consider this a debt paid."

"What do I owe you now?" the Dwarf laughed.

"I believe that brings you down to only one hundred and eleven favors to go." Black Peter grinned.

"That'll teach me to use favors to gamble." Nigel shook his head. "Never again, I tell you!"

"You'll be at poker night Thursday, though, right?" Peter said over his shoulder as they prepared to leave.

"With bells on," Nigel called after them.

Back at Oberon House, they were settling in as much as they could. It had been a long day. Kringle could come bursting through the door at any minute, but Abney hoped he could wait till tomorrow. The house wasn't ready yet and, honestly, neither was she. Honali and Domino sat on either side of her, both looking exhausted and scared.

"Zoey's so scared right now. I can feel it in my bones," Domino croaked, holding back tears. "I swear, if I get her back, I'll never take her for granted again."

"We're going to get them back," Honali said with determination.

Abney put her head on Honali's shoulder. It was the closest to a hug she could manage comfortably, and it was somehow less awkward. She didn't want to say anything, because all she felt was fear and guilt for feeling fear. Her friends probably guessed her feelings with the small puffs of steam escaping her, but it somehow felt traitorous to say it aloud.

Agatha appeared in the doorway. "Come on, you ragamuffins. Soup's on. Everyone needs to eat something."

None of them felt hungry, but they followed her anyway. Nothing ever came from arguing with Agatha.

When they walked into the kitchen, Peter, Lady Maurelle, the Hobgoblins, and a few of the KRAMPUS guards, including DiGott, were lined up by the counter to fill their bowls. A sort of pseudo-merriment was running rampant like wildfire. They laughed and joked like nothing was happening, but if one paid close attention, a flicker of fear around the eyes or in a half-hearted smile was apparent.

"What are you doing here?" Abney asked DiGott.

"I'm in the KRAMPUS reserves," he told her proudly. "I'll be the one giving the orders to the other Elves when the time comes."

"They put you in charge of something?" Honali teased as she joined her friend.

"They let you stay, even though you can't see the enemy and are likely to be more of a hindrance than a help." DiGott jabbed back. He was a quick wit.

"Touché," Honali stuck her tongue out at him. Abney couldn't take the bickering and went to sit down at the breakfast nook.

"Nervous?" Peter sat down next to her. Abney nodded. Words felt too complicated. "If you weren't, I'd be worried. Fear is a good instinct. It keeps you alive. Just make sure that it's only there as an advisor, not a ruler."

"I don't think I can do this," Abney admitted.

"Of course, you can't," he said incredulously. "You're what, thirteen? I have a thousand years plus some on you, and I can't do this without help. My brother is old and strong. Orina was made from pure magic, and my brother is half of each parent. Not to mention the spells Baba Yaga put on him to protect him. He is powerful in ways I can never be, and he's almost killed me a few times. We have you, though, and that's something. You may be my great-great-great—You know, the number of greats isn't important. What is important is that you, Abney Kelly, also carry the same magic in you. Now, this is a lot to put on the shoulders of a young Fae, but you have more in you than you realize."

"Thanks," Abney said, but he hadn't made her feel any better.

"Put on a brave face, kid," he said. "Even though you don't feel it right now. You will, and it will happen when you least expect it." Abney nodded and watched him walk over to talk to some of his fellow KRAMPUS guards. She wished he hadn't called her kid. That's what her dad called her, and she was missing him a lot at this particular moment.

"Come on." Honali grabbed her hand. "It's been a long day. Tomorrow will probably be longer. We need to get some sleep." Abney and Domino followed her to Ocean Room where they found themselves camping out yet again.

✦

Kringle didn't come. Everyone was part relieved and part anxious to just get it over with. Since everyone was full of extra energy, they decided it was time to booby-trap Oberon House. This was not easy. Agatha had many objections and yelled at them that they could kill Kringle in her house, but if they so much as chipped a wall frame, she'd be taking it out of their hides.

They settled for the basics. Elves were stashed in all the rooms because every single one of them had a fireplace, and that would be where Kringle and his associates would come from. The stairs up and down were greased with Yeti mucus, which was slicker than any ice rink, and set up with spider yarn as a tripwire. Spider yarn was nearly invisible and incredibly durable. They needed every advantage they could get. Something as small as a fall or trip could mean the difference between them getting the drop on Kringle or him getting the drop on them.

Feo stopped by to help them grow a small, Agatha-approved thorn patch at the bottom of the stairs. She seemed to enjoy helping, but Honali said she thought the real reason Feo dropped by was to flirt with Taticus. Abney never noticed before, but Feo was rather chummy with the Puca. Taticus seemed pretty interested in her too. Good for him, Abney thought.

It made for a fun afternoon. Abney, Domino, and Honali pretended they were in the *Home Alone* movies, and the Sticky Bandits were going to burst through the door at any moment. The others humored them. Agatha even begrudgingly allowed Domino to set up swinging paint cans at the top of the staircase. Abney and Honali lit the hearths with the fire from Vern's torch and hid marbles in the thorn patch when no one was looking. Taticus said marbles were a stupid idea, but they wanted to keep with the *Home Alone* spirit.

The lighthearted mood Feo brought with her couldn't last though. Evening drew near again, and Feo had to get back to Puck House. She took Lady Maurelle with her. Maybe it was all the emotions flying around, but Abney felt like she was going to miss that neurotic mess of a Fleetling. Everyone was leaving. Lunetta hadn't been too off the mark. The goodbyes were starting to feel final. This time they all watched from the window as Feo led Lady Maurelle away.

"All right," Peter said. "Time to wrap the windows and doors with the rope from my father's forest. From here on out, no one but my brother comes in, and no one gets out."

CHAPTER 24

THE HANGED MAN

The trap was set. It was designed to bring Kringle right to them after a few bumps and bruises. Then the real fight would begin. Peter, Taticus, Blythe, and Wilbur would lead the charge on Kringle. Abney, Honali, and Domino were to stay out of the way until they had him subdued. Then they would beat the location of Sümeyye and Zoey out of him. As soon as they had the information, Abney would blow herself and Kringle to high heaven, hopefully without killing herself in the process. It was Honali's job to stick Le Coeur de Maurelle through Abney's back at just the right moment to prevent that from happening.

Abney was very nervous about letting her emotions overtake her, especially since the primary emotion had to be love, not fear or anger, either of which would have been easier to conjure. Taticus worked with her on summoning images of those she was doing this for and remembering that this was an act of love. She loved her friends and family enough to possibly sacrifice herself. The problem was that Abney was having a bit of trouble buying that story. You have to believe it, she told herself, you have to, or it won't work.

It had been eight days of waiting so far. They took shifts sleeping, but there hadn't been a peep. Feo sent the yellow mini-pixie, who Abney learned was named Leo, to check on them often. He would carry messages and jokes back and forth for the Changelings, too, in exchange for food and other goods, which helped pass the time.

"I thought you said your spirit guide indicated that Nicholas would come to us? This is getting boring, and I'm sick of sleeping on the floor," Taticus complained.

"She did say that," Abney said defensively.

"We're not going anywhere until my brother graces us with his presence," Peter said. "That's the end of it. So settle in. We may be here for a month or a year. We'll sit here as long as it takes."

"As you wish," Taticus bowed sarcastically and took a seat on the chaise lounge.

"You know what song I have stuck in my head?" Domino asked.

"What?" Honali nodded for him to tell them.

"'He'll be Coming Down the Chimney' by that old country guy, Gene something or other." Domino said.

"You know, most of the songs from Christmas that I grew up loving have really morbid undertones now," Abney complained. They were never going to mean the same things to her again.

"Yeah, I can see how they're all a little spooky now," Honali agreed.

"I haven't felt Zoey in days," Domino said. "I'm starting to worry that I can't feel her because she's gone." A tear crept down his face, and Honali put her arm around his shoulder.

She spoke softly. "Don't talk like that. We're going to get our girls back. I have to believe that."

Suddenly, loud thuds crashed above them. They all froze, listening for the next bump. They could hear smaller plops now, like footsteps.

"*And then, in a twinkling, I heard on the roof the prancing and pawing of each little hoof,*" Abney recited.

"You're not helping," Domino murmured irritably.

"Shhhh," Taticus hissed at them. They could hear creaks, groans, and scutterings in the walls. Then loud thumps shook the floor above them. The lights swayed, agitated by the movement. Yelling started above as the Elves began their attack.

"Abney, you and your friends get in your place, now. Stay out of the way until it's time," Taticus instructed them.

"Here we go." Peter stood up with a smile. He cracked his whip, daring the first Fleetling or Fae to come down the stairs.

"Where the hell are they coming from?" Abney heard a gruff voice gripe.

"They're tiny," another voice observed in panic. "I can't keep track of them!"

"It bit me!" A female voice followed by a long string of profanity.

"Jesus Christ, they're like gremlins!" another shout declared.

"We're Elves, bitch." Abney recognized DiGott's sassy voice. She covered her mouth, trying not to smile. Screams and thunks ensued. Then there was the roar of something more vicious. Heavy footsteps made the ceiling rattle above.

"He's here," Peter announced. Abney, Domino, and Honali crowded against the wall unconsciously. They were all fighting the voices in their heads telling them to get out now! The hair on all the Pucas was standing on end, and their teeth were visible. Abney could hear the sound of tiny bodies hitting the wall. She began to shake. The footsteps made it into the hall.

"What the—" a voice started, but didn't finish. They could hear him trying to regain his balance and then the thwack as something crashed into one of the paint cans. They saw the top of his white head first as he fell forward and hit the trip wire, sending him tumbling down the stairs and into thorns with a mighty howl. Three more thumps followed suit. Two of them were Zoey and Sümeyye. Honali and Domino both went to run for them, but Abney grabbed their arms.

"Not yet." she reminded them, though this certainly changed things a bit. Nicholas Kringle struggled to his feet. He was towering and his beard long. His skin was the same ice-blue as Abney's, his hair the same white with the hint of greens and pinks dancing in it, his ears were a good deal more triangular, and his teeth sharpened to a point. But even with the changes, Abney knew this man.

"Ol' Chris?" she said confused. She looked at his hands. They were monstrous claws, how had she missed those? Then she remembered: He always wore gloves.

"I knew you'd recognize me," he said, brushing the thorns from his sleeve. "I used only a small bit of glamour. I wanted you to know me when this moment came, daughter." Everyone's mouths dropped open.

"You're not my father," Abney said, willing it to be a lie. "You can't be. Algernon is my father." Suddenly, he seemed a lot more preferable.

"What? That sour old meddler? No, he's your uncle, your mother's twin. He's the one who spirited you both away from me. Arabella was a KRAMPUS guard at my prison. We fell in love. She was such a lovely creature. It grieved me that she didn't survive your birth. There's something in the way you move that reminds me of her, though there is no doubt you are the spitting image of my mother. Baba Yaga promised you would be."

Abney felt sick and dizzy. Her legs came out from under her. Honali grabbed her arm and helped her regain her balance. The truth slapped Abney across the face. There was no Harpy-girl. She'd been there to meet Nicholas so he could give her Isodanelli's journal. Baba Yaga knew who she was and had been expecting them, but she wasn't helping them. She was still helping Kringle. This was not the way it was supposed to happen. Would their plan even work, or had Baba Yaga simply set them up to fall into his trap?

"What does he look like? Where is he?" Honali looked desperately around to try to see Kringle.

"Calm down," Abney told her. "It's not your job to worry about him."

A thin woman in a plague mask stood up, holding their captives by their arms. Zoey and Sümeyye looked frightened and disheveled. Abney wanted them back and safe. Honali and Domino looked like they wanted to tear the woman limb from limb.

"No one else has to get hurt," the woman announced. Abney recognized the voice from the battle in the Arctic. "Come with us willingly, Abney, and we will release your friends."

"Not a chance," Taticus stepped between Abney and Kringle.

"That's not a wise decision, Hobgoblin," Kringle warned him. Taticus leapt at him before he had a chance to make another threat. Feet first, he knocked Nicholas to the ground, who was up again in a flash. Kringle backhanded Taticus, who went flying and hit the wall hard. Blythe jumped in and scratched him across the face, but it didn't leave so much as a mark. He swiped his claws across her legs, and she faltered.

Abney noticed the woman in the mask stumbling over the marbles as she tried to make her way toward Abney and her friends. Wilbur saw too and moved to intercept her. Peter stepped forward with a crack of his whip, which wrapped itself around Kringle's right hand before he could swipe at Blythe again. Taticus was still hunched over on the floor. Abney ran to his side.

"Brother!" Peter's voiced boomed. "It's been too long."

"You're no brother of mine," Nicholas snarled and used the whip around his hand to pull Peter toward him.

"You're right," Peter admitted, letting go of the whip and kicking Nicholas's legs out from under him. "We're only half-brothers, thank goodness. I'd hate having to explain how a full sibling of mine was so ugly. You must take after your mother's side!" At that, Nicholas jumped to his feet. He was spry for an old man and landed a blow across Peter's face. He shook it off. "I think you're losing your touch."

"You're lucky you have the blue fire draining me," Nicholas said, hitting Peter's face again, "Or you'd be dead already."

"Back away or I'll kill her," the woman in the plague mask threatened Wilbur, dropping Zoey on the floor, and holding a knife to Sümeyye's throat.

"No!" Honali screamed. Domino held her tight, fearing if he let her go, the women would carry through with her threat. Wilbur backed away, making sure his hands were visible. Nicholas and Peter froze to watch the transaction.

"Come on, Abney. Your life for your friend's. Are you willing to let two innocent girls die for you?" the woman yelled for all to hear. Taticus was still out cold. Abney looked at him and then to Sümeyye's tear-filled face. There was only one thing to do. She kissed Taticus on the top of his head and walked toward the woman. She could hear her friends screaming no, but her feet walked forward. She felt strangely calm.

"Let them go," Abney demanded. "I'll come with you, but you have to let them go first." The woman kicked Zoey forward. She crawled on her knees with her hands tied behind her back to her brother. Abney took another step forward. "Now, Sümeyye." She pushed her last captive into the awaiting arms of Honali. Abney stepped within reach of the woman, and she grabbed Abney's wrist, pulling her painfully to her side.

Nicholas had his brother pinned to the floor. Just like in the story, Abney watched Peter turn an hourglass that hung around his neck. Time appeared between his two sons. The whole room froze except for Abney and her grandfather. He walked toward her.

"Oh, my god," Abney said with relief. "You're here. You can take Nicholas back to his prison now, right? It's all over?"

"Why would I do that?" he asked. "We've been waiting for you a very long time." Abney stepped back.

"What do you mean?" Abney said.

"You think my son has accomplished all this on his own?" he asked. "Do you have any idea how many children I've led to his cell over the past thousand and more years? Nicholas was too impatient. Attracted too much attention. I had to put him behind bars to protect our mission. When those idiotic Fleetlings liberated him this year, we only needed one more heart, which we got. Then there was just the matter of getting to you. Do you have any idea how many grandchildren I have?" Abney shook her head and backed away from her pursuer.

"Four thousand three hundred and six and you are the only one to bear any resemblance to Orina. Now all my son has to do is rip your heart out and replace it with the one we've made from the hundred pure ones! We are finally going to have her back! My Orina," he said, brushing his hand on her cheek. "We are going to be together again." Abney shied away from him. Nicholas unfroze and kicked his brother as hard as he could before walking over to his father and daughter. Cesare pushed Abney toward him.

"Do it!" he ordered his son. "Let's get your mother back and be done with this." He grabbed Abney roughly. Tears were pouring down her face.

"You don't have to do this," Abney told him between sobs. She didn't worry about letting off steam, she was about to die anyway. "I'm your daughter. Doesn't that mean anything?"

"Not really," he said, but Abney could see some remorse behind his eyes.

"You could have taken me anytime in Avalon; why didn't you?" Abney grasped at straws.

"What is she talking about?" Cesare asked Nicholas. "You couldn't get into Avalon. You said it was too well guarded."

Nicholas turned to his father and explained. "I did get in with the help of the Hobgoblin Hatsuko and her pet Wizard. I've never met any of my children. I just wanted to see what she was like. I wanted to see Mom. When Baba Yaga said she would look just like her, I couldn't resist seeing her."

Cesare stroked his son's hair. "I understand," he said. "I have missed her too. Now finish this, and we will never have to miss her again."

Nicholas looked at his daughter. Her silvery eyes were brimming with tears. He raised his hand.

"Dad, please," Abney said, making a final attempt and apparently hitting her mark. Nicholas's face softened, and Abney could see a shadow of the Fae he used to be. He looked at his father and looked back at Abney. He put his hand down.

"I can't," he said. "She looks just like Mom. I can't hurt her."

"Don't be an idiot. This has been over a thousand years in the making. That girl is not your mother!" Cesare flared. "How many of hundreds of thousands of children had to die to get us here, and you're just going to give up?"

"Please, Papa, I can't. She's my daughter," Nicholas begged.

"Your daughter?" Time scoffed. "You don't even know her. She's nobody! Nothing! Just a vessel so that we can get your mother back."

"I can't," Nicholas said, tears running down his face. Abney had a very strong impression that none of this had been Nicholas's idea in the first place.

"Get out of the way," Cesare ordered. "I'll do it myself." He reached for Abney, but Nicholas knocked him away.

"I said *noooo!*" he screamed. The others popped back to life, well aware of what was going on as Father Time hit the ground. The old man was up faster than they expected and at a dead hobble for Nicholas and Abney. Nicholas braced to stop his father, and a loud whistle pierced the air. DiGott had appeared from seemingly nowhere, and his trunk was on a collision course for Father Time. Abney pulled Nicholas back as the trunk smashed into his father.

By this time, Peter had regained his composure; his hooves clopped across the floor, and his whip wrapped around the old man's ankle before he could try to stand again. "I trusted you," he said and knocked his father unconscious with his spare hand. Everyone paused for a moment to process everything that had just gone down. Nicholas got it together faster than the others.

"Abney," Nicholas said, "you have to do what Baba Yaga sent you to do." He looked at her kindly. Abney looked back at him.

"She wants us to kill you," Abney said, shaking her head. Nicholas hugged her tightly and wiped her tears. Abney was steaming again.

"She wants you to release me," he said. "Until a moment ago, I didn't know if I would murder you to get my mother back or not. I couldn't. I'm ready, Abney. Mine has been a long, sad life, and my black heart bears a curse only you can remove. If you leave me alive, my father will try to use me again to get my mother back. He lost his mind when she died. It's what's best for everyone."

"If you leave him alive," Peter said, "the Queens will put him in the Graveyard of the Undying." Abney thought about all the possibilities, and there were no good ones, no happy endings. She sucked up her tears and looked back at Honali who was holding Sümeyye's hand tightly.

"Ready when you are," she said.

Abney nodded and wrapped her arms around her father. She let herself feel everything she'd been holding back. Anger, fear, sadness, hate.

She thought about all he must have gone through, all he had done, and that in the end, he had done the right thing. She found forgiveness for him and let everything else go. Forgiveness is, after all, a type of love. An icy knife sliced into her heart, and a blinding light burst from her chest.

Everything went black.

EPILOGUE

bney awoke two weeks after the incident with both Queen Titania and Queen Mab sitting at the foot of her bed. She thought she was dreaming, but when she sat up and shook off sleep, they were still there, waiting for her to gain her faculties. Abney, helpless and frightened, looked at them. Was this nightmare ever going to end?

"Abney Kelly," Queen Titania said. Her expression was neutral and impossible to read.

"Yes?" Abney croaked; her voice hoarse with disuse.

"You have defeated a great evil, saved your friends' lives and the lives of untold others," she said, still seemingly impartial.

"Thank you?" Abney replied. She wasn't sure that was the correct response.

"You also used a Ouija Board unsupervised, which is against the rules while you remain in school. You used the Traveler within Avalon, opening it up to attack. You got two of your friends kidnaped after sneaking out of Avalon for a second time. You used a Ouija Board for a second time unsupervised. You recruited outlaws, dug a tunnel into a sacred Fae fortress, and you removed one of my prized possessions from that fortress." Queen Mab looked at her harshly. Abney nodded, this was it. They were going to feed her an Evermore and make her get in a coffin.

"The Fae owe you a great debt despite everything you have done," Queen Titania acknowledged.

"Considering your transgressions, we are going to call the whole situation a draw for you and your friends. There will be no punishment and no reward," Queen Mab said, still looking unamused. Abney sighed, relieved.

"Abney," Queen Titania snarled and looked deep into her eyes. Abney stared back, frightened again. "I advise you to stay under our radar from here on out. Next time will not end in your favor." Abney nodded. Abney nodded and watched breathlessly as the monarchs left her room without another word.

✦

3 Months Later

Abney sat quietly in her window seat with the window open. It was a gray October morning. Fall always smelled like magic to her. Something about the aroma of decaying plant life mixed with the crisp air always filled her with feeling of utter euphoria. She smiled; it was so good to be home with her family. She felt nostalgic. There was a time before she knew she was Fae, a time when things were simpler, a time when sleep came easy.

The last few months of school had flown by between regular classes and the extra tutoring from Algernon to catch them up. There had been no time for any of them to deal with what had happened, and that was probably just as well. Dwelling on it didn't make any of them feel particularly happy. Abney had nightmares every night. She didn't need to face it when she was awake too.

Two good things had come from it all: First, Abney had found real family through the incident. She had two real uncles, and they weren't opposed to being in her life. She was the only Fae her age with any real idea of her parentage. Algernon hadn't given her any information on her mother yet—it was a sore subject—and he shut down completely whenever she brought it up. He promised he would tell her, eventually. Abney was grateful to have them both. It was a comfort to know that when she had to give up her Fleetling life, there were Fae who would still want her.

The second good thing was that Abney's heart was no longer volatile. The glass fused around it, creating a permanent casing. They weren't sure what that meant as far as her fire abilities went, but she and Master Blewitt would be exploring that next semester.

All of her friends had come out as well as could be expected, except Sümeyye, who had been quiet and distant ever since her kidnapping. She and Zoey both had mandatory counseling twice a week, but Zoey seemed to be recovering more quickly. Abney had attended some counseling too, but she wasn't ready to talk.

Her real father was a child-murdering monster. He was also one of the most well-known and beloved legends from around the world. He'd killed hundreds of thousands, yet at the end, she'd been able to see the Fae he'd been before his father tracked him down and used him to get his wife back.

Abney had killed her own father. That was hard to deal with or think about at all. He wanted her to end his life, but that didn't make it any easier. He was the only casualty of the invasion of Oberon House. The HAFWITS had all escaped, including the woman in the mask.

Cesare Kringle was being jailed for the time being in Mist Marrow Castle. The Queens hadn't decided what to do with him. He was Father Time; they couldn't execute him or put him in the Graveyard of the Undying, but he couldn't just be set free at the moment either. Abney was relieved that she wouldn't have to worry about him for a long while yet.

As for Maurelle, Queen Mab had been most reluctant to allow her to keep her freedom, but Peter reminded her that they had used her heart to break a curse. If they went back on the promise, there could be serious ramifications. Magic was funny like that. It was always wise to keep any bargain made with it. Mab begrudgingly allowed Maurelle to remain free.

The Lady did not end up in the Arctic though. She and the Dwarf Nigel had a whirlwind romance and were married only one month after their first meeting. Abney hoped that Maurelle would finally be happy. Queen Titania talked with the Wyvern Dragon personally. She was not amused by the deal he'd made with an underaged Fae. He was forced to forgive the debt, but was then rewarded with a more suitable companion for his assistance in bringing down Kringle.

Abney squeezed her eyes shut and enjoyed the smell of waffles and bacon that wafted up the stairs. She was already three weeks into break from Tír na nÓg, and she wasn't missing it yet. Fleetling school and problems were much simpler. She wasn't sure she wanted to go back to the Faerie Realm. Then again, she didn't really have a choice.

She sprung from her window seat and opened her closet. Taticus tossed her Halloween costume out at her and slammed the door. He was enjoying his break too. Abney was letting him use her tablet. He'd recently discovered MeTube and had been watching videos for almost a week straight. She also loaned him headphones so that he could watch without her having to hear it as well. She'd never seen anyone so amazed by technology.

"Hey," he called out to her. She opened the door. "Happy Birthday."

"Thanks," she said. "When's the gang coming through?"

"They'll be here any minute," he said. Abney was a little nervous about having them all over. Her father had been overly interested in where all these new friends had come from and down-right suspicious about where she'd managed to meet boys at an all-girls school. It had all been explained away by a few white lies. Abney had a feeling he didn't believe a word of it; he just wasn't ready to call her out yet.

"Hey kiddo," her father called up. "Get your birthday tushy down here! Breakfast's ready."

"Coming!" she shouted back.

"Don't yell in the house," Granny stopped at her door and smiled.

"Okay!" Abney hollered after her.

"Kids these days," she grumbled as she descended the stairs.

Abney just managed to get into her costume when she heard a rush of voices fill her closet. She opened the door again. There they were, Fleetling glamour, Halloween costumes on, and all. Gus was the hardest to get used to. At this point, he looked a little weird with skin. Abney had to do a double take when he spoke to make sure it was him.

"Okay," Abney told them. "Taticus is going to fly you down from my window one at a time. Then you'll run around to the front of the house. I told my dad you'd all be arriving together. Ring the doorbell; don't knock."

"You get lost?" Mr. Kelly bellowed up the stairs.

"Coming!" Abney shouted and waved to her friends as she closed the door behind her.

Here we go, Abney thought nervously as she headed for the staircase. She jumped up on the banister, balanced herself, slid down gracefully, and landed perfectly on her feet.

"Ladies should not be sliding down the banister." Granny shook her head in disapproval. "Olly, discipline your daughter." Abney smiled. Everything was just as it should be.

ACKNOWLEDGMENTS

First, I would like to tip my hat to survival mode. Depression and anxiety are very real, and if I hadn't needed an escape, this book would not be a thing. On that note, I have several people who deserve thanks for supporting and pushing my neurotic-self to finish this book: Mom, Dad, Brad, Andy, Hailie, Kaitie, Nicole, Sara, Diane, Lura, Amber, Darlene, Gil, and all of my other friends and family who have been so supportive! I love you!

ABOUT THE AUTHOR

SamiJo McQuiston is a first-class shenanigator, decorated coddiwompler, narrator, and author of, The Abney Kelly series. She lives in North Dakota with her dog, two cats, and four chickens. She participates in tomfoolery frequently and plans to get into waggishness in the future. Vive La Pete!

Made in the USA
Coppell, TX
14 December 2022